ANNE BENNETT

A Girl can Dream

HARPER

This novel is entirely a work of fiction.
The names, characters and incidents portrayed in it are
the work of the author's imagination. Any resemblance to
actual persons, living or dead, events or localities is
entirely coincidental.

Harper ·
An imprint of HarperCollins*Publishers*
77–85 Fulham Palace Road,
Hammersmith, London W6 8JB

www.harpercollins.co.uk

Published by HarperCollins*Publishers* 2014

9

Copyright © Anne Bennett 2014

Anne Bennett asserts the moral right to
be identified as the author of this work

A catalogue record for this book
is available from the British Library

ISBN: 978-0-00-735925-7

Set in Sabon LT Std by Palimpsest Book Production Limited,
Falkirk, Stirlingshire

Printed and bound in Great Britain by
Clays Ltd, St Ives plc

MIX
Paper from
responsible sources
FSC™ C007454

FSC™ is a non-profit international organisation established to promote
the responsible management of the world's forests. Products carrying the
FSC label are independently certified to assure consumers that they come
from forests that are managed to meet the social, economic and
ecological needs of present and future generations,
and other controlled sources.

Find out more about HarperCollins and the environment at
www.harpercollins.co.uk/green

A Girl
can
Dream

Anne Bennett was born in a back-to-back house in the Horsefair district of Birmingham. The daughter of Roman Catholic, Irish immigrants, she grew up in a tight-knit community where she was taught to be proud of her heritage. She considers herself to be an Irish Brummie and feels therefore that she has a foot in both cultures. She has four children and five grandchildren. For many years she taught in schools to the north of Birmingham. An accident put paid to her teaching career and, after moving to North Wales, Anne turned to the other great love of her life and began to write seriously. In 2006, after 16 years in a wheelchair, she miraculously regained her ability to walk.

Visit www.annebennett.co.uk to find out more about Anne and her books.

ACKNOWLEDGEMENTS

I wrote this book primarily because I wanted to highlight the really valuable work the Women's Land Army did in the Second World War. Although the organisation was started in 1917 in the First World War, then called The Great War, it was revived again in the summer of 1939 just before the official clarification that we were actually at war, which by then everyone knew was inevitable. Young women from all walks of life and most with no experience of farming at all, joined the Land Army and in the main they were dedicated, eager to learn and extremely hard working. It was a good job they were. for Hitler, instead of immediately bombing our towns and cities, as people expected, concentrated instead on sinking our merchant ships. We are an island race and we were far from self sufficient then, so he thought he could perhaps starve us into submission. Without the Land Girls he might have succeeded for many of the farm hands were called into the armed services at the very moment when farmers were told they had to drastically increase their yield if Britain's people were not going to starve to death. And yet, after the war, the Land Girl's vital contribution to the war effort seemed largely forgotten and it was only in the last year or two that they have been recognized and have taken part in the Remembrance Day Memorial Service at the cenotaph.

When I read about this I started to research the Women's Land Army and was left full of respect for this valiant band of women and decided to include one of them in my new book.

I was inspired further by *Wartime Britain*, which I saw on the television and later I bought the book that accompanied the series, compiled by Peter Ginn, Ruth Goodman and Alex Langlands. I also bought *Land Girls* compiled by Joan Mant, which told of women's true stories and experiences in the Land Army. I trawled the internet too and some of the Land Girl's lives on the various farms were documented in *The People's War* series compiled by the BBC. I used *Life On The Home Front* as well, which was a *Reader's Digest* book and Carl Chinn's book *Brum Undaunted*.

And so with most of the research completed I began to write the story of Meg Hallett, starting off with a most traumatic and upsetting event that meant her future was not the one she thought it would be.

It is when I begin the book that I value greatly the Harper team behind me, my editor, Kate Bradley and my publicist, Amy Winchester. My agent Judith Murdoch too is always there on the end of a phone or e-mail to help and advise and I appreciate all you do, so thank you. Thanks to Yvonne Holland for the copy edit, we know each other well.

Thanks too to my lovely friend Judith Kendall and all the fellow dog walkers I meet on West Shore every day. Most know nothing about writing but they are very interested in what I do and how it works and how the current book is coming along. They are a great bunch and some of them I have known for the 21 years we have been living here though in that time the dogs have changed. In this part of Wales too there are a lot of fellow Brummies and they have told me things that I have included in the books sometimes and they love it when I do that.

My family too give me immeasurable support, my husband, Denis and my daughters Nikki and her husband Steve, Beth, Tamsin and soon-to-be-husband, Mark and my son Simon and his wife Carol. The grand-children are a source of delight, Briony now in a flat of her own that she shares with Josh and working in a lab which is what she wanted to do, and Kynan at Sixth Form College beavering away for his A levels, Jake is studying for his GCSEs and Theo, who becomes a teenager this year, is also working hard and doing well. As for Catrin, now three and a half, she keeps the rest of us laughing for she is a sunny-natured, happy little girl very like her mother and it is a pleasure to have her around. I often feel very blessed to have them all.

Another group that I am a member of and I feel very grateful to are the "Novelistas" that this book is dedi-cated to. We meet once a month and I hate missing a meeting for the company is good and we have a lot of fun, though we do discuss issues to do with writing and listen to everybody's news as well. Book launches mean that there is cake after the nice lunch and bubbly for the toast and really there is not a lot to dislike.

I have left the most important group of people to

last and that is you the readers for without you there would be no point in my writing a word. A special thanks to the very many who write to me, I appreciate every letter. There has been a long wait for this book "A Girl Can Dream" and I hope now it is on the shelves you enjoy it as much as any of the others. To each and every one of you I owe an immense debt of gratitude.

I am dedicating this book to all the "Novelistas"
for the help, support and encouragement
they are always ready to give.
I appreciate it all a great deal . . .

ONE

1937

Meg Hallett would never forget that terrible day. Her mother, Maeve, had been having labour pains since the early hours of the morning. The other children had gone to Mass with their father but, with the new baby obviously on its way, Meg had stayed behind to tend to her mother. The baby was trying to push its way into the world far too soon and Meg wondered if this was due to the fall her mother had had in the yard the day before.

Suddenly Maeve turned anxiously to her fourteen-year-old daughter. 'Meggie, you will see to the others, won't you?' she begged. 'I know it will be really hard for you . . . I know I'm asking you to give up all the dreams you have of a future for yourself, the job you had lined up at Lewis's and everything but you must promise me to keep them together. I'd not rest easy if I thought the family were torn apart.'

'Mom, please don't talk this way,' Meg cried. Beads of sweat were standing out on Maeve's brow and Meg wiped them away gently with the damp cloth she had ready, noting that her face was as pale as lint and so thin her high cheekbones stood out.

Maeve had always admired those cheekbones. People always said she was a carbon copy of her mother, but though she had inherited her fine bones, luxurious dark hair with a coppery tinge, and deep brown eyes, she doubted her skin was as flawless, or her cheekbones so high. Now, though, her mother's rosebud mouth looked bruised from where she had chewed it when the pain was bad, her face had lost all vestige of colour, and her hair was lank around her face.

'Why don't you lie down, Mom, and try to sleep?' Meg suggested gently.

Maeve, however, was too perturbed to sleep and she continued as if Meg hadn't spoken. 'And you must help your father. Charlie's a good man and he will be lost. You will manage between the two of you – you would have been leaving school in a fortnight anyway – and Billy will be starting at the school himself in six months. May will be on hand if you need her.'

Meg nodded. Their neighbour had always been very helpful. 'I know, Mom.'

'You will do this for me then, sure you will?' Maeve said, clutching at her eldest daughter's hand.

'Mom, you know I would surely take care of the children and the house – and Daddy too – as well as I am able to,' Meg said in as firm a voice as she could muster. 'But I hate to hear you talking this way. You're going to be fine.'

'No, my dear girl,' Maeve said. 'I haven't much time. My family in Ireland might say you are too young to deal with all the children and they'll offer to take one or two off your hands but, I beg you, don't let them go. My father will have them working their fingers to the bone, as he did me and my siblings.' She stared intently at Meg, reliving her sad memories of home. 'If he didn't feel we'd worked hard enough, then we didn't eat. We were beaten with his belt for the slightest thing. I escaped my life of abuse, thank God, and now I would hate my parents to get their hands on my children.'

Meg's mouth opened in surprise. Her mother had never spoken about her growing up in Ireland before. She remembered her father warning her not to plague Maeve with questions about her homeland; she hadn't had a good time of it there. Meg doubted he knew much more than that. He himself had never raised a hand to any of his children – not even Terry – and there was always food on their table. To her knowledge her mother's family had never written her one line since she left home, and she had never written to them so, Heaven forbid, should anything happen to her mother she doubted they would be involved in any way. So she said confidently, 'They will never take any of the children, never fear, Mom.'

Maeve sank back on the pillow with a sigh and said, 'Or the authorities might say they'd be better off in a home.'

'How could they be?' Meg asked in genuine puzzlement. 'Daddy's in work and a good provider, and I've virtually left school and am able and willing to see to them. Terry and Jenny will help, so you needn't worry about that either. But you are fretting for nothing. You'll be as right as rain when the baby is born and you have recovered from the birth and all.'

But her mother went steadily downhill after that. When, in trying to make her more comfortable, Meg discovered the blood pumping from her, she stopped only long enough to pack her with a towel before setting off for the doctor, leaving their neighbour May Sanders sitting with her mother.

The doctor ordered Maeve straight to hospital. Charlie's brother, Uncle Robert, had been alerted to what was happening, and he and his wife, Rosie, took the younger children home to care for them. Meanwhile Meg would go with her father to the General Hospital.

'Someone's got to go with the poor sod,' Robert said to Rosie. 'I've never seen our Charlie in such a state,' 'The others seem totally traumatised by it all, too,' Rosie said. 'It's the suddenness of it, I suppose.'

'That's why I thought the nippers would be better with us,' Uncle Robert said. 'I mean, neighbours are all well and good, and I know May Sanders to be one of the best, but families should step in at times like these.'

Meg was glad that Uncle Robert and Aunt Rosie had the care of children. It was one less thing for her to worry about. She felt the burden of her father's distress lodge on her shoulders and was glad that he hadn't seen just how sick her mother looked. By the time the ambulance came she'd been semi-delirious, her face contorted from the agonising contractions. All he knew was that Maeve had started in labour and had been taken to the General Hospital.

They sat alone on hard chairs in a dismal corridor, white paint flaking off the walls, for what seemed like hours. Eventually Charlie's head sank into his hands.

'If she dies it will be my fault,' he wept. 'I should

never have allowed her to get pregnant again. The doctor warned us both it would be dangerous.'

'Oh, Dad, stop this,' Meg said, 'Whoever's fault it is, I'd say Mom's in the best place.'

Charlie got to his feet. 'Well, I'm away to find out how she is,' he said. 'I can't sit here any longer and know nothing.'

Just at that moment, a harassed-looking young doctor in his white coat, a stethoscope hanging around his neck, came through the double doors at the end of the corridor. As he approached, the look on his face turned the blood in Meg's veins to ice.

'Mr Hallett?' the doctor asked Charlie.

'Yes, I'm Mr Hallett.'

Meg suddenly didn't want the doctor to say any more, as if not knowing the news would make it not true. But the doctor went on quietly, 'I'm terribly sorry, Mr Hallett. Your wife died on the operating table just a few moments ago.'

The terrible words hung in the air. Meg and Charlie stared at the doctor as if they couldn't quite believe what they had just heard. Despite her mother's apprehensions about the birth, Meg had comforted herself with the thought that women had babies all the time; once they'd got her to hospital, everything would be all right.

Charlie sank back onto the chair, unsure his legs could hold him up. He just couldn't take it in. Maeve dead, and through his own selfish fault. He was aware of Meg breaking her heart on the bench beside him, tears coursing rapidly down her cheeks, and he put his arms around her.

The doctor said sincerely, 'I'm sorry to give you such bad news.' And then, to give them some vestige of hope: 'We may be able to save the child, though she is very small.'

Charlie and Meg jolted upright. Neither of them had considered that the baby would have survived.

'Child? You mean the child is alive?' Charlie asked, astonished.

The doctor nodded solemnly. 'When I left the theatre she was alive, yes.'

'Better if it doesn't survive,' Charlie snapped abruptly. 'Because I don't want it.'

Meg pulled herself from her father's embrace and turned to stare at him, utterly shocked. 'Not want this baby? Dad, what are you saying?'

'How could we raise such a wee child without its mother?'

'It has been done before,' the doctor said, as Meg burst out, 'I don't know how you can even think such a thing. This poor wee baby is an important part of our family.'

'And who will look after it?'

'I will,' Meg declared. 'I promised Mom I would look after them all if anything happened to her. Are you suggesting abandoning the youngest one, the one Mom died giving birth to?'

Charlie already felt ashamed of his initial reaction, and yet he saw the burden the baby would be for his daughter. 'Meg, you have your life before you,' he protested.

'Yes, I have my life before me and I won't consider it a wasted one rearing my brothers and sisters,' Meg replied, her eyes sparking angrily. 'I promised Mom I would do it and I will, and that includes this little one just born, if she should survive.' And then she turned to the doctor and said, 'Please, do what you can to help her.'

'I'd say you have little to concern yourself about with a daughter like that,' the doctor said to Charlie, and to Meg he said, 'Try not to worry. I can make no promises, you understand, but I assure you we will do our best.'

When the doctor left them, Meg could barely look at her father. Her heart felt as if it was breaking at the loss of her mother, a loss she was barely able to comprehend. Yet she couldn't blame an innocent baby for Maeve's death, as her father seemed to be doing.

It was a couple of hours later that the doctor came to see them again and told them that the child was holding her own and that the next twenty-four hours would be critical. Meg would have liked to stay at the hospital, willing strength to the sister she hadn't even seen, who was fighting for her life, but there were the other children to deal with. Sorrow-laden and in silence, she and Charlie headed for home.

Telling her siblings the dreadful news was even worse than Meg had imagined. The children were inconsolable, and Meg felt as if her own heartache had to be put on hold in order for her to deal with the others. She doubted that four-year-old Billy could comprehend the finality of death, or that Sally really understood, as she was only three years older, but they wept anyway. They were missing their mother already, and were frightened because everything was strange. The others were well aware that they would never see their mother again, and their anguish was hard for Meg to cope with. Charlie, too, was beside himself with grief, and she was glad when her uncle, who was stunned and upset himself, took him off to the pub.

'I'll call for our Alec too,' he told Meg, as they were about to leave. 'He needs to know, and families should be together at times like this.'

Aunt Rosie was very upset as well, for she had loved Maeve. When the men had gone, she said to Meg: 'Robert's right and families should do that, but I don't think there will be much support from Alec's wife, your aunt Susan. Anyway,' she added, 'no one wants help to be given as grudgingly as it would be from her. Trouble is, there's only one person she really cares about besides herself, and that's Nicholas, her darling boy.'

Meg nodded. Nicholas was her own age, and an only child, and her aunt had big ambitions for her clever son, who was now at King Edward's, a posh grammar school on the other side of town.

'May Sanders is a different person altogether, though,' Meg said, 'and she needs to know about Mom, too, for I'd hate her to hear from someone else.'

'Yes, go straight on and tell her,' Rosie advised. 'And I must think about getting all the children fed.'

'Food would choke me just now.'

'Me too,' Rosie said. 'But growing children have to eat.'

'Yes,' Meg agreed, 'and there could well be another mouth to feed before long.'

'What d'you mean?'

'The baby was alive when I left the hospital.'

8

'Heavens,' Rosie exclaimed. 'Why didn't you tell the children?'

'Because she may not live,' Meg said. 'She's very small, they say, so the next twenty-four hours will be critical. What was the point of telling them all they have a new sister and then tomorrow telling them they have not? It would just be another loss to cope with.'

'Oh, my dear girl,' Rosie said sympathetically, 'what a load you have taken on.'

'Don't,' Meg warned. 'If you are too nice to me, I will blub.'

'Well, do,' Rosie said firmly. 'Tears will do you no harm. You have been too controlled by half.'

'Oh, no, Aunt Rosie,' Meg said. 'I cried when I heard and I have the feeling that if I allow myself to cry again, I will never stop. Then Dad and the children might feel more adrift than ever.'

Rosie nodded. Meg was the eldest, to whom the others all looked for direction, and would do so even more now their mother was gone.

And then another thing occurred to her. 'Meg, if the baby is very poorly then she has to be baptised right away.'

'I don't know what name was decided,' Meg said. 'Mom never would discuss it. Said it was bad luck.'

'What about your father?'

'Oh, he always left the decision about names up to Mom.'

'And she really gave you no inkling?'

Meg thought for a moment or two. 'Well, there was just one thing. She hardly ever talked about Ireland, but she told me once, many years ago, that she'd had

9

a little sister who died of TB when she was only two years old. Her name was Ruth – maybe she would like this little one named for her?'

'Ruth Hallett.' Rosie nodded and smiled. 'Meg, that's a fine name, and I'm sure if your dear mother is looking down on us this minute she will be as pleased as punch. When you've seen May, go down to the priest as soon as you can. If that wee mite is just hanging on to life it is better to have her baptised as soon as possible. I'll send word to your dad.'

'He won't care,' Meg said. 'He doesn't want the baby.'

'No, I think you've got that wrong,' Rosie frowned.

'No I haven't, Auntie,' Meg insisted. 'He even said that to the doctor.'

'I'm sure that was just the effect of the shock he had,' Rosie said. 'Charlie is a good father. Why ever would he say a thing like that, unless he wasn't in his right mind?'

'He said he was thinking that I would have another child to bring up before I can have any sort of life.'

'Well, there you are then,' Rosie said, obviously relieved. 'He was thinking of you and he phrased it badly, that was all. I'm sure he wants the child to live as much as anyone else does.'

Meg wasn't convinced, though, and she thought her new little sister had had a poor welcome into the world so far. She vowed that if she lived, she would never ever let her feel in any way responsible for her mother's death.

When she had sat with Maeve while Meg went for the doctor, May had been worried sick as she watched her

10

good friend's condition worsen. At eleven o'clock Mass she'd prayed earnestly for Maeve's recovery.

However, she had only to look at Meg's face as she opened the door that afternoon to see that her prayers had not been answered. In fact, Meg didn't speak at all at first. Overburdened with sadness, she went straight into May's outstretched arms and cried her eyes out. It was some time before Meg was able to tell May what had happened.

May agreed with Rosie that the baby had to be baptised immediately to ensure her immortal soul was safe.

May went with Meg to see the priest, Father Hugh. When Meg explained how premature and small the baby was, he said that the hospital should be his immediate port of call, as the baby's life hung in the balance.

'Where's your father, Margaret?' he asked Meg. 'Why isn't he here?'

Meg knew better than to say that her father was at the Swan, so she said instead, 'He's with my uncle Robert, Father. He is ever so upset.'

'Doubtless he is,' the priest said. 'But it should be the child he is thinking about now. He must come to the hospital.'

'I'll fetch him, Father,' May offered.

'Good,' Father Hugh said. 'I think no time should be lost. Come along with me, Margaret.'

Meg was glad to go with the priest; she'd rather not be the one to prise her father from the pub.

Little Ruth was in a room of her own and swaddled so well that only her face was visible. Meg was immensely moved to see that tiny face. She wasn't wrinkled as Meg had half expected her to be, just very beautiful and vulnerable-looking. Her eyes were closed so that her lashes lay like perfect crescents on her cheeks, which were slightly plump and even had colour in them, though the nurse tending her said that that was a sign of jaundice. Meg had no idea what her hair was like because it was covered, like her hands, to keep her warm. Her crib was lined with cotton wool and there was a light bulb shining above it.

'How ill is she?' Meg asked, looking down on the child she was told not to touch because of the risk of infection.

'She is holding her own so far,' the nurse answered. 'And each hour that passes increases her chances. Jaundice is not a good sign, but many newborn babies have that, and if it gets no worse it won't harm her.'

That was good news, but she was not well enough to be taken from her cot and have cold water poured on her head, the doctor was adamant about that, despite the priest's protestations. When Charlie turned up with Robert he fully supported the doctor.

'Give over, Father,' he said. 'The doctor knows what he is doing.'

'I am worried about her immortal soul,' the priest maintained.

'Well, I'm more worried about keeping her alive,' the doctor countered. 'Can't you put water on her forehead with your thumb or something?'

The priest shook his head. 'The water should be flowing,' he said.

'Well,' remarked the doctor drily, 'I'm sure a loving God will understand, in the circumstances. And may I suggest that you scrub your hands first?'

Father Hugh was annoyed but sensed that the doctor was inflexible. 'Have you a name for her?' he asked Charlie as he washed his hands thoroughly in the basin the nurse brought for him.

Charlie was nonplussed. 'No, we never talked about names.'

'She discussed it with me once,' Meg said, thinking the small lie justified. 'She said she would like a girl to be called Ruth, after her sister who died of TB.'

'Did she?' Charlie asked. He gave a slight shrug. 'I suppose Ruth is as good a name as any other.'

And so with Robert as godfather and May as godmother, little Ruth Hallett was baptised. They each held one of her mittened hands, and the priest prayed for little Ruth's recovery as they stood round the crib.

Later, however, as they all walked back towards the Halletts' house, Meg's father turned sadly towards Father Hugh. 'Maybe it's better that she doesn't recover, Father,' he said.

Meg saw the priest's shocked expression as he said, 'I can't understand you talking that way, Charlie. All I can say is that grief for your wife has coloured your outlook.'

'What chance has she, growing up without a mother's love?'

'The same chance as the rest of us,' Meg burst out. 'I can do nothing about the lack of a mother's love, but I have sisterly love in abundance for little Ruth, as well as the others, and that's better than nothing, surely?'

'Come on, man,' Robert said encouragingly. 'Won't we all be on hand to give the little one a good start in life?'

'And count me in on that,' May added. 'As Meg said,

she can do nothing to bring Maeve back, but I know that she will do her best to slip into her place.'

Meg could have told her father that the two red spots in May's cheeks were a bad sign; it showed she was in a temper and she proved this as she rounded on him. 'Little Ruth, if she should survive, deserves the same care as your other children. She is not like a parcel left at the hospital because it is not convenient to have at home. She is a child, your child, and every child should ideally be with their family.'

Charlie looked morose and sighed heavily while May leaned forward and squeezed Meg's hand. 'You are a grand girl, Meg, but only a girl yet. If you want anything, anything at all, you know where I am.'

'I know,' Meg said in a low voice. 'And I am grateful. You were a good friend to my mother.'

'I was very fond of her,' May said with a slight catch in her voice. 'It was no hardship.'

'Even so,' Meg said. 'If only Dad . . .'

'He'll come round,' May said in little more than a whisper. 'You'll see. Time is a great healer and meanwhile you have something to tell the others that might cheer them a little.'

Meg nodded and they parted at the Halletts' door. Once inside, Father Hugh said Maeve's parents must be informed of their daughter's death and the birth of Ruth, and advised Meg to send them a telegram the following morning.

'But Mom didn't really get on with her parents,' Meg told him.

'And how do you know that they are not sorry for that now?' the priest asked. 'Maybe they regret any harsh words spoken.'

14

'Whether they are sorry or not,' Charlie said, 'her parents must be told about Maeve's death. I would be failing in my duty if I didn't tell them. Isn't that right, Father?'

'Yes, Charlie,' the priest said. 'And Maeve was once telling me that she had family in America.'

'Yes, three brothers and a sister,' Charlie said. 'Better send telegrams to them too, Meg.'

Meg nodded. She didn't mind sending telegrams to those in the States, for her mother used to write to them regularly and the letters they sent back often made her smile. She would read snippets out to them all. Meg knew much more about them than she did about her maternal grandparents. Still, if they had to be told, then that was that.

Now she put it out of her mind and concentrated instead on what she was to tell the children about their little sister. They were a sad little bunch, and Meg's heart went out to them all. When she told them of their tiny wee sister fighting for her life in the hospital, they made no sign that they had even heard her. A small, frail baby was little consolation for their mother, who had been taken from them so suddenly. Meg, dealing with this loss herself, felt suddenly dispirited.

When a knock came on the door a while later, she wondered who it could be; for few neighbours knocked in that area.

'Miss Carmichael,' she exclaimed with all the eagerness she could muster. Miss Carmichael had been Meg's teacher at school; Meg had loved her with a passion and worked hard to please, so achieving higher marks than anyone in her leaving exams. Meg knew Miss

Carmichael had visited her parents to ask them if she could stay on at school longer, but she knew her father, like many, regarded education for women as worthless, and that her parents would expect her to earn wages as soon as possible.

Kate Carmichael noticed that the wan smile did not reach Meg's large, dark eyes, which were glazed with misery. Normally teachers were excluded from the inner circle of gossip, but news that Maeve Hallett was very ill and about to give birth prematurely had filtered through. When Meg told her what had happened since, she was shocked to the core.

She knew that Meg would have to step into her mother's place and the thought that her life would be stunted before it had really begun saddened the young teacher. She sensed that now Meg needed time to mourn her mother: grief was etched all over her face. In fact, so moved was she by Meg's obvious distress that she put her arms around her and held her as Meg began to sob afresh.

TWO

The following day, Meg pushed her brothers and sisters off to school. Though they might not want to go, she felt it was best that they should keep to their usual routine, and in any case she had plenty to do that would be best done without the young ones getting under her feet. Rosie offered to look after Billy as he wasn't yet at school and Meg accepted gratefully for she had the telegrams to send first, and then there was a pile of washing needing attention, and sometime during the day she had to squeeze in time to visit her wee sister in the hospital.

When she eventually got there the doctor told Meg that she should be proud of the baby's tenacity, that after everything she'd been through, she was going to make it.

Meg let her breath out in relief. To her it made some sort of sense to her mother's death that the baby she had been carrying had survived.

'When can I take her home?' she asked.

'Oh, that's a little way off yet,' the doctor said. 'She

17

must weigh at least five pounds, and that might take a week, possibly two.'

'Can I come and see her?'

'Of course,' the doctor assured her. 'She is still in the special care baby unit and when she is a little stronger you may be able to give her a bottle. You will have to get used to doing that anyway.'

'Oh, yes,' said Meg. 'I would love to . .'

Afternoon was turning into evening as Meg scurried home, collecting Billy on the way, knowing the children would all be sitting there with their tongues hanging out; her father, too, because he hadn't gone to work that day. However, if Meg had thought he might be some support for her, then she was disappointed. She'd known he had taken himself off to the Swan after the meal she had put before them all, but the children told her that while she had been at the hospital he had staggered home at closing time and was in bed sleeping it off . .

'It's how many men deal with things,' May told her when they met in the yard as Meg was bringing in the washing. 'I often think that it is women who are the copers in this world. A man loses his wife and goes to pieces, and yet if a woman loses her man she will roll up her sleeves and work to feed and clothe her children and get on with it without moaning much. Now your father has lost the love of his life, so don't expect him to just get over it as you will have to.'

In the light of May's words, Meg was patient with her father when she woke him to have his dinner, and she bit her lip when he sat at the table bleary-eyed and complaining that the food wasn't a patch on what

Maeve would put before him. Meg had been too busy to make anything more than a scratch meal using the meat and vegetables intended for the previous day, and was stung by the criticism.

However, to prevent herself either flying into a rage or dissolving in tears, Meg told her father about her visit to see the baby.

'Ruth is definitely going to make it now,' she said. 'So that's good news.'

'Is it?'

'Oh, Dad, of course it is.' Meg insisted. 'She will be able to come home when she is over five pounds in weight. I can't wait for that.'

'Don't see why,' Sally said.

'Why do you say that, Sally?' Meg said. 'I thought you liked babies.'

'I do,' Sally maintained. 'But not this one, not Ruth.'

'Why on earth don't you like our own baby?'

''Cos if she hadn't been born, our mommy would still be alive,' Sally said.

Meg was astounded. Sally was only seven years old and Meg wondered if she had overheard the others talking about it. 'Is this how you all feel?' she asked, glaring at them all around the table; she knew by the uncomfortable glances they exchanged with one another that they did.

'You can count me in as well,' Charlie said. 'Don't expect me to get excited over a baby that robbed me of my wife.'

'How can you blame one small helpless baby for Mom's death?' Meg cried, patience with her father gone. 'The truth is, Mom shouldn't have been expecting at

19

all, and the fact that she was can't be laid at little Ruth's door. I take it you won't be going to see her?'

She was met by a wall of silence. 'All right then,' she screamed. 'Have it your way, but I will visit every day until the time I can bring Ruth home. And when that time comes, she is never to feel any sign of this resentment. And that goes for you all,' she added, looking at each one of the children in turn.

The children looked aghast, waiting for their father's reaction, but he didn't respond. Meanwhile Meg felt such misery envelop her that she knew if she stayed in the house a minute longer, she would burst into floods of tears. She strode purposefully to the door, stepped into the street and shut it behind her with a resounding and very satisfying slam.

She had no plan of where she wanted to go. She felt all churned up inside and so she set off for Calthorpe Park, where she walked alongside the Heath, passing the bandstand where the brass bands played on Sundays. She could see boys having a kick-about with a football on the far side, and a couple of families packing up after a picnic. It was a peaceful scene and began to soothe Meg's bruised soul.

Courting couples arm in arm were strolling along the banks of the river Rea, which were overhung with weeping willows, or walking under the canopy of trees by Pershore Road. And the bees taking in the last of the sun busily buzzed amongst the flowerbeds, which were a riot of colour. Meg gave a sigh that was almost one of contentment.

She strolled all over the park, drinking in the peace and tranquillity, taking her time, so that the sun was beginning to sink below the horizon when she turned for home. It was quiet when she went in and all the pots and pans, she saw, had been washed, dried and put away. Only Terry was up, reading a comic.

'Where is everyone?'

'Jenny, Sally and Billy are in bed.'

'And Daddy?'

Terry's eyes met Meg's and she burst out, 'He has gone back to the Swan, hasn't he?'

Terry shrugged. 'S'pose. He said he was going to see Uncle Robert.'

'And that's where the two of them will make for,' Meg said grimly. 'May said men often deal with loss by drinking too much, though I can't for the life of me see what good it does. I hope Dad gets a grip on himself soon.'

'And me,' Terry said gloomily.

'Did you just stay up to wait for me?'

'And to say sorry,' Terry said. 'Maybe Mom shouldn't have had this baby, but I know a bit of how babies are made and once you are having one, it's too late then to wish you weren't. But I got to thinking that the baby hasn't had any say in it either, has she?'

'No,' Meg said. 'And that was the point I was trying to make.'

'I know,' Terry said. 'I should have had more sense, and I will try and make the others feel the same before she comes home.'

'Oh, Terry, that's great,' Meg cried, for she was very fond of her twelve-year-old brother and had been disappointed with his initial reaction. 'It will be a poor welcome for Ruth to come to a house where no one wants her.'

'I got to thinking that too after you left,' Terry said. 'Anyway, I'm sorry for upsetting you.'

'None of us is thinking straight since Mom died,' Meg said. 'Concentrating on the baby helps me, because it's something positive.'

'Here's something else positive,' Terry said. 'Though maybe not so pleasant.'

'What?'

'A telegram was delivered while you were out,' Terry told Meg. 'Mom's parents are coming for the funeral.'

When she finally met them, Meg didn't care for either of her maternal grandparents one bit. Sarah Mulligan was a small woman, but a stout one. Her face was the colour of putty, and so creased and wrinkled it reminded Meg of a dried-up old prune. The wrinkles didn't hide her thin tight lips, though, or her blue eyes that looked so cold that shivers ran down Meg's back.

Conversely, everything about Maeve's father, Liam Mulligan, was oversize. He was a tall man, and beefy, with enormous shoulders, a very large stomach and hands twice the size of her own father's. He had an exceedingly red face with rheumy brown eyes and slack, bulbous lips.

However, it wasn't just how they looked that Meg found off-putting, it was also their manner. They expressed no sorrow at the loss of a daughter, nor any sympathy for the family. They gave the children scant attention and little affection, but they were very quick to find fault and Meg found them very unwelcome guests.

On the morning of the funeral, all the Halletts – even

Billy – were dressed in black. Meg's long dark brown hair was up in a chignon, which Miss Carmichael had shown her how to do when she was going to the interview at Lewis's and it had immediately had made her appear older and given her confidence – she thought she needed both qualities that day. The sun shone from cornflower-blue skies, though it seemed a mockery for the day to be such a bright one when their spirits were so low. The children's aunts and uncles and grandparents had already gone to the church, and it was just the Hallett family left to walk together, Meg leading the way and her father bringing up the rear, as they walked along Bell Barn Road and down Bristol Passage on to Bristol Street, where St Catherine's Church stood. All those not attending the Requiem Mass stood at their doorways in respectful silence and watched them pass.

The church was packed and Meg told herself she shouldn't be so surprised, for her mother had been very popular, but it still warmed her heart to see so many there, including Miss Carmichael and the doctor standing at the back.

The Requiem Mass was a long one, but none of the children fidgeted or whispered together. Even Billy seemed awed by the solemnity of it all. And after it, as they began the short walk to Key Hill Cemetery in Hockley, where Maeve was to be buried, Meg caught hold of Billy's hand. His very shiny eyes grew bigger when, after the murmured prayers around the graveside, the coffin that Meg had told him housed his mother was gently lowered into the prepared hole. The lump in his throat threatened to choke him as his father stepped forward and threw a clod of earth on top of the coffin. *Thud.* That seemed to Billy to bring home the fact that his mother really was dead. One by one the family threw a handful of earth onto the coffin.

'You don't have to do it, Billy,' Meg told him kindly.

'I want to.' Billy shook his head emphatically and, dropping Meg's hand, he stepped forward boldly. People started to cry afresh as the small boy took a handful of earth, but Billy didn't cry till the clod hit the coffin. Then the enormity of it all seemed to get to him, the realisation that his mother was dead and gone, and he ran back to Meg and buried his face in her skirt as tears threatened to overwhelm him.

Charlie, too, felt stricken as he watched his children step forward one by one. Unbeknownst to Meg, the Mulligans had offered to take Billy and Sally back with them to what they said was a much better life in Irish countryside, and he had been very tempted,. They painted a powerful picture of the idyllic life the children would have and Liam Mulligan promised that Billy would inherit the farm one day if he took to the work. Charlie felt he couldn't just dismiss the offer out of hand, but looking at the kids now, they were so lost and vulnerable. They were his children, he realised; they only had the one parent now. The children needed time to grieve for their mother; surely they could do that better in familiar surroundings with people that loved them.

He suddenly peeled Billy from Meg, lifted him into his arms and, carrying him like that, led the way to the Swan, where Paddy Larkin had given him the use of the back room. Rosie and her daughters had worked very hard to put on a good spread for the mourners, and Meg was immensely grateful to them as she took her place beside her father.

As tea and beer flowed, and neighbours got chatting, Charlie drew Meg into the corridor and closed the door against the noise.

'Are you all right, Dad?'

'Child, it will be many years before I am all right,' Charlie told his daughter. 'Indeed it might never happen.' He gave a sigh and went on, 'But I wanted to talk to you.'

'Talk away then,' Meg said.

'It's about the children,' Charlie said, and he told her what Liam and Sally Mulligan had suggested, Meg gasped for it was just the very thing her mother said to guard against. Charlie hadn't noticed her reaction and went on. 'I know you don't like Maeve's parents and you want to keep us all together, but would it be selfish of us to keep Billy and Sally here when they can offer them a much better life in Ireland?'

Meg took a deep breath. She knew she had to remain calm and rational. He was clearly genuinely asking her opinion, so she had to push down her desire to tell him that she could see cruel malevolence in her grandmother's gimlet eyes, and how much she hated her grandfather's coarseness and belligerence, particularly when he had a drink in him. The thought of either Billy or Sally being beaten by that hulk didn't bear thinking about. And there was also the promise she had made to her mother. But it was more than that: she knew the only way for them all to get over their

25

loss was to stay together, so that they could offer support to one another.

She chose her words with care. 'If I had to choose between health and happiness, I think I would choose happiness every time,' she said. 'Mom said she was desperately unhappy at home.'

Charlie nodded. 'I remember. But I suppose people can change.'

'Not those two,' Meg declared determinedly.

'So you don't think they should be given this chance?' Charlie asked her seriously.

Meg shook her head. 'If you send them away I won't be able to keep the promise I made to Mom and that will distress me greatly. But, more importantly, I think both Billy and Sally will be desperately sad.'

Charlie still looked hesitant and Meg took his arm. 'Come on, Dad. Their place, the place for all of us, is in the bosom of the family where we are loved and understood.'

Meg saw with a measure of relief that her words had hit home as her father nodded his head. 'You're right. I think you are right.' The image of his young ones standing by their mother's coffin came into his mind again. 'I don't want to send the two young children away like that, however healthy it is. Their place is here – and more especially now, but have you no qualms at all about how you will cope?'

Meg put her hand on his arm. 'Dad, I'll never be another Mom, but I will do my best, and when I make mistakes I'll learn from them. I know this is what Mom wanted above anything else, and that helps.'

'Right,' Charlie said, squaring his shoulders. 'I am away back into the room and will tell Maeve's parents that the children won't be going with them.'

'That's the spirit, Daddy,' Meg said, and she smiled with relief as she followed her father.

THREE

No one felt particularly easy until the Mulligans had left. Charlie ran to the expense of a taxi to take them to the station as their train was leaving very early in the morning. But still the whole family got up to see them off, or, as Terry said, to make sure they really went. As Meg watched the taxi drive down the road she felt the sudden desire to dance a jig.

Terry had done his work well and soon Meg had her siblings all helping her with the weekly wash. Terry filled the large copper in the brew house, and when the clothes had had a good boil, Meg hauled the white shirts and the like into a shallow sink, She'd already added Beckett's Blue to the water and Billy and Jenny swirled the clothes through there before wringing them out and taking them to Jenny who was operating the mangle. The rest of the clothes were heaved into the maiding tub and then Meg pounded them up and down with the dolly stick, That finished they all had a go at turning the mangle, while Meg hung the damp clothes on the lines criss-crossing the yard. This was all done to cries of encouragement from the women from the yard, who knew that Meg was keeping them busy for their own sakes.

And when the family wash was completed Meg fished out all the baby things their mother had put in a trunk in the attic and these too were washed in the sinks by hand for as Meg said, 'There will be nothing new for this baby, so the least we can do is welcome her with sweet-smelling clothes and bedding.'

Later that evening Meg laid down the iron after pressing the last of the little smocked dresses and said to Terry, 'You know, small as these clothes are, they are going to swamp Ruth. She is so incredibly tiny still.'

'She must be all right to come home, though.'

'Yes, she's five pounds now.' She began folding up the clothes. 'I suppose I'm just nervous generally. I mean, I really want to bring Ruth home, it's where she belongs, but I am worried how I'll cope with everything.'

'We'll all help as much as we can,' Terry said. 'I think we'll have to because I can't see our dad giving you much of a hand with her.'

'No,' Meg said, shaking her head. 'I can't understand him. How can he blame a tiny baby for Mom's death when it's more his fault than her's?'

'What d'you mean?'

'Nothing,' Meg mumbled, not wanting to discuss the sexual side of marriage with a boy only twelve years of age. 'Don't mind me. I'm just cross with Daddy generally. I mean, we're all suffering, but he just can't seem to pull himself together. Where did he slope off to at dinner-time and where is he now?' That didn't need an answer. They both knew he was at the Swan.

29

'Quite apart from anything else,' Meg said, 'he can't afford to go to the pub every night.'

'He says he is bought drinks,' Terry pointed out.

'Maybe he is being bought a few drinks at the moment,' Meg said, 'especially with Mom's funeral just over, but that's not going to go on for ever. And I doubt people buy him enough for him to get in the state he seems to be in some nights. I hear him stumbling around and muttering to himself.'

'So do I,' Terry said. 'And I know it was agreed that you move into the bedroom with the baby while she is so small and needing night feeds so she won't disturb us, but Dad disturbs us much more coming home drunk.'

'Maybe he'll take a grip on himself with another mouth to feed,' Meg said.

'Yeah,' said Terry, with a rueful grin. 'And maybe pigs fly.'

The following day, Meg and her aunt Rosie went to fetch the baby home. The nurse seemed a bit surprised and said, 'I thought your father might be here with you today to discuss the little one's care in the future.'

Meg's eyes met those of her aunt, but she felt she had to defend her father. 'He . . . he had to work,' she said. 'You know the funeral and all was a great expense.'

'Of course, I understand,' the nurse said, but Meg knew that she didn't. It was small wonder: Meg herself didn't fully understand why her father had never been to see his baby daughter since the day of her birth.

But she said to the nurse, 'What do you mean about the baby's care? She is all right, isn't she?'

'Oh, yes, she is,' the nurse said, 'but she is a month

premature and so her feeds will have to be little and often – every two to three hours.'

Meg nodded and the nurse went on, 'And she will be unable to regulate her temperature so you must ensure that she is kept warm. Be aware of that and add an extra blanket if the nights are cold. And guard against infection. Don't let anyone nurse her if they have a cold or anything. In fact, keep visitors to a minimum for now.'

'Little chance of that,' Rose laughed. 'Every woman in the street has been on pins all day, knowing the wee one is coming home. They mean her no harm, but want to welcome her properly.'

Meg nodded. 'And they have all been good to us since Mom died and I'd hate to offend them, but if I see anyone with a cold, I will ask them not to touch her.'

'Well, do your best,' the nurse said. 'And we will keep our eye on her too. So for now I'd like you to bring her in every week to be weighed to make sure she is gaining enough.'

Meg could see the logic of it but it was yet another thing she had to fit into her week. Rose had seen the resigned look flit over her face and said, 'It doesn't have to be you that brings the child back here. I could do it sometimes. Don't be too independent. We can't help you if you don't let us.'

Meg smiled gratefully at her aunt and felt the burden of responsibility that had lodged firmly between her shoulders lighten a little.

Rose insisted on paying for a taxi as she said little Rose couldn't be expected to travel home on a tram, which rattled alarmingly and was probably full of germs.

Meg thoroughly enjoyed her second-ever ride in a car, while Ruth, snuggled tight against her, went fast asleep.

Rose was right about the neighbours eagerly awaiting the arrival of little Ruth Hallett. The children barely had time to ooh and aah over their little sister before they were invaded. Everyone brought something: matinée jackets, dresses, nighties, leggings or pram sets. One neighbour brought a rocking cradle and another an enormous pram she no longer needed, and a woman who had had twins five years before brought a selection of clothes that Meg was sure would fit Ruth because the twins had been tiny too.

That evening, Meg showed the things to her father, but he showed no interest in either the clothes or the child, his only comment being, 'That bloody pram is too big for this house.'

Stunned and hurt – Meg could not believe that her father would keep up this antipathy to his own child – she snapped back, 'Where d'you suggest I leave it then? In the street?'

'I'm just saying.'

'Yes, well, you've said, and unless you have an alternative place for it, it stays right where it is,' Meg told her father firmly.

For a moment he glared at Meg for speaking to him that way in front of the children, but he said nothing. Instead he stood up so quickly that his chair scraped on the lino, and then he lifted his coat from the back of the door and went out, slamming the door after him with such gusto that Ruth, lying asleep in the pram, woke with a start and began to cry.

Meg felt desolation surround her as she lifted the baby, realising at that moment that her father was a weak man. She had hoped against hope that when she brought the baby home he would finally mellow towards her and start looking after her in the way he should. But she recognised now that he was unable to take responsibility for his part in making her mother pregnant, and knowing by doing so he had put her life in danger. Instead of accepting any blame, he laid it all on the shoulders of a tiny, innocent baby.

The children began to clear the table and wash up the pots as Meg dealt with the baby. Then Terry supervised their getting ready for bed before putting a cup of tea down beside Meg. None of them had spoken about the incident after dinner, or their father's indifference to Ruth, and she imagined that they were as confused as she was.

'Not looking forward to him coming home tonight,' Terry said.

'Don't blame you,' Meg said. 'Maybe I shouldn't have gone for him the way I did, but . . .'

'None of us can understand the way Dad is with Ruth,' Terry said. 'I mean, when you see her, she's just so helpless.'

'I know,' Meg said with a sigh. 'I suppose I should be worried about his state of mind, really – I know he's lost his wife – but I just feel angry with him for being so weak when we are all doing our best to muddle through.'

And muddling through it was. Despite the help that Meg had given her mother bringing up her siblings, she had quickly discovered that it was very different being totally responsible for a child. She hadn't realised how loud and siren-like a baby's cry was in the dead of night, and how crushingly tired she felt, having been roused every couple of hours. The fitful sleep that Meg would drop into eventually was shallow and far from refreshing, and she would be jerked out of it again and again before the night ended.

After four nights of this, she was bleary-eyed on the Friday morning as she ladled porridge into her father's bowl, poured them each a cup of tea and sat down opposite him. As it was the school holidays she had left the others in bed until they needed to get up, and she was just about to broach the subject of housekeeping with her father – because she hadn't a brass farthing to her name – when, as if he knew what was in her mind, he handed over what was left in his pay packet. Meg knew he got paid on a Thursday, but when she looked in the pay packet there was only one pound and one ten-shilling note left in there. She had no idea what her father used to give her mother to buy the food for them all, but she could bet it was much more than she had been given.

'Is this all?' she asked.

'Aye, that's all,' Charlie snapped. 'Your mother never moaned. Great manager, your mother was.'

'Great manager!' Meg repeated. 'The rent is seven and six a week.'

'I am well aware of that,' Charlie said. 'And you may as well know it all. We are three weeks in arrears. Our landlord, old Mr Flatterly himself, came and offered his condolences when Maeve died and told me I wasn't to worry about the arrears, that I had enough on my plate.

He's a decent sort, not like his son, who I hear is taking over the properties from him now.'

'Great,' Meg said. 'So I've got to meet with this son, who isn't a decent sort, and give him just one week's rent when we owe three weeks. And how am I going to find the money to pay even one week if we are going to eat as well?'

'You'll not likely meet him,' Charlie said. 'You know it's Vince O'Malley collecting the money, and if you tell him you can't pay anything off the arrears yet, he's not going to bother about it, is he?'

'But I don't like owing money,' Meg said doggedly. 'Mom never held with it, but even with the basic rent paid I don't see how I will make the money stretch. We have another mouth to feed now and little Ruth has to have milk.'

'Well, you know how I feel about that.'

'Don't start that again,' Meg said. 'She's your daughter just as much as I am, and so she is your responsibility and she has to eat.'

Suddenly, Meg saw her father's shoulders sag and the eyes he turned to her glittered with unshed tears. 'Don't fight me at every turn, Meg,' he said. 'I am doing the best I can.'

It was on the tip of Meg's tongue to snap that her father's best was not good enough, but she stopped herself. Instead she said, almost gently, 'Perhaps things might be better for all of us if you stayed in more.'

'And do what?' Charlie demanded. 'Stare at four bare walls?'

Before Meg could reply, Terry entered the room, followed by Billy, and Ruth started to wail. With a glance at them all, Charlie lifted his coat from the door and set out for work.

He, Alec and Robert worked in the same place, Fort Dunlop, so they tended to go to work together. As Charlie waited for them that day he went over Meg's words.

Before Maeve's death he had never been a heavy drinker, nor an habitual one, but whereas during the day he could keep his thoughts in check because he was busy, they came back to haunt him in the evening. To drink heavily was the only way he could try to blot out that dreadful day when his beloved Maeve had died. The doctor had warned them before that another pregnancy would put her life at risk, but he had been selfish and careless and he couldn't help but blame himself. And now the presence of the child – whose birth had caused his wife's death – ensured that he would never totally forget. He knew he was wrong to feel this way but he just couldn't help it; he wished he'd stood up against them all and left her at the hospital. She'd have been taken to some orphanage and adopted, and he would eventually have been able to come to terms with the loss of his lovely wife.

When Meg heard the imperious knocking on the door that morning, Meg guessed it must be the rent man. But instead it was a young man wearing a dark blue suit, and a trilby hat over light brown hair. His tanned face had a haughty look to it and his eyes were piercing blue, as cold and hard as granite.

'I am Richard Flatterly,' he said. 'I am here to express condolences about the death of your mother.'

'Oh, your father—' Meg began, but the man cut her off.

'My father's unwell and so you'll be dealing with me from now on. I see you owe three weeks' rent.'

'I can pay this week's.'

'I was hoping for something off the arrears.'

'I'm afraid I haven't got it at the moment,' Meg said, 'with Mom's funeral and all.'

'I am not interested in excuses, my dear,' Richard Flatterly said, and there was no doubting the slight menace in his voice. 'I am just interested in getting the money owed me. I do not run a charity, and if you can't pay your rent I shall have to let the house to someone else. Do you understand that, my dear?' He looked her slowly up and down.

Meg nodded dumbly and handed the man the rent book and the ten-shilling note.

'If I take it all,' Flatterly said, 'it will be two and six off the arrears.'

'I know that,' Meg said. 'But I need it for food.'

Flatterly smiled but his eyes remained cold. 'I understand your father is in full-time work.'

'Yes, he is.'

'Then the rent should present no problem to him,' Flatterly said, handing Meg back half a crown. 'So next week I will return myself. I will want the full rent and a good bit off the arrears, otherwise I can make life very uncomfortable for all of you.'

Meg scuttled inside as soon as she could, shut the door and leaned against it. She felt really shaken. Flatterly's animosity had been almost tangible.

'Phew, sis!' Terry said.

'You heard that?'

'Every word.'

'We must make Daddy realise that Richard Flatterly will have us out of this house without a qualm if we don't pay off something next week,' Meg said.

'I think so too.'

'We *have* to make Daddy see that,' Meg repeated. 'But just for now, the problem is making the money I have left stretch, so tomorrow night you and I will go to the Bull Ring just before the stallholders close up and see what they are throwing out that we can use.'

It was what the really poor people did. Meg had seen them a few times: be-shawled women holding keening babies, usually with stick-thin children in tow as well, dressed in little more than rags. She had pitied them. Never had she imagined that she'd be joining them. Terry was looking at her, appalled.

'Don't look at me like that, Terry,' she cried. 'I like this no better than you, but it's what we must do to survive.'

'There's no other way?'

'Not that I can see.'

Terry sighed. 'S'pose we must then.'

So the following evening, Terry and Meg grabbed two shopping bags they hoped to fill with cheap meat and vegetables. Ruth was safely in her cradle in the bedroom, and she was sound asleep, as was Billy. Sally and Jenny, were also drowsy, yet still Meg hesitated to leave them as her father was down at the Swan.

'We'll have to go if we're going,' Terry said. 'It's a fair step.'

'D'you think they will be all right?'

'Of course,' Terry said heartily. 'What could happen to them?'

Then, as Meg still dithered, he opened the door. 'Come on, Meg. We'll go past May's and ask her to keep a lookout. And Dad's not a million miles away.'

'Huh,' said Meg, stepping onto the street beside him. 'He might as well be in Outer Mongolia. A fat lot of use he'll be with a bellyful of beer inside him.'

'I don't know so much,' Terry said. 'When we told him about Richard Flatterly and what he said, it did shake him up.'

'Yes,' Meg said, 'but how much? Didn't bother him enough to offer me extra money . .'

'Mmm, I suppose you're right,' Terry said. 'But you would hardly let him near Ruth.'

'He wouldn't go near her anyway, Terry, not by choice,' Meg said. 'I really think he would like to pretend that she doesn't exist.'

Terry knew what Meg said was true but there was no point keeping on about it so after a while he said, 'I wish we didn't have to skulk around for leftovers, but it will be nice to see the Bull Ring on a Saturday night,' Meg smiled. 'Yeah, it will and we can have a little look around. The stallholders won't be giving stuff away till they're near to closing up.'

When they reached the cobbled streets of the bustling market place it was almost as busy as it was in daytime, but they weren't surprised, for they'd heard lots of stories about the entertainment to be had on Saturday nights in the Bull Ring. It was even better when darkness seeped into the light summer night because then the spluttering gas flares were lit and the Bull Ring was transformed into something resembling fairyland. Terry and Meg walked around looking at the stalls, edging between men dressed up to the nines, even wearing top hats, moving effortlessly on very tall stilts.

Elsewhere a boxing ring had been erected and inside it was a bare-fisted burly boxer, challenging the watching men to a fight. There was a prize of five pounds if any knocked him down, but there were no takers.

'Too early see, ducks,' an old woman said to Meg and Terry as they turned away. 'When the men have enough beer inside them, they'll think they can climb Everest and beat the champ with one hand tied behind their back.'

'Have you ever seen it done?' Terry asked. 'Has anyone knocked him down?'

The woman gave a cackle of laughter. 'Well, if they have then I've never seen it,' she said. 'And I don't know how that man gets out of the chains either, 'cos I've examined them more than once.'

'What man? What chains?' Terry asked, and the woman pointed to a corner in front of Hobbies shop. They wandered over to see a man trussed up like a chicken. A table was put over him and a large shimmering gold sheet laid over that by his assistant. There was a lot of movement behind the sheet, a roll of drums, and then before they knew it, the man stood in front of them, unfettered and unharmed.

Even Meg was impressed. Then, as they were making their way to the area behind the Market Hall where a group of ragged-looking women were beginning to gather, Terry suddenly sniffed the air.

'What's that smell?'

'Hot potatoes,' Meg said. 'And they taste as delicious as they smell, but I'm afraid we have no money for such things.'

'I know,' Terry said resignedly.

Meg suddenly felt very sorry for her young brother, but there was nothing she could do about it. They passed a man prostrate on a bed of nails. Terry's eyes were standing out on stalks, for not only was the man lying there as if it was the most comfortable bed in all Christendom, but there was a young man standing on top of him. The girls standing around were giving little cries of alarm, but the man, whose brown skin gleamed in the light from the flares, and who was scantily clad with only a white cloth wrapped around his loins, appeared to feel no pain. Indeed, he had a big smile on his face.

'How does he do that?' Terry whispered to Meg when they were out of earshot.

'Search me,' Meg said. 'There must be some sort of trick to it, but for the life of me I can't see what it is. I mean, you could see the nails pressing into the man's skin.'

'Not half,' Terry said.

Some of the stallholders were getting ready to close up and Meg handed Terry one of the bags. 'It is better if we stand apart from one another,' she said. 'We may get more that way.'

When Meg took her place in the small group, though, she looked at the scrawny-looking woman with gaunt-faced children and felt as if she had no place there. Some of the children looked as if they had never had a square meal in the whole of their lives and their mothers seemed resigned to the fact that they were not able to feed their children adequately. Meg knew she needn't have been there if her father had tipped up enough housekeeping. But then she reminded herself that her father was not the only man in Birmingham who put his love of drink above the welfare of his family. Any of these women could be in a similar boat to herself. Thinking of her siblings, she stepped forward determinedly.

She had expected to feel embarrassed and ashamed, accepting food without paying, but the stall owners didn't mind that much – if they didn't give the food away, they would have to throw it away. The butcher and his assistant nearest to Meg tried to be fair and give something to everyone in the jostling crowd surrounding them. Meg was given a sizeable piece of pork and she was also offered some wizened-looking carrots from the stall selling fruit and veg and some peas still in their pods. Terry, standing by another butcher, had come away with a large ham bone with lots of meat still on it, and some slices of liver. He had also dived under barrows to collect anything that might have fallen off in the course of the day and had come up with a few apples, a cabbage and a fair few potatoes.

A group of musicians set up in a corner just before they left; they began playing the sort of jolly, foot-tapping tunes he remembered his mother lilting to him when he had been younger, and for a moment he felt the pang of loss so sharply that he gasped.

'What's up?' Meg asked, but she knew what it was when she saw the shadow that flashed across his face.

Terry gave himself a mental shake. 'Nothing,' he said, and to stop Meg asking any more questions that might cause him to think of a situation he could do nothing to change he said, 'What do you think of tonight's haul, then?'

'I think it's wonderful,' Meg said, catching Terry's mood. 'We have the makings of a few good meals in these bags. The wolf shall be kept from the door for a wee while yet.'

FOUR

The food had virtually gone by Wednesday so Meg did
something else that she had never done before: leaving
Ruth with the children she went to Moorcroft's and
asked for tick. Mrs Moorcroft knew the Halletts as a
respectable family touched by a terrible tragedy that
had made Charlie Hallett turn to the bottle. She
assumed, like most other people, that in time he would
pull himself together; meanwhile he was in reasonably
well-paid work so she was prepared to give Meg some
money on account.

Meg, though, found the whole thing mortifying, but
there was no other way she could find to feed everyone.

She bought a tin of National Dried Milk for Ruth,
a small bag of sugar and another of oatmeal to make
porridge, one loaf, sausages, onions and a pound of
potatoes. It made Terry's blood boil to see the bread
with a scrape of marg on, which was the meal for him
and Meg and the others, while that same evening his
father tucked into a plateful of succulent sausages in
onion gravy and mashed potatoes.

'He has to have the best food,' Meg said later that

night when Terry complained after his father had left. 'He has to keep his strength up to go to work. He provides for us all.'

'Not very well he doesn't,' Terry said mulishly. 'Not when he spends most of what he earns behind the bar of the Swan.'

'Hush, Terry.'

'Why should I hush?' Terry demanded. 'And why are you making excuses for him?'

'I don't know,' Meg admitted. 'I suppose because he is our dad, the only one we have, and I once loved him so much. I suppose I still do, really, and I feel guilty that I can't fill Mom's place. I mean, I can look after all you lot and everything, but I can't fill the hole in Daddy's life. For all he has us, I think he is incredibly lonely.'

'So what can we do about it?'

'Nothing,' Meg said. 'Just wait. Only time will help Dad now.'

But Terry wasn't prepared to wait, and when his father alighted from the tram the following day, Terry was there, glad to see that his uncles Alec and Robert got off just after his father.

'Why, Terry,' Charlie said, catching sight of his son, 'what are you doing here? Anything up?'

'No,' Terry said, almost contemptuously. 'Not "up" exactly. It's just that knowing you are paid tonight, I wanted you to give me some housekeeping for Meg before you go to the pub and blow a big portion of it.'

Charlie just glared at his son but Robert burst out, 'Terry, that's a terrible way to talk to your father.'

Terry tore his eyes from his father's wrathful scowl

and faced his perplexed uncle. Meg might want to make excuses for their father, he thought, but he had no intention of doing the same. 'Uncle Robert, we owe three weeks' rent,' he said. 'The landlord came round himself and threatened Meg, but she hadn't any money to pay off the arrears because Dad hadn't given her any. She had so little money we had to go to the Bull Ring on Saturday night and get the stuff left on the barrows.'

Robert gave a start – only the very poor in the city resorted to that – and he glanced at his brother.

But Terry hadn't finished. 'Even then it wasn't enough to feed us. By yesterday Meg didn't even have milk for the baby and she had to go to Moorcroft's and ask for tick. Only Dad had a dinner; the rest of us made do with thin porridge and bread and scrape.'

Robert saw embarrassment and shame flood across Charlie's face but he still asked him, 'Is this true?'

Charlie shrugged. 'I suppose if Terry says so. I didn't know about them going to the Bull Ring.'

'Then how did you think we would eat?' Terry burst out. 'And you knew the landlord had been demanding the arrears the other day because Meg and I told you.'

'Dear, dear,' Robert said, shocked. 'You know that you haven't the money to drink every night *and* provide for your family,' he told Charlie firmly. 'Something has to go and it shouldn't be the children. Now you give young Terry here three pounds ten shillings and that will enable Meg to pay off any tick and still have enough. And now Terry . . .' Robert drew his own wage packet from his pocket and withdrew two half-crowns from it, '. . . this is for Meg to help pay off the arrears.'

Charlie might have protested more about the amount

he'd been made to hand over, but before the determined eyes of his brothers and the resentful ones of his son, he could hardly do that, especially as his eldest brother had put his hand in his pocket to help them all.

Meg was astounded at what Terry had done and enormously grateful to both him and their uncle Robert. She immediately added seven and six to her uncle's five shillings and put it away in the box with the rent book. She also set aside the amount of tick she had run up at Moorcroft's, intending to pay it off first thing in the morning.

The following morning, Meg was able to pay the rent and five shillings of the arrears. Richard marked it all in the book but emphasised he would want the same every week until all the arrears were paid off. Meg decided she would be only too glad to keep her dealings with him to the minimum each week. He had stroked her hand in a rather unpleasant way as he handed back the rent book, and he had a slow way of looking at her that made her feel uncomfortable.

Early the next morning Meg meeting May in the yard told her what Terry had done, and of her uncle's generosity. May was pleased something had been sorted out and she said, 'let me give you a bit of advice. Spend as much of the money your father gave you as you can, because towards the end of the week when he is running out of beer money he may take any you have left off you. He will be unable to do that if you have bought food with it.'

Meg saw the sense in that and with the children looking after Ruth she went along to Moorcrofts and paid what she owed. Mindful of her neighbour's words,

Meg came back with brimming baskets of food. 'I've not bought many vegetables and only a bit of meat,' she told May who popped in to see how she'd got on. 'Because I think they are cheaper in the Bull Ring'

'I agree with you,' May said. 'Are you leaving little Ruth here? I'll mind her for you if you like.'

'Thanks, May, but I mean to take her with me,' Meg said. 'She was difficult to settle just now, and a pram ride will probably send her off nicely. Anyway, I can pack all the stuff I buy around Ruth; she barely fills a quarter of that enormous pram.'

'Aye,' said May with a grin. 'She looks lost in it right enough.'

'You can give an eye to the others if you like,' Meg said, settling Ruth in the pram. 'Terry's in charge, but Billy plays it up sometimes, as you know, and Sally and Jenny can fight. They've been warned – not that that will make any difference.'

'Don't worry,' May said, and added with another grin, 'I will be in with my big stick if I think it necessary. Now you get yourself away.'

Meg smiled as she wrapped Ruth in a lighter shawl, as the day was a warm one. It was a fair step, but it was a pleasant day for a walk, warm but with a breeze, and as Meg set off at a lick along Bristol Street, she reflected on how good it felt to have enough money in her purse to feed them all that week, and pay something off the rent arrears as well, though she did wonder if Terry would be able to get money off their father every week in the same way. Still, she chided herself as she turned into Bromsgrove Street, why worry about things before they happen?

She pushed the pram down the incline through the teeming mass of people and into the Bull Ring itself. Ruth slept peacefully, not disturbed in any way by the bumpy, cobbled streets or the clamour of the people. The flower sellers were lining the railings that enclosed the statue of Nelson, and the fragrant smell hung in the late summer air as Meg passed the vast array of stalls. Those selling bedding, curtain material, cookery and kitchen utensils, antiques and junk were interspersed with others selling vegetables, fruit, fish, meat and cheese, and the smell of those rose in the air as well.

She had bought quite a few good-value vegetables and was just reaching for a cabbage from one of the vegetable stalls when someone beside her said, 'Hello. Margaret, isn't it?'

Meg swung round and her big dark eyes met the merry ones of the girl she had met at Lewis's in July. Just before Meg was due to leave school that summer, Miss Carmichael had encouraged her to apply for somewhere more upmarket than the factories or domestic service and Meg had managed to get an interview at Lewis's, a city centre department store. Although she had done well at the interview, events with her mother had prevented her actually taking the job. But here was the girl with the head of dark brown curls who had put her at her ease that day with her wide smile and friendly chatter. Meg remembered thinking that her name perfectly matched her character.

'Yes,' Meg grinned back. 'Joy, isn't it?'

'I say,' Joy said, indicating the slumbering baby in the pram. 'Not yours, is she?'

'Not in the way you mean,' Meg said.

'It's just that when I asked about you, Mrs Matherson in the office said you wouldn't be able to take up your place at Lewis's due to personal circumstances.'

Meg nodded. 'Fact is, my mother started in labour the next day, only she haemorrhaged and died, but they were able to save the baby.'

'Oh God,' Joy cried. 'You poor cow.'

'It was a terrible time,' Meg said. 'Still is, I suppose, because I miss my mother so much.'

'I bet,' Joy said. 'I would miss mine loads. And you are landed with the baby?'

Meg shrugged. 'Wasn't something I chose but there was no one else. But it isn't only the baby. I have a brother, Terry, who is two years younger than me, two sisters, Jenny and Sally, and my youngest brother, little Billy, who is going on for five. Oh, and a dad who is like a lost soul and who has taken to the bottle.'

'Typical man, then,' Joy said. 'And I will say it again. I think you are a poor cow.' She glanced at her watch suddenly and said, 'I have to get back; I'm only on my lunch hour. Nice to see you again.'

Oh, yes, it was nice, Meg thought. She missed her old school friends and envied them as she saw them tripping down the street arm in arm, sharing confidences or else laughing and joking together as they made their way to the pictures or a dance somewhere.

But her life was totally different from that of most girls her age, and money was a constant problem. She watched Joy threading her way through the stalls in the Bull Ring and turned regretfully to continue her shopping.

She didn't bother telling any of the others about

meeting Joy, and anyway, Terry had news of his own. He announced he had taken on a paper round.

'A paper round?' Meg repeated. 'Who gets their papers delivered around here?'

'It's not round here,' Terry said. 'It's Neil's uncle's. You know Neil Drummond.'

'Drummond Stores,' Meg said. 'His sister, Claire, was in my class. She said it's at the far end of Bristol Street.'

'It is,' Terry said, 'not far from where the big houses start – and that's where they deliver papers, the big houses.'

'It will be one hell of a trek for you,' Meg said.

Terry shrugged. 'Don't care about that,' he said. 'It's half a crown a week, Meg.'

Meg lifted the baby from the pram and started to feed her as Terry went on, 'As long as I can get a decent amount of money from Dad before he blows it in the pub, the money I earn will help to pay off the rent arrears.'

Meg's sigh of relief was audible – she hated to be beholden in any way to a man like Richard Flatterly. 'It will be a godsend, right enough,' she told Terry. 'But you must have something for yourself.'

Terry shook his head emphatically. 'Don't want nothing,' he said. 'I ain't done it for that.'

'I know, but—'

'Meg, we need every penny,' Terry said earnestly. 'I want no money for myself, but what I do want is for you all to keep quiet about this to Dad. And that goes for all of you,' he said, his eyes raking the table. All the children nodded soberly.

'He'll get to know, Terry.'

'How would he?' Terry asked. 'I am out before him in the morning and I'll be done and back home before he finishes work. He works most Saturday mornings, and him getting up early Sunday is a thing of the past.'

Meg knew that was too true; it saddened her that her father had become such a drunk. She hadn't a clue how to stop him and to help him revert to the father they all remembered. But her priority had to be the children and keeping them fed and clothed and warm, she wanted to give no excuse for the Welfare to get involved, and she knew that even with the rent arrears paid off, Terry's paper-round money would come in very useful.

The holidays were drawing to a close and Meg would miss the children when they returned to school; they had been a great help to her and there was always someone available to run an errand, or mind the baby, or take her for a walk. She had been able to avoid Flatterly who had come in person to collect the rents till the arrears were fully cleared by giving the rent to one of the children when he called. Meg found his blatant salaciousness hard to cope with and his lewd, lustful eyes ogling her with such intensity. She thanked God that the arrears were paid off in full before the end of the holidays and it was the nice Vince O'Malley knocking the door on Friday morning.

She was glad that Billy wasn't old enough for school yet because he was quite good at amusing Ruth and he seemed able to do it for hours which was how long the washing seemed to take and most of it was all down to her, though Jenny came to help before she had to make breakfast for the others and get them off to school.

She knew May would help her if she needed her, but she was getting on now and Meg hated to put on her, but when she said this the following Monday, when they met in the brew house, May dismissed her age.

'I'm as fit as a fiddle,' she said. 'And well used to it – I've been at it years. You'll have the hang of it eventually, but for now if you want a hand you shout. All right?'

'All right, and thanks, May,' Meg said. 'There is so much washing with four children and the baby, who has a wash load of her own, plus my clothes and Daddy's.'

'Aye, there will be a fair bit of it,' May agreed. 'And the nappies alone will fill one line.'

'I know, and the ironing takes care of Tuesday.'

May chuckled. 'A woman's work is never done.'

'I'm beginning to see that,' Meg said.

She wasn't the only one working hard, for Terry was finding the paper delivering job heavy going. He had a notebook with the roads and numbers and what each house had delivered each day marked down. The houses he delivered to were not squashed together like back-to-backs, but spaced out and hidden behind walls and privet hedges, with sweeping drives, so that it was hard to see the numbers until you were up close.

The first week he was very tired, especially when school reopened, but he never said a word about it. His paper-round money, however welcome, was a fraction of what was needed to run the house though, so he still went to meet his father from the tram on Thursday evening. His uncles were there again so Charlie didn't protest or bluster, and later Terry was able to deliver three pounds ten shillings into Meg's hand. She was delighted with such an amount and she put it in a tin box that she'd hidden in the false bottom of the baby's pram.

The next day she set out for the Bull Ring again, with Billy holding the handle of the pram till his legs got tired, and though she hoped to see Joy, there was no sign of the girl that day. Still, Meg was well satisfied because she'd managed to end up with a pram packed with vegetables and fruit for the family, and she had plenty of money left for the groceries.

As she lifted the baby out of her pram when they'd reached home, Ruth gave her a huge smile that seemed to split her face in two and set her eyes dancing.

The doctor at the hospital had warned Meg that Ruth might be later meeting her milestones as she had been a month premature, but here she was smiling away when she was just over seven weeks old. The smile that she bestowed on Meg made up for the exhaustion of the first few weeks, the night feeds and the fractiousness; it caused a lurch of pure love in Meg's stomach that took her by surprise because it was so powerful. She gave a cry of delight and hugged her tight.

Now that Ruth had got the hang of smiling, she seemed to do a lot of it; Billy was trying with her all afternoon and Meg told the other children about the smile when they came home from school and they were as delighted as Meg had been when she smiled at them too, but her father only grunted when he was told. Meg refused to let her father's reaction pull her down or prevent her feeling more positive about the future; she told him that as Ruth only woke once in the night now and was much easier to settle, she would move back into the attic. She knew her decision would be a popular one with everyone – her father would like his own bedroom back and the children would be glad because he would often wake them up when he came stumbling in at night, and Terry said he took up the lion's share of the bed and snored loudly once he had fallen asleep.

So, life began to fall into a pattern. Meg still found washday hard, but the worst washdays were when it was wet and the washing couldn't be hung on one of the lines festooning the yard, raised up on gigantic poles to flap in the sooty air. On wet days the washing would be draped around the house, the nappies airing over the fireguard so that everything smelled and felt damp. Sometimes it wasn't always dry by Tuesday, so the ironing would hang over to Wednesday.

Often May came in to help Meg a bit while she dealt with the baby's needs. Her aunt Rosie called around regularly too, usually armed with a casserole or a pan of stew, and Meg was glad of this because she was able to save a little money, now that the arrears were paid off fully.

She knew the money would be needed soon to buy coal for the fires and for boots for them all. Maeve had had a new pair of lovely warm lined boots that Meg remembered her father buying the Christmas before, just as she had begun to suspect that she was pregnant, and she had kept them for best so they were like new. Meg's boots, on the other hand, were worn and shabby and had begun to pinch her feet; yet she hesitated to use any of her mother's things and all her clothes still hung in her wardrobe or were packed into the drawers.

'Is it awful to think of wearing things that once belonged to my mother?' she asked May one day when she popped in for a cup of tea.

May settled herself on the settee and put the tea down on a small table in front of her before saying, 'How could it? I would call that sensible. What else would you do with them? Give them to the rag-and-bone man?'

'Well, no, I suppose not,' Meg said. 'But I feel awkward about it.'

'Don't see why you should,' May said. 'You could do with the things, couldn't you?'

'Yes.' Meg couldn't deny it. In the past year or so her dresses had become extremely short and difficult to fasten over her growing breasts. 'Mom thought so too,' she said. 'She said she would buy me new clothes and shoes for starting work.'

'There you are then,' May said. 'She wasn't able to do that, so you adapt her things to fit you now. You're good with the needle. And there's something else to think of.'

'What?'

'Your father,' May said. 'I imagine he finds it hard to see his wife's clothes and shoes still there in the bedroom as if she had never died at all.'

Meg had not really thought about that, but she saw now that May was absolutely right. 'He's never mentioned her clothes or anything to me,' she said to May.

'Probably hurts him to speak of it,' May said.

'I suppose,' Meg said, and gave a sudden sigh. 'I don't half miss her, May.'

May leaned forward and squeezed Meg's shoulder. 'I know, and, God knows, I miss her too,' she said. 'But what can't be cured must be endured, as my poor mother would say.'

She took another sip of her tea as Meg said, 'It might upset me, but Mom's things have got to be taken out of that room, haven't they?'

'They have,' May said firmly. 'You shouldn't do it all on your own, though. I'll give you a hand if you like.'

'Would you?'

'I would and gladly,' May said. 'And I say no time like the present.'

'Now?'

'Why not?' May said. 'Little Ruthie is asleep, Billy's out playing and I have nothing pressing, so come on, let's strike while the iron is hot.'

Afterwards, Meg was so glad that May was there with her ready banter to keep misery away, for every garment she lifted from the wardrobe, or drew from the chest of drawers evoked poignant memories of her mother.

But at last all was done and packed away in two tea chests, which Meg got from the attic; a cardboard box that May produced took all the combs, brushes and creams and so forth that littered her dressing table.

Meg was apprehensive about their father's reaction, but she needn't have worried. When she asked him to go upstairs to see what she had done, he went straight away and stood for a moment in the doorway.

'You . . . you've cleared out Maeve's things,' he said to Meg.

'Yes,' Meg said. 'Only as far as the attic, though, in case you want to keep anything.'

'I don't need a keepsake to remember Maeve. She will be in my heart for ever,' Charlie said. 'I'm glad, relieved that you cleared her things away. I couldn't bring myself to do it and I thought it would be too upsetting for you.'

'It was a bit,' Meg admitted. 'But May helped me.'

'She's a good neighbour, that May,' Charlie said.

'None better,' Meg agreed, and then took a deep breath. She didn't know how her father would take to the idea of her wearing her dead mother's clothes. 'The point is, Daddy, what do you want me to do with Mom's things now?'

'What d'you mean?'

'Well, Mom was going to buy me some new things for starting work,' Meg said. 'The ones I have now don't fit too well.'

Charlie looked at his daughter and saw that she was right. Her skirts were far too short and her buttons were strained across her bodice. He was ashamed that he hadn't seen these things for himself.

'My boots pinch my feet too,' Meg said. 'But if you wouldn't mind me adapting Mom's clothes to fit me, Jenny could have my things and Sally have Jenny's and it will only be the boys who will have to have new things for the winter – and Ruth, of course.'

Charlie drew in a deep breath. 'I don't say that it won't cut me to the quick to see you in Maeve's things, but if she were beside me this moment she would berate me for being stupid. She has no need of clothes and you have, you all have, so take what you need and I will learn to deal with it.'

Charlie's eyes were like pools of pain and Meg cried, 'Oh, Dad, are you sure?'

Charlie shook his head. 'I'm not sure of anything much anymore, Meg,' he said. 'But I do know that it's the sensible thing to do. Oh, Meg, Meg, I've been little help to you these past weeks.'

'Oh, Dad, don't,' Meg said, embarrassed.

'I know I've been selfish,' Charlie said, 'and I don't blame you looking like that. My brothers have both been on about how I was behaving, but somehow I couldn't see any way forward and drinking blurred it a bit. I missed your mother so much, and then the child . . . every time I looked at her, it brought it all back.'

'I know, Dad,' Meg said. 'I feel Mom's loss too, but it isn't Ruth's fault.'

'I know that really,' Charlie said, 'but somehow I can't feel for her the way I do about you and the others.'

'Oh, Dad.'

Charlie looked at the tears sparkling in his daughter's eyes. 'Don't take on, old girl,' he said. 'I'm doing my best and I'm determined to change. I reckon I have wallowed in grief long enough. Time to take up the reins again.'

Meg was delighted to hear her father's words; if he meant them, their way forward would be easier. She thought of saying more about Ruth, but in the end said nothing. If he didn't spend all the time in the pub and saw more of her, Meg thought he was bound to fall under Ruth's spell, as the others had. Until that happened, she didn't want to rock the boat. One day at a time, she told herself as she mounted the stairs to the attic.

FIVE

Billy had his fifth birthday and there was a little tea party for him with all the delicacies that he liked. May had helped her to make a cake with five candles on it and had also given Billy a couple of toy cars that he was thrilled with. Meg bought him a small blackboard and a packet of chalks that she had seen in the Market Hall at a very reasonable price. Billy's attention had been taken at the time with the animals at Pimm's pet shop, so he hadn't known a thing about it. 'You can practise for going to school.' She told him. 'Only you'll have a slate there, but it's more or less the same thing.' He unwrapped it and gave a cry of delight.

Billy's fifth birthday seemed to bring the thought even closer that he would soon be a school boy and Meg realized that she would miss his company though Ruth would miss him more because they had become very good friends. And every Friday morning after paying the rent, rain or shine, she would push Ruth in her pram to the Bull Ring to shop for the bargain vegetables and meat. It was a hefty walk for little legs, so Billy would usually be hoisted up on the end of the pram for part of the journey there. He could sometimes hitch a ride back too. It would depend on how much produce Meg could pack around Ruth, or stuff into the large bag she had hanging from the pram handle.

Meg loved going to the Bull Ring now that she didn't have to hang about to be given meat and vegetables no one else had wanted, but could buy from the costers, like any other respectable person. She seldom went to the Bull Ring without remembering her meeting with Joy. She knew it was unlikely she would see her again but, Joy or no Joy, the Bull Ring was an exciting place. Meg liked the noise, the riotous energy of the place, the special smells that rose in the air and the banter and cries of the costers.

Billy was always as good as gold on these trips because he knew that if he behaved himself there was a chance Meg would take him into the Market Hall to play with the animals in Pimm's pet shop and see the clock strike. It was the highlight of his visit, and willing hands were always around to whisk the pram up and down the steps to the Market Hall, as if it weighed nothing at all. While Meg scrutinised the prices of the various goods on sale, Billy was entranced by the twittering canaries, the colourful budgerigars and the squawking parrot that called out incessantly, 'Who's a pretty boy, then?' He also liked the fish swimming endlessly around their bowls and the baby rabbits and guinea pigs, but best of all were the mewling kittens and the playful boisterous puppies that nipped at his fingers.

When the clock chimed as a prelude to striking the hour it drew everyone's attention. A sort of hush came over the place as the figures of three knights and a lady struck the bell denoting the hour.

Billy always gave a sigh when it was over. 'I love that clock.' he'd say nearly every week as they made their way home. Meg could have said she liked the clock too, for waiting for the clock to strike was the only time in the day that Billy stopped chattering for two minutes at a time.

Though Terry had been doubtful that his father would change that much, he had been pleasantly surprised. He no longer slipped into the pub on his way home on a Thursday, when one swift drink would turn into half a dozen in the twinkling of an eye, but instead brought his wages home to Meg as he had done to Maeve and took out some pocket money for himself that would pay for his ciggies and beer.

He began to go again to the football matches on Saturday afternoons with his brothers and Terry, and promised Billy he would take him along soon, and he gave all the children money to go to the thruppenny crush on Saturday morning. Meg was pleased to see all of them warming once again to the father who had been lost to them for a little while.

Aunt Rosie, who greatly admired Meg and the way she had stepped up to take over the family, popped in one afternoon for a cup of tea and asked her if she had ever resented giving up her dreams.

'No,' Meg said. 'Resent is the wrong word. I promised Mom I would look after them all and I want to keep my word, but I can't help being envious of other girls who don't have my responsibilities.'

'And what of your own future?'

'That's on hold until all the children are grown and settled,' Meg said, but she said it without the slightest shred of self-pity. Rosie was impressed by her maturity and she said this to Meg.

Meg smiled. 'Nicholas said almost exactly the same thing the day of Mom's funeral.'

'Did he?'

'Yes,' Meg said. 'I think in many ways he feels a bit like a fish out of water.'

Rosie nodded. 'Robert thinks that too.'

'Well, he's neither one thing nor the other,' Meg said. 'He hardly knows your lads or our Terry because he has never been allowed to mess around with them, and yet he never brings friends home from that posh school or talks about going to their houses or out with them at the weekend.'

'Susan says he has lots of homework.'

'I suppose he will have,' Meg said. 'But surely not every hour of every day? All this studying is making him look different and, however clever he is, no school-work is as good as having friends to knock about with.'

'It does sound very lonely,' Rosie said. 'But the worm might be turning because your uncle Alec was saying that since the funeral Nicholas has been pulling against the apron strings and he hasn't been as keen as doing his mother's bidding as he was. Even argued with her, he said, and he had never heard him do that before.'

'I'm surprised Uncle Alec has had nothing to say about it before now,' Meg said.

'He did try to have a hand in raising the boy at first,'

Rosie said, 'but Susan made it plain that rearing her child was her business. A man can be too easy-going, and that is our Alec. The general consensus is that Alec is a decent enough fellow, but that Susan is rather snooty, and the way she keeps her lad to his books is neither right nor healthy. Turning him into a mommy's boy, people say. And for a quiet life Alec has sat back and let her ruin the lad.'

Meg hadn't thought Nicholas ruined, just lonely, and so she was pleased when Terry came in the following Saturday morning after playing football in Calthorpe Park with his friends to say that Nicholas had not only turned up to play with them but had brought a proper leather ball. Charlie, who had just come home from work for his dinner, was also surprised at what Terry had said. 'That's a turn-up for the books, ain't it?'

Terry nodded. 'I'll say it is.

'Never even knew he owned a football.'

'Nor me,' Terry said. 'It's brand-new, like: never been used.'

'Is he any good at football?' Meg asked.

'No he ain't,' Terry said emphatically. 'He's flipping useless. Our Billy could play better than him. He don't even play football at his school. He plays summat called "rugger". Anyway,' he added, 'he said he'll have to learn the rules so he is going with his dad to a match this afternoon.'

Nicholas didn't enjoy the football match because he barely knew his cousins. In the company of Uncle Robert's sons, Stan and Dave, he felt like a baby. Dave was the same age as Nicholas but in September he had joined his father at Dunlop's, where sixteen-year-old

Stan had been working for two years. As they barely knew Nicholas they tended to talk mainly to Terry.

And Nicholas decided it was all very well for his mother to crow on about how getting a good education now would mean a better job in the future, Nicholas thought, but in the meantime these were his relatives and the people he lived among, and he hardly knew them. He hadn't made friends with many boys at school either, because most of them came from much more affluent backgrounds and he was nervous about their finding out he lived in a back-to-back house. There were bullies at the school who he was sure would make his life a misery if it ever got out. In contrast, there hadn't got to be any pretence with his cousins, so he decided there and then to get to know them better, to take charge of his own life and try and make his mother understand that he wasn't a little boy any more.

By the end of October Meg knew she had to get some winter clothes for Ruth, when she did the usual Friday shopping. Charlie had given her the extra money she had asked for and Terry had told her to go ahead and not to rush back, that they could make something for themselves at lunchtime.

Meg thought it was nice to be able to take her time and not have one eye on the clock, so after she had bought her usual purchases, she and Billy made for the Market Hall. As usual the pram was carried up the steps by willing helpers and Billy had his play with the animals at Pimm's pet shop before they set off to look around the stalls for clothes for Ruth. They watched the clock strike midday and then Meg found a stall with some beautiful baby clothes, including a fair number of winter-weight dresses. Most were not new, but Ruth wouldn't care about that. They were very pretty, for although they were mainly white or cream they had pretty designs on them or beautiful smocking or contrasting collars. There were fluffy little cardigans and warm pram sets with matching bonnets and bootees, and they were all so reasonable she was pleased to be able to buy a big bundle of clothing.

'All for you, this is, miss,' she told the baby, who rewarded her with a smile.

'Well, long time no see,' said a voice beside her.

Meg swung round. 'Joy,' she cried. 'How lovely to see you again.'

'Yes,' Joy agreed. 'I come here most Fridays and have a mooch round and a bite to eat usually, in the café. Like to join me and we can have a natter?'

'Oh, I don't think . . .'

Joy knew what was bothering Meg. 'My treat today,' she said.

'Oh, no, I couldn't possibly—'

'Course you could,' Joy said. 'Got paid today so I'm flush at the moment.' And then she glanced at Billy and with a wink she said, 'Bet you'd like something to eat?'

Billy, who was always hungry, nodded his head with gusto. 'Not half,' he said.

Joy laughed. 'Come on,' she urged. 'You can't leave yet anyway 'cos it's pouring.'

Joy was right, Meg realised, for outside the rain was coming down in sheets. 'Just a cup of tea then,' she conceded.

But Joy wasn't content for Meg to sit there with just

a cup of tea and she ordered egg on toast for the three of them, followed by doughnuts. What impressed Billy most was the fact that she got tea for him too, which he often didn't get at home, and she didn't mind that he put three spoonfuls of sugar in it. Although he saw Meg frown at him, he took no heed of that, knowing that she was unlikely to tell him off in front of her friend.

After they had finished Meg fed Ruth, and still they talked on. Billy swung his legs and listened while he licked the sugar off his fingers. Joy felt immeasurably sorry for Meg, who, though her little brother was sweet and the baby delightful, wouldn't be able to have any sort of life for many years.

Meanwhile Joy was enjoying her new-found freedom and the money she earned each week. Some she had to pay to her mother, but what she had left was enough to buy clothes in the Bull Ring, or C & A Modes for better-quality clothes. She also went to the pictures once a week and had started taking dancing lessons with friends she had been to school with. She had been drawn to make friends with Meg from the day she had taken her up for her interview in Lewis's and now she felt she would like to help her in some way.

'How about if we meet up here every Friday?' she suggested.

Meg shook her head. 'I have to be back by lunchtime. The children come home for dinner, you see. Today they are seeing to themselves,' she added, 'because I had to buy Ruth some new clothes.'

'How old is your eldest brother?'

'Terry's twelve.'

'So say you left soup or something?' Joy persisted. 'He's old enough to dish it up and get them all back to school on time.'

'Oh, I don't know,' Meg said. 'My dad might not like it.'

'What difference would it make to him?'

'None, I suppose,' Meg said. 'It's just I've got out of the habit of thinking about myself.'

'Then start again,' Joy said. 'God blimey, Meg, you're a long time dead.'

Meg's laugh startled the drowsy baby a little and Joy said, 'Why don't you put it to your dad? I'm sure he will see no harm in it. Anyway,' she said, getting to her feet, 'must be away or I'll be getting my cards, but I'll be here next week about the same time if you can make it.'

'I'll try,' Meg promised, and she sat enviously watching her friend returning to work while she held Ruth against her shoulder, rubbing her back in case she had wind.

SIX

Meg might never have got round to mentioning her meeting Joy if it hadn't been for Billy telling them that evening about meeting a kind lady.

'And who is this kind lady?' Charlie asked.

Billy shrugged and said, 'Dunno, but she bought us egg on toast and doughnuts and her name is Joy and she don't half talk a lot.'

They all laughed and Terry put in, 'Surprised you noticed that, Billy. Bit like pot calling kettle.' for everyone knew Billy was a chatterbox.

Charlie, though, was more interested in who the 'kind lady' was. He knew because of what she had taken on that Meg had few friends now, and certainly not one who would treat her and her young brother to egg on toast and doughnuts.

'Billy's right,' she told her father. 'Her name is Joy, Joy Tranter. She's the girl from Lewis's that took me up to the interview the day Mom fell in the yard.'

'Fancy her remembering you all this time.'

Meg nodded. 'Yeah, I know. I mean only saw her for

a short time and yet we sort of hit it off. I thought we might have become friends if I'd worked there.'

Charlie heard the wistfulness in Meg's voice and felt guilty that she had no friends her own age. 'Haven't you seen her since?'

'Just once before today,' Meg said. 'She goes to the Bull Ring often on a Friday because it's her pay day and she has a mooch around the shops and treats herself to a snack in the Market Hall café, but normally I have to be home for the children at twelve so I leave before her dinner hour.'

'So what happened today?'

'I had to buy some winter clothes for Ruth today, remember?' Meg said. 'The children sorted themselves out.'

'And it did them no harm, I would say,' Charlie said. He looked from one child to the other. 'Did it?'

'No, Dad,' they chorused.

'So can you do that every Friday so Meg has a chance to meet her friend?'

They all nodded solemnly, and Meg was touched by her father's consideration and the children falling in with his plan so readily. 'I didn't think you would be so keen on me going every week.'

'Why on earth not?' Charlie said. 'God, Meg it's not much to ask.'

'And I am not helpless,' Terry said. 'I am twelve, you know, not two.'

'I could leave you some soup or something just to heat up.'

'There's no need.'

'Well, I'll leave the details up to you,' Charlie said. 'But in the meantime, Meg, while it was very nice of your friend to treat you today, I shouldn't think she earns that much so she wouldn't want to do it every week.'

'I shouldn't want her to do it either,' Meg said.

'No, I will give you separate money for yourself.'

'How?' Meg asked. She knew how finely the finances were balanced.

'Never you mind how,' Charlie said, knowing he would have to cut back on the ciggies and beer to give Meg an extra five bob a week, but he thought there was nothing to be gained by telling her this.

Christmas grew nearer. Although it was only six months since their mother died Meg wanted to make Christmas Day a special one for Jenny, Sally and Billy, who still believed in Santa Claus.

Her aunt Rosie could see her point and suggested Meg talk to her father lest he be upset, so she mentioned it to him as they sat over a cup of tea one evening. He was quiet when she had finished and she feared she had offended him.

'Do you think me awful, Dad?

'For what exactly?'

'You know, planning to celebrate Christmas and all with Mom dead less than six months?'

Charlie thought for a little while and then he said, 'No, Meg I don't think you're awful. You knew your mother almost as well as I did and she wouldn't have wanted us to mourn for ever.'

Meg nodded. 'I know.'

'Or for the young ones to miss out because she isn't here anymore. She loved everything about Christmas,' Charlie said, and a smile tugged at his mouth as he recalled his wife's excitement in past years as the season approached.

Meg smiled in memory too. 'Yes, she was worse than the children, stringing up the streamers and decorations and adorning the tree.

'She never minded all the cooking,' Charlie said. 'She revelled in it, she did, and the house used to smell beautiful with all the delicious food and cakes and puddings and all she cooked. Do you remember?'

'Of course.' Her mother's enthusiasm had engendered a love of Christmas in all of the children; even Meg's toes would curl in anticipation as it grew near.

'Do you know what I think we must do?' Charlie said suddenly. 'This is our first Christmas without Maeve and we owe it to her to have the very best Christmas we can in her memory. That would be what she would want us to do, and for children that means presents.'

'I've been saving for months,' Meg said proudly.

'So how much have you saved?' Charlie asked.

'Nearly two pounds and ten shillings.'

'Well done,' said Charlie. 'You're almost as good a manager as your mother.'

That was high praise indeed, for her father was always saying her mother could make sixpence do the work of a shilling, and then he surprised her still further by putting a ten-pound note in her hand. She had never seen so much money at one time and she stared at it in amazement. 'Where did you get it?'

Charlie laughed. 'You can get that look off your face,

girl, because I didn't rob a bank. It's part of the Christmas Club that I have to pay into every year. It's taken out of my wages and ensures that we all have a good Christmas. Use it to get some things for the young ones, at least.'

'I will, Daddy,' Meg said. Joy's going to help me choose because she said it is lovely to buy presents for children who still believe. And it is, so thanks for this.'

'I don't need thanks,' Charlie said. 'I'm their father and I know it will be a tough time. Perhaps it will help if they have presents they will enjoy opening on Christmas morning.'

Meg bought skipping ropes for the girls and more toy cars for Billy and a spinning top for each, which Joy encouraged her to buy. Seeing Meg hesitate, the coster wound up three spinning tops. 'Just a tanner each,' he said. 'Watch this.' And he set them off so they danced along the stall, twirling like dervishes so that the patterns on them melded into rings of vibrant colours. 'On the table, on the chair, little devils go everywhere,' he chanted. Meg, knowing the children would be delighted with them, parted with one and six.

'What about your older brother?' Joy asked as they turned away from the stall.

'A model,' Meg said decidedly, heading for the Hobbies shop. 'He loves making up sailing ships. He has quite few but there are bound to be some he hasn't got yet.'

There were, of course, and then Meg picked up the Swiss army knife that she had seen Terry lusting over, a large bag of marbles for Billy, and a set of rattles and building blocks for Ruth. And from Woolworth's opposite the Market Hall she got some ribbons and slides for Jenny and Sally's hair, colouring books and crayons for the three youngest and a bottle of whiskey for her father.

'I just love Christmas, don't you?' Joy said a little later in the Market Hall as she placed her bowl of soup on the table.

'Yes,' Meg said. 'And Mom did.'

Joy gasped. 'Oh, Meg, I'm sorry.'

Meg shrugged. "S'all right,' she said. 'Dad said we must make it a special time for the others, that she would want us to. Like he said, we can't mourn for ever.'

That night, with the children in bed, Meg showed Terry and her father the things she had bought for her younger brother and sisters. Charlie smiled proudly and said she was getting more like her mother every day.

The children entered into the spirit of the occasion, weaving garlands to be pinned around the house, helping decorate the tree Charlie had unearthed from the cupboard in the attic, and making a wish as they stirred the Christmas pudding Meg had made with more than a bit of help from May.

A few days before Christmas Eve, a large crate was delivered to the house. The children were at school and Billy was at May's house 'helping' her make mince pies, so Meg could open the crate from her mother's family in America, which she found was filled with presents for them all.

There were beautiful rag dolls for Sally and Jenny. They had pretty painted faces and dark brown hair in plaits, the ends tied with shiny ribbons. The clothes, too, were magnificent: they were dressed in Victorian costume, even down to the pantaloons and petticoats, with velvet dresses. Jenny's doll wore dark red and Sally's midnight blue, and the dresses were decorated with lace at the neck and cuffs of the sleeves, with a matching jacket over that and black leather boots covering their cloth feet. Meg knew that the girls would be almost speechless at owing such beautiful dolls; even Jenny, who had said only the other day that she was getting too old to play with them. But not dolls like these, Meg was sure – no one in the streets around them would have anything so fine.

Billy had a wind-up train on a track. From the box lid it looked a tremendously exciting thing and Meg could guess that her father and Terry would play with it just as much as Billy would. For Ruth there was a soft fluffy teddy and a Jack-in-the-box, which Meg felt sure she would enjoy, though they might have to work it for her at first.

They had sent Meg an elegant watch with a silver face and a leather strap, in its own box. She laid the watch over her wrist and turned her hand this way and that, for it was the first watch she had ever owned. When she lifted out the large box for her father and realised it contained cigars, she suddenly remembered her mother had always bought a few cigars for her father at Christmas, because he always said it properly completed the dinner. Terry's box was even larger and contained Meccano, the lid decorated with all the things that a person could make with all the metal rods and plates and screws and bolts.

Underneath the toys there were clothes. Hat, scarf and glove sets for the three girls, a soft grey cardigan for her father, seamen's jumpers for Terry and Billy. And for Ruth there was a little pink padded all-in-one that would cover her clothes and could be zipped up snugly. It had a little fur-trimmed hood and mittens attached and Meg knew, whatever the weather, Ruth would be as warm as toast in that.

She decided not to mention the presents at all; she wrapped everything up again, put them back in the crate and bumped it up the stairs to hide it in her mother's side of the wardrobe, where her father never went.

Downstairs once more, she opened the small parcel she had taken from the very bottom of the crate to find it contained cards from all her American relations and a letter from her mother's eldest brother. He said that the presents were from all of them.

This will probably be a sorrowful time for all your family, because it is the first without your mother, and so we all hope the things we've sent, especially the toys for the children, will help a little on Christmas morning and hope, despite the inevitable sense of loss, you still manage to enjoy the day.

As she read the letter, tears prickled behind Meg's eyes at the kindness of her mother's brothers and sister. Strange to think that she had relatives miles away that she would probably never see, though she knew plenty more were in the same boat.

Christmas Day began very early. The children exclaimed in delight as they pulled one item after another from the stocking they had hung on the bedhead, and declared themselves pleased as punch with everything. Despite the early hour they were so interested in playing with them that Meg had trouble getting them all ready for Mass in time.

After a wonderful roast chicken dinner, praised by everyone, followed by the sumptuous pudding they had all stirred, Charlie said that he would wash up the dishes and Terry could dry them and give Meg a break. She was really touched by such thoughtfulness and when all was finished she asked her father to give her a hand bringing something downstairs and so produced the crate. As they examined the contents they were almost speechless with pleasure and Meg blessed those kind people in America. The excitement the children felt at being given things they never in their wildest dreams imagined they'd ever own drove any sadness they might be feeling to the back of their minds, and the day took on an almost magical quality. Charlie smoked his cigar and treated himself to a small glass of whiskey, with a look of delighted pleasure on his face, and later, when the boys set out the clockwork railway, he was as interested as they, while Ruth sat on Meg's knee and waved her arms excitedly, fascinated by the trains running around the track.

The girls had taken their rag dolls out on the street to be admired by their friends, and when the cold and darkness drew them in they did some colouring with the new books and crayons. No one was interested in much tea, but Meg made a few chicken sandwiches and put them on the table with the Christmas cake that was May's present to them. There were mince pies as well, some of which Billy had helped May make, so they were a bit squashed-looking but they tasted all right.

When everyone had eaten what they wanted, Charlie led them all in carol singing. Her father had such a pleasant voice that Meg would have been happy just to listen, but Charlie would have none of it and soon she was singing along with the rest. They sang till the children were yawning and Ruth had fallen asleep on her knee, and when Meg got up to make a last drink for the children before bed she placed her in her father's arms.

He was about to protest but Meg said, 'This is your baby daughter and she has just enjoyed her first Christmas. Is it too much to ask that you nurse her while I make us all a drink?'

Charlie looked down at the sleeping child, her warm body snuggled into him. He knew he would never feel the same for her as he did the others, but that knowledge would upset Meg and he had no desire to do that today of all days. So he said, 'No, Meg, 'course it isn't.'

Meg made tea for them all with a smile on her face. Christmas Day was almost over and she had done more than just survive it, she had enjoyed it and she thought she could look to the future with confidence.

SEVEN

In late February, as the weather became just a little warmer, Ruth suddenly rolled over on the mat in front of the fire and drew her legs underneath her. May, who was having a cup of tea with Meg, chuckled. 'That young 'un will be crawling afore long,' she said. 'Then the fun will start.'

May was right. The next day Ruth crept forward a few hesitant paces, but by the end of the week she was going at a hefty pace. 'One body's work, they are at that age,' May remarked, and Meg knew she was right. The children were great at minding their baby sister when they were home, but there was still the washing and housework to be done during the day when Meg was alone now that Billy was at school too.

'Without May next door I would be lost,' Meg told Joy when they met in mid March . 'She minds her when I am in the brew house doing the washing or ironing the stuff the following day.'

'What about your auntie?' Joy asked. 'Rose – isn't that her name? Doesn't she give a hand?'

'She used to, but she won't be able to soon,' Meg said.

'Why not?'

'She's getting a job. Says the money will come in handy. It was a shock to me because there was no mention of her getting any sort of job before.'

'Well, there weren't jobs about for many people,' Joy pointed out. 'Lots of men couldn't get jobs either. You'd see lines of them just standing on street corners.'

'Yes,' Meg said. 'There's not so many of them now.'

'That's because they think there might be a war and they are getting prepared,' Joy said. 'What's your aunt looking into?'

'Sewing parachutes,' Meg said. 'Says it's really well paid.'

Joy grimaced. 'Our dad says if there is going to be a war it will be fought from the air and they'll drop bombs on us like the Germans did in that Spanish town a while ago. I suppose people are getting windy now because of the Anschluss a few days ago'

'Oh, yes,' Meg said. 'My cousin Nicholas keeps going on about that. But I don't see it's that much of a problem. I mean, Hitler's Austrian, isn't he, and the Austrian Government seemed to welcome him with open arms.'

'Hardly that.'

'All right then,' Meg conceded. 'But there was no fighting or anything.'

'No,' Joy agreed.

'So Hitler's happy and Austria must be too or they would have done something about it, so what has it got to do with us?'

Joy shrugged. 'I can see what you are saying, but I

reckon we just might be dragged into it somehow. I mean, your Nicholas thinks there's going to be a war, doesn't he?'

'He's certain sure of it. He goes on about the way Germany is treating the Jews and how we can't stand by and see it happen, but no one in their right mind wants another war.'

Meg was right: no one did, especially those who remembered the carnage of the last one. But the papers were full of the atrocities Germany was committing against the Jews; even the voices of the announcers on the wireless seemed doom-laden. 'Fascism' was the word bandied about a lot, like the Nazi Party that Hitler led in Germany, and Meg had been quite surprised that Britain had its own Fascist party, led by a man called Oswald Mosley, who seemed to dislike the Jews as much as Hitler did.

She didn't really want to think too much about it, and when talking to Nicholas she tried to steer any conversation away from the subject of war. But it seemed like it was all Nicholas wanted to talk about until one day she snapped, 'Oh, go on, Nicholas, you can clap your hands with joy at the thought of another war because you will be safe as houses away at school while others fight your battles for you.'

'No, you're wrong,' Nicholas said. 'If we were to go to war, I would enlist as soon as I was old enough, sooner if they'd have me.'

'And what about your studies?'

'What about them?'

'Your mother would never stand for you leaving school.'

'She would have to.'

'Well, thank God we shall never have to put it to the test,' Meg said firmly.

On Saturday 1 October 1938, when Nicholas called in with Terry after football, Meg had the pictures in the *Despatch* ready to show him. 'So much for you going on about war all the time, Nicholas Hallett,' she said, stabbing her finger at the picture of Prime Minister Neville Chamberlain waving a piece of paper in his hand as he walked down the steps from an aeroplane.

'"Peace for Our Time".' She read the headline out to him. 'Peace – see, it's what every sensible person wants. Peace, not war.'

She knew why Nicholas had thought that there might be a war, because her father had told her that many European countries, especially those near – or sharing borders with – Germany had become uneasy after the Anschluss, especially when Hitler starting grumbling about Sudetenland.

'Where is this Sudetenland?' Meg had asked him. 'I've never heard of it before.'

'Well, it's part of Czechoslovakia now,' Charlie said. 'It used to be part of Germany once and was taken off them after the Great War.'

'Why?' Meg asked. 'I didn't think you did that sort of thing to countries.'

'It was like punishing Germany,' Charlie said, and he shrugged. 'Anyway, now Hitler wants it back because he claims most of the people there speak German and think of themselves as German, so leaders of countries, including our Neville Chamberlain, are meeting in Munich to decide what to do.'

Meg had not wanted to think very much about politics up until then, knowing whatever government was in power did little good for ordinary people. But now, knowing some of the background, she was interested in the outcome of the meeting. However, the news was good. They'd all agreed to Hitler's demands and given him back Sudetenland, and any problem with Germany had been averted.

However, almost immediately things changed. Meg knew, for instance, that the Birmingham Small Arms Company had begun making guns because two men in the same street, who had been unemployed for years, got jobs there. Then her father, told her that Dunlop's had started making different tyres for military vehicles.

In late October she discussed these changes with Joy as they ate lunch and Joy shared her concern.

'The thing that bothers me most,' Joy said, 'is the fact that I really doubt they would go to all this trouble just to be on the safe side? I mean, I have an uncle who's begun work in what they call a shadow factory beside Vickers in Castle Bromwich, and they're assembling aeroplanes.'

'Aeroplanes?' Meg repeated, and felt a flutter of trepidation. 'It's like my aunt sewing parachutes. Like you said, in peacetime why would we want so many parachutes, or planes either?'

'Maybe Chamberlain was just playing for time,' Joy said. 'You know, giving us a chance to get ready.'

A chilling shiver ran through Meg. 'Oh, Joy, I hope you're wrong.'

'So do I,' said Joy. 'Two of my uncles were killed in the last war, leaving my aunts widows. Each of them left a son. They are worried to death. The Great War was supposed to be the war to end all wars; although they lost their husbands in that, they thought at least their sons wouldn't be sent to fight.'

'It doesn't seem fair, does it?'

'No it flipping doesn't,' Joy said. 'And if the unthinkable happens and we do go to war, people say it won't be a war like any other. If they bomb us like they did in Spain, what are we going to do?'

'But surely they'll find some way of protecting us if we do go to war?'

'I'd like to think so,' Joy said. 'But maybe we're worrying before we need to – you know, like meeting trouble halfway?'

Meg nodded. 'Mom always said something like that. She maintained that you should cross bridges only when you come to them.'

'That's what we will do then,' Joy declared. 'And we may find in the end we won't need a bridge at all.'

Charlie bought a wireless. He said it was best to keep abreast of things. Meg thought the plays and comedy shows were very entertaining and that nothing lifted the spirits like a bit of music, and the children always listened to *Children's Hour* as they drank their cocoa before bed. However, Meg soon discovered the downside of having a wireless was the fact it often brought disturbing news. Somehow she found it far worse to hear about things spoken directly into the living room than to read about them in the newspaper. She could always put the paper aside if a certain article upset her, but she couldn't do that so easily with the wireless, especially when her father was so interested in the news. On the evening of 10 November, with the younger children in bed, Meg and Terry were sitting with their father drinking a cup of tea and listening to a play when the commentator interrupted to tell them of a pogrom against the Jews in Munich that had begun the previous day. The attacks were carried out by storm troopers, members of Hitler Youth and other interested parties, in retaliation for the assassination of a German official in Paris at the hands of a Jewish youth.

The commentator went on:

It is estimated two hundred and fifty synagogues are burned and seven thousand Jewish businesses destroyed and looted. People have been thrown from their homes and many have perished while their homes have been looted. Jewish cemeteries, hospitals and schools have also suffered the same fate, and so much glass has been broken they are calling it 'Kristallnacht' or the 'Night of Broken Glass'.

Meg sat and stared, stunned, at the wireless, and Terry, she saw, was little better. Charlie reached over and snapped the wireless off as Meg cried, 'Dad, I've never heard anything so horrific.'

'There will be further repercussions to this, mark my words,' Charlie said.

'There needs to be,' Meg said hotly. 'We can't let people be treated this way.'

'No, I don't mean that,' Charlie said. 'At the moment we're letting Hitler get away with murder because everyone is afraid. I think he will impose even more sanctions on the Jews to drive the message home that the German Government doesn't want them there, and yet some have lived there for generations and a great many fought for Germany in the Great War. They think of themselves as German.'

'But where would they go – and *why* should they?' Meg asked.

'Because in Hitler's Germany things are done his way, and he is a racist,' Charlie said. 'Already they are barred from using public transport, entering public buildings or attending school. What's next, I ask myself.'

Suddenly Meg got up, crossed the room, pulled the curtain back and looked out at the rain-sodden streets. She tried to imagine what it would be like if it had been they who were thrown out into the night, the house looted and destroyed, and felt a *frisson* of fear trickle down her spine.

Nicholas had told her of the maltreatment that Jews in Germany were suffering and she hadn't really listened, because she had thought that anything, however bad, happening in Germany wouldn't affect her life in any way. Strangely a disembodied voice on the wireless made much more of an impact.

Over the next few days, Meg listened to the wireless as avidly as her father. They heard that a rigid curfew had been imposed on the Jews in Germany. They were forced to repair the damage done to their homes and businesses, though they were not allowed to claim any insurance to help with the cost, and then the repaired houses were occupied by Aryans and allies of the Nazi Party, who also took over their businesses.

It was reported that 274 synagogues had been burned and 7,500 businesses destroyed on the Night of Broken Glass and subsequent nights of violence. No details were given of the 300,000 people who had disappeared, the 91 who lay dead in the street or the 600 driven to take their own lives.

The weeks slid one into another and Meg tried to shake off her despondent mood. None of the younger children could understand why she felt so low, and there was no need for her to frighten them with her unease about the war. Another crate arrived from America in time for Christmas, and Meg felt better about accepting the gifts now.

After the first crate had arrived out of the blue, she'd felt she should get to know the relations that had sent them such fine and thoughtful things, and she now wrote to them regularly. She felt she had got to know them all so well: her mother's eldest brother, Bobbie, the two younger ones, Martin and Jimmy, and her sister, Christie. She loved their replies, which were often humorous, and if she asked specific questions about her mother they never ignored them, or told her not to think about such thing like they all did in Birmingham – just as if Maeve had never existed – but would answer her questions honestly and she appreciated that.

She even knew what they looked like now, because they had sent photographs, all of them standing with their families, looking happy and healthy, and Christie so like Maeve it gave Meg quite a jolt. She had borrowed May's Brownie box camera to send pictures of them back and Bobbie wrote that they looked a fine bunch. Later Christie wrote asking all their sizes so Meg had guessed that they would be sending clothes. The crate contained good thick winter coats for them all, even Charlie, all beautifully made and with fleece linings. Ruth's all-in-one this year was dark pink with lighter pink fur lining. There was also a selection of books, board games, boxes of chocolates, and a pair of silk stockings for Meg.

By the end of January 1939 world events ceased to concern Meg as much as the foul weather, and she was immensely grateful for the new winter coats. A heavy snowfall had frozen, then further snow had fallen on top of the ice; then this had frozen, too and so on all week. It played havoc with the sports fixtures, with many events cancelled, and so, on the last Friday evening in January as they ate their dinner Charlie had said that Terry mustn't even try to play football in the park the following morning.

'Not worth it,' he said. 'You'd only have to fall on that frozen ground and you'd end up with a broken leg or something.'

Instead, Terry had gone to get his hair cut, and their dad had given the younger ones money for the pictures, so Meg and Ruth had the house to themselves for once, but the children hadn't long left the house when Meg was surprised to see Nicholas come in the door. 'Terry's not playing football today,' she said, 'because of the weather.'

'I know,' Nicholas said. 'I spotted him going in to the barber's and took a chance on getting you on your own.'

'Oh?'

'Yeah. I need to tell you something, but it's sort of delicate.'

'Can't be that delicate,' Meg declared, with a smile. 'Come on, spit it out.'

Nicholas's expression didn't alter, yet he didn't answer and Meg felt the first stirrings of unease. But she was the sort of person to meet trouble head on so a little impatiently she said, 'Come on, Nicholas, you can tell me and if you don't do it soon Terry may well be in on top of us. Doesn't take long to do a short back and sides.'

Nicholas blurted out, 'I – I . . . look, this is really awkward but look, I think your dad has a girlfriend.'

Meg was flabbergasted, and extremely relieved that there was no one else there to hear words that surely couldn't possibly be true. It was nonsense, it had to be nonsense, and that was what she told her cousin.

He shrugged. 'Thought it better to prepare you, like.'

'Prepare me?' Meg said. 'Shock me, more like, coming here telling me things that are not true.'

'If you say so.'

'But it can't be true.'

'Look, Meg, I've told you something and you don't want to believe it,' Nicholas said. 'There's nothing I can do about that, so we'll have to leave it there.'

'Oh, all right then,' Meg said impatiently. 'What have you seen or heard that has made you think that my father is having some sort of affair?'

'I overheard my parents talking about it,' Nicholas

said. 'I was supposed to be doing my homework in the attic but I was coming down for a drink and I heard them.'

'So what did they say?'

'Dad said he hoped your dad knew what he was doing, messing about with the likes of Doris Caudwell. And Mom said there was no fool like an old fool, and Dad said he's a bit of a laughing stock at the pub and that she'd set out to get her claws into him from the start.'

Meg groaned. 'I bet he's a laughing stock,' she said grimly. 'But who is this Doris Caudwell?'

'Search me,' Nicholas said. 'I think I've seen her, though.'

'How have you done that?'

'She met your dad from the tram the other evening,' Nicholas said.

'I thought all the men come home together?'

'They do. I don't know if she meets him regularly or how long it's being going on or anything, because I'm not usually on the same tram, but a couple of nights ago I had a detention for not handing my homework in on time.' And here he grinned at Meg ruefully and went on, 'Not that I told Mom the real reason why I was late home. Said I volunteered for extra maths. As if?'

'Get on with it,' Meg said impatiently.

'Yeah, anyway, Dad and Uncle Robert and your dad wouldn't have known I was on the same tram because I was on the top deck and they were already inside when I got on but I didn't know that and I was coming down the stairs as the tram pulled in to Bristol Street and saw this woman waiting by the stop. I didn't take that much notice at first, but then I saw your dad seemed mighty pleased to see her, and my dad and Uncle Robert were talking to him on the pavement, sort of arguing, and didn't see me sneak past. As I went up Bristol Passage, I looked back, and it was as if they were trying to reason with your dad, but he suddenly pulled free of my dad and went off down the road with the woman. I didn't wait to see any more. I made for home and was in quite a bit before Dad. I reckon he and Uncle Robert were talking about it.'

Meg was chewing her thumbnail. She knew Nicholas was right. Her father had been coming in late for a week or two now, always blaming the traffic and she had thought the traffic was going slower because of the snow and the ice.

'Why didn't they talk it over with me?' she demanded. 'Surely that would have been the thing to do.'

'They probably didn't want to upset you.'

'It's not them would upset me,' Meg said. 'It's my dad with this sort of secret carry-on.'

'Maybe they thought it would amount to nothing in the end,' Nicholas said. 'You know, a flash in the pan, and you wouldn't have had to know a thing about it.'

There was a silence between them and then Meg said, 'What's she like, this woman?'

Nicholas shrugged. 'Just a woman, you know. I only caught a glimpse of her. Sort of ordinary.' He paused and then asked her, 'What are you going to do?'

'Nothing for now,' Meg said after a moment. 'If your dad and Uncle Robert are right and this is just a fling, it will all blow over. I might make things worse if I say anything now. I think I'll wait and see. And, Nicholas, I don't want the others to know anything about it.'

'I won't say a word,' he promised.

EIGHT

By March, which had come in like the proverbial lion sending icy gusts of wind funnelling down the street, Charlie began leaving the house on Saturday nights as well as being late on Fridays, and then he started disappearing on Sunday afternoons too. By the time the month was drawing to a close, he was out a couple of nights in the week as well. Meg said nothing, but Billy and Sally had begun to ask where he was going.

'Just out,' Charlie would answer them. 'When a man works all week, he values time to himself.'

Meg had thought he might be reverting to the drink, but she never heard him staggering about the place, and he seemed to have no trouble getting up in the morning. Although she still worried that his lady friend might be unsuitable, she had to confess that she'd seldom seen her dad so cheerful since her mom died. He came home from work with a smile on his face and whistled around the house, or sang snatches of songs like he used to do.

One evening, Meg decided to tackle her dad about the mysterious Doris Caudwell for all their sakes. The night was a cold one and she pulled the curtains tighter

94

across the windows and shook more coal onto the fire, then put the wireless on for company so that big band music filled the room as she settled to wait for his return.

By the time Charlie came home, Meg was asleep, but she roused herself as he came in the door. She was still bleary-eyed as she snapped off the wireless and faced him.

'What is it?' he asked anxiously. 'Is everything all right? The children . . .?'

'The children are fine,' Meg said.

'So, why are you waiting up?'

'To ask you something,' Meg said. 'Something that I shouldn't have to ask you.'

'What?' Charlie asked, but he knew full well what his daughter was getting at and she knew it too.

'Oh, come on, Dad,' she snapped impatiently. 'Don't play the innocent. Are you going out with a woman called Doris Caudwell, or aren't you?'

The red blush that flooded over Charlie's face told its own tale, and Meg felt as if a lead weight had settled in her stomach.

Shamefaced, her father nodded. 'Who told you?'

'That doesn't matter,' Meg said, and added a little bitterly, 'It could have been any of a number of people, because one thing I am pretty sure of is that it wasn't a secret to anyone but us, and for the life of me I can't think why that was.'

'I didn't want to upset you.'

'D'you think this is any less upsetting?' Meg snapped. 'And when did you intend to tell us, or were you just going to install her in the house as your wife and the

95

children's mother without any sort of consultation about it at all?'

'Of course not,' Charlie said. 'I just thought you might feel it too soon after your mother.'

'If you feel that way, you shouldn't have begun any sort of relationship,' Meg said icily.

'I . . . I don't feel that way,' Charlie said. 'At least . . . goddammit, Meg, you know what I thought of your mother, and when she died I didn't go looking for someone else or anything.'

'So how did you meet this woman?'

'I met her in the Swan where she had come in for a drink with another woman,' Charlie said.

Meg curled her lip. Women who went into public houses alone were considered to be the lowest of the low.

'Now don't look like that,' Charlie censored. 'She's not loose or anything like that, but the other woman was going to see her chap and didn't want to go into the pub alone, and as Doris is a widow she agreed to go in with her. She is actually quite alone in the world, for she has no children and no siblings, and neither had her late husband. Their parents are long dead. She's also a stranger here, drafted from Yorkshire.

'You seem to know a lot about her from one meeting,' Meg commented.

'That first time we met it was your uncle Robert who did most of the talking.'

That surprised Meg. 'Why?'

'Because she works at the same place as Rosie,' Charlie said. 'She doesn't know her. Apparently they work in different areas. Doris actually doesn't know many people, unless you count the woman she came out with. She says she hasn't had time to make friends yet.'

'Where does she live?'

'She has a small flat on Bristol Street.'

'Why did she come here from Yorkshire?'

'Because she said she didn't mind where she went,' Charlie answered patiently. 'See, she was a seamstress and not getting that much money and, as she said, she had to provide for herself after her husband died. So when she heard that war-related work was paying more, she made enquiries. They asked what she could do, and when she told them, they asked if she wanted work near to home. She said she didn't mind where she went and so she arrived here.'

'So that was the first time you saw her,' Meg said. 'So why didn't you leave it there?'

'Because when she was there again the following week, I couldn't just ignore her.'

'And you asked her out?'

'Yes,' Charlie said. 'I did,' and added a little defiantly. 'To tell the truth I felt a bit sorry for her. And I know how she feels because I'm often lonely myself.'

The plaintive note in Charlie's voice gave Meg a bit of a jolt, for she had wondered before if her father might be lonely and she felt sorry for him until he said 'Do you know, I really envy Robert and Alec going home to loving wives and warm beds.'

'Oh,' Meg snapped 'Is that what you were hoping for: a warm bed with a woman you had just met?'

''Course not,' Charlie said. 'There was nothing in it then. Just two lonely people being company for one another. We saw a film at the cinema in Bristol Road and popped into the Trees for a quick drink afterwards and that was the extent of it.'

'But it didn't stay like that?' Meg tried to hide the deep hurt flowing through her body.

'No, it didn't stay like that,' Charlie said. 'That's how relationships do develop. Doris thanked me and said how much she had enjoyed it, and I realised I had too, and I took her out the following week, and so it went on, but I never went looking for it.'

'But you did nothing to stop it once you did see what was happening,' Meg said. 'How could you, Daddy? Mom has been dead only just over eighteen months.'

'There isn't a timescale on these things, Meg.'

'Then there blooming well ought to be,' Meg burst out. Even recognising her father's lonely state, she felt such pain at what she saw as his betrayal, and knowing how powerless she was to change the situation, she lashed out. 'Just what sort of father are you? You knew Mom was risking her life to carry another child and she died giving birth to the child of that union, a child that you then refused to have anything to do with. Little Ruth will grow up without the love of a father or a mother, but it isn't her fault that Mom died. And now, when she is barely cold, you are seeking to replace her.'

Charlie stared at her. 'I will forgive you for your outburst,' he said. 'I can see you're extremely upset.'

Meg could feel a pulse beating in her head as white-hot fury filled her body and she screamed, 'I am not upset, I'm bloody angry. Do you think you are the only one that's lonely? There isn't a day goes by when I don't miss Mom and wish she was here, and I am very lonely at times, too, but all you care about is your bloody self.'

Charlie was taken aback by his daughter's vehemence but tried for a conciliatory tone. 'I did it for you, too, if you would only see that.'

'Oh, don't make me laugh,' Meg said. 'You did it for you. The rest of us don't matter.'

'You do matter,' Charles insisted. 'But Doris will be here to see to the children now and that means that you can have a life of your own.'

Meg's head was whirring. 'She knows about us then, this Doris?'

'She knows that I am a widower and that I have children,' Charlie said, and added a little nervously, 'I didn't tell her how many. Didn't want to scare her off. After all, she isn't that used to children.'

'So how do you know she'll take us all on?'

'If she marries me, of course she'll take you on,' Charlie said. 'It's a wife's duty.'

Meg knew how traditional her father's views were. He would expect his wife to get up before him in the morning, make him breakfast, pack up his sandwiches, keep house all day and be there when he got in after work with a hot meal on the table. 'What if she really likes her job and doesn't want to give it up?' Meg asked. 'Or really can't cope with the house and kids and that?'

'Meg,' Charlie said, 'Doris is a lonely woman who I'm sure wants to be married and I am willing to marry her. I don't know if I love her like I did your mother, but I am fond of her. She will be grateful to have another crack at marriage and will give her job up without a qualm when we wed. And of course she'll cope. She is a woman, and caring for husband, children and a house is what women are born to do.'

Meg knew her father really believed that. She gave a sigh and realised how bone-weary she must look when her father said, 'Why don't you go up to bed now, Meg? We have talked enough for one night.'

However, once in her room, sleep eluded her; she was too agitated to relax enough just to let go and drift off. She knew the children would have to be told about Doris. They might easily see her as an interloper, and while Meg wouldn't blame them, for their sake she would have to help them accept the inevitable. She tossed and turned as she rehearsed what she would say, eventually falling into a fitful sleep that was filled with lurid nightmares.

Meg decided the children had been in the dark long enough so she told them all together the following morning as they sat having breakfast after Charlie had gone to work.

There was a howl of anguish from Billy at the news. Ruth, sitting on Meg's knee, turned startled eyes on her young brother as he blurted out, 'I don't want no new mother. We got you, ain't we?'

'I don't want one either,' Terry said.

Meg knew it was up to her to get the children to feel at least more positive about the woman, because if their father decided to marry her, they would have no choice in the matter. 'Now come on,' she said. 'You haven't given the woman a chance. You have never even met her.'

'And whose fault is that?' Terry said. 'We never even knew about her till now.'

Sally burst into tears as Billy said mutinously, 'Anyway, I don't want to meet her.'

Sally scrubbed at her eyes with the edge of her cardigan and said, 'Nor me. I don't want someone to come in and try and be our mom. We had a mom and now we have you and I don't want no one else.'

Meg sighed as Ruth, picking up the atmosphere in the room, began to grizzle, and as she cuddled her she said, 'Now you've upset Ruth with your goings-on. You must all realise that if Daddy wants to marry this woman then he will, and none of us can do anything about it.' She looked at the woebegone faces of her brothers and sisters and felt for them, but it was doing them no favours letting them feel that they could influence their father in any way.

'Don't know why he wants another wife anyway,' Terry said. 'We're all right as we are, aren't we?'

'Daddy obviously isn't.'

'Didn't he love our mom?' Jenny asked.

'He did,' Meg said emphatically. 'You know he did. I think maybe he's lonely.'

'How could he be lonely when he has us?' Sally asked.

'It's a different kind of loneliness when you an adult,' Meg said, 'and I know Daddy feels sorry for this Doris, because he told me so.'

'Feels sorry for her?' Terry repeated. 'You don't marry someone because you feel sorry for them.'

'Oh, I should imagine there's more to it than that,' Meg said. 'And really you can't help feeling sorry for her because she's completely alone. Her first husband is dead, and their parents, they had no brothers or sisters and she had no children of her own. You must admit that's sad.'

'Yeah, I suppose.'

'And added to that, she knows very few people here,' Meg went on. 'She comes from Yorkshire but was sent here to sew parachutes like Aunt Rosie.'

'Where did Daddy meet her?'

'In the Swan.'

Jenny's eyes opened wide. 'Was she on her own?'

'I think there were two of them.'

'Mom said she thought women who went to the pub on their own like that were no better than they should be. I heard her telling May one day,' Jenny said.

'You shouldn't have been listening.'

'I couldn't help it,' Jenny cried. 'Anyway, that's what she said. D'you think that?'

Meg did a bit, but it would hardly help Doris's case to say so. She chose her words with care. 'I don't know really. The world is changing all the time. I mean, there are more women working now, married women with families like Aunt Rosie, often doing a man's job. And more women in the Forces than there have ever been, and maybe that changes your perception a bit. Anyway, let's not condemn the woman out of hand. Let's give her a chance, because if Daddy has chosen her, then it would be better for all of you if you try to get on with her.'

As the family were worrying about Doris, news came of discontent spreading throughout central Europe with Hitler's invasion of Czechoslovakia. Not only was the British Government alarmed, but also the governments

102

of many other European countries, especially those near to Germany. Hitler, rumours of war and now Doris Caudwell – Meg felt weighed down with her anxieties.

Meg spent an uneasy couple of weeks with the children. But they were off school from Wednesday for the Easter holidays and she would be meeting Joy on Good Friday. Her father was off work then too, but he declared on that morning he had plans of his own and he would be out all day. Meg could barely bring herself to talk to him and so she said nothing to this and later he came up behind her as she was washing up.

'You seeing Joy today?' he asked.

'Yes, of course.'

'Then take this.' He pressed a pound note into her hand. 'Get some chocolate eggs for the children.'

Meg nodded. 'All right.'

She had intended doing that anyway, as the children had given up sweets for the whole of Lent, so she thought they deserved chocolate eggs on Easter Sunday. She also relished the freedom of going out without Ruth because her siblings would look after her and, she thought wryly, she might be able to have a proper conversation with Joy and a hot cup of tea as she wouldn't be charging around after Ruth all lunchtime.

That day, though, Joy had news of her own that was so upsetting it put Meg's problems with her father and Doris into perspective.

'My brother Colin's joining the Territorial Army . . He has to report next week to Thorp Street Barracks. Our cousin, Barry, is joining as well.'

'But what's it all about?'

'War, that's what it's about,' Joy said. 'They don't ask for a whole lot of young man to volunteer and train them to fight for nothing.'

'No.'

'And there's something else,' Joy said. 'One of our neighbours is in the TA already and he had been doing manoeuvres abroad somewhere. Anyway, his wife was telling Mom he's been recalled. People say if we go to war they're going to be used to guard key installations.'

'Golly,' Meg said. 'It's really getting serious, isn't it?

'I think so. Dad said Hitler had cast his eyes at Poland now, and if he attacks them we will be at war because we have a pact or some such thing.'

'So Nicholas was right all along,' Meg said.

'Looks like,' Joy said. 'Don't you wish he hadn't been?'

'You bet I do,' Meg said. 'But if war comes there isn't a thing we can do about it.'

'I know,' Joy said. 'And that's what's really scary.'

NINE

Despite the worrying world news, life had to go on and what was interrupting Meg's sleep was not Hitler's invasion of Czechoslovakia, but this Doris Caudwell that her dad appeared to have such a fancy for. She knew for the sake of her siblings she was going to try very hard to like the woman but whatever she said, the children could not be persuaded to warm to the idea of a stepmother of any size, shape or description. They had no desire to meet her and were cross and difficult when they heard that their dad had invited her to Sunday tea.

Meg felt she had to make an impression so cleaned the house to within an inch of its life on Saturday while Terry emptied the ashes and black leaded the grate before laying the fire afresh. Meg polished with such vigour that the scent of lavender still lingered in the air on Sunday morning. When Charlie came down dressed ready for Mass the following morning he found Meg on her own apart from Ruth. She was looking around the room in some satisfaction for she felt she had done all she could and the room looked as cosy and inviting as she could make it. Her father said, 'Your mother would have been proud of you for the mature way you are dealing with this, Meg looked at her father coldly, hardly able to believe that she once thought him the greatest man in the universe. 'I would rather you didn't mention my mother today of all days,' she said crisply. 'If Mom was still alive, we wouldn't be having this conversation, nor would we be having a visitor. As for being proud of me, well, it is just to show this Doris that we know how to treat guests.'

'I wish you wouldn't call her "this Doris",' Charlie said.

'Well, I wish lots of things were different too, and "this Doris" is how I think of her,' Meg said. 'But don't worry, I know how to conduct myself. As for me being mature, I'm as heartsick as the children, if you want the truth, but I am keeping a lid on my feelings for their sakes. Today they will have to welcome a person they don't want and didn't think they'd ever need.'

'I know,' Charlie said.

'No, Dad,' Meg replied, 'I don't think you have the least idea how any of us are really feeling. All I'll ask is that you don't rush into this. Take it slowly and make sure we all get to know Doris much better before you make it permanent. It will be better for the children that way.'

As they walked to Mass together later, Charlie was deep in thought. He knew that Meg was right, but he had a feeling things might be taken out of his hands because of what was happening in Europe. He had discussed it with his brothers.

'I reckon I'll be called up if we go to war,' he'd said. Robert had been astounded. 'Surely not?'

'Well, I'm only thirty-eight,' Charlie had said.

'It's the young fellows they'll need.'

'It's every able-bodied fellow they'll need to beat Hitler, if you ask me,' Charlie said. He glanced at Alec, two years his senior. 'You might be going along with me. I was talking to a bloke at work and he said when war is declared there will be a call-up of men from the ages of eighteen to forty-one.'

'How do people get to know these things?'

'I don't know, but if he's right, that's the two of us.'

'Susan will go mad.'

'Think the War Office will care about that?' Charlie said. 'She'll have to cope like everyone else. It's my kids I worry about.'

And he did, because if he wasn't around at all maybe the authorities would take a dim view of Meg looking after all the children on her own. She was only just sixteen now. The children might be taken off her and put into care. He had heard dreadful tales about children placed in care. A man he worked with, having no handy relatives to look after his two children – a baby of twelve months and a little boy of two and a half – had them placed in care while his wife was undergoing surgery in hospital. He tried to see them quite a few times but was prevented from doing so and told it would be upsetting for them. He thought probably that was right, and concentrated his energies on helping his wife get better as quickly as possible.

A couple of months later, when his wife was home and recovered enough to care for the children, they were told that as the children had had no contact with either parent for some time, they had both been adopted and were settled now with new parents. They were not allowed to know where and there was no way they could fight the decision through the courts. Their children were lost to them. The man said his wife was destroyed by the thought she would never see her beloved children again, and six months later she threw herself under a train.

If war was declared, Charlie might have to marry Doris quicker than he had really intended to. He knew she would have him. She'd been hinting at marriage for some time, though initially she had balked when he'd told her how many children he had. She certainly hadn't banked on that. She didn't even like children.

Charlie didn't notice her initial reaction, however, comfortable in the assumption that all women wanted children and considered it a tragedy if they couldn't have any. So he expressed his sympathy to Doris for her childless state and said that it must have been a great cross to bear.

Doris could see that Charlie was nervous about her meeting his children as he called for her that afternoon. She knew all there was to know about men and was aware that while Charlie lusted after her, when she wasn't driving him mad with passion he cared deeply for his children. It was plain to her that to have him she would have to have them, at least for now. The eldest, though, he'd said was sixteen, and the second was fourteen, so soon they'd be off his hands, out to work and sorting themselves out. The other three were coming up and she'd soon have them working for their keep. Pity he'd been landed with the baby. She wondered why he'd kept it when he admitted that he hadn't taken to the child, but that could be gone into later. But still, the children were there for now so a lot hinged on how they would get on that day.

Doris started as she meant to go on. But she dressed with care. She'd had a marcel wave the day before and her hair tinted so there was no hint of grey in her dark blond locks, which fell in folds very becomingly. She had a lovely figure, though she was inclined to be busty, which Charlie took to be an advantage, and the navy-blue costume she'd chosen accentuated her figure to perfection. She wore it over a lacy pink blouse that showed no hint of cleavage, and a pale blue cloche hat that did not disturb her hair too much, and she had on silk stockings and smart black patent shoes with a small heel.

She applied many cosmetics to accentuate her features. Maeve had used very little other than a pot of Pond's cold cream, so Charlie was unaware of how Doris was using her products. He just knew that he had seldom met a woman of Doris's age, which she said was thirty-five, with such flawless skin and a dusting of pink on her cheeks, or one with such long eyelashes, almost perfectly shaped eyebrows, dark, mysterious eyes and a wonderfully kissable, red pouting mouth. When Charlie arrived to escort her he thought his Doris the picture of loveliness and when he took her in his arms the potent waft of perfume she was wearing almost made him light-headed.

'Oh, my darling girl,' he cried. 'You look terrific, just terrific. My children will soon love you as much as I do. What a pity it is that you were blessed with no children of your own.'

Doris said nothing, but suppressed a smile as they walked along Bristol Street toward the Halletts' home. She had never intended having any children. Her husband, Gerry, had agreed with her and said there were ways of preventing pregnancy and he had dealt with that side of things.

Their lives had consisted of going out and having a good time. Drink and drugs featured highly, and though Doris had been trained as a seamstress, she had given that up when she had moved in with, and later married, Gerry. He was a drug dealer and an inveterate gambler. All sorts of shady characters came to their flat and Doris had to be 'nice' to many of them. A gambling debt that Gerry had incurred could be cancelled out, or substantially reduced, if she gave the punters a good enough time. She knew many ways of pleasing a man and thought prostitution easy money, and she was always in great demand.

However, Gerry had killed someone in a drunken brawl and had taken off into the night, leaving her with the dead body and the knife. She had been taken into custody. There was no evidence to charge her – her fingerprints were not on the handle of the knife – and she was released. However, witnesses said she had been as drunk as a lord herself and, rather than trying to stop the fight, she had egged them on, calling on Gerry to 'stab the bastard'. She couldn't remember whether she had said that or not, but she knew the family of the dead man were gunning for her and that if she stayed around they would find her.

Her troubles were compounded when she arrived at her flat to find her landlord had moved all her belongings onto the pavement, piled into a variety of containers, and while she was deliberating about her next move, a group of heavies approached to extract the gambling debts Gerry had run up. She had little money of her own – Gerry took care of that and she hadn't a hope in hell of paying the debt – but she managed to stall the men and agreed to meet them the following week when she would give them all the money she owed. Instead she immediately registered for war work, claimed to be a widow and a trained seamstress wanting work away from the North because it held too many memories, and two days later she had gone south to Birmingham.

However, Gerry's debts were considerable and Doris knew the type of men to whom he owed money didn't give up easily; their nets were wide. Though she had covered her tracks well, she really needed to change her name, and the easiest way to do that was to marry someone – and preferably someone respectable. The fact that she was already married didn't worry her one jot. She doubted she'd ever see Gerry again because he was wanted for murder, and if he was stupid enough to put his head over the parapet he would hang if he was caught.

That first night in the Swan she'd noticed Charlie Hallett straight away and recognised him as a malleable man, one she could manage easily enough, and so when she heard he was a widower with his own house and in good steady employment she made a play for him. It was her chance to be respectable and could work as

111

long as Charlie Hallett did not learn of her past life. She had been a good judge of his character because Charlie seemed remarkably uninquisitive about the life she had led before she'd arrived in Birmingham and, being an easy-going sort of chap, he had been like putty in her hands.

She knew Charlie's brothers didn't like her – not that she cared; she had overheard them talking to Charlie outside the pub one night. 'Look, have your fun,' she'd heard the elder one, Robert, say. 'Just don't marry her, that's all I ask. I think that woman is bad news and I'd hate to see you chained to her for life.'

'She'll suck you dry if you do,' the other one, Alec, had warned. 'I've met her type before as well.'

Doris didn't care because the more they said against her, the more Charlie defended her. She had slept with a great many men, so she knew how to please, though she had held him off at first. She allowed only chaste kisses so that she always left him wanting more, especially as she teased and tormented him.

Eventually, though, she allowed further liberties, so their lovemaking grew more ardent and exciting. He saw her almost every day; everything else took a back seat as all he could think about was Doris and how she made him feel. She could and often did take him to the peak of desire, and in that state nothing else mattered to Charlie, not his brothers' disapproval, nor even his children's unhappiness. He was enthralled by Doris and the heights of sexual gratification he never knew existed.

She told him that she wouldn't totally submit to him until she had the ring on her finger; she wasn't that type of girl. He believed and respected her, and felt bad for pressing her, despite the fact that he was often almost consumed with craven lust as the blood pounded round his veins. Even his sleep was punctuated with sexual and lurid dreams. He was a virile, red-blooded man who missed sex a great deal, and though he had truly and deeply loved Maeve, by the time he was ready to take Doris home to meet his children, he knew he needed her in a base and carnal way and he would never be able to let her go.

As soon as Charlie left the house to fetch Doris, Terry was dispatched to take Ruth and Billy for a walk as arranged, and, Jenny and even young Sally helped Meg to prepare the table. First they draped it in the white lace cloth their mother had used on special occasions, and then brought in the dishes and plates and laid them out. There was one filled with slices of ham and a dish of tomatoes and a larger one filled with green salad. Beside it was a plate of salmon paste sandwiches and another of crusty bread and a tub of butter. On the sideboard, laid on a folded tablecloth, was a trifle and some little choux buns dusted with sugar, which had been Maeve's speciality, and which she had taught Meg to make.

Meg was proud of all she had done and thought the room looked inviting with the easy chairs drawn up to the fender, gleaming in the light of the glowing fire that she had lit to take the chill from the room, even though it was the last week of April.

Meg thought that though Doris Caudwell's clothes were lovely, especially her hat atop her beautifully waved hair, her face was caked in powder with pink rouged cheeks, so different from the her mother's natural beauty. The smokiness around Doris's eyes and the fluttering ridiculously long lashes did not hide the fact that those black eyes were as hard and cold as steel, and her lipstick was like a crimson slash across her face. Meg didn't like what she saw and she castigated herself for not giving the woman a chance. She remembered her manners and turned to greet her, trying to push down her uncomfortable feelings at seeing another woman by her father's side and in her mother's home.

Charlie was aware of the slight silence. He smiled encouragingly at Meg and all the children and said, 'Where are your manners, children? Aren't you going to welcome Mrs Caudwell, our guest?'

Rather than even try to put the fear of God into her siblings for their behaviour towards Mrs Caudwell, Meg had appealed to their better nature, stressing again how alone in the world she was. 'And she might be a bit awkward with us because she isn't used to children,' she'd added, so now the children looked to Meg for direction. She gave an almost imperceptible sigh. God, sometimes it was hard to be the eldest, she thought as she nailed a smile to her face and offered her arm outstretched. 'We're pleased to see you, Mrs Caudwell,' she said. 'Would you like to take off your hat and I'll put it upstairs until you leave?'

Doris smiled and despite herself Meg thought it was like the leering sneer a crocodile might give before he takes your head off, for it didn't touch her eyes. 'Thank you,' she said in clipped tones. 'But I prefer to keep my hat on.'

Meg gave a brief nod and chivvied her brothers and sisters, and one by one they moved forward and shook hands. Doris turned her leering smile on them too and Meg knew that they didn't care for her much either. But to be fair she realised they would like nobody who might come into their home and, as they saw it, take the place of their mother.

To cover the awkward silence that fell after Billy had shaken Doris's hand, Meg scooped the drowsy Ruth from the pram and planted her in Charlie's arms, saying to Doris as she did so, 'This is the youngest member of the family.'

Her father looked awkward holding Ruth, and as Meg made tea she thought it strange that Doris seemed ill at ease with her too. But she didn't have children of her own, so probably that was the reason. 'Her name is Ruth,' Meg said, and Doris patted the baby awkwardly on the arm.

To Meg's dismay, Ruth burst into tears and struggled in her father's arms. 'Hey, hey, there's no need for that,' Charlie chided, setting Ruth on the floor where she continued to cry. 'What's the matter with her anyway?'

Meg swallowed her irritation and put the teapot on the table before picking Ruth up, stopping the tears in an instant. 'Still tired, I imagine,' she said and, to prevent her father saying anything else, she added, 'Would everyone like to come up to the table?'

'We'll do that all right,' Charlie said briskly, pleased to have a diversion. 'Meg, you've done us proud. This all looks delicious. Come on, my dear,' he said to Doris, and he pulled out a chair for her. Terry and Meg exchanged glances for they had never seen him do anything like that for their mother.

Charlie had told the children the tea table would be their chance to get to know Doris. Meg found that wasn't going to be so easy, though, because any questions they asked her, she answered politely but briefly, so that it began to sound more like an interrogation than a conversation.

Doris had some questions of her own. 'So you don't go out to work?' she asked Meg as she finished her last cup of tea, and Meg turned to her father for support.

'It would have been difficult for Meg to go out to any sort of job with all the others to see to,' Charlie said.

'Yes, I see,' Doris said to Meg. 'Weren't there relatives able to help, take a child or two off your hands?' Her tone was courteous, but Meg's hackles rose a little once more.

'I had promised my mother to keep us all together,' she explained.

'That seems quite a burdensome, selfish sort of promise to extract from a young girl,' Doris observed matter-of-factly.

Meg bridled again, perceiving criticism of her mother, and she faced Doris and said, 'No, Mrs Caudwell, that's not so. My mother never had a selfish bone in the whole of her body. It was a promise I willingly made.'

Charlie smiled gently and said conciliatorily, 'I'm sure Doris understands that. Don't you, my dear?'

Doris smiled pleasantly. 'Of course I do, Charlie.'

'Yeah,' Sally put in. 'Daddy didn't want us to go anywhere, anyway.'

'Like those horrible people from Ireland who wanted to take us to live with them,' Billy said.

'Billy,' Charlie said sternly. 'Those people are your grandparents.'

Billy shrugged. 'Don't care. Don't mean they can't be horrible. You didn't let us go to them, did you?'

'No, but—'

'You said you loved us too much,' Jenny reminded him. 'And you do.'

'Yeah,' Billy said in agreement, but added, "Cept for Ruth. You ain't that keen on her.'

There was a collective gasp and Charlie's cheeks were so red the scarlet stain had even spread to his neck. Billy, on the other hand, just looked puzzled. He looked around the people at the table and said, 'What?'

Meg knew she had to say something so she said, 'Billy, you shouldn't say things like that.'

'Why not?' Billy asked. 'You said I had to tell the truth and it is the truth.'

Doris smiled beatifically at their father and said, 'Lots of men have no time for babies. Isn't that right, Charlie?'

Meg watched her father nod and smile fondly back at Doris, and yet Meg knew as well as he did the true reasons for his finding contact with Ruth so difficult.

'You see,' Doris asserted with a smug smile.

Meg fumed inside at Doris's proprietorial attitude towards her father, but she supposed there was no point in feeling angry. 'Let's change the subject, shall we?' she

117

said brightly. 'Would you like any more to eat?' she asked Doris.

'I couldn't eat another thing,' Doris said to Meg. 'It was delicious food.'

Charlie was relieved that Doris and Meg seemed to be getting on well because he knew that the younger ones took the lead from Meg.

'Another cup of tea perhaps?' Meg said.

'Not even that,' Doris said. 'We will have to be making tracks, Charlie, if we are going to see that film.'

'Oh, you're right, my dear,' Charlie said, glancing at the clock. 'I will just go and get my good coat.' And he made for the stairs.

With the tea party broken up, Sally and Billy were playing with Ruth in front of the fire and Terry was carrying the plates out to Jenny, who was washing them in the scullery, and so there was no one near Meg when Doris leaned towards her and hissed, 'I would have thought it was your father's place, not yours, to bring the matter to a close. I think you take far too much upon yourself.'

Meg was taken aback, for though the words were spoken quietly there had been real venom in the way they were said. But no one else had heard so what could she say in reply, especially as her father came bouncing into the room at that minute, smiling fondly at Doris as he said, 'Are you ready, my dear?'

Meg swallowed her anger so that she could bid Doris a civil goodbye, but her sigh of relief was audible as she watched Charlie take Doris's arm and set off down the road towards Bristol Street.

'Thank you for introducing me to your family,' Doris

said as they walked along. 'The tea, as I said, was delicious, but . . .'

Charlie turned to her quizzically. 'What, my dear?'

'Well, I know your children haven't had a mother around,' she began carefully, 'but you really should keep an eye on them, especially the younger ones. They seem to think they can say what they want without any fear or favour.'

Charlie blushed and shrugged helplessly. 'What can I do?'

'Insist on better manners before the children are ruined altogether,' Doris said. 'In my day, children were seen but not heard.'

Charlie wondered if it was true that he had been too lax, had abdicated his role as a father. He knew he'd been neglectful for a while after Maeve's death and probably he should have kept a firmer hand on the tiller. It was obvious the children needed more guidance. It was true they could be undisciplined and, small wonder: Meg hadn't the authority of a parent. Not that he was much good in that department anyway. He had always left that type of thing to Maeve.

Back at the house, Meg looked at Terry. 'Thank God that's over,' she whispered.

'I know,' Terry mouthed back.

'I don't like that lady,' Billy said loudly.

'Now that's enough, Billy,' Meg said. 'It's not up to you who Dad sees.'

She felt she had to defend her father in front of the younger children, but she knew that underneath the fixed smile was someone who could not be trusted and could be really nasty. Look at the way she had spoken to her, and over nothing.

Meg asked her Aunt Rosie about Doris Caudwell when she saw her next.

'I just felt she was trying to avoid answering any personal questions,' Meg told her aunt.

Rosie burst out, 'She's just the same at work. In the beginning, when Robert told me about your dad having a fancy for this Doris Caudwell, and me working at the same place as her, I sought her out and tried to be a bit friendly, like. Well, I might as well not have bothered because she made it clear she wasn't really interested in any sort of friendship with me. It's not just me, either; she barely talks to the women she works with. They know as little about her now as they did the day she started.'

'What about the woman she went to the Swan with first?' Meg said. 'Surely they must be friends?'

Rosie shook her head. 'No,' she said. 'No, Daisy's a nice girl. See, her chap's in the army and he was passing through Birmingham and the driver of the truck agreed to stop off in a pub near where his girl-friend lived so that they could spend an hour or two together. He didn't know what time he would get there and so he told her to go and wait at the Swan pub. She was desperate to see him, but had never gone into a pub on her own before and wanted someone to go with her. Doris agreed to go. Don't know why because she isn't known for her kind gestures. But Daisy told me herself that as soon as Doris saw your father she might as well not have existed. She did talk more to Robert first, but she said anyone with half a brain could see that she had earmarked your dad, and more especially when Robert let slip that Charlie was a widower. And since that day she barely looks at the side Daisy's on.'

'Isn't that rather strange, Aunt Rosie?'

'I'll say.'

'What does Dad see in her?'

'Well, now, Meg, this might be hard for you to take just now,' Aunt Rosie said. 'But, you see, your father is a normal, healthy man – and you know what I mean by that, don't you?'

Meg nodded mutely, blushing slightly, and her aunt Rosie went on, 'Doris can obviously give him what he can get nowhere else, and if you read what these magazines say about such things, it seems in men the sexual urge is much greater than in women. Men find it hard to do without it for very long.'

Meg didn't say anything to her aunt but she was remembering back to Billy's birth and the doctor saying her mother wasn't to have any more children, and so there must have been minimal relations between her parents in the final few years. It made her uncomfortable thinking of her father and Doris in bed together, but that was what her aunt Rosie meant.

Then Rosie said gently, 'If Doris is providing something your father needs and enjoys, he will not want to upset her, so if he is taking her part instead of yours, that's probably why.'

That sounded very depressing to Meg. 'That isn't very fair, Aunt Rosie. Will it always be like that?'

Rosie shrugged. 'In my opinion, men do anything for a quiet life,' she said. 'And this is a new experience for your father. Personally, I can't take to the woman, but at the moment in your father's eyes she can do no wrong. When they are married and settled down together, speak to your father quietly and on his own if there is something upsetting you. He does value your good opinion. I know that.'

'No magic solution, then?'

''Fraid not. Did you expect there to be one?'

'No, not really,' Meg said. 'I long ago stopped believing in fairy tales. But I can't understand her not wanting to make friends with people. Maybe she would be a kinder, more understanding person if she let others into her life.'

'Ah, but maybe she has secrets she doesn't want others to know about,' Rosie said.

'Has she?'

'How would we know?' Rosie said. 'But there is certainly something amiss, if you ask me.'

Rosie had been more astute than she knew. Doris couldn't risk making friends because they would ask questions and expect answers. Charlie never did that for, just as he had never quizzed Maeve about her traumatic childhood, he had not been overly curious about Doris's life in Yorkshire. He believed her when she explained her husband, Gerry, had died of a tumour and that she had nursed him till the end. He didn't ask for details, nor did he keep on about it, in case it upset her. He quite understood that after his death she'd decided to move away and make a new start elsewhere.

'But you can look on the bright side,' Meg's aunt concluded.

'What bright side?' Meg asked.

'Well, this releases you, doesn't it, if your father and Doris marry?'

Meg nodded. 'Dad seems to think so,' she said slowly. 'But at what cost to the children, I wonder.'

TEN

The following Friday morning, there was a knock at the door. Meg assumed it was the rent man, though he usually came much earlier. She had the money put aside on the mantelpiece so she picked it up and the rent book, but was astonished when she opened to door to find Richard Flatterly outside.

'What are you doing here?' she asked in surprise.

'Why shouldn't I be here?' Richard asked. 'I happen to own the houses.'

'I know, but Vince O'Malley collects the rent usually.'

'Well, he's laid up at the moment,' Richard told her. 'So, you're stuck with me for a while. Don't mind that, do you?'

Meg did mind very much. The last thing she wanted was to see Richard Flattery's leering face every week, but you couldn't say that sort of thing to the man who owned the house you were living in, so Meg contented herself with a shrug. 'Doesn't bother me.'

'Oh, I'm sure that's not true,' Richard said seductively, touching her hand as he had once before as he gave her back the rent book.

Meg took a step backwards, almost tripping over Ruth, who was peeping through her legs to see who was at the door. She picked Ruth up and held her almost protectively against her. Ignoring Richard's comment, Meg said, 'You must excuse me, but I am meeting a friend in town,' and she shut the door quickly lest he put his foot in the way to prevent it closing.

'It's not what he says so much, but it's the way he says it,' she said later to Joy.

'I hate men like that,' Joy said. 'They give me the creeps. They need a good slap.'

'I agree,' Meg said. 'But I can hardly do that when the man is my landlord.'

'No,' Joy agreed. 'I can see your problem there all right.'

'Mind you,' Meg said, 'he probably won't want to pound around the houses collecting money for long. I should think he will get another rent man in soon enough. I can't imagine he has any sort of loyalty to his employees.'

'Few have,' Joy said. 'What about you? Now you're nearly free, why don't you think about what you're going to do with your future?'

'I may do,' Meg said. 'I really would like to work and better myself, but not just yet. I can't leave Daddy in the lurch till I know what's happening.'

Joy's words did make Meg more hopeful for her own future, though, and that night as they sat eating the evening meal, she mentioned to her father that Richard Flatterly had called for his own rent that morning. 'I expect he'll engage another rent man before long, though,' she added. 'With the numbers of unemployed, I'd say that he'll be spoiled for choice.'

125

'There's not the lines of unemployment there were once,' Charlie said. 'But whether there are or not, they will not be engaging anyone else.'

'Oh?'

'Oh, you can bet that it isn't young Richard's idea,' Charlie said. 'He wouldn't give a body the skin off his rice pudding, that one. His father now, he's a decent sort – in fact our rent man, Vince, saved his life in the Great War. He told me about it one night in the pub. Vince played down his part in it at the time, but others filled in the details after. He risked his own life to save the officer's and was shot to bits for his trouble, riddled with shrapnel, and apparently his life hung in the balance for some time. He recovered, but you must have noticed the limp.'

''Course.'

'Well, that was what he was left with,' Charlie said. 'Still gives him gyp, that leg. That's what's wrong with him now. Anyway, old Flatterly promised him a job for life in gratitude. He is an honourable man, so Richard will have to collect his own rents till Vince is better.'

Meg wrinkled her nose. She hated the thought of dealing with Flatterly every Friday morning, but there was no point in complaining about it.

Doris Caudwell had never had any interest in the news or what was happening in the world around her, and tended to dismiss as overreaction all the worries and anxieties about Germany. Charlie, in contrast, was fanatical about what was happening, knowing any war could involve him. When listening to the latest news broadcasts, she was surprised to hear many were talking about the war as if it was a foregone conclusion. Doris asked Charlie about it one night as they sat having a drink in the Trees public house. When Charlie said he might be called up, it gave her a start.

'I thought you'd be too old.'

Charlie laughed. 'Thanks.'

'Oh, you know what I mean, Charlie.'

'Well, I know at the moment it's only supposed to be blokes aged twenty or thereabouts, but I'm told by quite reliable sources that forty-one will be the cut-off point if things get more serious. And if I am called up I must go.'

'So what are we going to do?' Doris asked, frowning.

'Well, we could get married, although then our time together might be very limited till this war is over. Are you prepared for that?'

Doris didn't even have to think. 'Of course I'm prepared, though I never thought of us being at war again after the last time.'

'Yeah,' Charlie agreed. 'Must be hard on the old ones who maybe left the bodies of family and friends in the fields of France – and now we're starting again. They must wonder if they died in vain.'

'True,' Doris said. 'And I wish you hadn't got to go and risk your life too, but if you have to then I don't want you sailing over the bright blue sea without making an honest woman of me first. Think what delights will be in store for you when we are married,' she said seductively, running her hand up the inside of his leg beneath the table.

Charlie felt himself harden. 'Stop it, for Christ's sake,' he said huskily. 'Or I won't be able to walk out of here.'

'Let's finish these drinks and go back to my flat then,' Doris suggested. 'And I can show you a good time, even if you won't get the cherry on the cake just yet.'

Charlie was more than willing and that night Doris stripped off completely. She had a lovely body and was not coy about showing it off and Charlie realised that it was the first time he had seen a totally naked woman, despite the years he had been married to Maeve, the love they had shared and even the children she had borne. Then Doris took him in her arms and they fell back on the bed. She put his hand on her plump breasts as she wriggled her body beneath him, driving him wild. Her hands were over every bit of him and he bent his head and gently took one of her nipples in his mouth. He felt as if he was drowning in exquisite bliss, and then Doris was astride him and leaning forward so that he took the other nipple in his mouth and he was licking her breasts, running his hands between her legs, and she too was moaning with desire.

'Do you love me, Charlie?' she asked.

'My darling girl, I adore you.'

'D'you love me more than Maeve?'

'I love you more than anyone,' Charlie said, for at that moment he did; he needed to ease the ache inside him more than he'd needed anything in the world before.

'And are we going to marry, Charlie?' Doris whispered in her throaty voice that sent shivers running up and down his spine.

Charlie was in the throes of passion and he said almost impatiently, 'Of course, and as soon as it can be arranged. I'll see the priest after work tomorrow and arrange for the banns to be read.'

'Do you promise?'

'I promise.'

The intensity of the kiss that Doris gave Charlie surprised him; her tongue darted in and out of his mouth and as his excitement and passion rose higher her hands on his body were electrifying. Just when Charlie felt he couldn't bear any more, that he would be engulfed by it all, Doris flipped herself onto her back again and pulled Charlie on top of her. As he entered her for the first time, he felt as if he was drowning in rapture.

Later he lay beside her in the bed. 'Oh, my darling girl,' he said. 'How I love you.'

'I love you too, Charlie,' Doris said, for they were the words that Charlie wanted to hear.

'Thank you,' Charlie said. 'You don't know how much I have wanted to do that.'

'Oh, I do.'

'Why did you let me tonight?'

'Because you think there is going to be a war, and we are as good as married and we might not have long together. Anyway, I wanted it too, you know. That's the trouble with being a widow or widower – you're used to sex and you miss it. Don't you miss it?'

'Oh, yes,' said Charlie. But to him that experience had not the slightest resemblance to the sex he had thought he'd enjoyed with Maeve. Not that he could remember much about sex with her because for so long before she died he had lain beside her like a board, and they had seldom even kissed in case his feelings had overtaken him. There was just the once he had slipped up and the result had been catastrophic.

No, thought Charlie, my children can moan and

perform all they like, but I am sticking to this woman who can transport me to the door of paradise.

Doris's arms were creeping around him again. 'Are you ready for some more, big boy?' she asked provocatively.

Charlie's arousal was immediate and he turned to her with a little growl of pleasure. After that he had no will to go home. He slept the night with Doris, waking before the alarm went off to make love again before getting up for work.

Meg had lain in bed wide-eyed all night, waiting to hear her father come in. She dozed eventually, but when she woke she crept down to the bedroom to check whether her father had come in. His bed had not been slept in. Terry had already left for his paper round, and though she was thoroughly worried, she tried to keep any concern out of her voice and manner as she got the children up and off to school.

As the house fell silent, Meg picked Ruth up and headed next door. She was so agitated she knew she had to talk to someone. May made the usual cup of tea and gave Ruth her button box to play with as Meg explained to May that her father hadn't come home the previous night.

'D'you think should go round the hospitals?' she asked.

'No,' May said. 'Bad news travels faster than good. If anything had happened to him, then you would have heard, I'm sure. Did he see Doris last night?'

'Are you kidding?' Meg said. 'May, he sees Doris every flipping night.'

'Then I would wait until this evening,' May advised. If he doesn't come in from work, then there's time enough to raise the alarm.'

'You . . . you can't think that he stayed with Doris all night?'

'I think it is the most likely explanation,' May said sagely.

Meg was relieved but also irritated when her father came home from work that evening at about the usual time and on his own for a change. He seemed totally unabashed about the fact that he had stayed out all night, and offered no explanation, though Meg felt really annoyed with him for the worry he had put her through.

When their meal was over, however, Charlie told his two younger daughters to see to the dishes as he had something to say to Meg. He suggested taking a walk. She gave a brief nod because the evening was a fine, warm one, and it would give her the chance to tell her father how inconsiderate he had been.

They hadn't left the house far behind when Meg demanded, 'Where did you get to last night, Daddy? I was so worried I barely slept, and when I crept down and your bed hadn't been slept in, I didn't know what to think. I nearly did a tour of the hospitals.'

'I don't know why the fuss,' Charlie said. 'I am a grown man.'

'I know that, but you ought to have let me know.'

'No, Meg,' Charlie insisted, 'you have to realise that I am not answerable to you, not any more. In actual fact, that is one of the things I wanted to tell you.'

'You're marrying Doris,' Meg said. 'That's not really news.'

'Yes,' Charlie said. 'But you should know I'm seeing the priest this evening about calling the bans and getting married as soon as possible.'

'But, Dad—'

Charlie lifted his hand to still the protest he knew Meg was about to make. 'I know that you're going to say it's for the children's sake that you advised me to take it slowly, but the war looming over us has forced my hand.'

'Why has it?'

'Because the chances are I will be called up.'

Meg stopped dead still on the road. Such a possibility had never occurred to her. 'Called up?' she said incredulously. 'You?'

'Don't look at me like that,' Charlie said. 'I'm not totally decrepit.'

'No,' Meg said, resuming the walk. 'But it's the young men they've been calling up so far, isn't it, and we're not even really at war yet.'

'We will be, and soon,' Charlie said grimly. 'And that initial call-up is just for starters. When we declare war on Germany – and it is "when" and not "if" – they will need every man jack of us. And if I was in the Forces, would the Welfare people let you live all by yourself with the kids and no adult?'

'I've proved myself so far,' Meg said hotly.

'But I was here.'

Meg fell silent. She knew her father had a point. Everyone was terrified of the Welfare people getting their tabs on their children and she knew they could

132

easily because she was only sixteen. 'So if you marry Doris . . .'

'Then the kids are safe.'

'Safe from the Welfare, maybe,' Meg said. 'But, Dad, I am worried because she really doesn't seem to like them much.'

'Rubbish!' Charlie said. 'She's just not used to them like you are. Doris will be fine once she has a bit more practice being around a family.'

'I just wonder what Mom would have thought,' Meg said, almost to herself.

'Meg, your mother is dead,' Charlie said. 'I have to think about what is best for our family, and what I think is best for us is for me to marry Doris so that the kids have a stepmother if I am called up to war. And now,' he said, 'I must be off, because after we have seen Father Hugh, Doris wants us to go dancing to celebrate our engagement.'

Meg felt very despondent after her father had left her and very close to tears. She made her way home and got Ruth ready for bed in an almost mechanical way, and then sat the others down and told them the general gist of the conversation she had had with her father.

'I know it's difficult, but Dad is trying to do the best thing by us, and by Doris, and we'll just have to accept his decision. It'll be fine,' she told the children brightly, even though she had deep-seated reservations herself.

Once she and Terry were alone, Terry burst out bitterly, 'I don't know, Meg. He used to be a great dad when Mom was alive but since then . . . well, he just seems so easily led.'

'Terry!'

'Well, he is,' Terry said, unrepentant. 'He's bloody useless, frankly.'

Meg sat in silence, waiting to hear what else Terry wanted to say.

'Anyway, that has finally decided me,' Terry told her. 'You know my mate at school, Neil Drummond, has an uncle that owns a shop on Bristol Street – where I already do the paper round?'

Meg nodded.

'Well, just the other day, he asked Neil if he had a friend looking for a full-time job. Neil said what about me, and his uncle was great about it because he knows me already. I'd have to give a hand in the shop and cycle round with the grocery orders, but he said the people who have their groceries delivered are more or less the same ones who have papers delivered, so I already know the route. He said if I want the job I can have it.'

'You haven't left school yet!'

'I've only got a few weeks and they sometimes let you leave early if you have a job to go to. Neil's uncle is going to see about it. No good asking Dad 'cos he's a dead loss when it comes to anything we want to do.'

Miserably, Meg had to own that that was how it seemed. 'And this is what you want to do?'

'Yeah.'

'You'll have to work all day Saturday,' Meg reminded him. 'No kick-about on Saturday morning or going to the Villa in the afternoon.'

'I know,' Terry said. 'But I still want to do it. Neil's been helping out for a bit on Saturdays already and he loves it. When he starts full time, though, he's going to live with his uncle and aunt, because the papers are delivered really early. Anyway, the shop is going to be his one day because his uncle and aunt never had any children.'

Meg nodded. 'I know that,' she said. 'Claire always said she felt cheated because she was the eldest, but it was always earmarked for Neil, 'cos he's the eldest boy.'

'I know,' Terry said. 'But it isn't his fault and there's not a lot he can do about it. Anyway, Neil said I could stay as well because there's a three-bedroom flat above it. I said no to that at first because I thought I should stay here and help you out, like, but if now our dad is marrying Doris, then I'm off as soon as I can.'

Meg had never expected that, and she felt her heart sink as she realised how much she would miss Terry.

'And in the meantime I'm stuck here with that woman,' Meg said bleakly, upset and a little hurt by Terry's decision.

'Oh, cheer up, sis,' Terry said. 'I can't live with her and I know she don't want me here either. She doesn't want none of us, if the truth be told, and if I were you I'd look to your own future. 'Cos I tell you what, no one else will.'

ELEVEN

When Charlie was told Terry's news the next day he was astounded that all this had been decided without even consulting him, never mind asking his permission.

'You didn't ask our permission to marry Doris,' Terry said to him bluntly.

'I don't need your permission, boy,' Charlie barked out. 'I am your father, though that seems to have escaped your notice.'

'No it hasn't,' Terry said. 'And all right, you don't need our permission officially, but it would have been nice to ask if we minded. Anyway, it's all arranged now. You might not be pleased, but I'm sure Doris will be – it'll be one less of us for her to worry about, so there's no point in making a fuss about it.'

In fact Charlie found that Terry was right, because when he expressed concern at Terry living away from home at such a young age and with people he didn't know that well, Doris told him not to fuss. 'It was the boy's own decision and he's living with a mate from

136

school, you said. What can happen him? And for heaven's sake, he is only around the corner.'

A week after Terry moved, Doris told Meg that she wanted her to find a job of work and somewhere else to live after the wedding. Meg wasn't that surprised because Doris's attitude to her after Terry left had been such that she almost expected the ultimatum. She was seriously worried about leaving her brothers and sisters to Doris's indifferent, almost neglectful care, and anyway she didn't know of anywhere that she would earn enough to afford to live on her own.

'War-related work pays better than anything, I do know that,' Joy said. 'Munitions and that.'

'My mother was totally against me going into a factory,' Meg said.

'Your mother didn't know there was going to be a war,' Joy pointed out. 'That changes all the boundaries, though I must admit,' she added, 'I don't fancy factory work.'

'But you have a job and place to stay,' Meg said. 'Yours is nothing like my position.'

'Yeah, but if war comes, I want to do my bit to help,' Joy said. 'And anyway, with all the men gone, the girls and women will have to take over doing their jobs, as well as make things for the war.'

'Yes, of course,' Meg said. 'Dad said it was like that in the last war and that it was odd seeing lady conductresses on the trams, or sometimes even driving them, as well as delivery carts and petrol vans, and they were in all the factories or in machine shops sewing uniforms.

He told me that some of the girls in the munitions sometimes had their skin go yellow and their hair used to get a reddish tinge to it because of the chemicals they worked with. He said everyone knew the girls who worked in the munitions and they used to call them the canary girls.'

'Ugh, I shouldn't like that,' Joy said. 'Why would anyone want to work there?'

'Maybe it wasn't want, but more necessity, because they got really good wages,' Meg said. 'Mom said they deserved every penny because sometimes there were explosions and girls were killed and injured. Actually, I wouldn't mind moving out of that place anyway to get away from the clutches of Richard Flatterly.'

'Is he still being a nuisance?'

'Yes,' Meg said. 'Right pain in the neck he is, and thinks he's God's gift. Ever since he learned that I had turned sixteen, he has been hinting that I could have the rent reduced or pay none at all if I was "nice" to him.'

'Good God, nothing like being blatant about it.'

'And you should have seen what he did just this morning.'

'What?'

'Well, I knew it was him at the door,' Meg explained. 'But when I opened it, he pushed so hard and so suddenly and the next minute he was over the threshold, kicked the door shut with his foot and had me crushed up against the wall and I could feel every bit of him. You know what I mean?'

'Only too well,' Joy said, shuddering. 'What a creep. Did you scream out or anything?'

'I tried, but he clapped his great, greasy hand over my mouth. I was nervous because there was only me and Ruth in, so I struggled and kicked out as much as I could.'

'What did Ruth do?'

'Oh, that's the best bit,' Meg said. 'Flatterly frightened her at first and she just watched and snivelled a bit and then – as if she realised what I was doing – she ran and punched out at him with her little fists. 'Course, it made no difference, and she must have realised that, and so she bit him, didn't you?' she said to the little girl beside her, swinging her legs as she tucked into a bun.

'You bit him?' Joy said, staring at her.

'It was on his bum, wasn't it?' Meg reminded her, ''cos he was a bad man, wasn't he?'

Ruth nodded slowly. 'Bad man,' she repeated.

''Course,' Meg continued to Joy, 'it was probably the last thing he expected. Ruth bit him hard enough to make him cry out and loosen his hold on me. I lost no time then in pushing him off me so he knocked his head against the wall. Then I opened the door and told him to get out. I shouted it you know so that everyone could hear. He couldn't do anything then, see, in front of the neighbours.'

'I bet he wasn't that happy with you, Ruth,' Joy said, but Ruth just smiled as Meg lowered her voice and said, 'He would have hit her. She was stood beside me at the door and I caught hold of his hand and said if he laid a hand on her it would the last thing he ever did in his life. I did say too that if he touched me in that way ever again I will tell my father, but he knows I shan't, for, as he said, the streets are not that comfortable just now. I mean, what could Daddy do? Someone like Flatterly would say it was all my fault, that I came on to him. Doris would probably believe that as well. I was shaking afterwards I was so scared. I'll have to be prepared for him the next time he comes round.'

'Well, you did right to bite him,' Joy declared, smiling at the little girl. 'Bloody right.'

'Loody right,' Ruth repeated.

Meg glared at Joy and she said, 'Sorry, I forgot, but isn't it terrible that people like him get away with things all the time?'

'Yeah, it is,' Meg said. 'And I think that's what will tip us into war in the end, stopping Hitler getting away with things.'

'Oh, I think you've hit the nail on the head there, Meg,' Joy said.

There was a spate of marriages in the following weeks, for most people now thought war was inevitable, and Charlie and Doris couldn't get a date on which to be married as quickly as they wanted.

As Meg thought about her father being called up, she remembered the men who would stand with trays around their necks on the steps to the Market Hall in the Bull Ring, selling bootlaces, matches, razor blades and the like. One was blind and led about by friends, and another was missing an arm; one had no legs at all and was pushed about in a homemade trolley, and there were a couple who shook badly. Dad had told her they were like flotsam from the last war: men who had served their usefulness now thrown on to the scrapheap. Sometimes he would complain that they had enough razor blades and bootlaces to stock a shoe shop because Maeve had always found it hard to pass the men without pulling out her purse. 'We owe these men such a lot,' she'd tell the children. 'It grieves me to see them reduced to this.'

There hadn't been so many ex-soldiers around of late, though, and Meg could only imagine that they had obtained employment somewhere and that would more than likely be war-related. The lines of the unemployed had dwindled vastly, which must have been good news for many families.

'Well, it's an ill wind,' Joy said when Meg commented on this.

'I suppose.'

'I should imagine that if you want to wage war you will need a great deal of stuff that you wouldn't want in peacetime.'

'That's true enough,' Meg said. 'Even at Dunlop's they are making tyres for military vehicles now.'

'There you are,' Joy said. 'And many of these jobs will have to be managed by women.'

'Not at the Dunlop factory and places like that, though?'

'Well, who will do it if the men aren't here?'

Meg wrinkled her nose. 'I wouldn't fancy it,' she said. 'I mean, Dad stinks of rubber; it's ingrained in his skin, his hair, everything really, and I can't see any woman wanting to do that.'

'If it comes to war, Meg, maybe we can't just do the things we'd like to do,' Joy said. 'I mean, do you think all the lads called up wanted to be soldiers? Do you think they will enjoy finding out how to kill people and trying not to get killed themselves?'

'I see what you say and you're right,' Meg said. 'So we have to do our bit as well.'

She had a lot to think about as she made her way home that day, weaving the pram between the stalls while Ruth lay back against the pillows drowsily. And so lost was she in thought that she almost cannoned into a woman standing at one of the stalls.

'Oh, I'm so sorry,' she burst out, and the woman turned.

She was about to reassure Meg that it was all right, but the words died in her throat and instead she cried, 'Meg Hallett.'

Meg was equally surprised. 'Miss Carmichael.'

The teacher recovered herself first. 'How lovely to see you, my dear, and your sister looks well,' she said, gazing at Ruth fondly. Ruth smiled at her drowsily as Miss Carmichael said, 'She is a credit to you, Meg.'

'Thank you,' Meg said, and added a little wistfully, 'but I won't have the children to look after much longer.'

'Oh?'

'Dad's getting married again.'

'Oh, that is good news,' Miss Carmichael said, surprised Meg wasn't more pleased.

'Yes,' Meg said in flat tones, and Miss Carmichael deduced that all was not well.

'Look,' she said, 'have you to rush back home?'

Meg shook her head. 'Not till four, when the children come out of school.'

'And Ruth looks as if she won't be any trouble,' Miss Carmichael said, for Ruth's eyes were closing. 'So let's go and have a cup of tea and a real catch-up?'

Meg moved Ruth gently down the pram, and though she wriggled about a little getting comfier, her eyes stayed closed. 'But what about school?' she asked her old teacher.

'I'm playing hooky,' Kate said with a broad smile. 'I haven't to go anywhere either in a hurry, so shall we try Lyons Corner House on New Street and I'll tell you all then?'

As they started up the incline that led from the Bull Ring to High Street, Miss Carmichael said, 'And as we're no longer in the school, you can call me by my given name – Catherine – though I am usually called Kate.'

Meg wondered if she'd ever have the neck to do that, but she nodded anyway, remembering how she had once thought the world of her lovely young teacher. She had spent hours gazing at her in the classroom. Her hair, as dark brown as Meg's own, was always put up for school and fastened with lovely tortoiseshell combs, and her soft eyes were dark grey. Her smooth skin reminded Meg of her mother's but her lips were fuller and her teeth absolutely white. Meg hadn't seen her for two years, since she had come to the house to express her condolences at hearing of her mother's death, for though she had glimpsed her at Mass a time or two, even if Kate Carmichael had been inclined to chat, Meg never had much time to linger.

The eyes she fastened on Meg were sympathetic and a little curious but the tea and buns were in front of them before Kate asked Meg directly why she was unhappy with having a stepmother.

'None of the kids like her,' Meg began. 'It's like she's replacing our mother, who hasn't really been dead that long. I told Dad to take it slow, let them get used to it, like and . . . I don't know, maybe he would have done but for this war. Dad's worried that if he is called up, the Welfare people might say I'm too young to look after the kids by myself and take them away.'

'There is a chance of that,' Kate Carmichael said. 'Do you like her?'

Meg shook her head. 'No, and she doesn't like me. I think she resents the fact that because I had to take the place of my mother, especially as my father was lost for a time and someone had to steer the ship, I am used to making decisions that I probably shouldn't have had to make.'

'What about your siblings?'

Meg gave a rueful smile. 'They would like no one that tried to take the place of our mother and Doris doesn't really understand kids because she's never had any, so I thought I could stick around for a bit after Dad married her and give her a bit of a hand, but she's made it clear she doesn't want that, I think because she doesn't want me to have any undue influence on Dad.'

'Well, I suppose it might help that situation if you try and get some kind of job.'

Meg nodded. 'My friend Joy thinks we should do something for the war. I mean, it really does seem inevitable now, doesn't it?'

Kate nodded. 'I'm afraid it does. You could enlist, join one of the services.'

'I thought of that,' Meg said. 'That's what my cousins Anna and Lizzie are doing. They are getting married soon and said if their husbands are prepared to put their lives on the line, they want to do their bit too.

But I couldn't keep an eye on the kids if I enlisted and I'm hoping that I'll be able to do something a bit closer to home.'

'Well, the children may not be with her long anyway, not if she doesn't want them to be.'

'Why not?'

Kate ignored Meg's question and instead said, 'I'm in town for a medical.'

'Medical?' Meg repeated. 'Is something wrong?'

'Not a thing,' Kate said. 'In fact the doctor said I am a very healthy specimen, all told.'

'Then why . . .?'

'It's because of the evacuation plans,' Kate said. 'Getting the children out of the cities to safer places in the countryside. Our school is being evacuated along with many more, and I offered to go with ours because – unlike some of the other members of staff – I have no ties. They insisted I have a medical.'

Meg felt quite agitated. 'But, Miss Carmichael,' she said. 'Kate. People can't just send children away from home like that.'

'It's what's proposed.'

'But they will be with perfect strangers,' Meg said, and she shook her head. 'It can't be right and I can't see Dad agreeing to it. There was talk of sending Billy and Sally to Mom's parents in Ireland after she died and, although Dad was tempted, he wouldn't do it in the end.'

'But there wasn't a threat of war then,' Kate pointed out. 'If it comes we will be attacked from the air.'

'I read in the paper that we are two hundred miles from the coast.'

'That's nothing, in the modern planes they have today,' Kate said. 'Anyway, I think keeping the children safe is only part of the Government's plan. Another thing is to release mothers from childcare so that they can go into war work and we'll need them to do that because if here is a war it will be one that we must win. Have you considered the Land Army?'

'Land Army?' Meg repeated with scorn. 'How will it help the war effort growing potatoes?'

'Meg, people have got to eat,' Kate said. 'How can the farmers produce the food we need if their sons and farm hands are called up? It's really essential work and you would be out in the air and not enclosed in some factory. They provide housing too. And I suppose you could ask to be billeted close to home, or at least near a train line that comes this way.'

Meg laughed. 'Don't be daft, Kate. There are precious few farms in Birmingham.'

'Plenty just outside, though,' Kate said. 'Put it to your friend next week and see what she thinks.'

The idea of joining the Land Army played on Meg's mind, and the more she thought of it, the more she liked the idea, but she did wonder how her father would cope with the fact that she would be leaving home. As the date for the wedding grew closer, though, Doris began to really irritate Meg to such an extent that she only had to hear her voice to set her teeth on edge. She knew that there was no room for her and Doris in the one house, but she could hardly tell her father that and so she decided she should find out all she could about the Land Army.

At first she didn't know where to start, but May helped out there. One day when they had both finished the ironing and stopped for a cup of tea, Meg told her about meeting Kate Carmichael and her suggestion for war-related work.

Immediately May said, 'My youngest sister, Phoebe, did that in the last war. God! Our old man kicked up shocking. I was glad I was married and out of it.'

'Was it about her leaving home?'

'Yes,' May said. 'Well, you see, girls didn't, not till they were married, like. Anyway, she stuck to her guns. She said if Dan and Derek could go to war then she wanted to do her bit too.'

'Were Dan and Derek your brothers?'

A flash of sadness showed in May's eyes as she nodded. 'Yes, and they were called up along with John, who was the husband of my sister Sadie, and my Mick. And,' she added, 'Mick was the only one to make it home.'

'Oh, how sad,' Meg said. 'I never knew that.'

'No reason for you to know,' May said. 'It was many years ago and it was only brought to mind because of what you said about the Land Army.'

'Did your sister like it?'

'Well, she would say she did even if she hated it, because she had to fight so hard to be allowed to go,' May said. 'That was the type of girl young Phoebe was. She did tell me that the work was harder than she'd thought it would be and Dad needn't worry that she was up to no good for all she wanted to do at the end of the day was sleep. But she said no one bothered complaining and they all put their backs into it, whatever they were asked to do, because they knew what they did was vital. If it didn't get done we could all have starved to death.'

'Do you really think it's that important?'

'I don't *think*, I *know* it is,' May said. 'If I were you, I would go down to Thorp Street Barracks and find out all about it.'

TWELVE

In the end Meg never got to Thorp Street Barracks because as Doris went on with her elaborate plans for her wedding, Ruth's second birthday passed with barely a ripple from her father. Meg, determined the child should not be side-lined, had been saving for weeks to buy her a beautiful rag doll she had seen in the Bull Ring and Aunt Rosie had knitted clothes for it. Jenny and Sally, with no money for presents, unearthed the pram and crib they'd had when they'd been younger, which they cleaned up beautifully, and Terry bought Ruth a 'Monkey on a Stick', which he had seen at the Bull Ring. Yet from her father she didn't even get a card.

When Meg reminded him of his own child's birthday, he just shrugged.

'I have no money to spare, and that's the truth,' he said. 'And sure, she's little more than a baby and will hardly notice.'

Meg was too angry even to speak to him after that, but she went ahead with having a little tea party. Aunt Rosie came with a jelly and blancmange and a large tin full of fancy fairy cakes, and even Nicholas came laden with a massive plate of sandwiches his mother had made. Added to that, Meg had made a large chocolate cake, into which she had stuck two candles. Everyone tucked into the food and helped Ruth blow out the candles and she clapped her hands with delight. 'Happy birthday, Ruth,' Meg said, and planted a kiss on her little sister's head.

Ruth beamed. She had no idea what all the fuss was about, but she liked it none the less and, not used to presents, was enthralled by those she had been given. 'Appy birday,' she said in an attempt to imitate her sister, and made everyone laugh.

Best of all, though, in Meg's opinion, was that when her father and Doris came home there was no dinner for them. It was light summer evening, and when she saw them turn in the road, Meg sent the children out to play, taking Ruth with them. With the children safely out of the way, she faced her father and Doris and told them there was no meal ready and she had no intention of making any. 'Even if I wanted to cook you something,' she said, 'I have no money left for I spent it all on a present and little party for Ruth. It was up to us to give her a nice day and make up for your lack of attention. Her needs came before yours and if you don't like that, then you'll have to lump it.'

Charlie knew nothing he could say or do would work when Meg had that set face on. Doris had plenty she wanted to say, but she saw what Meg had said to Charlie had made him feel guilty and so she tucked her arm through his. 'Come, my dear,' she said, and they left the house together – and that was another night Charlie did not come home.

That night Meg did a lot of thinking. Because Ruth had been born on the day her mother died, on her first birthday, the loss of her mother was still very much in Meg's mind and she thought in her father's as well. She could well understand that perhaps he did not want to celebrate the anniversary of his wife's death. However, she imagined that he would eventually come to terms with the fact that Maeve's death was in no way Ruth's fault and start acting as a proper father to her.

Now, though, the situation was different. He was no longer grieving for her mother, but was instead planning to marry another and yet his antipathy towards Ruth was more entrenched than ever. She imagined the scenario if Ruth was left totally in the care of her father and Doris, or Doris alone if her father was called up. The children would be evacuated, she was certain, as soon as Doris got wind that it was happening, so there might be just her and the small child in the house together.

She gave a sudden shiver because she had seen enough of Doris to guess that latent cruelty lay just below the surface. So how could she think of waltzing off in the Land Army and leave her little sister totally unprotected? She had to stay close by. Maybe it might stay Doris's hand if she knew she was popping in every evening and she could take her totally off her hands at the weekends. No, until Ruth was a lot older Meg's life was on hold again. She would tell Joy all about the Land Army in case she wanted to go for it, but accepted that it was not for her yet.

The children broke up for the long summer holidays on Thursday and so were at home and willing to mind

151

Ruth while Meg met Joy in the Bull Ring the following day. It meant Meg could avoid the rent man completely if she left early enough.

Since Ruth had bitten Flatterly, Meg had dreaded meeting him again and though she had decided to tell her father nothing of the encounter, she had told the children an edited version and they promised to keep Ruth out of the landlord's sight. Once Doris took over she would be paying the rent and Meg wished her well of it. Dealing effectively with the lecherous Richard Flatterly was one problem she didn't mind relinquishing.

So that day she was in the Bull Ring earlier than usual and had a good mooch around the stalls, listening to the banter from the costers as they plied their trade. Eventually she hailed Joy, whom she saw weaving her way towards the Market Hall. A little later over a cup of tea and a sandwich Meg told her friend about her old teacher's suggestion. Joy thought it sounded just the thing, though she had a somewhat idealised view of what it might be like.

'Better than a noisy, dirty factory any day of the week,' she said. 'Can you imagine it? We'll be breathing in fresh air for once in our lives.'

'I won't,' Meg said, and told her friend about the party, her father's reaction to it and her subsequent decision.

'Oh, what a shame,' Joy cried. 'I thought we'd be going together.'

'I hoped we would,' Meg said. 'But you see why I can't just go off and leave her?'

Joy nodded. 'I do. I just wish it wasn't all down to

you. It certainly was awful way to treat a child on her birthday . . . I can't understand that at all.'

'He ignores her just as if she isn't there,' Meg said. 'And in his heart I still think he wishes she wasn't.'

'Ah, Meg, I feel really sorry for you,' Joy said.

'Don't,' Meg warned, 'or I will be in floods of tears.' And to turn the conversation to another tack she said, 'So you're still going ahead with the Land Army, then?'

Joy nodded vigorously. 'You bet. Never really thought of that side of things but now I quite like the idea of being instrumental in feeding the nation if the country is plunged into war.'

'Yes, that does sound great,' Meg said wistfully. 'What will you do?'

Meg shrugged. 'Go in the munitions, I suppose – that pays the best – and rent a room or something near to the house. That should suit Doris but I know Dad won't want me to leave home to live even a short distance away.'

'Why don't you stay then?'

'I can't,' Meg said. 'Doris and I would end up killing one another. Dad chooses to imagine that Doris and I get along fine and that I will stay on at home to give Doris a hand, but that's not going to happen.'

'Does your dad always give in to her?' Joy asked.

'Yeah, he does. He was never like that with Mom, but she never made demands on him like Doris does and she always deferred to him for the final say. He seemed stronger-willed then, somehow. I mean, I know that he didn't want Terry to leave home, 'cos I heard him talking about it with Doris. But she eventually convinced him it was a great idea. She mentioned evacuation the other day though I don't think she knows that much about it at the moment.'

'Evacuation seems an awful thing to do,' Joy said. 'Our area is up for evacuation as well. Mom says it's criminal to post children around the country in that way.'

'I agree,' Meg said. 'But I bet that eventually Doris will get Dad not only to agree, but also to think it is his idea. Still, sometimes I think that if the children are sent to a "place of safety" and go to live with someone kind, they might be better off than being left with Doris, especially if Dad is called up.'

'Why is your dad marrying a woman like that?'

'I have asked myself that same question over and over,' said Meg. 'And Dad has given me reasons such as feeling sorry for her and worried that if he didn't marry her and was called up the children might be taken away – and while all those things are true, I honestly think it is all to do with sex!'

'Meg!'

'Well, what else?' Meg said, unabashed. 'My aunt Rosie said the same. I mean, isn't that what the women's magazines are always on about, "a man's needs"? As my aunt said, Doris offers Dad comforts that no one else could. He was lonely and she was there and they got together.'

'She sort of satisfies him, so he ignores all the negative points?'

'Yeah, that's it more or less,' Meg said. 'He often doesn't come home at night now, and however we feel about it, or her, we can't fight anything like that.'

Joy felt immensely sorry for Meg because she wasn't one to lie or even exaggerate. 'Oh, Meg,' she said. 'I

154

would say you need to be away from that unhappy house and that woman as soon as possible.' Joy's words brought Meg up sharp. She had never considered her home as an unhappy one before. It had been when her mother died, for everyone had missed her so much, but Meg had worked hard to alleviate that, and before the arrival of Doris they had been happy. But now that happiness was being slowly eroded.

Everyone at the parachute works had been talking about evacuation all week, some very much for the idea and an equal number against. Doris took no part in the discussion but listened carefully. If what they said was right it was the answer to a prayer for her.

The same day Meg was meeting Joy, Doris took a few hours from work and went into the Town Hall to find out what was what. A very smart lady of middle age, dressed in a black suit and pristine white shirt, could quite understand that she wanted to know what was being proposed, and she hadn't been the first by any means to make enquiries. 'Unless parents have made private arrangements schoolchildren will be usually evacuated with the school they attend,' the woman said. 'However, a lot depends on where the schools are. Not every school is considered at high risk. We are compiling lists of schools who will be in the evacuations schemes now, and it is voluntary, you understand,' the women added. 'Parents are not forced, but it is what the Government are advising.'

'And a jolly good idea, if you ask me,' Doris said. 'And could you tell me if St Catherine's School is included in this scheme?'

155

The woman checked the list in front of her and said, 'Yes, yes, it is. Are you a parent of one of the children at the school, Mrs . . .?'

Doris didn't supply her name, but instead said, 'No, I have no children of my own but I am shortly to be married and my husband-to-be is a widower and has three children in that school. Naturally he is concerned for their safety, especially as, in the event of war, he will in all likelihood be called up.'

'Yes,' the woman said. 'I do understand, and as the children's natural parent, your husband-to-be will have to sign the forms when the system is in place.'

'Yes, of course,' Doris said, knowing she could soon convince Charlie that that was the best plan. 'And what of those not of school age? My intended's youngest is not yet five.'

'It is proposed under-fives are evacuated with their mothers.'

That didn't suit Doris's plans at all. 'Can't they go with a nursery?'

The woman gave a rueful smile. 'Not many women would like their very young children to be housed away from them, though there are some plans afoot in special circumstances. Is the child concerned at a nursery?'

'Not at present.'

'Then I can do nothing for you,' the woman said regretfully. 'As the child's stepmother you will be entitled to be evacuated with that child but that is all.'

'I work sewing parachutes,' Doris said. 'And if I didn't have the care of the children I had thought to go into the munitions.'

'Very commendable,' the woman said. 'Mothers with

small children, who are engaged in war work, will have priority at the city's day nurseries. You might easily find the child a place there, but there are no national plans to move the very young away from home.'

It wasn't what Doris wanted to hear, but the woman couldn't help her further and so Doris went home deep in thought. Once war was inevitable – and every day that seemed more likely – she could get rid of all Charlie's children except Ruth, and there was no way she was going to be landed with a snivelling two-year-old. It wasn't as if Charlie even cared for her. Better for everyone if the child was away in a home some-where where she could be adopted by people who did love her, and the sooner she convinced Charlie of that the better. She knew the other kids would probably object but they couldn't stop their father if that's what he decided, and she'd make sure he saw sense before he was much older.

The following day, Meg's cousins Anna and Lizzie were married at St Catherine's Church, which was packed with relatives and friends. They had elected to be married together and had bought very smart matching costumes in cream and navy, which they said were more practical and could be worn again. They also thought it unseemly to have lavish arrangements with the country in the state it was, and with weddings pushed forward out of necessity.

Doris said Anna and Lizzie had a right to an opinion and to have the wedding of their choice, but she thought a person's wedding day was the one day no one should use the word 'practical'. However, the lack of fancy clothes and pomp and ceremony didn't seem to detract from the wedding, for the beauty of the girls came from within and warmed the hearts of everyone. True abiding love sparked between the two young couples as, with the Mass over, the priest pronounced them man and wife.

The service had also had a poignancy to it, as they, like many young couples, had been desperate to tie the knot before the balloon went up. Their futures were uncertain, but with the declaration of war hanging over them, they would almost certainly be parted – maybe for many months or years – and face immeasurable dangers. Meg suddenly closed her eyes and prayed fervently that they would all return safely.

When she opened her eyes it was to find Terry's eyes fastened on her and she smiled, glad to see her brother because she had missed him. She had seen him at Mass most Sundays, but they only spent a few minutes together and he never came to the house. The wedding celebrations spilled out onto the street, because the house could not accommodate all the people who had attended the Nuptial Mass, but it didn't matter for the day was a fine one, sunny and warm.

Meg told Terry about bumping into Kate Carmichael and her suggestion about joining the Land Army. 'Joy is really keen,' she said, 'only a bit disappointed I can't go with her.'

'And why can't you?'

'Oh, Terry, think why not,' Meg cried impatiently. 'Doris came home last night full of the Government's evacuation plans.'

'Dad won't agree to that.'

'Have you forgotten already that Doris makes the decisions in our house?' Meg said. 'And she's in favour of evacuation so it will happen. Then if Dad is called up that will leave Doris in sole charge of Ruth. You are growing into a big strapping lad but I bet you wouldn't want Doris to be in sole charge of you.'

Terry grinned. 'No,' he said, 'I wouldn't. Tell you the truth I would rather take my chance with a sabre-toothed tiger. I think it would be more trustworthy.'

'Yes, but it's no laughing matter, is it?' Meg said. 'I mean, what chance will Ruth have with her? And even though I am not joining the Land Army, I'll have to work at something so however close to home I am Doris will have her all day. You can do a lot to a little child in a day and she will be too young to tell me.'

'Oh, yeah, that's right,' Terry said. 'And Ruth is bound to do things that will annoy her because little kids do.'

'What's up?' said a voice behind them.

'Nicholas!' Meg said, swinging round to face her cousin. 'Don't you know it's rude to sneak up on people?'

'I didn't sneak up,' Nicholas assured her. 'That wasn't the intention, anyway. Just saw you talking and it looked serious.'

'Not really,' Terry said. 'Just moaning about Doris. We do it often.'

Nicholas looked as if he could quite understand that. 'I think a lot of people feel a bit sorry for your dad,' he said.

'Well, they needn't waste their sympathy,' Terry said fiercely. 'I have no respect for my father because he is spineless. He allows things to happen to him rather than taking charge of his own life.'

Meg hated to hear her brother talking that way about the father she still made excuses for. 'It isn't all his fault. You know how he missed Mom.'

'Oh, don't give me that,' Terry said with an impatient shake of his head. 'I missed Mom too. We all did. But we had to get on with things like she'd have wanted us to. Look, it didn't take him long to find another to warm his bed. I may not go to the wedding at all; I have no desire to. No, Meg. You defend him all you like, but in my opinion Dad and Doris Caudwell deserve each other.'

That night, Doris and Charlie lay on the bed in Doris's flat and again Doris broached the subject of evacuation. This time Charlie had had enough to drink to feel mellow and very amorous, and as Doris spoke she allowed him to fondle her body and gave him little teasing kisses to punctuate her words, the words that mentioned evacuating the children for the first time. 'It's just sending them so far away that worries me,' Charlie said with a slight slur that made Doris smile. She had drunk little herself because she thought the evacuation of the older children and the problem of Ruth had to be dealt with and she knew just how compliant Charlie was in this stage of drunkenness. 'Meg was s'posed to keep them together.'

'When Maeve laid that charge upon Meg she didn't know there was going to be a war, now, did she? Did any of us?'

'No, no, you're right. None of us did.'

'And doesn't war change everything?'

'I suppose it does, yes.'

'And haven't you told me that everyone's saying that this will be a war fought from the air?' Doris prompted. 'You saw the pictures of that Spanish place a few years ago. What if that happens here and your children are in the thick of it? You might be called up by then and I can't be with them every minute.'

Charlie had had enough talking with Doris's luscious body lying tantalisingly close and he reached for her, but she evaded his grasp. 'The pleasure comes later,' she said, kissing him on the lips lingeringly so that he groaned in desire. 'There are decisions to make first.'

Charlie was thinking more about the pleasures of the flesh almost within his grasp and he didn't want to waste time, but yet he couldn't risk annoying Doris so that she wouldn't give him what he craved, as she had occasionally before now. Anyway, what she'd said more or less made sense to his fuddled brain. 'You're right,' he said. 'The children need to be evacuated.'

'So you'll see about it?' Doris said. 'You must sign the forms.'

'I will, I will,' Charlie said. 'I promise. Now come here, woman.'

'Not yet,' Doris said, evading him with ease.

'Christ!' Charlie cried. 'I'm burning up inside.'

'Ah,' said Doris, and she put her arms around Charlie's neck and kissed him passionately. 'I'll make it up to you, Charlie, when you decide what we're going to do about Ruth.'

'About Ruth?' Charlie repeated. He hadn't given the child a thought.

'Well, she can't be evacuated with the rest, so what are we going to do about her?'

'What d'you mean?'

'I mean that you can't seem to stand the sight of her, because Maeve died giving birth to her and I can't take to her at all either. Anyway, with all the children away I could earn good money – have a little nest egg for when you come home again – and I couldn't do that with a two-year-old around my neck.'

'No,' Charlie agreed.

'Anyway, are we being fair to her?' Doris said. 'I mean, if she went into an orphanage I bet she wouldn't be there long because she's a pretty little thing and she could be adopted by people who would really love her.'

Charlie was silent so long that Doris thought maybe she had gone too far too quick; that she had really offended him. Then she saw the tears in his eyes because Charlie was reliving the day he had been told that his beautiful wife and mother to his children had died and then, as if some sort of consolation prize, that the baby might pull through. He wished she had died too and prayed that she would, but she was here, a living breathing child of his blood, yet he felt little or nothing for her.

The tears he shed were for Maeve and he let them trail unheeded down his cheeks as he said brokenly, 'That's what I wanted to do in the hospital. I thought the baby wouldn't have survived and against the odds she had, though it was touch and go at first, and I wanted to leave her at the hospital, but Meg insisted on bringing her home.' He looked at Doris and asked, 'Could I really do that now? Would they take my child like that?'

'They will if you play it right,' Doris said, who had already given it some thought. 'Go before we are married

162

and say nothing about getting married. You can tell them truthfully that you are a widower and yet you want to do your bit in the war that's coming. Explain about the evacuation of the others and ask them to take Ruth until you return for her.'

Even in his confused state, Charlie could see that that just could work. 'It will be no wrench for me; more relief, if I'm honest,' he said. 'But the children – Meg in particular!'

'Oh, she'll be upset, I grant you,' Doris said. 'But she'll get over it. It will allow her to have a future for herself. What would you have her do, give her life over to the care of Ruth while the others grow up and leave? If you do that you could be stopping her having any sort of life and maybe children of her own.'

Doris let that sink in before letting her hand trail up Charlie's leg. 'She might never know the delights of sex as we do, Charlie. Think on that.'

'Yes,' gasped Charlie.

'So what do you say, big boy?'

'I say yes, you're right.' At that moment Charlie would have said anything Doris wanted him to say. 'I will take Ruth to the orphanage.'

'Are you ready to claim your reward?' Doris asked with a slight smile. 'You have gone very hard all of a sudden.'

'Oh, my darling girl,' Charlie cried. 'Come to me, please, for God's sake, and I'll do anything you want.'

Doris pulled Charlie down on top of her and as he entered her he felt as if he'd exploded inside and he let out a cry of exultation, and Doris smiled because she knew she had Charlie under her thumb. She pulled the strings and he danced to her tune, and that was how she liked it.

The next morning Charlie had only a vague memory of the night before, but Doris remembered it and she reminded him. Charlie was badly hung over. He felt as sick as a dog, a thousand hammers were drumming in his head, and he was no match for Doris. He could see no reason for her to lie to him and so if he'd promised to see about evacuation for the older ones and an orphanage for Ruth that was what he would do.

They had both agreed that it was better to take Ruth when Meg was out of the way but didn't really know how that was to be achieved. Doris was thinking up errands to take Meg into town when fate played into their hands. because on the following Wednesday morning, Meg received a letter.

'Oh, it's from Joy,' she said.

Joy's interview for the Land Army was that Friday morning but she had booked the whole day off and suggested that Meg could meet her afterwards for lunch and then either go to the pictures or for a mooch round the shops, as once she left they would see very little of one another. When Meg told her father and Doris that evening she missed the look that flitted between them.

'Will you go?' Doris asked.

Meg thought that strange because Doris wasn't usually interested in anything she did, but she had asked pleasantly enough and so Meg said, 'Oh, yes. She is such a lovely person and I am going to miss her so much when she goes off to the Land Army.'

'Is that where she's bound for?' Doris said. 'The Land Army. Wouldn't that suit you too?'

'Maybe,' Meg said, and she lowered her head as she muttered, 'Circumstances are different for Joy.'

Again she missed the look Doris gave Charlie, the look that said plainly, 'You see, the family, and particularly Ruth, are stopping Meg doing what she wants.' Charlie understood her perfectly. However upset Meg would be initially at Ruth's been sent away, they were doing her a favour. Not that he wanted Meg leaving her home at such a young age. There were plenty of jobs she could do in Birmingham and still be around to give Doris a hand if she needed it.

THIRTEEN

On Friday morning, when Charlie said he was having the day off because there were some legal things he had to see to concerning the wedding, Meg, who took as little notice of the wedding as she could, wasn't the least bit suspicious and went off to meet her friend unconcerned.

She hadn't been gone more than half an hour when Charlie said to Jenny, 'Get Ruth's coat. I'm taking her out.'

Jenny stood stock-still on the floor and stared at her father. 'But you never take her out.'

'Well, today I'm going to,' Charlie said.

Jenny felt concern prickle the back of her neck and she asked herself why that was. Wasn't it a normal thing for a father to take his young daughter out for a walk? Perhaps, but not in their family. 'I'll come with you,' she said. 'No, better still, I'll tell the others and we'll all go. We haven't had a day out with you in ages.'

'Have to be some other time,' Charlie said. 'Today I'm taking Ruth on her own.'

'But Meg told me to care for her.'

166

'I am her father, in case it has escaped your notice,' Charlie said.

'It certainly seems to have escaped yours.' Jenny clapped her hand over her mouth because she hadn't intended to let that slip out. She saw her father's eyes smouldering with anger in a way she had never seen before. He was usually a mild-mannered man, but in that instant she was afraid of him.

'Get Ruth's coat,' he said through gritted teeth and she ran to get it.

Ruth didn't want to go with the man that, despite her tender years, she had learned to avoid and she struggled and cried. Even when he held her hand her other was stretched towards Jenny. Her eyes, awash with tears, were fastened on her elder sister's and seemed to be begging her not to let her go as she cried out, 'Jenny. Jenny. Want Meg.'

Exasperated, Charlie lifted her into his arms and stepped out on the pavement, and Jenny stood biting her lip to stop her crying because she didn't know what was going on. Billy and Sally tumbled into the room. They both saw the flash of their father pass the window holding the threshing, protesting Ruth in his arms.

'Where's our dad taken Ruth?' Billy asked.

'God knows.'

'He never takes Ruth anywhere,' Sally said.

'I know,' Jenny said, 'and it bothers me that he has just decided to do it now so I'm going to follow him and try and find out what he's up to.'

'And me,' Billy said.

'No, just me,' Jenny insisted. 'It wouldn't do for him

167

to know he's being followed. You stay here. I shouldn't be long.'

By the time Jenny was out on the street she saw her father turning down Bristol Passage and so she was able to hurry along Bell Barn Road to the top of the passage, where she followed more slowly. He went on to Bristol Street and she watched him wait at the tram stop, and a few minutes later she was flying down Bristol Street in the opposite direction.

Terry wasn't that pleased to see Jenny because the shop was really busy, but Mr Drummond told Terry to have a word with his agitated sister because it could be important. Terry took Jenny into the stockroom at the back and when she blurted out that she was worried because their dad had taken Ruth out, Terry gave a low whistle.

'That's a turn-up for the books, ain't it?' he said.

'He ain't never done it before.'

'I know.' Terry said. 'Maybe he's had a change of heart.'

Jenny shook her head. 'He was really strange, Terry,' she said. 'I suggested we all go with him 'cos you know he doesn't know the least thing about Ruth, but he said no, and Ruth didn't want to go with him anyway and she played up shocking. It really upset me seeing her crying and trying to pull away and calling for Meg.'

'Where is Meg?'

'Gone to meet Joy in town and that's where Dad was heading with Ruth too, into town.'

'Didn't you ask him where he was going?'

'He probably wouldn't have told me,' Jenny said. 'Like I said, he was strange. But I didn't expect him to get on a flipping tram, and Ruth was still roaring her head off.'

Terry had to admit it was concerning, but he refused to get worried about a man taking his young daughter out for the day. 'There's likely some simple explanation. Dad ignores Ruth, or has done up till now, but he wouldn't harm her or anything, would he?'

'No, I don't suppose so.'

'Well, then, wait until he comes back and I'm sure he will explain everything.'

But Charlie didn't come back. Jenny made them all something to eat in the end, and still they waited. It was almost tea-time when Meg came home and Jenny was so glad to see her and yet a bit anxious in case she blamed her for letting Ruth go out with their father.

Meg was as concerned as anyone else but she didn't blame her young sister. 'What could you have done?' she said. 'You couldn't have stopped him. But he will get the length of my tongue when he does decide to come home, worrying everybody like this.'

Meg's words were said to help her sister, but she had a deep dread feeling inside that something was very badly wrong.

And then suddenly her father was standing in the threshold and he was alone.

'Where's Ruth?' Meg shrieked at her father. 'What have you done with her?'

Terry's words of assurance that their father wouldn't hurt Ruth rang hollowly in Jenny's head as she cried, 'Have you hurt Ruth?'

'Of course not,' Charlie said. 'Ruth is where she should have gone long ago. I've placed her in a children's home.'

'You did what?' Meg screamed. She was having trouble drawing breath as if the heart had been cut from her, like her worst nightmare coming true, the one thing she had dreaded and guarded against. It was too much, she couldn't bear it and with an anguished cry she fell to the floor.

When her eyes flickered open she groaned as the memory of what her father had done returned to her. She closed her eyes again and wished she could pull up a mental drawbridge and retreat into herself so that no one could hurt her any more. 'How are you feeling, my dear?'

Meg forced her eyes open to see she was lying in her father's bed and her aunt Rosie was sitting on a chair beside her. 'Aunt Rosie . . .'

'I know it all, my dear.'

'Why did he do it?'

'He said he was thinking of you.'

'I don't believe that for a moment.'

'He said he was giving you your life back and said something about your friend going into the Land Army and you wishing you could have gone with her.'

'I never said that, and I was going to get a job here and a place to live, seeing that Doris doesn't want me living at home.'

'Did she actually say that?'

'Oh, yes,' Meg said. 'And I was doing that to keep an eye on Ruth, for Doris cares as little for her as her own father and I was worried about her.'

'Even so, it seems a grievous thing to have done, to put the child into an orphanage when she has a family willing to care for her,' Rose said. 'Robert is raging

170

about it because, as he said, surely between us all we could care for one small child. We will all feel the loss of her but yours will be the greater.' Rose gave her niece's hand a squeeze.

Meg eyes were deadened and her words seemed wrung from her very soul as she said, 'There are no words to tell you how I feel, but it is as if a part of me is missing and the pain of losing that part is agonising. I suppose there is no chance of getting her back?'

Rose knew there was little chance once a child was in the system, but instead of answering directly she said, 'I'll tell you what I know. According to your father, the first place Ruth will be sent to is the Children's Hospital to be examined and make sure she is healthy and carrying no infectious diseases.'

'And then?'

'Then, as we are Catholics, she will be sent to Maryville Orphanage in a place called Kingstanding, which is run by the Sisters of Mercy.'

'And once she is there, can I visit?'

Rose shook her head. 'They say no. It just upsets them.'

'I'm never going to see her again, am I?' Meg said plaintively, and then the tears came in a torrent and great gulping sobs like a paroxysm of grief. Rose relinquished Meg's hand, gathered her into her arms and rocked her, crooning softly as she had done to her own children, quite understanding Meg's agony for she felt tears prickling behind her own eyes.

All evening Meg was left in bed and treated as if she was ill and she didn't care because she could work up no desire to get up. She was brought a meal she was too upset to eat and numerous cups of tea by Jenny, who was as heavy-eyed as Meg was. She held herself somehow responsible for what had happened, despite many reassurances from Meg, and, wrapped in her sister's arms, she shed bitter tears.

Eventually, though, she was calmer and said, 'Dad said we won't miss Ruth that much because we're going to be evacuated.'

That was no surprise to Meg, and Jenny went on, 'They say they send you to the country. I ain't never been there, so I don't know if I'll like it or not.'

'You will, I should think,' Meg said. 'It gets you away from Doris and that's got to be good.'

'Oh, yeah,' Jenny said with a wobbly grin. 'That might be the only good thing about it.'

All the children came to see Meg. Last of all was Terry, who said he had wiped the floor with his father that night.

'I don't blame you,' Meg said, 'but what am I to do now? I feel like I've been sort of cast adrift.'

'Listen to me,' Terry said, holding his sister's shoulders and looking deep into her eyes. 'I don't agree for one minute with what Dad did, nor that he has arranged and signed the forms for the kids' evacuation, but he has done it and it can't be undone, so you have only yourself to think about. So why don't you go for the Land Army like Jenny tells me your friend is doing? It will get you away from this place and that pair.'

'It is tempting,' Meg said. 'I don't think I'll ever be able to forgive Dad for this and I know Doris will have had a hand in it.'

'Probably her idea,' Terry said. 'Most things are.'

'Probably was,' Meg said with a heavy sigh. 'Tell you the truth I can hardly bear to think about them, never mind talk to them or look at their smug faces, but with the evacuation the kids will have new things to think about and they won't miss me for long.'

'No,' Terry said, 'and I never thought I would say this, but I think it's better if the kids are evacuated away from that she devil.'

'I think so, too,' Meg said. 'Where's Dad now?'

'At Doris's,' Terry said, 'and Uncle Robert said he can stay there. He says from what he hears he spends enough nights there already so a few more won't hurt and he is not to come round here and upset you.'

'Oh, I'm glad,' Meg said with a sigh of relief. 'I wondered how I would face him.'

'Well, you won't have to,' Terry said. 'Not yet awhile.'

However, Meg found she couldn't just walk away from Ruth, and the next morning she asked Rosie to go with her to the Children's Hospital to see if Ruth was still there. Rosie agreed readily, intending to tell whoever was in charge that Ruth had a loving family waiting to welcome her home.

They hit a solid brick wall. The hospital authorities wouldn't even verify that Ruth was there and both were told pointedly that her father had freely given the child into the care of the Social Services and that was where she would stay.

Meg was tearful on the way home, but this setback strengthened her resolve.

'I must leave here,' she told her aunt. 'It would be worse in a way if I stopped here, being so close to Ruth

173

and not able to see her, and at the moment I can't look at Dad and Doris.'

'You can stay with us if you like,' Rose said. 'We'd love to have you, you know that.'

'Thanks, Aunt Rosie,' Meg said. 'But it has to be a more permanent solution and I have made up my mind to apply to join the Land Army. Tonight I will write a long letter to Joy telling her everything, and much as I would like to stay with you while the formalities are completed I think the kids need me to be there as much as possible until I have to leave. They have lost a sister, too.'

But when Meg began the letter she found she couldn't write about what her father had done to her youngest sister and she said only that as it was obvious the children were going to be evacuated. Her way was clear to go into the Land Army.

Though Joy was delighted to hear that Meg was going to try for the Land Army after all, she knew she was holding something back. She never mentioned Ruth, which was odd. But she had said that Doris had talked about going to work in munitions because it paid better than sewing parachutes, and nursery places were given as priority to the children of working mothers so Doris probably had that in hand.

Joy explained the enlistment procedure and Meg went to Thorp Street Barracks to sign the necessary forms and arranged to have a medical.

The day of the interview, in early August, was warm and sunny. Meg stood at the bottom of the white marble steps leading up to the Council House, looking up at the imposing building. She had never been inside before, but now she ran up the steps and opened one of the two large studded wooden doors that gleamed in the sunlight.

She gasped as she stepped inside for it was an impressive place; an intricate and very beautiful glass chandelier hung from the ornate ceiling and her feet sank into a thick carpet that led to a desk at the back, in the alcove of the wide sweep of a staircase. It seemed a long walk to the desk, with her feet making no sound.

She presented her appointment letters to an incredibly smart girl. She had her fair hair caught in a bun at the back of her neck and her face was heavily made up, but her smile was genuine enough as she bid her go up the steps to the waiting room situated on the first floor. The stairs were as heavily carpeted as the reception hall, and the stair rods and banister burnished brass, and at the top of the stairs was a beautiful arched window and another chandelier.

There was already quite a cluster of girls waiting, and more joined them as Meg sat on one of the benches against the wall. They all looked at one another self-consciously. They were an assorted bunch, Meg thought: girls of all shapes and sizes, and mostly fairly young, though Meg guessed that none was as young as she.

The woman at Thorp Street Barracks had asked her age. She had thought of lying, but knew she would be found out as she had to bring her birth certificate to the interview, so she had told the truth and the woman had shaken her head.

'They may not take you,' she had warned. 'They are not as strict as the services and will take girls of seventeen sometimes – but sixteen, I don't know. All girls under eighteen have to get permission from a parent anyway. Will that be difficult?'

It would be very hard to get her father to agree, Meg knew, but Doris would sign anything that would get Meg out of her hair and so she said, 'No, that won't be a problem.'

'They might take you with that then,' the woman had said, handing over the forms. 'Best of luck.'

Well, forewarned is forearmed, Meg had thought at the time, but sitting in the room with the others she felt the confidence that had got her this far dribbling away.

Another girl, seeing the look on her face, whispered, 'Are you nervous as well?'

'A bit.'

'I think everyone is a little,' said the girl the other side of Meg. 'Bound to be, because we don't really know what we are letting ourselves in for.'

'You know nothing about farming then?'

'Does anyone round here?' the first girl said.

'Don't see as that matters,' another said. 'We'll have to be shown what to do, that's all. My chap knows nowt about killing folk, but he'll have to learn same as everyone else.'

'Well, that's true enough.'

'So why did you choose farming?' Meg asked the first girl.

'Do my bit, I suppose.'

Others chipped in. A few would have preferred to join one of the armed services but were prevented by parents, and in one case because a young husband objected. More than one was willing to join anything to put some distance between herself and a tyrannical father. As many reasons as there are girls here, Meg thought as the interviews began and the first girl was called in.

It was just the one woman in the room, Meg saw, when it was her turn. She was very smart and spoke dead posh, as if she had a load of marbles in her mouth. Meg was glad the woman at Thorp Street Barracks had warned her what would happen when she saw the posh woman scrutinising her birth certificate before saying, 'You are very young, only sixteen. Too young and small to be of any use, I feel.'

'I am only sixteen,' Meg said, 'but I'm not that small and I am very strong and not afraid of hard work either. When my mother died giving birth to my youngest sister, I took then all on – my other two sisters and my two brothers and the baby.'

'How long ago was this?'

'Two years.'

'I see. So what will happen to those children if you join the Land Army?'

Meg had decided it would do her no favours to tell the whole truth so she tried hard to keep any trace of bitterness from her voice as she said, 'They will have a new mother because my father is marrying again.'

'I see,' the woman said again. 'And tell me, Miss Hallett, have you any farming experience?'

'No,' Meg admitted, but remembering the chat in the waiting room she added, 'but soldiers don't come ready trained either, and I'm sure I will pick up all I need to know as well as anyone else.'

'You have great confidence in your abilities, Miss Hallett,' the woman said.

Meg knew it was important not to show one trace of the nerves that had affected her in the waiting room and so she answered, 'Not great confidence like I was a cocky person, who thinks they don't need to be taught, but I do pick things up quick so I will probably learn as fast as anyone else. And I can get a consent form signed by my parents.' When the woman still hesitated she pleaded, 'Please, won't you take a chance on me?'

The interviewer was moved by the emotion in Meg's voice and the look in those eyes that showed plainly that she had tasted sorrow and yet she had to say, 'I don't know. Possibly, but the final say rests with the committee. I will submit a favourable report on you, but get the consent form signed first, as we can't proceed without it. We will be informing you by mail if you are successful.'

Going home, Meg turned the woman's words over and over in her mind. She knew that she had to get the consent form signed as soon as possible and wondered how she was going to do it as Doris and her father seemed joined at the hip.

Then on the following Wednesday morning, Charlie told Meg he would be late home because there was a meeting after work to discuss air-raid precautions.

Meg's heart leaped – this was her chance. As soon as the evening meal was over, under the guise of popping out for a bit of shopping, she left Jenny in charge and, taking her coat from the nail at the back of the door and promising 'not to be long', she slipped out.

To say that Doris was surprised to see Meg at her door was putting it mildly. 'What do you want?' she asked truculently. 'And whatever it is, make it snappy, because I'm meeting your father later.'

'This won't take up much time,' Meg said, and without further preamble announced, 'I've joined the Women's Land Army.' She saw the glint of satisfaction in Doris's eyes as she continued, 'But I'm too young and need the permission of at least one parent.'

'And you don't think your father will give it?

'Do you?' Meg said. 'But you will, because you want rid of me as much as I want to leave here.' She withdrew the form from her pocket and passed it to Doris. 'I've filled it in,' she said. 'You just need to write Doris Hallett on it.'

'And I'll do that with pleasure,' Doris said, snatching it from Meg and signing with a flourish. 'When do you intend to start?' she asked, as she gave the form back.

Meg shrugged. 'Soon. They're just waiting for this form.'

'And when do you intend telling your father?'

'After the wedding,' Meg said. 'I'd like it if you said nothing to him about it yet.'

Doris grunted. 'Think I'm a fool? I don't want to spoil my wedding day and I expect he will kick up about you leaving home.'

'Yeah, I know,' Meg said and added a little caustically, 'But I'm sure you will be able to convince him it's all for the best because you have done that many a time.'

Doris's eyes narrowed and she thrust the form at Meg, 'There,' she said. 'You have what you need now.'

She seemed anxious to get rid of Meg, but that suited Meg anyway. 'So if that's all, you can clear off now. Like I said, I'm meeting your father.'

'Don't worry, I'm going,' Meg said, but on the stairs

as she went out she passed a man going up. For a moment she wondered where he was making for, because only Doris lived in the top flat, but she put it from her mind because, with the consent form signed, a new future was beckoning.

When the knock came to the door minutes later, Doris presumed it was Meg again, wanting something else. However, a glimpse of the weasel-faced man outside caused her to stagger in shock. 'Frank,' she cried. 'Frank Zimmerman.' He was an associate of Gerry's that she had thought and hoped she would ever see again.

'Hello, babe,' Frank said, pushing her back inside and closing the door with his foot.

'What're you doing here?' she said. 'And where's Gerry?'

'Questions, questions,' Frank said, walking round the room as he did so.

'Well,' Doris said, willing her voice to be steady for it was safer not betray weakness in front of this man, 'where's Gerry?'

'Gerry's dead, darling.'

'Dead?' Doris thought it was hard to think of Gerry as dead. She wondered at her lack of emotion, when once he'd meant the world to her, but then she had known when he fled to save his own skin that he was as good as dead, and her own instinct for survival superseded any sense of loss she might have felt.

'He went back for you,' Frank said. 'It was about a month after you left. We all said he was mad.'

'How did he die?'

'The family of that bloke he killed got him,' Frank

said. 'Did him over proper. I found what was left of him in an alleyway.' He looked at Doris then and said, 'They're after you as well. Said you're as much to blame as Gerry.'

'Why d'you think I got out of there?' Doris said. 'I knew his family were gunning for me and I had to give the heavies the slip as well.'

'Heavies?'

Doris nodded. 'From Big Bert's mob, I think,' she said. 'Paid me a visit the day I was thrown out of my flat. Gerry owed them one hell of a lot of money.'

'That's Gerry all right.'

'Huh, nearly the end of me,' Doris said. 'Anyway, how did you find me? I thought I had covered my tracks well.'

'You probably had,' Frank said. 'But Gerry went around looking for you and someone mentioned that they had seen you go in the Recruitment Office where people register for war work before you seemed to disappear off the face of the earth. He guessed what you'd done and thought they might have a file on you and so he broke into the office one night. He said the job was like taking candy off a baby 'cos the filing cabinet wasn't even locked – and there were all your details, including the address of the factory in Cregoe Street that you were assigned to.'

'What you can do, others can do,' Doris said in panic. 'Did Gerry tell you where I was?'

Frank shook his head. 'He wouldn't let on, but before I told the police where his body was I went through his pockets. He had a notebook in his inside jacket pocket and all your details were in that book. When

181

things got a bit hot for me up north I thought I'd look you up. All I had to do then was wait for you to come out the place you work and follow you home. Knew you'd put me up for a bit, for old times' sake.'

'I can't,' Doris said bluntly. 'I'm getting married this Saturday.'

'God, that was quick work,' Frank said. 'I've only just told you you're a widow.'

'Come on, Frank,' Doris said. 'I never thought I'd see Gerry again. He left me high and dry. I had no idea where he was, and two groups of people wanted my blood as they couldn't have his. I had to leave, and even this isn't really far enough. I thought if I could change my name I would feel safer and,' she added, 'this was my one stab at becoming respectable.'

Frank hooted with laughter. 'Respectable my arse,' he said. 'Too late for the likes of us to try and be respectable.'

'It's not just respectability,' Doris said. 'It's for my safety as well.'

'You got a nice pad here,' Frank said. 'So is he moving in here after the wedding?'

'No, he has a house in Bell Barn Road,' Doris said. 'I've given notice on this place.'

'Withdraw it,' Frank said. 'I'll take it on. the landlord won't care as long as he's getting the rent.'

'What do you want it for?'

'To store certain things.'

'What things? Drugs?'

'Amongst other things.'

'Look, Frank, you might scoff but I am trying to give up that sort of stuff,' Doris said. 'I don't think—'

Frank was across the room in seconds. He grasped Doris's chin tight between his fingers as he spat into her face, 'I don't think you really understand me. You go against me now and I will drop your address into the ears of people who just might want to know. You got that?'

Doris understood all right. She looked at his thin lips in that mean-looking face and his cold black eyes boring into her and she knew he meant every word he said. For her own safety she was bound to him and she couldn't prevent the little shiver running through her even as she nodded. Frank felt her fear and it amused him. He gave a cruel little laugh as he pushed her away. 'I knew you would see sense in the end, my dear.'

That night Doris couldn't quite hide her agitation from Charlie, but when he asked her what the matter was, she put it down to wedding nerves. That made him treat her more tenderly than ever. She was glad they went to the pictures so she didn't have to try to make conversation and could hide the deep fear probably evident in her face. She wasn't just frightened of Frank Zimmerman, she was absolutely bloody terrified. She had seen what he had done to others who had tried to stand against him or had offended him in some other way and it wasn't pleasant. He was brutal and merciless, and she knew she had to do what he wanted or he would have no hesitation in doing any of the things he had threatened to do. She felt as if she was sailing a boat through very choppy seas with snapping sharks on every side, and she wished heartily Frank hadn't bothered tracking her down.

Charlie had taken Doris to see *You Can't Take It*

With You, but she hadn't a clue what it was about, for her mind had been elsewhere. Afterwards, at the Trees, she drank far more than was usual when she was with Charlie, and so he had had to help her home. But when they got there, she put a hand on his arm to stop him following her up the steps. 'Not tonight, Charlie,' she said. 'I'm feeling ever so sick. My fault, I know but . . .'

Charlie hid his disappointment. 'Ah, well,' he said. 'No harm done. You need to get your head down, my dear.'

Doris said nothing and made her unsteady way up the stairs to the flat to find that Frank was asleep in the spare bedroom. One thing she knew was that he wouldn't try anything on with her, because he preferred men for sex, or, to be precise, boys and as young as he could get them. The man sickened her, but she knew she had to be careful not to show that. She feared for the future. It had all looked so rosy and now her past had caught up with her.

FOURTEEN

Charlie had wanted a quiet, unassuming wedding and had thought Doris wanted the same, but then she seemed to change her mind and said she wanted the works. Charlie had to tell her he couldn't afford a big wedding. He agreed that she needed a dress and so she hired a dressmaker to make her one, of powder-blue decorated with white satin and lace and tiny rosebuds, in a style that suited her enviable figure. The cost of that alone made Charlie wince.

He refused to let the girls have something similar, for he said finances wouldn't allow it. Instead Aunt Rosie took them all into C & A Modes and kitted them all out in clothes – at a fraction of the cost – that they could wear to the wedding and also afterwards.

But Doris wasn't finished. She wanted Charlie and even Billy to have new suits to wear, but Charlie objected. 'The suit I wear for Mass is good enough,' he said. 'And a suit for a wee boy is ridiculous. What wear will he get out of that?'

'He could wear it to Mass.'

'Doris, I know you've had no children and so maybe

don't understand. No boy of Billy's age has a suit,' Charlie said. 'You must put that idea out of your head.'

Doris sulked but Charlie held firm. He had to. He had already borrowed from both his brothers for the engagement ring, and even if they'd been able and willing to lend him more, he didn't want to go further into debt. Doris punished him by withholding sex; nevertheless, as frustrated as he was, he couldn't give in to her demands.

She had also approached Paddy Larkin at the Swan pub for the hire of his back room for the wedding breakfast, and arranged for it to be prepared by Paddy's wife, helped by outside caterers.

'Outside caterers?' Rosie said to her in surprise when she heard.

'I believe if you are going to do a job it is better if it is done properly,' Doris replied, and Charlie said nothing, for he didn't want to upset Doris again. He did truly care deeply for her and was grateful for the closeness they had and the wondrous sex they both enjoyed. But if he upset her there would be no sex and he was finding it difficult to do without it for long. Far better, he thought, to let her have her way this time, and then life ran much smoother.

The day before the wedding, Meg escaped to the Bull Ring again to see Joy for lunch and tell her about visiting Doris.

'And she signed the form just like that?' Joy said.

'Yeah, like I knew she would,' Meg said. 'She had to sign Doris Hallett or it wouldn't have worked, though she isn't officially that until tomorrow. Point is, I don't think they will be that bothered, not to check in minute detail, because she will be my official stepmother by the time I'm joined up properly and I didn't see when else I was going to see her on her own.'

'And how is she with you now?'

'Oh, she's all right,' Meg said. 'Got what she wants, you see, which is basically me and Terry – the older ones – out of the way. Point is, I can't wait to go either. I will worry about the kids, but I know for a fact I won't make it better by staying there. Maybe if I'm out the way she will be better with the others and they are going to be evacuated so they'll be out of her hair altogether. Anyway, there is nothing really I can do any more to ease the situation and so on the way here I dropped the form off at the Council House. The woman said she was only waiting for that form and they will process everything straight away now.'

'I hope we're billeted together.'

'We might be,' Meg said. 'In the regular army they do try to put people together, brothers and that. In the Great War they used to bunch people from an area together and call them the Pals' battalions.'

'Yeah, I know,' Joy said. 'But they stopped doing that, Dad said, because in some cases it was wiping out all the young men from one area, clearing villages and towns.'

'You can see why that was,' Meg said, 'And I suppose that is going to extremes, but at least they saw the value of people who knew each other working together. And, let's face it, the only battles we are likely to face is against the weeds threatening to strangle the crops.'

187

'Hardly life-threatening then?' Joy said. 'Might be bloody annoying, though.'

'Let's see how it goes, and if we are not together, one of us can ask for a transfer after we've been trained and everything.'

'Yes,' Joy said. 'I'm really quite excited, you know, though I know I will miss everyone like mad, except it's like a different house with my brother away. No one to argue the toss with now. Didn't know life could be so boring, 'cos he used to drive me wild at times.'

'I thought they only kept the young chaps they called up for six weeks.'

'They do,' Joy said. 'And he came home for a bit, just long enough really to tell Mom and Dad he was joining the Regular Army.

'He said there was little point in him settling back into his old job and that only to be called up again because war is staring us in the face. Anyway, he'd made good friends with some of the lads and they all decided to do the same thing.'

'Doing their bit like we're doing ours,' Meg said. 'It has given my life purpose. You know, I saw looking after the kids as an important job and when Doris indicated clearly that she wanted me out of the way I felt cast adrift, not knowing what I was going to do. Terry told me once to look to my own future and I suddenly saw, with the kids evacuated sooner or later, the field was clear for me to think of myself for once.'

'I know,' said Joy softly, wondering at the brooding sadness behind Meg's eyes. 'Looking forward to the wedding?'

'Are you kidding?' Meg said. 'And for all the fuss Doris made, they'll only be a few of us there.'

'How come?'

'Search me,' Meg said. 'Doris had been in charge of this, but basically it is only the family invited. Well, who else could be, really, because Doris knows such few people, having chosen not to become too friendly with the women at work, and so that's it really.'

'So no hen night then?'

'Not enough hens,' Meg said with a giggle. 'We did wonder if she would ask just the family round and, when she didn't, Rosie asked her if she wanted to have a few drinks with us, but she said she didn't believe in such foolishness.'

'And your father?'

'Oh, he's a great believer in stag nights and they have a grand send-off planned in the Swan,' Meg said, and with a wry smile went on, 'And you can bet your bottom dollar that I will have to put him to bed when he comes in. Times like this I miss Terry – he used to help me when Dad got home in a state.'

'Won't one of his brothers help?'

'I couldn't guarantee that either of them will be in better shape – even Uncle Robert, who is his best man,' said Meg. 'No, I've asked Nicholas.'

'Oh, I'm glad you'll have someone,' Joy said. 'You haven't mentioned him for a bit.'

'Well, he wasn't around,' Meg said. 'He was studying for his matric. Now he is kicking his heels waiting to see if he's passed. He will have, of course.'

'Then what?'

'Highers, I suppose, if the war doesn't get in the way.'

'Then university?'

'That's what Aunt Susan wants.'

'What about Nicholas?'

'He told me that if we go to war he will join up when he is eighteen.'

'D'you think he will?'

Meg shrugged. 'Who knows? 'Course, he will have no choice if he is called up, but if he wants to go before he has to, he will have a battle with his mother, especially if his dad is called up too.'

'Yes, I think it's harder for those left behind, in a way.'

'So do I.'

'Oh, let's stop talking about depressing things that haven't even happened yet,' Joy said.

'Hard to talk about anything else, though, don't you think?' Meg said. 'This impending war is on everybody's lips. Often followed by gruesome tales of dreadful things that happened in the last one. It makes you wonder if there will be any chaps left for us when it's our turn to get married.'

Joy hooted with laughter, 'Are you kidding?' she said. 'Look about you, the only men for us will be the leavings, the ones the services didn't want.'

'On that depressing thought, I will leave you,' Meg said with a wave of her hand. 'Wish me luck for tomorrow?'

'You have it but you won't need it,' said Joy. 'Because whatever happens, bite your tongue and tell yourself you will be out of there as soon as possible.'

Doris and Charlie's wedding was on 19 August 1939. Meg and her siblings were gathered in the porch, waiting for the bride, when they saw Terry come up the steps. Meg felt an immense sense of relief because he had threatened to boycott the whole affair.

'Well, don't you all look the business?' he said, for he had seldom seen all his sisters looking so pretty.

'So do you,' Meg said.

Terry had even semi-tamed his wiry hair with masses of Brylcreem. He was wearing a dark blue suit and a pure white shirt. His striped tie matched the handkerchief in his top pocket and he looked very grown up. 'Couldn't let the side down,' he said in a voice that had deepened since he had left home.

Meg could understand that he might want to look as well dressed as everyone else since he had made the effort to come, but she did wonder how he had afforded it. As if Terry had read her thought he said quietly, 'It's all right, sis, I didn't steal the suit or anything. I bought it on hire purchase.'

'Hire purchase?

'Yeah, you pay so much down as a deposit and then so much a week,' Terry said. 'I was too young to do it on my own so Neil's uncle stood surety for me.'

'Don't ever let Dad know that, because it might upset him.'

'Don't know why it should, or why you're so protective of him, Meg, 'cos he ain't worth your concern,' Terry said. 'He seemed to cease being our dad when he met Doris. Tell you the truth, I nearly didn't come at all, and then I thought if I didn't I would be letting you down. It was Neil's uncle said I had to wear a suit for my own father's wedding. He's been good to me, and his wife has. She never usually works in the shop, but she is taking my place today because Saturday is our busiest day.'

'That's kind of her,' Meg said. 'But I'm so glad that you made the effort to come. It would not have been the same without you and I need all the support I can get.'

There was a shout that the bride was on her way and Meg gave a sigh as she said to Terry, 'See you later.'

Despite herself, Meg had to agree that Doris looked gorgeous. She had spent hours in the beauty parlour that morning and her face was carefully made up so it accentuated all her good points. Her eyes looked smokier and more mysterious than ever and her lashes were the longest Meg had ever seen. Her eyebrows were perfect crescents above her eyes. Her face was so smooth, and rouge and lipstick had been delicately applied. Her hair wasn't caught up totally as it usually was, but held in soft waves that framed her face. Doris looked the picture of loveliness, and in the beautiful dress that showed off her fabulous figure to perfection she looked much younger than thirty-five, the age she had admitted to.

For the first time Meg saw what had attracted her father. Charlie was looking at her walk down the aisle towards him with such obvious love that Meg felt quite hurt. Even in her wedding dress Doris was a sexual and sensual woman and Meg knew that Rose had been right: her father was enthralled by Doris in a way he had never been with her mother, for he needed and wanted her in a purely sexual way. As long as she continued to satisfy, his life with Maeve would recede into the background more and more and, because Doris would want it that way, eventually so would the children. That realisation depressed her totally.

And yet, despite her father's so obvious devotion, the wedding service lacked that vital spark, the feeling that this was love to last a lifetime. There was a sort of stiffness about the whole thing that was uncomfortable, so uncomfortable that when the priest asked if anyone knew of any reason why these two people should not enter into holy matrimony they should *speak now or forever hold their peace*. Meg found herself holding her breath. She wouldn't have been that surprised if someone had spoken out to stop this fiasco. She wanted to speak out herself, but what could she say apart from that she felt the marriage wasn't right? She just wanted the whole Nuptial Mass to be over as quickly as possible.

Later, in the back room of the Swan pub, the children behaved impeccably, even Terry, and Meg was gladdened that Doris seemed fine with them, even pleasant. Meg felt the worry that she had at leaving them ease a little. She thought Doris, maybe because of circumstances, was a rather cold woman, but as long as she was kind, the children could cope with all that and she did seem to be making an effort with them.

Still, Meg found the whole thing a strain and she saw her Aunt Rosie's and even her Aunt Susan's eyes on her often and full of sympathy. She wondered what they would feel when she told them about joining the Land Army, which she would do today if the opportunity arose. And so a little later, when Meg saw her aunts stepping outside for a breath of air, she joined them and without any lead in told them what she intended to do.

'Oh, my dear,' Aunt Rosie said, 'I don't blame you

in the slightest. You will be sorely needed when war is declared and farm labourers are called up. But what will the children do without you?'

'Well, Doris and Dad will look after them, and they are down to be evacuated anyway so won't have time to miss me.' Meg said.

'Don't you think that it's harsh to send children off like that?' Rosie said.

Meg nodded. 'It's a really difficult choice,' she said. 'But if war comes – and that seems inevitable now – and is fought in the air, as everyone says with bombs raining down on us, however painful a decision it is, it may be better to send the children away from the cities to places where it's safer for them.'

'I suppose so,' Rosie said doubtfully.

'I think it will still be an incredibly difficult for all the mothers and fathers,' Meg acknowledged. 'I will miss all the children like crazy if they go before I do.'

'Yes,' said Susan. 'Thinking you're doing the best for them is the only way to handle evacuation, I think.'

'I suppose that's the way to look at it,' Rosie said. 'I think this war will be like no other, with civilians in the front line as much as the soldiers.'

'Yes,' Meg said. 'And after it, the world will never be the same again.'

On Sunday afternoon Charlie and Doris left for Blackpool on a brief honeymoon and when Monday morning dawned bright and clear Meg, wanting a lasting memory to leave with the children, decided to take a big picnic to Cannon Hill Park. It was a fair hike, but they were in no hurry. They set off in high spirits, Billy carrying

Terry's ball, which he'd left for Billy when he'd moved out, and the two girls cavorting beside her like the children they still were.

Meg's high spirits fell a little when she saw the men digging big trenches around the park, though she'd read in the newspaper what they were going to do. But to see it made it more real somehow.

'What are they doing?' Billy asked.

'What's it look like?' Sally snapped. 'Stupid.'

Jenny said nothing, but her troubled eyes met Meg's over the heads of the squabbling children as Billy cried, 'I ain't stupid.'

'You must be if you don't know a man digging when you see one.'

Meg knew that Jenny, at eleven, probably had a pretty good idea what those trenches might be used for, and she read the trepidation in her eyes.

'Well, what are they digging for then?' Billy asked Sally.

'How should I know?'

'Thought you knew everything,' Billy sneered. 'Little Miss Know-All.'

'Meg, tell our Billy,' Sally cried, bringing Meg's attention back to her, and she chided, 'I don't know, I take you for a nice day out and you two start arguing before we've even got there.'

'It's him,' said Sally.

'No it ain't,' Billy maintained.

'I don't want to hear whose fault it is,' Meg snapped. 'Personally I think it's both of you, and for two pins I will turn round this minute and take you home, depriving Jenny of a day out too. Is that what you want?'

Dolefully both children shook their head. 'Sorry, Meg,' said Sally.

'Yeah, sorry,' Billy said.

'But why *are* the men digging those holes?'

'Well, now,' Meg said, choosing her words carefully. 'There's pipes for all sorts of things underground, so maybe they're doing repairs on them.'

'Maybe,' Sally conceded.

But Billy said, 'Don't think it's that. They just seem to be digging.'

Meg decided diversionary tactics had to be brought into play. 'Whatever the men are doing, it's nothing to do with us, so it's better if we let them get on with it. And the question I want to ask you, young Billy, is, have you brought that ball to the park to cuddle it all day, or are you going to kick it, since there's two lads watching that I'd say would love a game?'

The distraction worked and Billy tore across the grass with Sally pounding after him. As Jenny watched them disappear, she said, 'Good move, and now let's go across to the playground. When more boys come to join Billy, as they surely will, Sally will be surplus to requirements and she'll come to find us.'

Jenny was right and soon Sally had left the male-dominated game, her pique immediately forgotten in the delights of the playground swings, roundabout and slide. When they were played out, Meg spread the blanket slightly away from the playground on an incline overlooking the lake, sparkling and glittering in the sun, watching the ducks weaving their way between the rowing boats.

Some children were paddling on the edge and Meg

couldn't blame them, for her clothes were sticking to her and she'd not been running about like they had, so she wasn't a bit surprised when Billy and Sally started clamouring to paddle as well.

'Eat first,' Meg said firmly. 'Then we'll see.'

The children polished off the jam and the cheese sandwiches and the bottles of cold tea in double-quick time, and then, Sally's dress tucked into her knickers, the two were off. Eventually even Jenny went to cool her feet and Meg lay back on the blanket, feeling suddenly drowsy herself, and closed her eyes. When she awoke she was disorientated for a moment or two and she knew they would have to set off for home soon.

But not yet, she thought as she sat up and surveyed the scene before her. It all seemed so happy and peaceful, the buzzing of the bees in the nearby flowers and the laughter and sometimes squeals of the children splashing in the water the only sounds. It seemed inconceivable that this country would soon be at war. That German planes might fly in that cloudless sky and drop bombs to kill and maim and destroy like they had done in Guernica. A sudden shudder ran all through her body.

'What's up?' Jenny asked, approaching at that moment. 'Someone walk over your grave?'

'Something like that,' Meg said. 'Better start tidying away. We'll have to set off for home soon because it's a tidy step back.'

'Been a brilliant day, though, hasn't it?' Jenny said

'It has, Jenny,' Meg said. 'A truly brilliant day.'

Meg was even more glad of the great day she had enjoyed with her brother and sisters when she saw the official letter waiting for her on the mat when she got up the following morning. She slipped it into her pocket to read later when she went out to use the lavatory. She had looked forward to the letter coming, but holding it in her hand made it suddenly very real and her mind churned with differing emotions. When she read that she had been accepted for the Land Army she felt exhilaration flow through her, though it was threaded through with slight trepidation and sadness, for getting away from Doris meant that she would hardly see her siblings, and that was very hard because she had been a little mother to them all since Maeve died.

She expected her father and Doris back that evening and decided that she would tell the rest of the family her news after dinner. So after breakfast she set off for the Bull Ring to see if she could buy maybe a bit of rabbit to make a nice meal for them all. She also wanted to buy a case or something to put her clothes in; although uniform would be supplied, she didn't know if it would be given straight away.

She wished she could tell Kate Carmichael that she had done as she'd suggested, but now that the holidays had started she wouldn't know where to find her. She had let slip one day that she didn't live at home but in a small flat in Edgbaston. That in itself was fast enough for girls and young women of Kate Carmichael's class, who usually stayed at home until they married, but then Meg reminded herself that Miss Carmichael didn't seem to have a lot of time for marriage.

Then, as she passed Bow Street, the small road off Bristol Street where the school was, she was hailed, and there, coming down the road away from the school, was Kate Carmichael.

'Oh, I am pleased to see you,' Meg burst out. 'I have done what you said and joined the Land Army. I wanted to tell you before I left but I don't know where you live.'

'No point telling you now,' Kate Carmichael said. 'I am leaving my flat in the next few days. Where are you heading for?'

'The Bull Ring,' said Meg.

'And so am I,' Kate said. 'So we'll go together.' As they walked a little way down the road, Kate said, 'Are you looking for anything special?'

'Mmm, sort of,' Meg said. 'See, Dad and Doris are coming back from their honeymoon today.'

'Where did they go?'

'Blackpool.'

'Well,' said Kate, glancing up at the cloudless, cornflower-blue sky and the warm golden sun lighting all before it, 'they've probably had good weather and that's not something that can usually be said of Blackpool.'

Meg agreed. 'I want to see if I can get a bit of rabbit or something to make them a nice meal, sort of buttering Dad and the kids up because they don't yet know that I'll be leaving.'

'You said your dad and the children—'

'Doris already knows.'

'And your father doesn't?'

'No.' Meg saw the arch of Kate's eyebrows and she said, 'It wasn't that I was being mean. I was thinking of Dad. He won't like the thought of me leaving home, so I didn't want to broach the subject before his wedding and honeymoon. But however he behaves when I tell him, upset or angry, Doris will soon convince him it's for the best. She's very good at that, and when I also assure him it's what I want to do, he'll be fine. He'll have to be fine. I'm in now and can't change my mind because my father doesn't like the sound of it.'

'I still don't see why you told Doris.'

'I'm underage,' Meg said. 'Doris wasn't exactly Mrs Hallett when she signed, but they'll hardly check that. Everyone says this blessed war will be declared any day and then everyone really will have to play their part, whatever it is. That is, if we have any chance of winning.'

'Well, losing is not on the cards,' Kate said.

'No indeed,' Meg said. 'Now it's your turn. You know all my news, now tell me yours – like, why are you giving up your flat? Where are you off to?'

'Goodness knows,' said Kate. And then at Meg's bewildered look, she went on, 'Like I told you before, I am going with the children being evacuated, so I'm going down to the area they have been allocated to check that there are enough homes for the children and to arrange how the school there is going to cope with so many extra.'

'So you do know where they are going?'

Kate shook her head. 'Not yet. I suppose I'll be told eventually. The important thing is that everything is in place for them. Richard Flatterly is coming with me.'

'Richard Flatterly?' Meg repeated in surprise. The very mention of his name caused a knot of distaste to form in her stomach. 'What's he got to do with anything?'

Kate glanced at Meg in a slightly puzzled way; it was unusual for Meg to speak so sharply. 'D'you know him?'

'Oh, I'll say I do,' Meg said vehemently. 'He's our landlord.'

'Well, you'll know then that he is on the council?'

'Yeah.'

'He's the one dealing with the evacuation of children from Birmingham.'

'Didn't think he cared that much about children,' Meg said, remembering when he might have struck Ruth.

'What's the matter with you, Meg?' Kate said. 'What have you got against Richard Flatterly?'

Meg thought of telling Kate, knowing she was the only one who would almost certainly believe her. But what could she do about it? Nothing, that's what, and Kate would still have to work with the man. Anyway, her family had nothing to do with him now because the old rent man was back. So she looked at Kate steadily and said, 'Nothing, really. I just find him a bit smarmy, that's all.'

'I don't see how you can say that,' Kate said. 'I have always found him charming and courteous. And he is very nice-looking, too.'

'Is he?'

Kate laughed. 'Maybe you're a mite young to notice things like that,' she said. 'But take it from me, he is. We have really got on well together. In fact, he is taking me to the cinema tonight.'

That gave Meg a jolt. She didn't realise Kate meant they were getting on *that* well. She could understand that Kate might find Richard Flatterly attractive, because he could turn the charm on when he wanted to, but surely Kate could see through that?

Obviously not, because she went on, 'We're off to

the Odeon in New Street to see *Wuthering Heights* and I'm really looking forward to it.'

Meg smiled and managed to say that she hoped Kate had a good time, but inside she felt a little sick because she had never seen a pink blush touch Kate's cheeks before, nor had she seen that bright light shining in her eyes, and it worried her. Surely to God, Meg thought, she had enough sense to steer away from the likes of Richard Flatterly, but then why should she when she thought him such a charming and courteous man?

They were due to part company at the Bull Ring and Meg suddenly said, 'How will we keep in touch? We must do that, but you don't even know where you are going and I haven't got a full address.'

'Oh, yes, we must write to one another,' Kate said. 'I would love to know how you are getting on. Tell you what,' she said suddenly. 'When you know your address, send it to me via Richard's offices in the Council House.'

Meg hated the thought of Richard Flatterly having anything to do with her life at all. She didn't answer for a moment but then finally she said, 'Do you think it's all right to do that?'

'I can't see any other way of doing it,' Kate said. 'Then, as soon as I know where you are, we can write direct. And remember to tell me when you finish training and are assigned a farm. I suppose that's how it works.'

'S'pose so,' Meg said. 'I haven't a clue really. I should imagine they will tell us all this sort of stuff.'

'Yes,' Kate said. 'It will be all new to you and so there will be lots to learn, but you learn quickly. I was your teacher, remember, and I know you're not as green as you're cabbage-looking.'

Meg laughed. 'Thanks a lot for that back-handed compliment.'

'My pleasure,' Kate said. 'Now we'd both best get on.'

And then, for the first time, Kate put her arms around Meg. 'You'll probably feel a little lost in the beginning,' she said. 'I was the same when I first went to teacher training college. But I ended up having a marvellous time, as well as learning how to teach. That is how it will be for you. This is your future, so grab it with two hands.'

Meg faced her family over the table that evening. She had given them all a lovely dinner. It was unusual to have a roast dinner in the middle of the week, but the butcher had prepared the rabbit and Meg had roasted it with potatoes all around, cabbage and carrots on the stove, and after they had done justice to that, she served apple pie and custard.

Charlie said back with a sigh of satisfaction. Rested and relaxed after his holiday and then to be served such delicious food was his idea of heaven. 'By God, Meg, you will make a fine wife for someone.'

'Not just yet a while.'

'No, plenty of time for all that,' Charlie said. 'And now, as you have all eaten, we have something for all of you.' He produced sticks of rock for the children, with 'Blackpool' written all the way through them, he said, and a box of fudge for Meg, and then of course the children wanted to hear about the holiday.

None of them had ever been to the sea and Charlie, who had not seen it before either, did his best to describe it for them. For a short while for the children it was like having their old father back as he painted pictures for them so they could see the vast sea sparkling in the sunset, the white-fringed waves lapping the shore that they both paddled in and the miles of golden sand. He told them of the gigantic fair and rides of all shape and sizes, the merry-go-round where they sat astride horses as if they were children; the ghost train where Doris screamed her head off and the waltzers where the men spun the cars to set the women squealing.

'Oh, Dad,' Billy said wistfully. 'It sounds great.'

'It sounds scary,' Sally countered. 'Was you scared, Dad?'

Charlie shook his head, 'No, I loved it all but Doris wasn't keen on the Big Wheel was you, Doris?'

'No I wasn't' Doris conceded. 'We were so high up. God, the ground looked miles away. And on the roller coaster I felt as if I had left my stomach behind.'

The children giggled at the thought and Charlie went on to describe the front and the shops selling all manner of things, and the arcades with machines to feed money into. 'What for?'

'To see if you can win some more.'

'And did you?'

'No,' Charlie said. 'It was the quickest way of losing money that I've ever known.'

He told them of the candyfloss that they'd eaten. 'Just like clouded cotton wool on a stick,' he said. 'Put a great wad in your mouth and it melts away to nothing in seconds.'

'Was it nice, though?'

'Nice enough,' Charlie said. 'What would you say, Doris?'

'It was all right,' Doris said. 'But I preferred the toffee apples we had.'

'Toffee apples,' Billy said. 'What's them then?'

'Just what they're called,' Charlie said. 'An apple on a stick covered with toffee.'

'Oh, I'd like to try one of those.'

'Maybe you will one day,' Charlie said. 'But Blackpool has something no other resort has, and that's a great big high tower. You can see for miles at the top of it, though it's really windy up there.'

'Supposed to look the same as the one in Paris in France,' Doris said.

'And does it?' Jenny asked.

'How would we know?' Charlie said. 'I've never been to France. Never likely to go, either, unless it's with the British Army, and then there will hardly be time to look at towers.'

It was the first time their father had said anything in front of the younger children about being called up, and it was Sally who said, 'Why would you go to France with the army?'

'I just might, that's all.'

'But why should you?' Jenny persisted. 'You're not in the army.'

'If we go to war I'll probably be called up.'

'Oh,' Jenny, Sally and Billy said all together. They all fell silent, so Charlie turned his attention to Meg.

'You're very quiet. What've you been up to while we've been away?'

This gave Meg the lead-in she wanted. 'Well, we all went to Cannon Hill Park yesterday,' she said.

'Oh, yes, that's a hike, mind.'

'We took a picnic and my football and everything,' Billy said. 'And they was digging big trenches round the park. Don't know what for, though, and Sally didn't either.'

Charlie looked at Meg and she shook her head slightly at him, but he thought it might be better to prepare the children and he said, 'It's probably because the trenches would be somewhere to hide if we were at war and the bombs come.'

'Why would they bomb the park?' Sally asked.

'They can bomb anywhere once they start,' Charlie said. 'But you are not to worry about that because you are not going to see any bombs. You'll be going to the countryside where you'll be safe. That's why I agreed to let you be evacuated.'

'And we really are going to have a war?' Billy asked.

Charlie nodded. 'It's only a matter of time now.'

'On the wireless this morning the announcer said this will be the first war when we will all be on the front line and everyone has to do their bit,' Meg said.

Charlie's eyes narrowed. He'd had the feeling since he arrived home that Meg had something on her mind and now he saw the way the conversation was leading and he snapped out, 'Don't you suggest working in one of those munitions factories, because I'll never agree to it.'

'Good job I don't want to work in one, then,' Meg said lightly.

'So what is this?'

'I'll tell you where I do want to work,' Meg said. 'In fact, where I'm going to work because I've had the medical and interview and everything.'

206

'Doing what?'

'I've joined the Land Army, like Joy.'

'Have you, by God?'

'Yes, I have, and next week I start training in an agricultural college just outside Wolverhampton.'

Billy began to cry as he grasped what Meg had said, and her father rapped out, 'You will be going to no college in some outlandish place. You'll be staying at home where you belong.'

Meg remembered May telling her of the fight that her sister had had to do the same thing in the last war, and so she faced her father and said, 'No, I'm not. It's an army, just like any other, and I have signed up for it. How else are the farms going to manage if we don't do this and the farmers and farm hands are called up?'

'But, Meg,' Jenny protested. 'You can't leave us here and go and live somewhere else.'

'But if you are evacuated you won't be here anyway,' Meg pointed out.

'Well, I think it's a wonderful thing Meg is doing,' Doris chipped in suddenly.

'Do you?' Charlie said. 'I thought you'd want Meg to stay on here and help you with the children. It isn't as if you have much experience.'

'Oh, well,' Doris said, 'the children are being evacuated in the event of war, aren't they? And I'd never have it said that I stood in Meg's way.'

'Did you know anything about this before?' Charlie asked.

Meg held her breath because Doris had to pretend she knew nothing about it; if her father should get a sniff that Doris had signed the form before she was officially

Mrs Hallett, then maybe he could overturn the whole thing. Fortunately Doris was no fool and she clearly wanted Meg out of her hair so she said, 'No, Charlie, I was as surprised as you, but I think it is a very brave thing that Meg is doing and we should be pleased for her because it's valuable work.'

'Well, I know that,' Charlie conceded.

'Dad,' Meg said, 'I think we'll all have to pull together in this war if we are going to win, and this is how I want to help.'

'Well, I can't say that I am totally happy about it,' Charlie said. 'But I won't stand in your way either.'

There was a howl of distress from the children and Meg did feel a little guilty yet she knew because they were being evacuated they wouldn't miss her so much because everything would be different for them too. Anyway, the die was cast now and she wanted the few days to speed past to Wednesday morning of the following week when she would meet Joy on the steps of the Council House where transport to the agricultural college would be arranged.

As the news filtered through the neighbourhood, there was a mixed reaction from the neighbours. Some thought Meg totally irresponsible to walk out on her brother and sisters in that way.

Only Terry fully understood. 'Don't let it get you down, Meg,' he advised. 'Why do other people's opinions matter anyway? You and I are the only ones who know the truth. You go for it, and do what you want. That isn't selfish, it's just normal.'

Meg was grateful for her brother's support but the last morning, when she said goodbye to all she held dear, she felt her heart was breaking in two. Even her father, who'd arranged to go in later to work so he was there to see her off, cried as he hugged her goodbye.

'I'll be back as soon as I get a spot of leave,' Meg promised brokenly, but she knew it was poor comfort to the children and she could do nothing more to ease the parting. Tears streamed from her eyes even as she made her way down the road, and a sad little group stood out on the pavement, and waved until Meg had turned down Bristol Passage and out of sight.

PART TWO

FIFTEEN

Joy was waiting for Meg on the steps of the Council House, along with a cluster of other girls of all shapes and sizes. Though most were young, there were a few older ones amongst them. Meg's tears were spent but her eyes remained red-rimmed and Joy examined her critically.

'Must have been upsetting, saying goodbye to them all.'

Meg nodded. 'I had no idea that anything could be that hard. I promised that I would write and I would be home as soon as I get leave, and to be honest as far as the children are concerned I might as well be in Outer Space .'

'Yes,' Joy agreed. 'But you can write as soon as we're settled. As for leave, I dare say we won't get anything significant until we've finished our training – whenever that is.'

'No, I don't suppose so,' Meg agreed.

Joy whispered, 'Plenty of girls here. Helps a bit to know that we're not the only idiots to join up for this little lot.'

'I never thought we were,' Meg said. 'Did you?'

'I wondered what I was doing a time or two,' Joy confessed. 'I mean, I don't know one end of a cow from the other, do you?'

Meg laughed. 'Yes, just about,' she said. 'But if I wasn't sure, I think I would work it out in short order.'

Meg's laughter had drawn some of other girls' attention on them and the nearest one said to Meg admiringly, 'You seem to be taking it all in your stride. I'm really nervous.'

'I am too really,' Meg said.

When an army truck with a canvas roof and sides stopped at the bottom of the marble steps another girl said, 'Don't you think our chaps were just as nervous as us? Mine was when he was called up when they took the younger ones in for training, but he still went.'

'Yeah,' Meg said. 'So let's stop moaning about our nerves. I mean, it don't help and it seems like we're all in the same boat anyway.'

'That's the spirit,' said a voice behind Meg, and she turned to find herself looking at the driver of the truck, who was a woman. She was more than twice their age, and though she wore no makeup, her face seemed very smooth. Her brown hair was daringly cut very short and she was wearing trousers. She smiled at them all and said in a rather deep voice for a woman, 'All right, girls, my name is Rita Partridge and I am here to look after you. We will just have a bit of a roll call and see that I've got everyone I should have and then we will be on our way.'

Everyone was there. Altogether there were twenty, and eighteen of those were directed to climb into the truck. Some did this with difficulty because of the unsuitable clothes they wore. But once the eighteen had clambered aboard, it was obvious there was no room for any more – as it was the girls were packed together tightly.

'God, it's sweltering in here,' one of the girls protested, and others agreed as the day was really warm, and so Rita rolled up the canvas sides to let some air through.

Meanwhile Meg and Joy were standing about like spare dinners. 'What about us?' Joy said.

'You'll have to squeeze in beside me, that's all,' Rita said. 'Be a bit of a squash but there you are. I did query the size of the truck but they said that's all there was.'

'It'll have to do then,' Meg said, and they both squeezed into the cab beside Rita.

She turned on the engine, swung the truck round effortlessly and it rumbled over the cobbled city streets. They were on their way and Meg felt excitement catch hold of her. Whatever lay ahead would be nothing like the life she had led this far, and that in itself was exciting.

The journey was a long one and at first there was a lot of chatter amongst so many, but gradually it quietened to a steady murmur as the city was left far behind. Fields were either side of them now, and here and there an isolated cottage. Despite the early hour, sometimes they'd see signs of activity, especially amongst the children. Some would watch wide-eyed as the truck rumbled past with their fingers in their mouths, while others might wave or run alongside the truck, which made them all smile.

Most of the fields were cultivated and Rita would name all the different crops to Meg and Joy. Some vegetables, such as cabbages, were obvious, and Rita pointed out the peas growing upwards supported by a frame.

Rita reminisced, 'When I was a child, that was my job on Sunday morning, to pod enough peas for dinner, but it was never a bother for me because I used to love to do it. Anyway it was worth it, because those fresh garden peas tasted delicious.'

'I love them,' Meg agreed.

'What about these fields we're passing now?' Joy asked. The land was furrowed and whatever was growing there was underneath the soil, for all that could be seen was a lot of greenery. 'Potatoes,' Rita said. 'And beyond that is sugar beet.' She waved to the people already working in the fields. 'And lots of root vegetables: carrots, turnips, swedes and onions – that sort of thing . . . Now girls,' she shouted into the back, 'we're passing by Oldbury. It's a nice little market town but the streets are narrow, not built for trucks like these.'

Rita was right. All Meg saw was a cluster of pretty houses and shops and a church spire peeping over the roofs. 'Now, apart from the odd hamlet, there isn't much until we come to West Bromwich,' Rita said when they were through the town and on the open road again. 'We'll pick up the Birmingham Canal there and follow it all the way to Coseley.'

'Golly, I haven't seen a canal in years,' Meg said.

Joy stared at her. 'You are joking?'

'No.'

'But Birmingham is threaded with canals.'

'Not our way it isn't,' Meg said. 'Dad took me and

our Terry to Gas Street Basin once and we saw all those painted barges and that, but I don't think the others have ever been. Mind you, I liked the barges, but I thought the water was really dirty and smelly.'

'That's because a lot of the factories were built to back onto the canals,' Rita said. 'And all their effluent and waste were just tipped into them.'

'Dad said we have more than Venice,' Joy said. 'Not that he's been or anything, but he read it somewhere.'

'Venice is in Italy, isn't it?'

'Yeah,' Joy said. 'And they sort of live on the water. They have river taxis and river buses and all sorts.'

However, before they saw the canal they passed a field that appeared to be empty until Meg spotted the horses sheltering under a tree.

'What enormous horses,' Joy exclaimed. 'And look at their shaggy feet.'

'Our Co-op milkman has one like that,' Meg said. 'He told me horses like that are called Shires.'

'That's right,' Rita said. 'Built for stamina and strength, not speed, and more important than ever now that tractors are hard to come by. Not that all farmers hold with tractors, anyway. A fair few want to stick with their horses.'

One of the horses gave a snicker and then a snort, nodding his head as if in disgust. 'Probably making a protest about horses being replaced by machines,' Meg said with a laugh.

'I think it's just that they don't like the smell of petrol,' Rita said. 'Cows don't seem to mind.'

Again Rita was right because the black and white cows in the neighbouring field had their heads over the fence, jostling for position, their large brown eyes fastened on the truck chugging past as they stood patiently chewing.

'Why are they eating like that all the time?' one girl asked, and her voice was so high-pitched that they heard it in the front of the cab, even over the noise of the engine.

'It's called chewing the cud,' Rita called out, as she negotiated the country roads with ease. 'A cow is able to regurgitate its food because it has four stomachs.'

'Ugh. That's disgusting.'

Rita laughed. ''Course it isn't, it's nature. That's how they make the milk, and you won't think "Ugh" when you have it on your porridge tomorrow, will you now?'

'Don't suppose so.'

'One thing we have plenty of is milk,' Rita said. 'And you might be glad of it before you are much older.'

They passed signs to West Bromwich. Rita turned the truck instead towards Coseley and there, running alongside the road, was the canal. Although Meg knew it was probably torpid and oil-slicked, it looked quite attractive with the sun shining on it, making the water gleam.

The truck rattled along merrily, and now and again, through a gap in the hedgerow Meg could see the towpath running alongside the canal. Sometimes people were on it and occasionally she got a glimpse of a vibrantly bedecked barge, but then at Coseley they left the canal.

'Is it much further?' she asked as they drove through a little place called Darlaston.

'Not much further,' Rita said. 'Are you uncomfortable?'

'I'm hot more than anything,' Meg said. 'And my bottom's gone to sleep and I'm not at all sure about the rest of me.'

Rita let out a gale of laughter. 'In a few minutes we will be driving through a place called Willenhall and Wolverhampton just lies to the west of it, but we have to go another ten miles or so to Penkridge.'

'Dad says Wolverhampton is a sizeable place.'

'Oh, it is,' Rita said. 'It is your nearest big town – well worth a visit if ever you have the time.'

'I presume we get some time off?' Joy said.

'Well,' said Rita, 'I think officially you work fifty hours, now reduced to forty-eight in the winter with one day off a week, but all I'm saying is there are times when the farms are extra busy, such as at harvest or spring planting, and the hours can't be so rigid; but they'll likely give you more time later when it is quieter.'

'Oh, I think we understand that well enough,' Joy said. 'I don't think in any kind of farming the hours can be as exact as that.'

'You'll soon get the hang of it,' Rita said. 'And look now, Huntington is just ahead and Penkridge Lodge where you're staying is just this side of the village. Only a step away.'

Meg couldn't quite believe it when Rita turned the truck through wrought-iron gates and down a gravel path. Her startled eyes met the equally amazed ones of Joy as Rita drew up in front of an enormous mansion set in its own grounds. It was three storeys high and built of honey-coloured bricks. A cream balustrade ran all along the first and second floors, and marble steps led up to the impressive studded oak door.

'Wow,' said Meg as the truck stopped with a squeal of brakes and a spray of gravel.

'Right, ladies, we're here,' Rita shouted to those in the back, and she leaped down from the cab like a woman half her age. Meg and Joy got down much more gingerly to see the others, equally stiff-limbed, staring around as if they too could hardly believe they would be staying in such a place during training.

'Blimey, look at all them chimneys,' one girl said.

'My mom was in service here before she got married,' another said. 'She told me what this place was like. And you've got to remember that every chimney leads to a grate for a little servant girl to clean out every morning, and then light and keep alight all day and into the evening, which involved carrying heavy buckets of coal up and down stairs all day. My mom swears that she has one arm longer than the other because of it.'

'I bet she had to clean the windows too,' Meg said. 'And there's hundreds of them, and some of them have got circles on them.'

'And if Mary's mother didn't clean them,' Rita put in, 'someone else must have done, and fairly recently too, because see how they are sparkling in the sun?'

'Yeah, it's lovely,' Meg said. 'It will be great to stay here.'

'Oh, I'll say,' Joy said. 'I can stand a bit of this. When I joined up they didn't tell us we would be living in the lap of luxury.'

'You probably won't be,' Rita warned. 'This is really

only while you're being trained. You might find many of the farms a bit primitive.'

'And we stay on the farms?'

'Ideally,' Rita said. 'But that really depends on the farm. If the farmer has a big family, or just a small farmhouse and there isn't room for you to stay, then you could come back here. Now pick up your bags and baggage and we'll go and meet Mrs Warburton, who will cook for you here.'

'Through the front door?' Meg asked in surprise as Rita mounted the marble steps.

'But of course through the front door,' Rita said, and swung it open. They all followed her into a large hall with a black and white checked floor and the magnificent sweep of a highly polished oak staircase. 'Dump your things in the hall till we have your bedrooms assigned,' Rita said. 'You must have had your breakfast early and I bet you're hungry.'

There was a murmur of agreement, though Meg hadn't realised how hungry she was until Rita mentioned it. They followed behind her a little nervously as she crossed the hall, and Meg almost expected an officious and pompous butler to pop up and direct them to the servants' entrance at the back.

'I know just what you mean,' Joy said when Meg whispered this to her. 'You can almost see the ghosts of women in long dresses with satin slippers and men wearing suits that make them look like penguins.'

Meg smiled as Joy went on, 'Seriously, though, who does this place belong to? Houses like this don't usually stand empty.'

But this one certainly was. Rita, ahead of the line of

them, had turned down a corridor and she was opening a green door. 'That's the green baize door Mom told me about,' Joy said.

'Did she know this house then?'

'No, not this house,' Joy said. 'It's in all big houses, and it separates the house where the posh people live from the kitchen and all the servants that look after them. It's supposed to close silently so it doesn't disturb them.'

And it did, Meg noticed, unless you could count the very slight 'Ssh' sound. It led into the biggest kitchen Meg had ever seen in her life. There was a huge old-fashioned cooker, gleaming copper pans hung from hooks, and floor-to-ceiling cupboards and shelves, and in the middle of the shiny tiled floor was a very large scrubbed wooden table.

Presiding over this was the woman Rita introduced as Mrs Warburton.

'Never trust a thin cook,' Joy whispered out of the side of her mouth, and Meg smiled because Mrs Warburton was a roly-poly kind of a woman, her brown frizzy hair was half covered with a hat and an apron was tied around her more-than-ample waist.

'You're very welcome,' the cook said with a smile. 'And though there is a dining room, it would hardly accommodate everyone, and anyway, I thought you might feel more at home in the servants' hall.'

'I don't care where we eat,' called a woman from the back. 'Just as long as we do it soon.'

They were all soon sitting around a table even bigger than the one in the kitchen. Three large steaming casserole dishes were put before them along with two bowls of buttered potatoes. The food was delicious and Meg tucked in with relish, wondering at her appetite because she had done nothing but sit in a truck half the morning.

The stew was followed by jam roly-poly and about a ton of custard, and it was as everyone was finishing and the girls leaning back in their chairs, replete, that Mrs Warburton said to Rita, 'Silas came in this morning.'

'Oh, yes. What did he want?'

'To see if you were here with the girls. I said that you wouldn't be here till lunchtime.'

'Why did he want to know?'

'He says their help might be needed,' Mrs Warburton said. 'There's a big storm coming.'

Meg looked at Joy and then at Rita, thinking of the heat of the day and for days past. It hadn't rained for weeks. Rita obviously thought the same. 'Surely not? It's lovely out.'

Mrs Warburton shrugged. 'S'what he said.'

'Who's this Silas?' someone asked.

'He's an old fellow who helps in the gardens and he can predict the weather.'

'Is he good?'

'Better than the bloke on the wireless,' Mrs Warburton said.

'Has he ever been wrong?' Meg asked, and Rita shook her head.

'So,' Meg said. 'There is going to be a storm.' She didn't see what a problem that could be.

'This could be catastrophic for the farmers at the moment,' Rita said. 'A storm now would ruin the hay. Many were late cutting it anyway after the young men were all called up. It has dried lovely in the hot summer we've had, but rain now we can do without.'

'Silas has been round the farms already and they're taking it seriously,' Mrs Warburton said.

'And so must we,' Rita said. 'How long did Silas say before this storm breaks?'

'Eight hours or thereabouts, but that was mid-morning.'

'Dear God!'

'Some of the women from the village have already set off to lend a hand.'

'Girls,' Rita said, 'I'm afraid I must throw you in at the deep end. Come with me quickly and I will give out your summer uniforms for now because there is no time to waste.'

They trooped behind Rita into what Meg imagined was the dining room, and on the beautiful shiny wooden dining table were piles of clothes. From each pile Rita selected a short-sleeved beige Aertex shirt, a green jumper, a pair of dungarees, one pair of Land Army issue socks, one pair of boots and a hat.

Meg changed in the room she was going to share with Joy and wrinkled her nose when she caught sight of herself in the mirror on the outside of the wardrobe. 'Not the most elegant of uniforms,' Meg said. 'But I suppose it's practical enough.'

'Well, I joined up to make a difference,' Joy said. 'So I'm not that bothered what the clothes look like as long as they are suitable for the job.'

'Oh, absolutely,' Meg said. 'And if this Silas is right in his predictions and we can get the hay undercover before the storm breaks, then it will make a difference.'

'I'll say – and I don't think we have long, and being new to it we're bound to be a bit slow and clumsy,' Joy said.

'We'll soon see,' Meg said. 'I can hear Rita calling us.'

However, Meg was not the only one who found it difficult to hurry in the heavy, cumbersome and very stiff boots; they all were complaining about them. One girl said, 'If you wee in the boots and leave them overnight, they soften up lovely.'

There was a combined cry of disgust. 'Ugh!'

'I'm not doing that,' Meg said, and there was a mumble of agreement from many of the others, but the girl was unabashed.

'Please yourselves,' she said. 'I thought that too at first, but my brother was one of the young ones called up and he got blisters on top of blisters at first, until an old hand gave him that tip and he had no trouble after.'

'Don't tell me you're going to try it?'

'Why not?' the girl said. 'I've got nothing to lose.'

'Get a move on girls, do,' Rita said. 'You can discuss your boots later.'

Outside, although it was still warm, it was muggy heat. Clouds had begun to drift across the blue sky, and in every hay field the truck passed the land girls saw people – old men and women and even children – working feverishly.

Eventually, Rita stopped at the top of one lane and said, 'Oakhurst Farm. This is where you will be, Meg and Joy. They have lost their son and two farm hands to the Forces, but we can only give them two Land

Army girls, so I'd say you'll have your work cut out. Name of Will and Enid Heppleswaite. Just do your best.'

'Are you dropping us here?'

'Yes,' Rita said. 'I can't risk the truck down the lane. I might get down and not get back up. Here's Will come to meet you now.'

Will Heppleswaite was in his early fifties, though he looked older, for his hair was white, bleached by the sun, and his face was wrinkled and weather-beaten. But his brown eyes were kind and Meg felt herself relax.

'Here you are, Mr Heppleswaite,' Rita said, as she climbed back into the truck. 'I'll leave them in your capable hands.'

Will smiled, crinkling all the skin around his eyes as he waved to Rita, but really he was dismayed at the sight of Joy and Meg. They wouldn't have known this initially, for his smile was warm and welcoming and his handshake firm.

'Now, as Rita told you, my name is Will, so we'll get the names out of the way first.'

'Meg Hallett,' Meg told him, shaking the proffered hand.

'Joy Tranter,' Joy said, doing the same.

'Well, I am very pleased to have the two of you here,' Will said. 'And never doubt that for a moment. 'It's just . . . well, you're such slight things. Do you think you are up to this sort of work?'

'We're stronger than we look, honestly,' Meg said. 'But we will do our best and work as hard as we know how, and surely any help is better than none.'

'Indeed it is,' Will said. 'And I have no time for arguing

226

the toss either. Come on, Enid and I will work alongside you and show you what to do. Between us all, and with God's help, we may save most of the hay.'

The mown hay had been made up into little hay cocks to dry thoroughly and Will told them these had to made into stacks, which he secured with ropes made out of straw. These tied stacks could then be transferred to the trailer that the farm horse they called Dobbin would pull down to the barn. They had already built one stack and it was in the barn, and they were halfway through another. Meg was assigned to work alongside Enid and found there was an art to getting hay to stay on a pitchfork so that she could throw it up to the top of the stack, as Enid did with such ease.

However, she was in the same mould as Will and unfailingly kind and patient. They had similar eyes, but Enid's face was plumper. In fact, she was plumper all over, and her brown hair, which was scraped back into a bun, was liberally streaked with grey.

As they worked Enid spoke of the difficulties of running a farm without help, and what a blow it had been when their son, Stephen, had been called up.

'He wasn't on his own, of course, because the other two young farm hands we took on were called up too. They joined the regular army. I mean, Stephen came and told us that he felt that's what he had to do. Well, now he's home again for a bit.

'Is he? Meg said, wondering why he wasn't out in the fields helping them if he was home. She didn't say this, but Enid must have guessed she was curious.

She said, 'And we are lucky to have him home in one piece because he was run over at the camp a month ago now. He hadn't signed to go into the regular army that long before this accident. The brakes failed on the truck one of the chaps was driving and Stephen wasn't able to get out of the way quick enough.'

'Goodness,' Meg said. 'Was he badly injured?'

'Nothing that won't fix, praise God,' said Will. 'He had some internal injuries but the camp doctor sorted those out. But he needs time for them to heal properly, we were told. His body is a mass of cuts and bruises and he also had a badly broken ankle and arm, and dislocated shoulder, and feels bad that he isn't able to help more. Enid and I think he was lucky that the injuries were not worse and I just tell him to be patient. Now he can be seen as an outpatient he has been allowed to come home for a bit.'

'And "patient" is not a word Stephen thinks much of,' Enid put in.and Will replied with a wheezy laugh, 'No indeed he does not.'

'We'll try and make up for the loss of the help you had,' Joy promised, and the two girls threw themselves into the work with even more vigour as the clouds gathered above them. The drop in temperature was welcome – Meg and Joy had already been forced to remove their jumpers – but the breeze that sprang up wasn't, because it scattered the little hay cocks and the hay had to be gathered up again.

When they could no longer throw up the hay from the ground, Will produced a small ladder to lean against the stack, and Meg and Joy laboured on. Meg was very glad that she had got the hang of keeping hay on the pitchfork at last. But as fast as they worked, they knew time was against them, especially as Will had to leave them to do the milking just as the third stack was completed.

The dark, dense, purple-fringed clouds that now filled the sky were so low that they turned the afternoon prematurely dark. It was difficult to see but they couldn't afford to stop, so Enid went down to the house and came back with two hurricane lamps, which helped a bit.

Sometime later, when Will returned, he was in time to tie down the fourth stack, which was then hitched to Dobbin. Enid led him down the lanes as fast as the horse was prepared to go.

The two girls and Will bent to their task again, but they had only made a smallish mound when the first large drops of water fell. 'Oh, bugger!' Will cried, and then the sky was rent open by forked lightning, cracking across it from one side to the other. Will leaped to his feet as the lightning was followed almost immediately by the extremely loud, rolling crash of thunder.

'Must give Enid a hand,' Will said. 'Damned horse can't abide thunder. If Enid can't handle him and he rears up, he might do himself a mischief, hitched to the trailer as he is. And we also risk losing the whole stack of hay.'

'Go,' Meg said to Will as the rain began to fall like solid sheets of water. They collected up the ladder, the pitchforks, the kerosene lamps and their jumpers, and made for the farmhouse. The lane was already filling with mud, and slippery, but it was hard to be careful, for with the dense, dark clouds and relentless, torrential rain, they could scarcely see where they were going. And then the lightning crackled and flamed, throwing everything into sharp relief for a second, and then the evening plunged back into darkness while the rumble and boom of thunder filled the air.

By the time they got to the farmhouse, a whitewashed two-storeyed building with shuttered windows painted red like the front door, they were soaked through, but went straight to the stable where they found that Enid and Will still had their hands full with Dobbin. Will had managed to unhitch the trailer, but the horse was so unnerved by the storm that he couldn't get near him to get the hitching harness or bridle or anything else off him. Meg could understand the horse's agitation, because she thought herself unafraid of storms, but she had never seen such a ferocious one.

'Can we help?' she asked.

'No,' Will said. 'Thanks anyway, but Dobbin is too spooked to have anyone here he doesn't know. Every time he hears the thunder and lightning he rears up, and I'm afraid of him hurting himself. But it would help if you could put the hens away before the fox pays us a visit. That would really put the tin hat on it today. Oh, and the sow and piglets better be shut up safe in the sty. Old Reynard might fancy a bit of pork for a change.'

'He might indeed,' Enid said. 'Cheek of the devil, foxes have. That would be such a help. Do you mind doing that?'

Meg minded very much going back out into the teeth of that storm and she could tell by Joy's rueful expression that she did too. But they assured Enid they didn't mind in the slightest, for as Joy said when they were again in the yard facing the elements, 'It isn't as if we can get any wetter.'

Joy was right, as the water was running off them, but the hens had also been disturbed by the storm and had scattered all over the farm. The two girls hadn't any idea of how many there should be and so they had to delve under every hedge and bush and search every ditch while the relentless rain hammered at them as if they were being beaten with stair rods.

'I'm sure if we get the rooster in, the hens will follow,' Meg said. But the rooster proved the most awkward of all. In the end they each took a handful of chicken feed they'd found in the barn and, using that, they coaxed and cajoled the cantankerous old rooster in and the hens followed behind. Eventually all the fowl were locked up safe for the night.

The indolent sow was another matter; she was in no hurry to move anywhere. She was feeding her numerous offspring under the overhang of the pig pen, so was in some shelter, and she completely disregarded Meg and Joy's efforts to move her into the sty, where there would be more shelter from the elements and where her brood would be safer from the attentions of the fox.

'What shall we do?' Meg said. 'We can hardly haul her inside.'

'I don't think so,' said Joy. 'Even with the two of us, we'd hardly manage it, and anyway she might not go without a fight. I think she could give you a hefty thump if she put her mind to it. Oh,' she added suddenly, 'I have an idea.'

'What?'

'You'll see in a minute,' Joy said. 'Keep her attention.'

'What?' Meg said, staring at Joy incredulously. 'What

are you on about, "keep her attention"? She's a flipping pig.'

'I know what she is and I don't want her to see me going to the back of her,' Joy said, moving around as she spoke. And then once at the back of the pig pen, she lifted her leg over the wall and – quick as a flash – she plucked the last two piglets from the sow's teats and they began to shriek lustily as she tossed them into the straw in the sty.

The sow moved surprisingly quickly for one so large, and Joy hastily pulled her foot back as, with a grunting roar, the sow got to her feet, spilling the piglets from her. She gave Joy a malevolent glare as she lumbered into the sty and the other piglets followed her.

Meg leaned over and shot the bolt, saying with a grin as she did so, 'Made an enemy there, I'd say.'

'Yeah,' said Joy. 'And do you think I'm worried? Now let's get inside, out of this bloody rain, before both of us catch our deaths.'

Enid threw her hands in the air at the state of them as they stood at the doorway shivering in their saturated dungarees, Aertex shirts and their sodden, muddy boots but all Meg's attention was taken by the young man beside the range, his plastered foot on a stool and his plastered arm in a sling. She thought Stephen Heppleswaite the most beautiful man she had ever seen.

It seemed odd to call a man beautiful but she couldn't think of another word to describe a man with hair so blond it was almost white, a handsome yet kind face and lively dark blue eyes. But those eyes, indeed, his whole face, looked troubled as he watched his mother fussing over the girls. Girls he had never seen before, but his mother said they'd been assigned Land Girls and so he presumed that's who they were for they had a uniform of sorts and they were so wet water was pooling at their feet

'Look how wet you both are,' he said as Enid ran for towels. 'Are you from the Land Army?

Still shivering the girls just nodded. 'Baptism by fire all right,' Stephen went on, 'while I just sit here like Lord Muck.' Even his voice had a musical quality to it, thought Meg.

'Well, that's not your fault is it,' Enid said, wrapping towels around the Meg and Joy. 'And I'll soon deal with the girls, never fear.' She took them to her bedroom and had them stripped and rubbed dry and their hair towelled, and then she pulled her spare nighties over them and wrapped blankets around them before they returned to the kitchen where Enid arranged their uniforms on a clothes horse and opened the door of the range to let the fire out to dry their clothes and their boots which were steaming on the floor.

'Is anyone going to try and fetch you tonight?' she asked.

'No one said anything about fetching us,' Joy said. 'I mean, we weren't given a time or anything, but I expect they will come for us eventually.'

'In the meantime you have this,' Enid said, and she handed the girls each a bowl of broth she had put on the range to heat, and gave another to Stephen. The girls took them gratefully, and the hunk of bread was very welcome too.

'Oh, that was so good,' Meg said sincerely as she drained the bowl.

'One thing about working on a farm,' Stephen said, 'you build up a rare appetite.'

'You might be right there,' Joy said. 'Though we've not done much farm work yet I was famished. Weren't you, Meg?'

'You bet I was,' Meg said. 'That was delicious broth, Enid. Thank you so much. I was so hungry I was beginning to feel I'd have to gnaw on the chair leg.'

Enid laughed. 'That's one thing you'll never have to do on this farm,' she said. 'I can always knock up a meal.'

'I can second that,' Stephen said. 'Tell you, if Dad hadn't kept me hard at it in the fields I'd be the size of a house by now.'

Enid was preventing replying for Will came in then and he looked at the two girls and said, 'You won't get back to Penkridge Lodge tonight because the lane is flooded. It's completely impassable, and the rain is still coming down, though the thunder and lightning has stopped, thank goodness, so the horse is settled at last. I thought at one point I would be spending the night in the stable.'

'Then you must stay here,' Enid said to the two girls. 'That will be better in a way because your clothes will be properly dried by tomorrow.'

Meg was immensely glad not to be going out into that cold, squally night again, but she said, 'Sorry to be putting you out like this.'

'You're not putting us out,' Enid insisted. 'And it's hardly your fault anyway. No, we'll be glad to have you stay.'

'I'll echo that,' Will said. 'You two girls have worked like Trojans today.'

Meg knew that to be true, for even when they chatted they never stopped and at times she had felt as if her back was breaking. But still they had left a quarter of the field where the hay would be lying flattened by the rain. 'Sorry we couldn't get all the hay in,' she said. 'There was at least one more stack left there, maybe two.'

'Listen,' Will said. 'We have four full haystacks in the barn, thanks to you, plus the one Enid and me did on our own, so you should be proud of yourselves.'

'Yes, you should,' Stephen said. 'I bet it's not work you are used to.'

'Well, no.'

'There you are then.'

'You are likely tired, though,' Enid said, 'so I'll just go and make the beds up for you.'

Meg was so glad to hear that because she was more than tired, she was exhausted, but hadn't liked to say, so she was thankful when Will said, 'When Enid has the beds made, you can go up when you want. I'll be following you myself shortly, for we don't keep late hours on farms.'

So when Enid came down, Meg and Joy, still with blankets wrapped around them, made their way to bed.

'What an eventful first day,' Joy said as she climbed into bed.

'I'll say,' Meg agreed.

'Wonder what tomorrow will bring.'

'Who knows?' said Joy sleepily.

'Well, we best go to sleep now or we shan't be able for whatever it is,' Meg said, but there was no answer from Joy, just the sound of her gentle breathing because she was already fast asleep. Meg gave a small sigh of contentment, closed her eyes and followed her friend's example.

SIXTEEN

When Meg opened her eyes the next morning, she was disorientated for a moment, and then she realised where she was, sat up in bed and pulled the curtain.

'Oh wow!'

'Wassup?' Joy asked sleepily.

'There's water everywhere,' Meg said. 'Don't mean a bit of water, like, but lots. I mean, there's no fields, just a proper sea of water.'

Joy joined Meg at the window. 'Look,' she said. 'It's the same everywhere, as far as the eye can see. Blimey, even in the yard the water is more than halfway up Will's boots.'

They watched as he ploughed his way across to the barn to let the dogs out, and when they jumped into the swirling water their legs almost disappeared. 'Will must be going for the cows,' Meg said. 'If they have been stood in water all night, that won't have done them any good.'

'No,' Joy agreed. 'And the cowshed might be water-logged as well.'

'Everywhere will be, I'd say,' Meg said, getting out

of bed. 'Good job they have those two steep steps to get into the house, or the water might have got in here as well.'

'Where are you going?' Joy asked as Meg struggled to her feet and wrapped the blanket back round herself.

'To see if I can help.'

'You'll be as good as useless without wellingtons.'

'Maybe they have spare ones,' Meg said. 'Stephen must have used boots. Maybe they kept the ones he grew out of. I mean, wellington boots don't have to fit like shoes. I used to keep a pair of wellies for about three years, stuffed the toes with old socks that were past darning, and I didn't get a new pair till they were small enough for the next one down. Anyway, I won't know till I ask. Come on, this is our chance to get our uniforms on while Will's out of the way.'

Enid was downstairs and was surprised to see them up. 'Thought you'd still be tired,' she said, pouring them each a very welcome cup of tea. 'You looked done in last night.'

'We were tired,' Joy said. 'But that was yesterday. We're young and fit and we bounce back.'

'We'd like to help,' Meg added. 'But we have no wellies.'

'No wellies,' Enid said. 'I'd say they were essential for farm work.'

'They might well be part of the uniform,' Joy said. 'They just gave us the basics to get us here as quickly as possible. I mean, Rita knew there was going to be a storm, but I shouldn't have thought she had any idea it was going to be as fierce as it was.'

'No one expected that,' Enid said. 'I have never

238

experienced such a storm. The man on the wireless said this morning that Staffordshire was the worst hit.'

'You have a wireless?' Joy asked in surprise.

'Yes, there it is on alcove by the chimney breast,' Enid said.

'Fancy us not noticing that yesterday,' Meg smiled as she struggled into her crumpled but dry uniform.

'We haven't had the wireless that long,' Enid said. 'And we're not really in the way of turning it on much, except for the news. We got it after our lad came home after his initial six weeks and said that he was joining the Royal Staffs because there was one holy bloody war coming and he wanted to be part of it. His dad was upset, you know, with him being in the last one. He never said much about it, always said he didn't want to relive it, but the odd thing he let slip was bad enough. I mean, I know that every man is someone's son or brother or father, but when it is your much-loved only son, it's very hard.'

Enid's eyes suddenly looked very bleak and then she said, 'And now he's home for me to spoil a bit before he's back in the fray again.'

'My brother did the self-same thing,' Joy said. 'And my parents were upset as well.'

Enid nodded. 'At the beginning, Will wanted Stephen to claim exemption as a farmer, but he wouldn't hear of it. Really I was proud of him and deep down Will was too. Anyway, when he'd gone, Will said we needed to get a wireless to keep abreast of any war news.'

'You get some good stuff on a wireless,' Joy said. 'Plays and all different kinds of music and comedy shows and that.'

239

'Maybe,' Enid said. 'Will turned it on this morning for the weather report. That's how he knew Staffs took the brunt of that storm, but he turned it off again because we run it with an accumulator that we have charged up every week in Penkridge. With the weather the way it is, who knows when we will get to Penkridge again.

'Anyway,' she said, getting to her feet, 'you were asking about wellington boots. We have a collection in the attic. I never threw the old ones away because Will said rubber was useful and he has mended more than one bike puncture with a pair of old wellies. Come up and see if there's some to fit you.'

There were, and soon Meg and Joy were sloshing across the yard to meet Will, who was leading the twenty cows down the waterlogged lane towards the cowshed, the dogs, Fly and Cap, beside him.

'Were they stood in water all night?' Meg asked, concerned.

Will laughed. 'Not they,' he said. 'Mind, I might have been in a pretty pickle by now if they had been. I might be facing foot rot and all manner of other things, but this little lot found this hummocky grass on the field. It goes up a slight incline, but there's not much of it and they were all squashed on and around that, and not that keen on moving off it either. See, they are usually waiting by the gate at milking time 'cos their udders are heavy and probably uncomfortable, but they wasn't moving through that water and I had to go and fetch them. In the end it was the dogs barking that made them shift.'

'Oh, I bet they enjoyed that,' said Meg, giving the

240

two sheepdogs a tentative stroke. 'Look at them with their mouths open like that. You'd swear they were laughing.'

'I often think the same myself,' Will said. 'Now I bet you want to have a practice milking these here cows.'

'It's one of the things we shall have to learn,' Joy said. 'Apparently, to teach you they have this contraption on a frame that has rubber teats filled with water attached.'

'Nothing like a real cow,' Will said. 'Let me show you.'

Will was very patient with the girls, first of all showing them how the udders had to be washed gently. Meg was almost too frightened to touch them (she had never seen udders before and thought them rather grotesque), but she also saw how uncomfortable the cows were, and so she washed them as tenderly as she could, then sat astride the three-legged stool the way Will showed her, pulled slightly and squeezed the first teat. She was ridiculously pleased that a squirt of milk hit the bucket held between her legs.

'Well done,' Will said. 'Now relax. Lean your head against the flank of the animal and get a rhythm going.'

It didn't come straight away, but Meg had more of a technique by the second cow and was better still with the third, and later she came to regard milking as one of the favourite of all her farming duties. This was despite the fact that there were rogue cows that could kick out and upset the bucket, depositing the milk all over the milkmaid and the straw, or the ones that would shuffle round to crush the unsuspecting, or knock a person off the stool altogether, and she learned the hard way not to stand at the back of the animal.

That first morning, though, Will only gave them the well-behaved cows, and both girls thoroughly enjoyed the experience. They were surprised, however, when Will told them that much of the milk would have to be thrown away.

'But why?'

'The lane is impassable,' Will said. 'So I can't get the churns to the top of it, even if the main road is clear enough to allow the milk lorries through.'

'It seems awful just to throw it away.'

'I agree,' Will said. 'I hate waste, but Enid will take the cream to make butter and she might make soft cheese too. Those are useful things for you to learn to do.'

'Oh, yes,' Meg said enthusiastically. 'I would love to learn those skills.'

'Now's your chance,' said Will. 'Just now, though, these cows have got to be delivered back to their soggy field and the byre mucked out and cleaned, so let's set to and get on with it because there will be no breakfast till all that's done.'

Meg and Joy needed no further bidding as they were both hungry.

Will was impressed by his land girls and so was Stephen. His parents had sung the praises of both girls when they had gone to bed the previous day. 'They look as if a puff of wind would blow them over,' Will had said to his son. 'I didn't think they'd be much use; I even said that to them and they assured me they were stronger than they looked. And, by gum, they've proved me wrong for they've worked their socks off, and without complaining once.'

'One looks very young. Young even to have left home,' Stephen remarked.

'That's one called Meg,' Enid said. 'And I agree with you. She does look young, but she must be old enough or they wouldn't have let her come.'

'Mmm, I suppose,' Stephen said. 'She's very pretty.'

'Now, Stephen.'

'I'm only saying, Dad,' Stephen protested. 'Young men are supposed to notice pretty young women. I mean, I'm not dead from the neck up and I have got eyes in my head.'

'Well, you put your energies into getting better and don't turn the heads of those girls away from their work,' Will warned.

'Huh, fat chance of that,' Stephen said. 'As soon as I am in any way improved they will ship me back to camp faster than the speed of light to work with the physio. They've told me this already, so your girls are safe.'

However, despite Stephen's words, his eyes were drawn to Meg as soon as she came into the kitchen after milking. Meg found she was amazingly hungry and she tucked with relish into a large bowl of porridge with sugar and lots of creamy milk, and then attacked the delicious home-baked bread Enid offered.

'This is just mouth-watering,' Joy declared, taking a big bite of a slice that she had spread liberally with butter.

'Oh, we don't do bad for food in the country,' Enid

told her. 'And there is nothing, I don't think, to beat homemade bread. Try some blackcurrant jam with it.'

'It seems almost a shame to put jam on top of such nice butter,' Joy said.

'I agree,' Meg said. 'But I bet the jam is nothing like the stuff we buy in the shops. Is that homemade too?'

Enid nodded. 'I make jam every autumn,' she said, and watched the girls eat with some satisfaction. Enid was born to be a homemaker and had wanted a family of children, but she had only had Stephen and never a sign of any more. She had fretted about this in the early years and, being a Catholic, she had been driven to ask the priest about it. She got little sympathy as the priest told her sharply that she had to be satisfied with what the Good Lord sent. 'Who are you,' he demanded, 'to question Almighty God?'

Well, Enid never considered herself anything special, but if God knew everything, as the priests said, then He would be well aware that, though she loved her son with all her heart and soul, she yearned for a daughter, and to that end for the next five years she had prayed earnestly, had Masses said and offered up a novena and though she had not discussed it much with Will, he sensed her inner sadness and guessed the reason for it.

Enid felt very alone in her quest for another child. Her sister, Lily Daley, who lived in Penkridge, was ten years older than Enid, and the one she looked up to, and usually she would discuss everything with her elder sister, for she usually valued her advice and opinion.

However, this time she could say nothing, for Lily had once had five fine healthy children, and one by one she had lost them all to diphtheria. She'd been on her own, for her husband, Arthur, had been conscripted into the army in 1914, and she'd had her youngest son three months later. By the autumn of 1916 the children had all died, but her husband was fighting a deadly war and could not come home.

Lily had become hollow-eyed and bowed down with grief, and for a time lived at the farm with Enid and Will, who had married in 1915. Enid, despite feeling anguished and sorrowful herself, often held her sister in her arms when abject misery threatened to overwhelm her.

Even worse was to come. A month after the last child's funeral, Lily received a telegram telling her of the death of her husband. It was too much, and Lily fell to the floor in a faint. Once she regained consciousness, she still lay in a coma-like state for a further fortnight as she remembered the husband who had walked away so proudly, convinced they would have the Hun on the run by the first Christmas of the war.

However, as time passed she recovered enough to return to Penkridge and, knowing that she had to provide for herself, she offered to run the grocery store, which was owned by an uncle of Arthur's. She still lived in the three-bedroomed house she had moved into on her marriage and would not think of moving to something smaller and more suitable for she said all her memories, good and bad, were bound up in that house.

Enid watched the courage of her sister as she rejoiced in the birth of Stephen in 1919, a year after that Great War ground to a halt, though she saw the ravaged look in her sister's eyes when she took the child in her arms and knew that she would give everything she owned for that child to be hers. How then could she tell her sister about her longing for a daughter, when she had a son growing tall, strong and handsome beside her?

But now Enid had two land girls living with her, due to the inclement weather, and she felt strangely drawn to them, although she knew so little about them. After breakfast she watched them slosh across the yard after Will and she wondered what would make two girls like them up sticks and come from – she imagined – comfortable homes to some of the more crude cottages, for there were a great many more primitive than Oakhurst Farm.

Will had taken them out to clear the ditches to help the water run away, and she knew they would come in drenched and dirty and cold, like as not, and she'd have to get a nice spot of lunch together.

In fact Meg was having the time of her life. It was so different from anything she had done before and she could see the relevance of what she was doing. It gave her little time for thinking and remembering. She soon realised it was impossible for anyone doing this type of work not to get to filthy-dirty and very wet, and once you took that on board you were fine. Anyway, she thought it a small price to pay for seeing the water level going down, even a little, and she was quite surprised when Will called a halt, then led them back down the oozing muddy waters of the lane to the farmhouse, where they removed their mud-encrusted boots and washed in the scullery as quickly as possible, for delicious smells were coming from the kitchen.

'Now,' Enid said to the two girls as she led the way to the dairy after lunch. 'Making butter is easy enough, just a bit hard on the arms.' She showed them the wooden churn and then she handed Meg a wooden stick with wooden flaps sticking out from the sides at the bottom.

'This is called the paddle,' Enid said. 'Put it through the hole in the top of the lid of the drum, fasten that on securely, and churn the butter by hauling the paddle up and down.'

'Is that all?' Meg said. 'Doesn't seem that difficult.'

'Tell that to your arms and shoulders in a wee while,' Enid said, and she turned her attention to Joy, who had been watching Enid intently as she explained things.

'Now, Joy,' Enid said, leading her over to a bench where there were a collection of smaller barrels. 'I have put vinegar in the milk to make it sour. Now we must strain it through muslin to separate the curds.' They lifted the heavy bucket together as Enid spoke, and poured it into another container to which Enid had already fastened the muslin. 'Do you remember the nursery rhyme about Miss Muffet sitting on a tuffet eating her curds and whey?' Enid asked as the liquid started to seep through the muslin. Both girls nodded and Enid went on, 'Well, on this farm we eat the curds, or soft cheese, and it is fair lovely spread on slices of homemade bread, and the whey is mixed in with the pig feed. Nothing goes to waste.'

'What shall we do now?' Joy said. 'All the liquid is drained off.'

'Bless you,' Enid said. 'Aren't you that come from big cities impatient? That will drip all night and tomorrow will be done except for the salt to be added.'

So saying, she tied a knot in the muslin and fastened

it to a beam above the container. 'There, that's done,' she said with satisfaction.

'You know,' said Meg, leaning on the paddle for a breather, 'when we lived in Birmingham I never thought much about how some foods are made. Did you, Joy?'

'No, I didn't,' Joy said. 'Butter and cheese and stuff were just things we bought in the shop. It sort of matters more here – and I suppose it's the same on any farm.'

'Yes,' Enid said. 'It would be similar anywhere, I would say. But we are lucky in many ways, because rabbits can always be killed for the pot and I can wring the neck of a bird that's not laying any more.'

'Ugh, don't.'

'No good being sentimental about animals if you live on a farm, young Meg,' Enid said with a slight chuckle. 'Rabbits are a menace and need to be culled, because the expression "breed like rabbits" is only too true. And any hen laying well will be kept because the eggs are very important, but if they stop laying, they are just a drain on the food supplies, which are hard enough to get. And we all get a piece of pig when one is killed locally, like we share ours in turn.'

'It's amazing,' Meg said. 'But you will have to be patient with me because I suppose the idea of killing animals wasn't in the forefront of my mind when I joined the Land Army.'

'What was in the forefront of your mind?' Enid said. 'What made two girls like you come to a place that was so different from anything you have done before?'

'I suppose that's part of the attraction,' Meg said.

'You know what they say about a change being as good as a rest?'

'Well, I wouldn't have said you two have had much rest so far,' Enid said. 'And you are stronger than you look, all right, because you have been paddling that churn like a good'un.'

'Oh, that's because it's not much different from the maiding tub and I had plenty of practice at that.'

'Maiding tub?' Enid queried. 'What's that when it's at home?'

So while Joy took a turn at the churning, Meg explained, and that led to her telling Enid about her mother's death and her rearing her brothers and sisters, as she had promised her mother she would.

'What a great pity for your mother to have all those fine children and to die just like that. What a great girl you were to take all that on.'

'And she did a great job too,' Joy put in, and added, 'Did you want more children?'

'Oh, yes,' Enid said. 'I wanted a big family. I fretted about it at first and even asked the advice of the priest. Not that he was any good, for all he said was that I had to be satisfied with what then good Lord sent and I hadn't to question Almighty God.'

'Are you a Catholic, Enid?' Meg asked.

'Yes,' Enid said. 'How did you know?'

'Because I'm a Catholic too and that is just the kind of thing the priests say,' Meg told her. 'And I bet it didn't help at all.'

'You're right, it didn't,' Enid agreed.

'What about Will?' Joy asked as she took a rest from the churning. 'Did he want more children?'

'He never said in so many words,' Enid said. 'I suppose he thought there wasn't any point in talking about something that he couldn't fix.'

'Yeah, men don't talk about things, though, do they?' Joy said. 'Not emotional things, anyway. I've noticed that.'

Enid shrugged. 'It's the way they are. Normally it didn't matter, because I have a sister living in Penkridge called Lily. She is older than me and I would usually discuss everything with her, but I couldn't tell her of my longing for more children.'

'Why not?'

Enid didn't answer straight away, but what she did say was, 'Afterwards, when I was coming to terms with the fact that I wasn't going to have any more children, I began to wonder whether it was more painful to have no children at all, or to have them and love them and care for them and have them all taken away.'

Meg gave a gasp as she thought of little Ruth and she thought that was painful all right.

Enid noticed the distress flood over her face as she said, 'That's what happened to Lily, see,' and she told the story of her sister. Meg wept for she thought that although Ruth hadn't died she was still lost to her and her brothers and other sisters. 'I know you've tasted tragedy too,' Enid said to Meg. 'The loss of your mother must have been grievous.'

The tears flowed freely down Meg's face as she said, 'It was terrible, truly terrible. Mom knew she was dying. I didn't want to hear, hoped she was wrong. She died giving birth to Ruth and then Ruth very nearly didn't make it. She was in Special Care for ages.' Meg gave a shudder that went all through her body as she said, 'I try not to think of that time too much.'

'Then I'm sorry for asking you questions and forcing you to remember things that are maybe best forgotten.'

'No, don't be sorry,' Meg said. 'Maybe it would be better to remember her more often, because memories are all I have and I need to keep them alive for my own sake, and in case the children ask about her.'

Enid watched her eyes while she spoke and realised the depth of love Meg had for her siblings. She wondered what had caused her to take this job, which would mean being separated from them. Birmingham surely had other types of jobs she could have done that would have enabled her to live at home a little longer?

However, when she broached this, Meg said firmly, 'My help wasn't needed at home anymore because my father married again.'

She tried to keep any resentment and distaste out of her voice and she told of her father meeting Doris and their haste to marry, as her father thought he would be called up. 'You see,' she said, 'I am only sixteen, and if Daddy was conscripted and not married, the Welfare people could say I wasn't old enough to look after my brother and sisters completely on my own.'

Enid nodded, for just the word 'Welfare' struck fear into people's hearts.

'Anyway,' Meg finished, 'Daddy did marry her so the children have a new mother now.' She had tried to speak lightly but her voice had betrayed her. Enid looked at her keenly and saw the desolate look cross her face before she recovered herself and gave Enid a wan smile. Enid knew Meg hadn't told her everything; she had the sudden

251

urge to draw her into her arms for she looked in bad need of comfort.

Stephen knew that too. Bored by his own company he had hobbled to the dairy to see what they were about, and the sight of Meg so sad affected him greatly. He sat awkwardly on one of the barrels, reached for her hand and drew her down onto the neighbouring barrel.

He continued to hold her hand as he said gently, 'What is it that is upsetting you so much? You don't need to tell me – any of us – if you don't want to, but I think you must tell someone because something is tearing you apart inside.'

Meg nodded and her troubled eyes raked over each of them in turn. Suddenly it was too much for her to hold inside any more. Even Joy had never been told the whole story.

Meg began to tell them everything since the dreadful time her mother died, all the tribulations they had gone though, reliving it all again so much that her eyes were two pools of heartache. She spoke honestly about her father's drinking, which had initially plunged them into poverty and debt, and his animosity towards Ruth, whom he thought had caused his wife's death.

Enid's eyes darkened in sympathy. She had heard of such things before, but not that often, and usually the man came round in the end. She thought of her longing for a daughter; this man had four and yet they were enough for him because Meg was talking about the arrival of Doris making their lives even harder.

'The children now have a stepmother,' Meg went on, 'yet the reality is they have no mother at all because

Doris hasn't got a maternal bone in her body. I bet she couldn't believe her luck when she heard about evacuation.'

'This area seems to be safer than many other places and so is earmarked for evacuees,' Enid said. 'Even the priest told his parishioners that if they had the room it was their Christian duty to take in a child or two, especially if those children were Catholics. I did think of it and if it hadn't been for all the lads leaving and us needing to apply for land girls I would have gone for it. So I suppose your brothers and sisters are to be evacuated?'

'Yes,' Meg said. 'Not Terry, though. He's already left home. As soon as he was finished with school at fourteen he went to work in a mate's shop and he lives above the premises.'

'Not your youngest sister either,' Enid said. 'I was told it was school-age children only.'

Meg gave a strangled sob and tears squeezed from her eyes and trickled down her cheeks, and Stephen's felt his whole stomach lurch at the anticipation of more bad news. She shook her head mutely as Stephen dropped her hand and instead put his arm around her. She hesitated for a moment, aware that what she had to say exposed her father in the worst light possible and she felt shamed by what he had done, but it had to be told. So pressed, against Stephen's shoulder and in a voice little above a whisper she said, 'My father put Ruth in an orphanage.'

There were gasps from all of them, for Joy hadn't known about that either, and then Meg said bitterly. 'All that talk about marrying Doris to protect them was just so much eye wash. If he wanted to keep the kids out of care why did he just deliver one into their waiting arms? I can't bear to think of what Ruth is going through, what she thinks has happened to us all. She is too young to understand, and as far as she is concerned we have just disappeared into thin air. It breaks me up inside when I think about that. I know in time she will forget us all and while that is upsetting, it is better for her that she does.'

She gave a sudden gulp and tears ran afresh as she said brokenly, 'I had the care of Ruth for two years since the day of her premature birth, and I loved her like she was my own child, and now it is as if she is dead to me for I'll never see her again.'

Joy's eyes were very bright and tears were pouring down Enid's face as she said, 'My poor dear, how you've suffered. Go into the kitchen and rest yourself.'

'Oh, but . . .'

'I insist,' Enid said. 'Joy and I will finish up here.'

'When Mom speaks in a certain way it is far better to do as you are told, I've found,' Stephen said with a faint smile at Meg.

'Better go then,' Meg said in as light a manner as she could manage. And she followed him into the kitchen. When they were sitting either side of the range she said, 'I feel a bit of a fraud because I'm not the only one has had bad things happen to her. Look at your aunt. What became of her in the end?'

'Oh, she got over it,' Stephen said. 'As much as anyone can ever get over something as traumatic as that. She has always loved me but has nothing to do with other children generally. I would stay with her in the holidays sometimes.' He grinned as he went on, 'She let me get away with murder and would spoil me rotten. I worried as much about her reaction to me enlisting in the army as I did Mom and Dad's.'

Meg nodded. 'I think your mom will really miss you when you go back.'

'I know, but Mom and Dad are not going to be the only parents missing their son, and to win this war everyone must be prepared to make sacrifices.'

SEVENTEEN

Enid mentioned the things Meg had told her to Will later that evening as they got ready for bed.

'She certainly seems to have been dealt a bad fist all right,' Will said.

'I'm really taken with her, Will. I mean, I like both girls but with Meg . . . Oh, I don't know, she is so young and looks sort of lost. She needs mothering.'

'Now, Enid.'

'Don't you "Now Enid" me,' Enid said crossly. 'That girl has been a little mother to her brothers and sisters since their mother died when she was only fourteen. Seems to me somewhere along the way her needs have been forgotten. Today I felt like giving her a damn good hug. Oh, don't worry, I didn't,' she reassured her husband, seeing the look on his face. 'Stephen did, though.'

'Stephen put his arm around her?'

'Yes, and I couldn't blame him. Will, she is like the daughter I never had.'

'No, she's not, Enid,' Will said firmly. 'She has a family of her own.'

'Huh, not much of a one,' Enid said. 'There's no

mother, a father who – reading between the lines – is more eager to please his wife than tend to his children. And as for her brothers and sisters, the only one that could have been a help to her, Terry, the eldest boy, left home virtually as soon as he left school. I mean, what child leaves their home at fourteen, unless something is very wrong?'

'So what do you want?' Will asked perplexed. 'She's here now and not at home.'

'I know and I want her to stay here.'

'What?'

'As one of our land girls,' Enid said. 'They said we'll be assigned at least two, so why can't we have these two?'

'I don't know if you can pick and choose like that.'

'Well, you won't know unless you ask,' Enid pointed out. 'And you'd better check that's all right with the girls, too, that they'd like to stay here.'

Will still looked doubtful and Enid cried, 'What's the matter with you? You know as well as I do that many farmers only agreed to have land girls on sufferance, and others are so mean they wouldn't give you the skin off their rice pudding.'

Will smirked at the picture this conjured up and Enid snapped, 'This is no laughing matter, Will. The girls could end up at some ungodly place where they are not treated right or even fed properly, and they need good food if they are supposed to work as hard as men.'

'All right,' Will said. 'I will ask if we can have the girls working this farm and they may as well live in; after all, we have the room and I'll need them every day early for the milking.'

'How will we get word to them at the hostel place?'

'We won't,' Will said. 'Provided it doesn't rain tonight – and there's none forecast – I should be able to get Dobbin up the lane tomorrow after the milking. I've got to try and get Stephen to his hospital appointment then anyway, and the girls will have to pick up their things and the rest of their uniform, and I need to go to Penkridge to get the accumulator charged. Times are too dicey now to be without a wireless.'

Both girls wanted to stay on at the farm if they could, but the following morning Joy said, 'We're both all for stopping on here and I'd like to get it all sorted as soon as possible, but do you think we will get to Penkridge today? The lane was still very muddy when we brought the cows in.'

'Yes,' Meg said, 'they were slipping all over the place.'

'Well, we will have to try it sometime,' Will said. 'Anyway, I'm going to load the churns on the cart as soon as we're done here and see if Dobbin can manage to pull them to the head of the lane. I hope he can because, especially in these austere times, I don't like throwing good milk away.'

Meg knew what Will meant. Glasses of milk had been pressed on the girls the previous day and, though Meg hadn't been that keen on milk before, she had an idea that she might develop quite a taste for milk that had just been taken from the cow.

Eventually the cows were milked and Will took them back to their marshy field while the girls cleaned out the byre. And when they were finished and crossing the yard ready to go back to the farmhouse for a welcome breakfast, it was to see Dobbin trying to pull the cart loaded with milk churns. Will was coaxing and encouraging him to walk upon duckboards that he had laid over the glutinous brown sludge at the bottom of the lane. The horse wasn't too happy about it, but Will was incredibly patient, and eventually the horse put his front hoofs on the board and Joy and Meg gave a little cheer, and this encouraged the horse to move further forward.

'He'll be all right now,' Will said. 'Go in and get your breakfast and tell Enid I'll be in shortly.'

The girls nodded, but removed their mucky wellingtons in the back porch and washed in the scullery before they went in and gave Enid Will's message. Stephen was already at the table and Meg smiled at him as she sat down. He really was nice, she decided, and he had been lovely to her the previous day. It reminded her of the talks she used to have with Terry, though she was always mindful that he was younger than she and she had tried to shield him a little.

'Hungry?' Stephen asked, and Meg nodded vigorously because she always seemed to be hungry.

'I'll say she is,' Joy said. 'And I can tell you that for nothing, because her stomach has been grumbling for the last half-hour.'

It was true as well. Enid laughed as she ladled porridge into their bowls as Meg retorted, 'I can't take responsibility for my stomach – and anyway, I bet you are just as hungry as me.'

''Course I am,' Joy said. 'I just make less noise about it.'

'Now, now, girls,' Enid chided, though she was smiling at their banter. 'Leave your mouths for eating, not arguing.'

It was easy to do as Enid said because she made the most delicious porridge, and for a while there was silence. Then Will was at the door saying that Dobbin struggled to get by in parts of the lane, but he had made it. 'What he can do once he can do again,' said Will. 'Anyway, I have left him chomping on hay and looking dead pleased with himself.'

'So we will get to the hostel this morning?' Meg said.

'I'd say so,' Will said. 'But apart from Stephen, who gets to ride, we'll have to walk to the head of the lane because I shan't expect old Dobbin to pull us until we get to the metalled road.' And then he added with a twinkle in his eye, 'Especially you two, who have us eaten out of house and home since you came. Dare say you will be a darn sight heavier going back than you were when you arrived.'

Meg remembered that she had sweetened her bowl of porridge with three teaspoonful of sugar before adding creamy milk from the jug, and now she was on her second piece of homemade bread. She flushed, wondering if she had been greedy.

Will saw the flush and Meg's discomfort and let out a bellow of laughter. 'I'm joshing you, Meg,' he said. 'No one works well on an empty stomach, and farms do better in terms of fresh wholesome food than those in cities and towns, so you can eat your fill of whatever we have.'

It was so warm and friendly here, and Meg felt a rush of affection for these people that until two days ago had been strangers to her. She could see that Joy felt the same and she was about to make some reply when Will said to Enid, 'Put the wireless on. There will be enough life in that accumulator to hear the eight o'clock news, I should think.'

There was, and they listened to the sound of Big Ben booming out the hour and then the newscaster's voice announcing the news at eight o'clock on 1 September 1939. The very first thing he said was that Hitler's armies had invaded Poland at dawn that morning. Meg didn't really understand the slightly panicky look that passed between Enid and Will, because though she imagined it was a blow that Germany had invaded Poland, it was only what had happened already to a place with a really long name – Czechoslovakia, yes, that was it. It had happened in Austria too, but her father had said that that didn't count because Hitler had been Austrian.

'Only to be expected,' Will said. 'He's been amassing troops on the border for a week or more. He wasn't doing that for nothing.'

'Why does it matter to us?' Joy asked.

'Because we have an alliance with Poland,' Stephen told her, 'saying we will go to Poland's aid if they are attacked.'

'Why?'

'Because of an important port in Poland that we don't want to fall into German hands,' Stephen said.

'Yes, but how can we protect Poland even if we wanted to and promised and everything?' Meg persisted. ''Cos it's miles away . . . isn't it? she asked uncertainly, because she had only a sketchy idea of geography.

'It's a fair distance,' Will answered. 'And I think the only thing to do for Poland is for us to declare war on Germany.'

'Oh golly!' Joy exclaimed. 'When d'you think this will happen?'

'Anytime soon,' Stephen said sombrely, and suddenly the heat seemed to have been sucked out of the day.

'Ssh now,' said Will. 'Let's hear the rest.'

They listened to the announcer telling them of the towns and cities all over Great Britain, where children were being assembled in school halls and playgrounds. They had gas masks that were purported to look like Mickey Mouse in boxes slung around their necks, and they were burdened with small suitcases, or even a carrier bag with a change of clothes and other sundries in.

And as they were marched to railway stations to be dispatched all over the country to 'places of safety' Meg knew neither the bewildered, tearful children nor the weeping mothers had any idea where these places of safety were.

Among those children were Jenny, Sally and Billy Hallett. They had a gas mask each around their neck, a coat over one arm and held a large carrier bag in the other hand. Billy's carrier held two vests, two pairs of pants, a pair of trousers, two pairs of socks, six handkerchiefs and a pullover, and the girls had two vests, two pairs of knickers, a petticoat, two pair of stockings, six handkerchiefs, a skirt, a blouse and a cardigan. In addition they each had a comb, towel, soap, flannel, toothbrush, and a pair of wellington boots.

Some parents put in a comic or two, or sandwiches and biscuits, some barley sugar in case they felt sick, and a piece of fruit, such as an apple. But the Halletts had just the bare essentials. They were also the only ones with no one to see them off, shed tears over them and say how much they would miss them.

Charlie had hugged and kissed them before he went to work that morning and said that he would miss them sorely and he hoped they wouldn't have to be away from their homes for too long. Billy and Sally had cried all over him but Jenny had stayed dry-eyed. She knew her father probably assumed Doris would see them off, but she had no intention of doing that and when the time came she had packed them off as if they were just going to school.

In fact, it was a relief to Doris to see the back of the children for Frank Zimmerman was making heavy demands on her, and though he wasn't a man to say no to – and Doris didn't dare – she did say that it was difficult to carry drugs all over the city when she had the children in the house. She also said she couldn't 'entertain' his friends in the evening the way she used to because of Charlie. He had smacked Doris about a bit when she said that. She was scared and nervous and it had made her temper shorter than ever and the children had borne the brunt of that . .

Jenny knew nothing of Doris's concerns but she was well aware of people pointing at them as they walked unaccompanied down to the school. She saw sympathy in people's eyes and heard them say it was a shame, and one woman said Doris was a heartless bitch.

Jenny had the urge to turn round and agree with her. Her bottom was still stinging from the caning she had endured at Doris's hands the day Meg left, for breaking a dish when washing up. Doris said she had done it deliberately and Jenny told her she hadn't, it was an accident. She got her face slapped for talking back and then she had eleven strokes of the cane because she was eleven. She knew it would please Doris more if she cried out, and so she bit her lip till it bled to prevent her doing just that, and only gave way to tears in her bed at night when she muffled the sound of her sobs in a pillow.

Doris was never that harsh when their father was there, but it was no good appealing to him as Billy tried to do. He had two strokes of the cane when Doris claimed he hadn't come straight in when she'd called him earlier the night before. So as Charlie was tucking him into bed, Billy told his father about it in a low voice. With his agreement, and because he had always left that kind of thing to Maeve, Doris had taken over the management and punishment of the children, whom she said they had been completely ruined under Meg's care. And she stipulated firmly that he was not to undermine her efforts to put some manners on them.

Charlie had seldom come the heavy hand and he had no desire to do so now, so he was grateful to Doris and he smiled down at his indignant young son and said, 'I believe Meg spoiled all of you, Billy, and Doris is just trying to undo the damage.'

'Yes, but, Dad, she used the cane.'

Charlie disliked that but he had made a promise to Doris to give her a free hand, so he swallowed any distaste and said, 'If she did you must have done something to deserve it.'

'No, no, I never.'

'Billy, you must have done. If you think hard you will realise that. Did you apologise?'

'She didn't give me the chance.'

'So you would have apologised?'

Billy thought about that and then said, 'Probably, if she'd told me what I'd done that got her so mad.'

'I'm sure you know,' Charlie said reprovingly. 'But you don't want to tell me in case I am angry with you too. I don't want that, especially because shortly you are being evacuated and will be living with another family and I want to know that wherever you are you have good manners and know how to behave. Doris is correcting you for your own good, and I hope you realise that. Isn't that the case, my dear?' he said, seeing Doris framed in the doorway.

Billy shot around in panic. Doris had sneaked up the stairs and listened to his conversation with his father and, looking at her malevolent eyes, he knew that he would catch it for complaining. The next morning his father had just left for work when Doris grabbed Billy out of the bed and hauled him downstairs. Knowing he would holler blue murder, she stuffed his mouth with socks, held his hands behind his back so he couldn't remove them, and administered six whistling strokes of the cane to his bottom.

Upstairs, Jenny lay almost too sore to move from her beating and though she heard the swish of the cane and knew the agony her little brother would be in, she could do nothing, for any interference by her could lead to Billy being punished more and she couldn't risk that. Jenny knew they were on their own now, and she was counting the hours till she could leave the house.

That is what she told her younger siblings as they assembled in the school playground. She spurned those who might pity them and told Billy and Sally to hold their heads high. 'Don't you dare cry,' she warned them. 'Wherever we're going, it's got to be better than what we've left behind.' And so the younger ones were dry-eyed as Jenny, with one either side of her, marched behind the headmaster as they made their way to Moor Street Station.

When Will, Meg and Joy arrived at Penkridge Lodge, it was almost deserted; the others – not trapped by the water as Joy and Meg had been – had all been taken to the designated farms. As it was, Rita Partridge was pleased to see them safe and sound.

'We did send the lorry around to fetch the girls back,' she told Will. 'But some of the farm lanes they didn't attempt, and yours was one of those. I knew that you would bring them back when it was safe to do so, but all the same it was a bit of a concern, given that I am responsible for the girls' welfare.'

'I can understand that,' Will said. 'That storm was certainly a ferocious one – even I've never seen the like. The thunder and lightning nearly drove the horse mad and I would imagine there's some damage hereabouts.'

'Sure to be,' Rita said.

'Well, as you can see, no harm came to the girls,' Will said. 'And they helped me save a sizeable amount of hay and have taken to the milking like they've been doing it all their lives. The missus has even had them learning how to make butter and cheese with the excess milk when we couldn't get the churns to the head of the lane. All in all, they have turned out a treat and we would like to keep them, but I didn't know whether they had been assigned to someone else.'

'Oh, no, Mr Heppleswaite,' Rita said. 'It isn't as organised as all that. You were assigned two girls and if you want these two to train up, they needn't go anywhere else. In fact, yours is a good farm for teaching them all aspects of farm work because you do arable as well as dairy, don't you?'

Will nodded. 'And I keep chickens and pigs.'

'And the girls can live in?'

'Oh, yes. We have plenty of room.'

'That suit you?' Rita asked Meg and Joy, and both girls nodded eagerly.

'Well, that seems to cover everything,' Rita said. 'I shouldn't think you had that much time to unpack when you arrived, but get your things together and I will give out the rest of your uniforms and then you are set. You know where to come if you have any problems, but I will come out to see you by and by anyway.'

A little later, as they were stuffing the few possessions – the civilian clothes they had removed on their arrival – back into their cases, Meg said, 'Yes, I'm glad to be going to the Heppleswaites because I really like them, but won't you miss living in this big house? You seemed very impressed when we arrived.'

'Oh, it's true that I was a bit awed by the size of the place,' Joy said. 'But I've been thinking about it since. None of us land girls will be living in the lap of luxury, it seems to me. Instead we will be toiling at physically hard and dirty work. This hostel might have mod cons in the shape of baths, and so on, but anyone staying here will not have much time to use them – they'll have to be up earlier than we will be in order to reach the farms they are working on, and they will get home later, too shattered to do anything but fall into bed, I should think. What about you?'

'I never wanted to stay here,' Meg said. 'I would have felt like a fish out of water.'

'Good job it worked out the way it did, then.'

'I'll say,' Meg said, picking up her case and giving the room a cursory glance. 'You ready?'

'I'm ready.' Joy said.

Penkridge soon came into view as the road was a long straight one, and Will said, 'Now, although lots of people call this a village, it is in fact a small market town and holds a market twice a week, Wednesday and Saturday.'

'Pretty enough place, though, for all that,' Stephen said as the cart rumbled along the cobbled streets. 'You'll soon see that for yourselves.'

Will pulled the horse to a stop in Market Street. 'I have to take Will for his hospital appointment, leave the accumulator at the garage, and it will take a few hours to charge, and then I have a few errands of my own to do, including fetching gas masks for us all.'

'Gas masks!' repeated the girls, looking askance.

'Yes, well, the Germans used mustard gas in the Great War,' Stephen said. 'It's only a precaution.'

'But also the law,' Will said. 'Everyone has to have a gas mask. There's no choice in the matter. Though let's hope we never have to use them. So why don't you forget all about gas masks for now and, while I'm busy, take a turn about the town and get to know your way round a bit? When all my business is attended to, you will find me and Stephen at the Boat Inn on the canal side. Join me there when you have finished your jaunting. Anyone will tell you where it is.'

The girls were pleased enough by that suggestion and quickly clambered from the cart outside the garage and set off, coming first upon a train station. It was small and very basic, but a few passengers sat on one of the benches on the platform and a porter wheeled parcels about on a trolley and looked very important.

'Didn't know there was a railway station here,' Meg said. 'Wonder where it goes to?'

'Be great if it went all the way to Birmingham, wouldn't it?'

'Yeah,' Meg said. 'If we ever get time off, we might be able to go home – not that I am in a great hurry to see Doris.'

'We'll ask Will and Enid,' Joy said. 'They are bound to know, but no chance of much time off yet, I'd say, so let's go and look at the rest of Penkridge.'

Stephen was right, it was a pretty place, with many old timbered and half-timbered houses both big and small. Some had thatched roofs and some of the larger ones had mullioned windows similar to the ones at the hostel. 'These must be really old,' Joy said. 'See, some of the beams are quite crooked.'

Meg nodded. 'But they are lovely, aren't they? I mean, I have seen pictures in books of houses like these, but never thought I would see the real thing.'

And whether Penkridge was regarded as a village or a town, it did have a proper village green with shops grouped around it, which the girls were delighted to find. They discovered the river overhung with weeping willows, babbling over its stony bed, the sun glinting on the ripples.

Eventually, though, they went back into the town and came upon a large and imposing old church. It stood in its own grounds through small, wrought-iron gates with a little graveyard beyond that. The stained glass

269

in the large arched window facing them sparkled in a myriad of colours in the early autumn sun, and there was a castellated turret above the main body of the church with a clock on the side of it.

'Looks very grand, don't you think?' Meg said.

'I'll say,' Joy agreed. 'And it's got a fancy name that fits it somehow, St Michael and All Angels.'

'Yeah, I know what you mean,' Meg said. 'That will be the parish church – Anglican, you know.'

'You looking for a Catholic one?'

'Well, as we're here, I thought I would have a look,' Meg said. 'I mean, as the Heppleswaites are Catholic too, it makes life easier for me, and Enid said they usually go to nine o'clock Mass on Sunday morning in Penkridge, so I'd like to have a dekko at it.'

St Mary's, the Roman Catholic church, was on the edge of town and, after the splendour of the Anglican church, Meg was rather disappointed by its square block construction Even the stained-glass looked not a patch on the beautiful windows of St Michael's. 'Oh, I don't know,' Joy said when Meg said this. 'It's got a lovely entrance. Anyway, does it really matter what it looks like? I thought it was what went on inside it that was more important than the building.'

'You're right, of course,' Meg said. 'Just now, though, we had better find this pub and Will and Stephen, 'cos we've been ages and they might be waiting for us.'

'Yes,' said Joy. 'I saw a gleam of water as we were making for the church. That'll be the canal.'

It was, and they walked along the towpath towards the town, watching the brightly coloured barges ploughing their way slowly through the water.

'At least it looks cleanish here, not like the dirty, oily canals in Brum,' Joy said. 'My brother learned to swim in the canal and my mother was always saying it was a wonder he had never caught anything. She never told him off much or anything for all the scrapes he got into. All our growing up she was fond of saying, "Boys will be boys", and that seemed to give my brother licence to do what he wanted.'

'I know,' Meg said. 'It's not fair, is it?'

'When we are older and in charge we'll have to change things round a bit,' Joy said.

'We will,' Meg agreed, and then suddenly said, 'Oh, look, there's Stephen waving.' They hurried towards him.

'Have you been waiting long?' Joy asked. 'I think we got a bit carried away looking round.'

'No worries,' Stephen said. 'I had a pretty long wait at the hospital for all I had an appointment, and now I'm stood here with a pint watching the world go round, and there is no better way to spend a Friday morning. Anyway, Dad says charging the accumulator takes some time.'

'Did you get the gas masks?' Meg asked Will when he came to join them.

'I did,' he said. 'Each one comes in its own little box. We'll examine them when we get home, and that is all I'm going to say about the gas masks now. I have a much better thing to ask you,' he went on, consulting his watch. 'There's time enough for another drink. Would you girls like a glass of lemonade?'

'Oh, yes please,' Meg said, for she had seldom drunk it and thought it one of the nicest drinks she had ever had.

Later, as they climbed into the cart to go home, Will said, 'Hope you like fish because I've got us some nice haddock for tonight. You'll find Enid can do a mean fish pie.'

'I eat most things,' Joy said. 'Though I must admit I've never had much fish, but I will eat it. I always find it doesn't pay to be fussy.'

'Well, you're right there,' Will said approvingly. 'And if I hadn't got hold of any fish today, we'd only have had eggs for the meal because we can't eat meat, see, with it being a Friday.' And he said to Meg, 'We'd best rattle through the milking Sunday morning then, because we'll all be going to nine o'clock Mass. And what about you?' he said to Joy. 'Are you a churchgoer?'

'No, not really.'

'Well, whether you are or not in the general way of things, I would go to some church this Sunday,' Will told her. 'And, once there, pray like you have never prayed before, because I believe that is only divine intervention that will stop this war now.'

At the farmhouse they found Enid using the treadle sewing machine, making curtains for the windows that didn't have shutters, using the horrible black material she had put by and hoped she'd never have to use.

'It's a two-hundred-pound fine if you let a chink of light show, they say, so I can't bury my head in the sand any longer,' she said. 'But I must admit it will depress me totally to have black curtains covering the windows.'

Neither Meg nor Joy blamed her one bit. 'Still,' Enid said, 'that's the way of it today and we have just got to get on with things.'

What everyone was really curious about was the gas masks, and a few minutes later, when Meg opened the box and hauled the mask out, she thought she had never seen anything so hideous in the whole of her life. When she fitted it over her face it was even worse, because she found it hard to breathe and the stench of rubber was overpowering. Joy felt the same.

'God,' she said, 'if we all have to wear these things for long, Hitler won't have any trouble invading us. No one will be able to stop him because we'll all be asphyxiated.'

'We may be glad of them if he uses poison gas,' Will said.

'I don't know whether I wouldn't rather take my chance with the gas.'

'No, you wouldn't,' Will and Stephen assured her.

'Let's hope it won't come to that,' Enid said soothingly. And she added, 'Let's not fight amongst ourselves. Hitler and his armies are what we have to focus our energies on. Mind you, the news just now is enough to make anyone tetchy.'

When they settled down to eat the steaming pie – which Will declared 'champion' – Enid said to Joy, 'What religion are you, Joy? C of E?'

Joy shrugged. 'Suppose so. Never really thought about it 'cos it's not as if we went to church or anything.'

'Would you like to go to St Michael's?' Enid asked. 'We could take you in on the cart with us?'

It was on the tip of Joy's tongue to say she wouldn't bother going anywhere, but with the world situation as it was, she thought a few prayers and church attendance couldn't hurt. She knew, though, that she would feel nervous of going to a strange church where she knew no one so, accepting the fact that one church was very like another, and that all Christian churches worshipped the same God, she said that she would like to go with them to Mass at St Mary's.

Later that day, now the girls were staying with them, Enid asked about the rates the land girls were paid and learned that Joy was to be paid thirty-two shillings because she was eighteen but Meg only twenty-eight shillings because she was younger.

Enid was annoyed. 'We paid our two male farm hands thirty-eight shillings a week and you two will be doing the work of three,' she said. 'And you must pay keep out of that.'

The girls nodded. 'Well, I've never heard the like,' Enid went on.

'The farm hands, because they were young, single chaps, used to sleep in the rooms we had made for them above the barn. You could have slept there too because we made them right cosy and warm, with a Primus stove and all, but we just thought being young ladies you might be more comfortable in the house. But what I am saying is we never charged them for those rooms. It was part and parcel of their wages, for farm work in general isn't well paid, but for you to get so much less and then to pay keep out of that doesn't seem right, especially as you are doing us a favour.'

'Have many hours a week are you expected to work for this princely sum?' Will asked.

'Fifty in the summer and forty-eight in the winter,' Meg said. 'And I think we must pay you something just for the inconvenience of us being here.'

'I agree,' Joy said. 'It might even be one of the rules or something.'

'Maybe,' Enid said. 'God knows, there are rules for every damned thing these days. So how about if I take a third of your money, that's seven shillings from you, Meg, and eight shillings from you, Joy.'

'Oh, are you sure that's enough?' Joy asked.

Enid never got to reply, however, because suddenly Will lifted his hand, crossed the room and turned up the wireless for the news. The newscaster was saying Poles were fighting for their lives although everyone knew that they had little chance against the disciplined German armies. Meg felt really dispirited as she went to bed that night.

EIGHTEEN

Sunday morning before Mass there were clusters of people standing about all talking of the possibility of war. Enid did interrupt the talk to introduce the two girls to her sister, Lily, whom she'd told them about, and Meg was surprised when Lily said the three children she had with her – one girl and two younger boys – were her new evacuees, because she had understood that Lily never bothered with children other than Stephen. These three looked extremely malnourished and were stick-thin and scrawny, reminiscent of many children in the streets Meg had been born in.

But she knew in the care of Enid's sister, Lily, they would be all right. She had been taken with the older woman straight away. She was a little on the plump side, like Enid, and had the same lovely, kind face, with twinkling blue eyes and round rosy cheeks. Her hair was cut much shorter than Enid's and worn loose, so dark curls peeped out from under the bonnet she wore for Mass. She had a beautiful smile, a soft voice, and a sort of goodness seemed to ooze out of her.

They went into the church as the strains of the organ

could be heard. Meg thought the inside of the church matched the outside for it too was rather plain. Around the walls were the carved figures of the Stations of the Cross and it had a simple high altar and the only ornamentation on it was a Lamb and a Flag etched in a recess underneath the altar table. There was a very old statue of the Virgin Mary that Enid whispered came from the Benedictine friars when their convent was ransacked by Parliamentarians in the civil war.

When the Mass began though Meg was impressed by the priest, who said that there might be testing times ahead and that they had to pray for courage to meet the challenges. She prayed earnestly for just that.

They didn't linger after Mass. Meg, Will and Enid had taken communion and no one had eaten breakfast, so they were all famished. They wanted breakfast over and done so they could concentrate on the Prime Minister, Neville Chamberlain's, wireless broadcast, which was due that morning.

It was almost a quarter past eleven when the sombre tones of Neville Chamberlain announced that because Hitler refused to withdraw his armies from Poland, Britain was at war with Germany. Although it was what they had all expected, for a few seconds no one spoke, stunned at the magnitude of the terrible reality.

'Thank God the doctor is removing the plasters next week,' Stephen said, breaking the silence. 'He said the bones have knitted together nicely.'

'So what happens now?' Meg asked.

'Back to camp,' Stephen said. 'A spot of physio will get me fully fit again and not a moment too soon I'd say.'

* * *

Immediately after the declaration of war, places of entertainment such as cinemas, theatres, concert halls – and any similar places where large numbers might gather – were closed, but that made little difference to life on the farm. The whole of the country was shocked, though, when the day after war was declared, news came in of a passenger ship, SS *Athenia*, carrying evacuated children and mothers to America, torpedoed and sunk with the loss of nearly 120 lives.

'Shows what barbarians we are dealing with,' Enid said fiercely, very agitated by the news. 'Fancy attacking and sinking an unarmed ship filled with civilians.'

'Well, maybe now you'll realise why I felt I had to join in the fight,' Stephen said. 'This man and his fearsome armies have to be stopped.'

'Yes, and it's a fight we must win,' Meg said.

'Of course,' Will said. 'And our bit is to grow enough food to feed the nation, because what has been done to an unarmed passenger ship can be done to unarmed merchant ships just as easily. The more we are able to produce here, the less we have to import and the more sailors' lives we can save.'

As the time drew near for Stephen to leave, he realised how much he would miss Meg, though he had known her for such a short space of time. He wanted to ask her to write to him, but she was only sixteen and so he asked his mother's advice. Enid was a wise woman. She had seen the lovelorn way Stephen had looked at Meg in unguarded moments and knew what he thought of Meg, just as she knew that Meg liked Stephen a great deal, but in a brotherly way. So she said that she was sure that Meg wouldn't mind writing to him but he shouldn't read anything into it other than a young girl writing to a soldier. He couldn't ask for what she wasn't ready to give.

Meg was initially a little wary about writing to Stephen. 'Doesn't it signify some sort of relationship, a girl writing to a man like that?'

Stephen, who very much hoped that they might eventually have some sort of relationship, was mindful of his mother's advice. 'Not today, with so many men leaving. All soldiers value letters from home,' he said.

'Who else writes to you then?'

'Mom and Aunt Lily.'

'No girls?'

'No,' Stephen said. 'I have never asked a girl to write to me until now.'

'I can write as a friend.'

'That's all I am asking you to do.'

'Then I would be pleased to write to you, Stephen.'

'He's sweet on you,' Joy said, when Meg told her this as they undressed for bed.

'No,' Meg said. 'I am just writing as a friend. He says the soldiers get lonely and like to know they not forgotten by those at home.'

'He's sweet on you,' Joy said again. 'It's as plain as the nose on your face, but if you can't see it then you can't see it.'

Meg knew Joy must be seeing things that weren't there because Stephen had never displayed anything but friendship towards her, and that was all she wanted as well, so she treated Stephen the same way as she had since she first met him.

His ankle and arm were very stiff when the plaster

casts were removed and he spent the next two days striding about the farm, swinging his sore arm. Meg was often inveigled into going with him. She didn't mind because she found him so easy to talk to. They discussed everything under the sun but the war he was returning to.

On the third day after Stephen's plaster casts were removed a military vehicle drew up before the farmhouse to take him back to camp. After embracing his parents he took Meg in his arms for the first time and kissed her chastely on her forehead and then he did the same to Joy.

The land girls and the Heppleswaites settled back into the rhythm of farm life again once Stephen had returned to camp. Meg was really enjoying her work on the farm and knowing it was so essential was an added bonus. She no longer thought five a.m. was the middle of the night, and though she was always ready to seek her bed, she didn't fall into it with the black exhaustion that had felled her originally. Because she was always so busy she was happy, but she felt guilty for feeling that way when there was a war on, a war that had already claimed lives and would claim many more before it was over.

The unfolding of the seasons was more apparent to Meg and Joy now they were living rural lives, and the daylight hours were so important to their work. Now the nights were really drawing in and there was a definite nip in the air most mornings. Winter wasn't that far away, but what was bothering Meg far more than that prospect was a lack of letters. She had written to all the children and asked Doris to pass the letters on to them. She eagerly awaited their replies so that she could write to them direct. Nothing came, though. She had also written to Kate via Richard Flatterly's office and got no reply from her either. Terry wrote spasmodically, and in fact the only one who wrote regularly was Stephen. Meg eagerly looked forward to those and just hoped she would hear something from the others by Christmas.

One week was very like another, but every Saturday Enid would go to Penkridge, where she visited the market, chatted with friends and neighbours, and called to see her sister. She took Meg and Joy with her, as she said they needed to get away from their farm work now and again.

Meg and Joy really appreciated this, for once they reached Penkridge they were left to their own devices. They would explore the town and would often met with other land girls, many of whom still lived at the hostel. It was soon obvious to the two girls that living with the Heppleswaites had been a good decision to make, for many of the other girls had a tougher life than they, sometimes due to the attitude of the farmers they were sent to. In contrast, Will and Enid were very kind and Meg and Joy were treated like members of the family. A real closeness had begun to develop between them, and this in turn made the girls work even harder.

However, it wasn't only the countryside that was quiet; so, according to the letters Joy's mother wrote, were the towns and cities; sometimes the absence of men and the dreaded blackout were the only signs that there was a war on. There were no bombs dropped, as the Government had indicated there would be, and many were questioning the wisdom of sending children all over the country away from their parents.

'Mind you, it opened the eyes of some in the village, taking in those evacuees,' Enid said one Saturday night as they sat round the table. Penkridge had taken in a great number of children. 'Our Lily said she doubted many of the townsfolk had ever seen such poverty and deprivation. She was no better, mind, for she hadn't seen it either.'

'Where were the children from?' Meg asked.

'Liverpool,' Enid said. 'Lily didn't put herself down to take evacuees, as she never has much to do with children if she can help it, so she didn't go down to the village hall the day they arrived. She was surprised to get a knock on her door later that evening and opened it to find the billeting officer there. All the children had been taken by their prospective foster parents, except these three. The billeting officer had trailed them all around the village, but nobody would or could have all three of them and the girl had promised her mother that they wouldn't be parted. Someone suggested they try Lily because she has this three-bedroomed house with only her in it.

'She said she felt so sorry for the children, whose thin, pasty faces were drawn with fatigue, and the little boy looked scared to death. He was crying and his nose had been running and snot was smeared across his face where he had wiped it with his sleeve. The elder boy was pretty near to tears himself and the girl looked kind of bereft, Lily said, as if the weight of responsibility that had been laid on her shoulders was too heavy a burden. The sight of the three waifs made her feel it was selfish to refuse to take them in when she had the room. She said she thought of our lad off to fight, and

282

the farm hands, too, and you girls leaving your homes and living elsewhere to work the farm in the place of men, and she knew she had to do her bit. And what an eye-opener she had.'

'In what way?'

'Well, that first night, she hadn't facilities for three children, and she just had one single bed that she had for Stephen when he stayed over, years ago, and she topped and tailed the two boys in that, gave the girl her bed and slept in a chair. Next morning she found the boys under the bed. It turns out they'd never slept in a bed before. Anyway, the evacuation society got more beds and bedding to her the next day, and she left it to them to use them or not. They had never sat at a table to eat either, and even the girl didn't know how to use a knife and fork properly.

'The children were very dirty as well. Lily didn't know how dirty till they all had a bath the next day and she had to scrape the muck off them, and their hair was crawling with lice. She had to go to the chemist for stuff to wash their hair with to get rid of them.'

'And every week they look better,' Meg said. 'To see them now – well, they are not like the same children.'

'Are they Catholics?' Joy asked.

Enid shook her head, 'No, they never went near any church, but as Lily said, she can't leave them in the house alone, they might get up to all sorts, so they have to come with her.'

Meg thought that though Lily might have to have been coerced into taking them in the first place, she was the sort of person to do the job properly. Lily's evacuees weren't the only ones who had arrived with body and head lice, and a fair few wet their beds and swore like troopers. An appeal was launched in all the churches and Women's Institutes for garments for some of the evacuees, who had come completely inadequately clothed for the autumn. They often didn't have a wellington boot between them, and in fact a good few just had plimsolls lined with cardboard in a vain effort to keep the rain out.

The shopkeepers had to keep their wits about them, too, because some stole with nifty fingers that moved like lightning. Having more space and freedom than was possible in the industrial towns, and not knowing the ways of the country, they caused havoc by churning up farmers' fields, or flooding them by damming streams, and they left farm gates open everywhere. Many of the village children resented the intrusion of these streetwise 'city kids', so fights were commonplace.

There was plenty of grumbling but, as Enid said, 'I think it takes time for children to learn to live together.'

'I think it was a massively optimistic to move half the country's children to somewhere so different from home, and expect them to adapt to country life just like that,' Meg said.

'Yeah,' Joy agreed. 'I missed city life at first, if I'm honest, and I had the choice to come here. The evacuees didn't and if you listen to them, they want the chippy and the pictures, the streets to play in, a kick-about down the park or the rec, and their nan living round the corner. It is all most of them have ever known, and they don't care how unsafe it is.'

'Well, that's just it,' Enid said. 'It doesn't appear to be unsafe, does it?'

'No,' Meg said. 'Sending the children away from the cities was just some sort of knee-jerk reaction.'

'Well, now,' Will said, 'I think that sending children away any time must have been a very difficult decision for parents. One that I am very glad Enid and I never had to make. I'm sure those who eventually decided to do it did so with the best of intentions.'

'Oh, yes, I agree with that,' Enid said. 'Most parents strive to do their best for their children, and if the promised bombs had come I think that they might feel more justified in keeping them away. But as it is . . .'

'I would think they can't risk bringing them home now,' Will said. 'Maybe that's what Hitler is waiting for them to do. We are dealing with an evil man and they can't afford to take chances. Remember, the only evidence they have to go on is what the German planes did in the civil war in Spain.'

Meg nodded. She remembered the harrowing newspaper pictures she had seen two years before of an air raid on a small Basque town: the dead and dying, and the devastated town just a sea of mangled and crushed remains of what had once been shops, buildings and houses.

'I think that was Hitler's way of showing the world what he could do,' Will said. 'And what he did there he will do here sooner or later, mark my words.'

Meg gasped, for the thought of something similar happening in Britain didn't bear thinking about.

The following day, Joy didn't accompany the others to church. She said she'd have the porridge ready for their return, and so Meg went off with Will and Enid. She had seen the lines of children at the front of the church, boys to the right and girls to the left many times but she'd never taken much notice of them because they were always in church when she arrived and were the last ones to leave.

That morning, though, Will was talking to some fellow farmers about the rules the County War Agricultural Executive Committees, known as War Ags, wanted to implement, and it had got quite heated, for as one said, how were they were supposed to get a greater yield with less help?

Meg knew Will would try his best to do as they asked because he was worried. Only the other day he had said to her and Joy as they milked the cows in the chill of the morning, 'We still bring in too much stuff from abroad; we're not nearly self-sufficient enough, and in these times it is criminal to have a field lie fallow because it's difficult to clear.'

Joy and Meg looked at him aghast. They knew what he was talking about, and that was the field at the far edge of the farm, complete with a derelict farmhouse. Will had told them it had belonged to a subsistence farmer who hadn't even tried to do anything with the land after his wife and son had died of the influenza bug in 1919 that he had inadvertently brought back from the Great War. Will had bought the field from him because he felt sorry for him, but he had never done anything with it, for it was literally full of gorse, brambles, high wild grasses and nettles.

Will caught sight of the girls' faces and said, 'All right, I'll not pretend that it will be easy, but it will be a lot easier than starving to death. Unless we all can grow more, Hitler could lay siege to Great Britain and starve us into surrender. Do you want that?'

No, of course they didn't, and they knew they had to clear that field whatever it took. Will was arguing the toss now with other farmers, saying the War Ags weren't the enemy, and Meg was idly listening to him as the children began filing out of the church.

'Meg? It is you, isn't it?' said a voice behind her, and she spun round.

'Miss Carmichael!' she exclaimed. 'What are you doing here?'

'I might ask you the same question,' Kate Carmichael said. 'To all intents and purposes, you seemed to have disappeared off the face of the earth.'

'But I wrote to you and Dad and the children as soon as I knew what farm I would be at.'

'I got no letters,' Kate said. 'Did they write back?'

'Terry did, but he is not a great letter writer,' Meg said. 'Why didn't you get the letters I sent you?'

'No idea,' Kate said. 'What did Terry say?'

'Well, I asked him to let me know how things were, with Doris and all, and had she heard from the kids, and in his reply he said he never went near the house, so he didn't know.'

'But Nicholas went to the house and asked Doris and she said she had not heard from you. He wanted your address, you see, because he was leaving.'

'Leaving?' Meg repeated. 'How do you know all this?'

'Because he's here,' Kate said. 'Well, in Rugeley, and I met him.'

'So you're in Rugeley? And what's Nicholas doing there?'

Kate laughed. 'One question at a time,' she said. 'You

knew I was travelling with the school because I told you. We were allocated a school that we share with other Catholic evacuees in a place called Upper Longdon, a tiny hamlet midway between Rugeley and Lichfield. With all the children to find homes for, I ended up renting a room from a widow in Huntington, which is nearer to Penkridge than anywhere else. We have been given a loan of a bus and each Sunday we collect up the Catholic children from outlying areas and bring them to Mass.'

'Oh,' said Meg. 'So how is Nicholas involved in all this?'

'He isn't,' Kate said. 'Not at all. Apparently he and his mother hightailed it out of Birmingham not long after war was declared. His mother has a sister in Rugeley and they are with her, and Nicholas is not best pleased about it.'

'Then he should say so,' Meg said impatiently. 'He isn't a child any more. And what about Uncle Alec?'

'Ah, well, Nicholas said that's what decided his mother,' Kate said. 'She'd been muttering about it for some time, but when his dad got his call-up papers, they were gone within a fortnight.'

'Call-up papers, Alec?' Meg said. 'I sort of hoped that they'd take the younger men first. What about my dad?'

'Nicholas said that they went together and they're both in the Royal Warwickshire's.'

Meg gasped in shock. 'I . . . never had a chance to say goodbye.'

'Your stepmother said they didn't know where you were.'

'She did,' Meg said through gritted teeth. 'I wrote.'

'Nicholas said your father was really cut up about

288

not seeing you,' Kate said. 'He went to that recruitment place for land girls but they would tell him nothing.'

'Terry knew,' Meg said. 'He wrote back, so he knew my address.'

'Terry wasn't there either,' Kate told her. 'He and his mate had gone on a first-aid course.'

'So he saw neither of us?'

'That's about the strength of it,' Kate said. 'Look, I must get the children back. Some have taken communion as I have, so they will be starving now.'

'Yes, of course,' Meg said. 'Could we meet sometime?' Kate's eyes slid away from Meg's as she said, 'Maybe, but I am really busy now and so, I imagine, are you.'

'Yes, but I get time off.'

'Lucky you!'

'Don't you sometimes?'

Again there was that glance away from Meg's face as she said, 'I'm so tied up. You've have no idea.'

Meg couldn't argue further, for she could see Will and Enid waiting for her.

'I must go,' Kate said. 'But here,' and she pressed a piece of paper into Meg's hand. 'Nicholas's address, where he is now. He will be able to put you in the picture better than I will anyway.'

Meg had no option but to take the paper and make her way to Enid and Will, leaving Kate to chivvy the milling children into the waiting bus. To her surprise and horror she saw that sitting in the driver's seat was Richard Flatterly.

Kate slid in beside him. 'That was Meg Hallett,' she told him.

'I know, I saw.'

'Why didn't you come out and say hello?' Kate asked. 'You know her too.'

'Oh, I know her all right,' Richard said, as he started the engine and, under cover of the engine noise, he added, 'When I used to collect the rents when my father's rent man was sick, she gave me every indication that she wanted to know me better . . . in the biblical sense, if you get my meaning.'

'You're telling me that Meg Hallett—'

'Came on to me,' Richard said. 'Yes, she did – and strongly. I know she was only young, but honest to God, she was offering it on a plate. It was really embarrassing and awkward, especially when she asked if she could she get money off the rent if she was "extra nice" to me.'

'You didn't do anything?'

Richard expressed utter indignation. 'Crikey, Kate, what do you take me for? She was little more than a child. She kissed me once because she took me unawares, but I told her firmly that I wasn't interested.'

Kate was stunned. 'I never thought Meg Hallett to be that type,' she said, but even as she spoke, she wondered how well she really knew the girl. She had barely seen her for two years. Her eyes slid across the cab to see Richard Flattery's crestfallen face and her heart contracted; this man was becoming very important to her. 'Poor Richard,' she said. 'I am sorry for even asking you, but it was just that I knew her so well when she was a child.'

'Well, now you know how she has grown up,' Richard said with satisfaction. He would teach the arrogant Meg

Hallett a lesson she wouldn't forget for repulsing his advances. 'And don't worry about me, I'll live.' And he smiled as the bus bowled down the country lanes.

As they were eating the delicious porridge Joy had ready for them, Meg filled them in about who Kate Carmichael was.

'How strange to find you are nearly living in the same place,' Enid said. 'Nice for you, though, being so far from everyone and everything you knew.'

'Yes, it is,' Meg agreed happily. 'I thought she might want to meet up today, but she said she has things on.'

Joy said, 'Well, I suppose she didn't know she was going to meet you, did she? And it is short notice anyway. Why don't you write to Nicholas and arrange to meet him next week? I'm sure he'll want to see you, and he might be able to tell you more about your brothers and sisters as well?'

'Yes, I will.'

'Actually,' Will said, 'I'm glad that you haven't made arrangements for today.'

'Oh?'

'Yes, because I am going to ask you a very big favour. It's the beginning of October and you have just over a week with us before your training is officially over and you are due a week's holiday. But I need to get that spare field ready for cultivation now, and if we leave it too late in the year the ground will be too hard for digging and ploughing. I really need your help, but it will mean you giving up your day off today.'

'I think this is more important than a day off,' said Meg, and she looked across at Joy.

'Me too,' Joy said, and they heard Will's slight sigh of relief.

'Put on your uniforms and your wellingtons then,' he said. 'You'll need them.'

The very first thing to do, though, Meg thought, surveying the field a little later, was to clear it of rubbish, because it was the place where unused or broken machinery and other assorted items had been dumped.

'What do we do with all of this?'

'Oh, that's easy,' Will said. 'Load it on to the cart. Penkridge is collecting scrap metal. Tomorrow, when I go to Penkridge to get rid of it, I'll try and get hold of some gloves because, when we have the rubbish collected, we must start on clearing out the ditches. These fields are liable to floods and, as they haven't been attended to for years, a lot of muck will probably have to be pulled up by hand. I doubt the billhooks and hoes will be strong enough.'

'Don't fancy clearing those fields without some protection on my hands either,' Joy said. 'Some of those grasses are as tall as me.'

'It isn't the grasses that bother me,' Meg said. 'It's the thistles and brambles that would rip our hands to ribbons, not to mention the stinging nettles – they would be very painful.'

'I'll see to it tomorrow,' Will said. 'But we might have to manage today, so shall we make a start?'

It took them all morning to clear the field of every bit of scrap metal, and then after a wonderful dinner they returned to tackle the ditches. It was stinking work, and muddy and unpleasant, for the ditches were full of putrid-smelling stagnant water, but they laboured on,

292

hauling and yanking on stubborn undergrowth that virtually covered the ditches and on which the billhooks were making little impression. They also had to plunge their hands into the scummy water to clear away the slimy roots and rotting foliage that were effectively clogging them.

But though the work was nasty, Meg knew how essential it was, and she was loath to stop for the milking; but as hard as they all had worked, they had been able to clear only a little. The field was a very large one and blocked ditches ran all along it.

Enid exclaimed at the state of their hands when they went into the farmhouse, for they were red-raw and covered in sores and scratches, some of them quite deep; their nails were broken and blackened. The warm water Enid poured into the basin for them to wash before milking was soothing, but Will felt guilty when he saw how sore the girls' hands were and marvelled that they had not complained.

'Maybe we should have left starting on that field till we got some gloves for you,' he said.

'We couldn't have done that,' Meg said. 'As it is we will be lucky to get it done in time. Don't worry, Will, we'll live.'

'Well, you might live,' Enid said, 'but if your hands are too sore tomorrow, then you will not be able to get so much work done, so, the pair of you, rub some goose grease into them before you go to bed tonight.'

They promised to do that, but later Meg – sitting astride a three-legged stool with her forehead resting on the velvet sides of the cow, and listening to the hiss of the milk into the bucket – thought of her cousin

Nicholas and wondered if he would be available to help them for a few days. No harm in writing to ask him.

When they had finished the milking and were eating the evening meal, Enid said, 'Why don't you stick at working at the ditches while you have the light and let me do the milking for the next few days?'

'Are you up to that?' Will said. 'I mean, you will have to fetch in the cows, milk them all by hand and then clean out the byre.'

'I know the work to be done, Will,' Enid said. 'Don't forget I was a farmer's daughter and had to do that and more when I was but a child.'

'But you are not a child any more.'

'I'm aware of that, but I'm not yet in my dotage,' she said firmly.

'All right,' Will said reluctantly. 'But you are not to lift the churns. Just leave them outside the byre and I'll deal with them. Just at the moment, it is the most tremendous help not to have to milk the cows.'

'It will give you more time,' Enid said. 'And with the blackout and all, what light we have is really important.'

'We need an extra pair of hands,' said Meg, 'and it came to me in the cowshed who that could be. Tonight, I'll write to my cousin Nicholas. As I said, he's living in Rugeley at the moment, so I'll ask if he has any free time to help us.'

'Maybe he has a job?'

Meg shook her head. 'Pretty certain he won't be working,' she said. 'He was at grammar school when his mother whisked him away, and he most probably will be doing nothing.'

'What age is he?'

'He's sixteen, the same age as me, but obviously taller and stronger. He could be a great help to us here.'

'He could that,' Will said in agreement. 'Well, you get your letter written, Meg, and when I go to into Penkridge to dispose of the metal early tomorrow morning, I'll post it for you.'

NINETEEN

Will set off the following morning. When the girls surveyed the day, Joy said that – even allowing for the time of year – the sky seemed very overcast, with thick, low-hung clouds appearing to promise rain.

'Shall we take our mackintoshes?'

Meg made a face. 'It will be hard to work wearing them.'

'But harder to be without them if the rain comes down in sheets,' Joy countered.

And so, after helping themselves to porridge, as Enid was dealing with the cows, the girls set out with their wellies and mackintoshes into the dawn. They hadn't yet reached the field when an icy drizzle began to fall.

'Oh, great,' Joy said.

'It's only rain.'

'I know, but how d'you think the mud will react to even more rain?' Joy said. 'We might both be spreading our lengths on the ground before we're much older.'

Joy wasn't far wrong. The two girls slithered through the mud to the ditches that ran the length of the field. They found it even harder work with the relentless, icy spears of rain attacking them as well, but they soldiered on. They had no idea of the time, but they could have blessed Enid when they saw her coming towards them. She was dressed in oilskins and thick-soled wellington boots, and either side of her were the two very damp and excitable collies, but, more importantly, she was carrying a tray.

By that time the girls were drenched through. Water had begun to seep through the thin mackintosh material and the mud had settled into glutinous sludge where they stood. So, with difficulty, the mud sucking at their boots, they moved to the partial shelter of a nearby tree and Enid presented them with a Thermos flask each filled with homemade broth. Meg had heard about such flasks. She knew they were supposed to keep hot things hot and cold things cold, but they were costly and until now she didn't know anyone who had one. She was immensely glad of the broth; the flask had lived up to its claim as the broth had been piping hot and it put new heart into the pair of them. Meg was intrigued as to how the Thermos worked.

'Will says it's because there is a vacuum between the inner and outer walls,' Enid said. 'When you look into an empty flask, that is not the wall of it, but a sort of liner made from glass, and so when you pour hot liquids in they are kept warm because the vacuum between the walls stops the heat or cold escaping quickly.'

'Aren't they very expensive?'

'Probably, in the normal way of things,' Enid said. 'But Will got these from the shop in Penkridge we buy our animal feedstuffs from. The owner was sent a job lot of these from America a couple of years before the war. He sold them to regular customers at a reasonable price, so Will bought a couple.'

'Well, whatever they cost they were cheap at the price,' Joy said. 'That hot broth has saved my life.'

'Any sign of Will yet?' Meg asked.

'No,' Enid said. 'And I'm surprised he's taking so long. I know he was anxious to get back to help you both.'

'Bet he can't find any suitable gloves,' Joy said. 'Gloves are not considered essential for the nation's survival.'

'What about my hands' survival?' Meg laughed.

'What about them?' Joy said. 'I reckon, by the end of the war, most women will have hands like ours.'

'You may be right,' Enid said. 'But I suggest you two put plenty of goose grease on them before bed like you did last night. It may help a bit, and in the meantime let's hope Will has found something to give your hands some sort of protection. Don't go on too long now either,' she said, picking up the tray. 'For in an hour and a half or so I will be dishing up dinner.'

Neither girl was wearing a watch, but they worked on for a while, glad that, while the rain hadn't actually stopped, it had slowed to a drizzle. Eventually, Joy threw down her billhook.

'That's it,' she said. 'My stomach says it must be dinner-time by now.'

Meg laughed, 'Come on then,' she said. 'My stomach is in no better shape.'

As they neared the farmhouse, they realised that Will was home, but they knew he hadn't been there long,

298

for while the cart had been run into the barn out of the rain, as they passed the stable they could hear the rhythmic strokes of the chamois leather that Will always used to dry the horse. When they walked in, sitting at the kitchen table, as relaxed as though he did it every day of his life, was Nicholas. Meg just stood on the threshold staring at him.

Nicholas laughed. 'You look as if you've seen a ghost.'

'How did you get here?' Meg asked him, astonished, crossing the room towards him.

'Will brought him,' Enid said as she stirred something on the range. 'That's what took him so long. Said he looked at the address on the envelope of the letter you were sending, and decided to deliver it in person and see if Nicholas was free to come now rather than later.'

'And, as you see, I was,' Nicholas said.

'Do you mind coming to help?'

'Mind? I'd say not,' Nicholas said. 'I was pleased because I was bored out of my brain, if you want the truth.'

'What were you doing?'

'Nothing.'

'See,' Meg said to Joy and Enid, smiling. 'What about school?'

'Not a chance about school,' Nicholas said. 'I should safely say my schooldays are over.'

'I can't see Aunt Susan agreeing to that.'

'She's had to,' Nicholas said. 'Oh, she had this bright idea of getting me into King Edward's Grammar School in Lichfield to do my Highers, but they have already had another evacuated school merge with them, so they are chock-a-block.'

'Were you upset about that?' Joy asked.

'No,' Nicholas replied. 'I was delighted because it meant I didn't have to tell my mother I had no intention of going anyway.'

'Why not?'

'Oh, I don't know,' Nicholas said with a shrug. 'Doesn't seem that relevant any more. I mean, if we lose this war, then what difference will it make that I have a degree in English and a very good grounding in Latin and Ancient Greek? I think everyone should do their bit, and until today I didn't know what my bit was. My father was called up just a few days after war was declared and my mother's answer to it was for us to fly to some obscure auntie living in Rugeley to keep me safe. She even told me that if I made it to university I could defer call-up.'

'Are you an only son?' Enid asked quietly.

Nicholas nodded. 'Only child. I often feel the pressure of that.'

'I wonder if my son does,' Enid said. 'He is an only one too.'

'But you let him go into the army,' Nicholas said. 'Will told me.'

'There wasn't any "letting" to it,' Enid said. 'In late April they called up young men of twenty and twenty-one. Both Luke and John, the farm hands, were twenty, and Stephen just turned twenty-one. They could have come home after the initial six weeks, but they all chose to stay. When Stephen had an accident at the campsite recently and was run over by an army truck I honestly hoped he had some injury bad enough to keep him away from active service'

She looked at the three young people listening to her and went on, 'I didn't pray for this to happen for I thought that totally wrong. But I did hope and I can't deny that.'

'No one could blame you for feeling that way' Meg said gently. 'It's natural to want to protect someone you love.'

'Didn't do any good anyway did it?' Enid said. 'He recovered and went back to it again and seemed glad to be going back.' She looked Nicholas full in the face as she said, 'To see your only son walk off to war is hard.'

'I know it must be,' Nicholas conceded, 'but my mother is treating me like some hot-house flower who needs protecting, cosseting, and I can't wait to get stuck in one way or another, to tell you the truth. But she never seems to want me out of her sight. I feel like I am being suffocated. I can't join up yet, but that doesn't mean that I can do nothing else. I had to fight her to let me come here, but fortunately Will is very persuasive, and the fact that Meg is also here made the difference.'

Enid sighed. 'Well, you are here for a wee while anyway, and after that maybe you should talk to your mother and tell her how you feel,' she said as she carried a heavy stew pot to the table. 'But now it's time to eat, so will you go out to the stables and tell Will to come in? He will have that horse rubbed away if he's not careful.'

The talk around the table was initially dominated by the work of the farm. For the first time Nicholas realised that if Great Britain couldn't become more self-sufficient, there would be a real danger of food running out.

'Oh, I see how important this is now,' Nicholas said. 'And why you are called the Land Army.'

'You'll understand it better after dinner,' Meg said. 'When you see the battle we will have to wage on a field full of brambles, thorns, thistles, stinging nettles, and grass nearly as high as me, and get it ready for planting.'

'You show me what to do and I will do my best to do it,' Nicholas promised. 'It was daft my mother panicking like she did. No bombs have fallen anywhere.'

'I don't want to see bombs falling in Birmingham when everyone is in the thick of it. Do you know where the children have been evacuated to?'

'No one seemed to know.'

'Don't be daft,' Meg snapped. 'Must be round Rugeley somewhere because Kate Carmichael came with them and she says most of the children were evacuated in and around Rugeley. They get a postcard to send home.'

Nicholas shrugged. 'Doris said she got no postcard.'

'Didn't she make enquiries?'

'Meg, you know as well as I do that all Doris wanted was the kids out of her hair,' Nicholas said. 'Evacuation fell in nicely with her plans, and that – as far as she is concerned – is that.'

'What about Miss Carmichael?' Meg cried. 'She was sort of organising it. Surely she knows where they've gone?'

'She says not,' Nicholas said. 'She said it was chaotic and she thought they may have returned home, and asked me how they were when we met in Rugeley. First I knew there was anything wrong.'

'But they could be living with anyone,' cried Meg in distress. 'Anything could be happening to them and we won't know.'

'I'm sure it's just some wee understanding,' Enid said calmly, patting Meg's hand. 'Though I fully understand your concern. You start your holiday next week and you'll be going back to Birmingham yourself then, so I'm sure you will clear it up in no time.'

'I will, don't worry,' Meg said rather fiercely. 'But for now it's best not to spend time worrying until I can do something about it.' She got to her feet. 'We've got a field to clear. Come on, we'd best get going. We're losing the light.'

Outside the rain had eased to a mizzle, and Will kitted Nicholas out with a sou'wester and wellington boots that had belonged to Stephen, though he rebuffed the heavy-duty rubber gloves the girls were so grateful for.

'Tracked them down in the hardware shop in the end,' Will said, as they set out for the field. 'Old Mac, who owns the shop, said there will be no more. Every bit of rubber is being syphoned off to help the war effort, so I got a few pairs. He said he will be lucky if he stays in business with this war on, because it's hard to get hold of anything made of metal, and that is mainly what he sells.'

'Of course,' Meg said. 'Never thought of that.'

'Yes,' Will said. 'I did feel sorry for him because he's been there years and he said he'll be reduced to selling the odd broom or mop. And that won't really keep the wolf from the door. Still, if we talk from now till doomsday it will change nothing, and meanwhile we are wasting the light, as Meg so rightly pointed out, so let's get cracking.'

It was amazing the difference an extra pair of hands made. Now more comfortable with gloves, the girls carried on cleaning the ditches, while Will and Nicholas were going to tackle the sprawling mess of vegetation threatening to take over the field.

'Never get the spade through this,' Will said. 'Reckon we need to scythe down as much as we can first.'

Nicholas agreed with that, though at first Will was reluctant to let Nicholas anywhere near the scythes, worried that he would slice his legs off. Nicholas insisted – though later that night, when they had eventually stopped for the day, he confessed that he ached all over.

With time of the essence, they decided on future days not to come home until the light failed. They needed the horse and cart anyway, so that they could fork the chopped-down thistles, gorse, brambles and grass onto the cart to be disposed of in the compost heap by the farmhouse. Enid would bring out their dinner, usually some warm pies she had wrapped in tea towels, and hot tea in the Thermos flasks, and even an old damp towel, so they could take some of the muck off their hands before they ate.

By the time they had started to dig the field on the third morning, the girls had finished cleaning the ditches, and they followed behind the men, turning over the soil and removing any large stones or anything else that might damage the plough. On the fifth day, Will began ploughing at one end of the field while Nicholas and

304

the girls finished off at the other end. By Saturday afternoon the field was ready: the rich, moist soil was now set out in neat rows and Will was dropping seed potatoes into the furrows.

Meg let out a sigh of contentment that began in her toes and spread in a glow all over her body. Never, in her whole life, could she remember feeling such pride as she did at that moment. In reclaiming a sizeable field they had achieved a considerable task, and one that she had originally thought might have been beyond them. Will finished his sowing and joined them as they stood surveying their handiwork.

'Well done,' he said as they began walking back to the house. 'I couldn't have done it without each and every one of you. Now I know Enid has a good dinner planned for tonight, because there was a hen not laying, she said yesterday, and she intended wringing its neck today.'

Then he let out a bellow of laughter at the look of distaste on Meg's face. 'No need to look like that, young Meg,' he said. 'We haven't got a handy butcher's shop at the end of the lane, and I'm sure you will enjoy the meal as much as the rest of us, especially as I intend to open a cask of cider to go with it. Have you tasted cider?' he asked. Meg, Joy and Nicholas all shook their heads. 'A treat in store then, 'Will went on, 'because you have done more than enough this week to deserve a drink.'

Meg enjoyed the meal and the drink, but she woke with a thick head the next morning.

'What's up with you?' Joy said as they dressed. 'You look as if you've lost a pound and found a sixpence.'

Meg made a face but didn't answer and Joy said, 'You best tell me. Will won't let you in the byre looking like that. You'll turn the milk sour.'

'You are a fool,' Meg said, and the ghost of a smile played around her lips.

'Oh, a smile,' said Joy. 'Or is it a touch of wind you have, perhaps?'

'Joy . . .'

'Let me guess,' Joy said. 'You are fretting about your brother and sisters.'

'Well, wouldn't you if the boot was on the other foot?'

'I suppose,' Joy said. 'It is worrying, I grant you, when they are so young, but I don't see what you can do till you get home.'

'One thing I am going to do this morning and that is talk to Miss Carmichael after Mass, and I am not going to come away without some answers.'

Everyone thought Meg was doing the right thing to try to find out what had happened to her siblings, and they waited for her in the cart so she could have a quiet word with Kate when she emerged from the church.

What Richard had told Kate about Meg's behaviour had shocked her to the core for she had thought she had known what manner of girl she was. Well, all goes to show, she thought and the look she threw Meg was one of disappointment threaded through with disgust.

Meg would have been puzzled by that look if she'd noticed, but her mind was filled with anxieties about the children and so without any beating about the bush, she asked Kate candidly, 'How is it that you don't know where my brother and sisters are when it was you who brought them?'

Kate saw how agitated Meg was and quite understood, for she had begun to feel uneasy herself. If the children truly were missing it was very worrying indeed and she wondered if she should have done more to find out where they had gone. She knew however she felt now about Meg Hallett she had to tell her the truth.

'I know I said I would be bringing them down, but at the last minute there was a change of plan,' Kate said. 'For so many extra children at the small village schools we needed more books, pens, pencils and things like that from an educational supplier in Birmingham city centre. As it was quite a big order, it might have been difficult to transport it by train so Richard offered to drive me down but we were delayed because the order wasn't quite ready. So when we arrived at the village hall, the children had all gone to their prospective foster homes and the billeting officer had left.

'It had been a bit chaotic, they said, because there was another school evacuated with ours, and that had a lot more children, so some of the children were not billeted in the village at all, but in isolated farms. It was only on the first Sunday I collected them all to take them to Mass that I realised your brother and sisters were missing.'

'So what did you think had happened?' Meg said. 'Weren't you worried?'

'A little,' Kate admitted. 'They were on the train because I checked the list, but they weren't on the billeting officer's list.'

'So what happened to them?'

'Well, I thought they had probably returned home because they couldn't stay together. Apparently that does happen. I wrote to your stepmother, but didn't get any sort of reply, but I only became really concerned when I met your cousin, Nicholas, and he said that Rose, who is still in Birmingham, wrote often to his mother and the children weren't back there.'

'Maybe Rose knows something but she can't put it in a letter,' Meg said. 'I've got a week off starting tomorrow.'

'You might find out more then.'

'I hope so, Kate,' Meg said sincerely. 'I really hope so.'

Meg was so white-faced when she climbed into the cart after she had spoken to Kate Carmichael that no one dared ask her anything, and the short journey home was completed almost in silence. Meg was glad of this, because what Kate had told her had shocked and worried her.

It was as they were sitting down to their steaming bowls of porridge that she told them what had transpired between her and her old teacher.

'It's monstrous,' Enid declared when Meg had finished. 'I thought in the beginning that posting children all over the country, like they were parcels, was wrong, but I did think that they would look after them properly.'

'But what shall I do? How will I find them?'

'Maybe if you found the billeting officer?' Joy said. 'Maybe she can tell you why they weren't on her list and what happened to them.'

'I think that would be pretty hard to do,' Nicholas said. 'Why?'

'Because I don't think that they *were* billeting officers as such.'

'What d'you mean?'

'I mean they were probably employees of some council drafted in to help with the evacuation,' Nicholas said. 'Once the evacuation was completed, they'd probably have gone back to what they were doing before, whatever that was.'

'If they were from the council, maybe Richard Flatterly will know who they are?' Meg said hopefully.

Nicholas shrugged. 'It's worth asking him,' he said. 'Only from what you said before, Richard Flatterly was there to oversee the evacuation on behalf of Birmingham Council, and yet he only arrived after all the children had been placed.'

'And Kate did.'

'Yes, but she's just a teacher in the school, not in overall charge,' Nicholas said. 'Flatterly should either have travelled with the children, or at the very least been here to welcome them and made sure it all ran smoothly, I would have said.'

'Yes,' Will said. 'I think you're right, young Nicholas.'

'And instead of doing what he was meant to be doing, he was probably canoodling with Miss Carmichael.'

'What makes you say that?' Meg said sharply.

'Well, they looked very lovey-dovey to me when I met them in Rugeley.'

That shook Meg a little, for it just confirmed what she suspected, but she had had more pressing concerns. 'But what difference does that make?'

'They arrived at Rugeley Village Hall together?'

'Yes,' Meg said. 'Kate said she had some things to

bring from the school and so he drove her. She said they were late because not everything was ready for them to just collect.'

'Well, he shouldn't even have been there.'

'I suppose not,' Enid said. 'But if this young woman had a lot to carry, it was nice to give her a hand.'

'Not if it meant neglecting the children.' Will said. 'That's what you're getting at, isn't it?'

'Yes,' Nicholas said. 'And if Flatterly had done his job properly, maybe three of my young cousins might not have gone missing.'

The words hung in the air, and for a moment no one could think of anything to say. And then Nicholas said, 'Anyway, there will be two of us searching once we get to Birmingham.'

'You're coming too?' Meg said in surprise.

Nicholas nodded. 'Before I came here my mother was talking about me collecting some thicker clothes for her because she only packed summer-weight stuff.'

Meg just stared at him. 'Will you know what to pack?'

'Not likely,' Nicholas said, 'I wouldn't have a clue. Mom sent a list to Aunt Rosie.'

'I was going to say,' Meg said, 'I would never ask Terry to pick out some clothes to send me. God knows what I might end up with.'

'I'd be the same,' Nicholas said. 'But Aunt Rosie will probably have the stuff waiting for me. I don't have to go back straight away, and between us we will do our best to find out where the kids are.'

'Oh, I would be grateful for that,' Meg said.

'It's all right,' Nicholas said. 'They are my cousins, remember, and I'm as worried as you.'

Joy, watching Nicholas, knew that though what he said was true, he was doing this as much for Meg's sake as he was for his own because he was another one who had a fancy for her. It was futile, of course, because there could be no relationship between first cousins, but forbidden or not, Joy was certain Nicholas carried a torch for Meg.

Proper *femme fatale* she was, Joy thought with a slight smile, and a totally unassuming one, because she could never see just how attractive she was and how people were drawn to her, like Stephen, who she saw as a friend when he really wanted to be her lover.

Meg had never experienced a day that dragged so much as that Sunday. If she could have, she would have left straight after Mass, but no trains ran on Sundays. The children never left her thoughts all day, and she hoped fervently that when she got to Birmingham someone might throw some light on their disappearance.

'Doris could be lying,' she said to Joy as they were eventually getting ready for bed.

'About the postcards, you mean?'

'Yeah. They all had to have them,' Meg said. 'Lily told me, and all addressed and stamped and just a short message written that they had arrived safely. She said the organisers even posted the postcards they collected from the children in the village post office, knowing that some of them might be going to isolated cottages.' She gave a shrug and went on, 'That was here, not Rugeley, but I imagine all evacuation points operate the same format, wouldn't you?'

'Bound to, I'd say,' Joy said. 'And franked at the post office so you'd know whereabouts they are.'

'Yeah,' Meg said, 'if they ever got to Rugeley at all.'

And if they didn't, Meg's mind screamed, then where are they?

TWENTY

Meg didn't expect to sleep well, and she didn't. When she did drop off for snatched moments, her mind was filled with images of the children. She was glad when it was time to rise and pull on her uniform. The day was a cold one with a definite autumnal nip in the air, and both she and Joy were glad of their thick green jumpers, yet despite them they shivered as they crossed the yard.

It was always warmer in the byre. Normally this was Meg's favourite time in the day and it never failed to soothe her, but that morning she viewed it as one more chore to complete before she could take the train back to Birmingham. As if the cows were aware of her distraction, they were more difficult to settle. Meg found milking more onerous than usual and she didn't get the same volume of milk from the cows.

She expected Will to say something to her, but he didn't. In fact, they were all uncommonly subdued, with none of the normal banter between them, because Joy was sharing her good friend's worry. An uncomfortable silence prevailed, and Meg was glad when the milking was over and the cows returned to the field.

She was like a cat on hot bricks during breakfast, and after it she said to Will: 'Can we go straight off to the station?'

'You'll be far too early.'

'Well, you know, Dobbin doesn't go very fast.'

Will had opened his mouth to defend Dobbin when he caught sight of Enid's face. She was staring at him and gave a slight shake of her head, and Will knew she was saying quite clearly that if Meg wanted to go early to the station, then she should be let go. So he said nothing.

Meg turned to Joy and said, 'Do you mind going a bit early?' and Joy, knowing that Meg really couldn't bear to stay at the farmhouse a moment longer than necessary, and needed to be at the station where the journey to Birmingham would begin, mutely shook her head.

'Well, I'll be away to get the horse and cart,' Will said, scraping his chair on the tiled floor as he stood up. Meg stood staring out of the kitchen window till she saw Will leading Dobbin and the cart onto the cobbled yard before the barn. The packed cases were ready by the door and Will lifted them into the cart before turning to the girls. 'When you're ready . . .'

Enid was fighting tears herself, for Meg's unhappiness had got to her and she doubted she could speak without breaking down, but in the end no words were needed, for she hugged both girls tight, and that hug expressed how she was feeling better than any words could have done. Then they climbed up beside Will, who gave a flick of the reins, and Dobbin started up the lane. Enid watched until the cart was out of sight and she turned back to deal with the breakfast dishes with a heavy heart because she just did not know what Meg would find at her journey's end.

A lot of the journey to Birmingham that day remained a blur for Meg. She was aware they met Nicholas and travelled together on the train, and that it was Joy and Nicholas who kept the conversation going because Meg felt worried sick, certain the children's disappearance was somehow all her fault. She remembered them all waving to her from the doorway the day she left. Now that picture seemed to mock her because she felt she had failed them by moving so far away, but when she burst out with this to Joy and Nicholas, they both said she could have done nothing else.

'Doris wanted you out,' Nicholas said. 'You know that.'

'But I could have got out,' Meg said, 'if I hadn't been so prissy, and taken a job in the munitions factory. I'm sure I would have been able to find lodgings somewhere that I could afford because the wages in the munitions are very good.'

'And the work is very dangerous,' Joy said. 'And you'd be no use to anyone dead or maimed.'

'Meg, none of this matters anyway,' Nicholas pointed out, 'because they were evacuated.'

'And you couldn't have done anything to prevent whatever happened to the children in Rugeley,' Joy pointed out. 'Didn't that Miss Carmichael say she didn't know they were missing till she checked the lists of Catholic children so she could arrange to pick them up for Mass?'

'Something could have been done then,' Meg said.

'If you had known,' Nicholas said. 'Miss Carmichael didn't follow it up. She just assumed that they had gone back home. If I hadn't bumped into her in Rugeley, we might not have known till you arrived home.'

'I know,' Meg said dolefully.

The platform at New Street Station was teeming with people. The majority were in uniform of one kind or another, and there was the trudge of many feet as the surge of people moved forward to the exit. Their voices rose and fell in a tumultuous roar as they laughed and cried and chatted and shouted. Weaving between this mass of people were porters with loaded trolleys calling on people to, 'Mind your backs, please.' In one corner the newspaper vendor was plying his trade in a nasal whine that penetrated the clamour. There was suddenly a clattering rumble as a train pulled into another platform, stopping with a squeal of brakes and a hiss of steam. Then there was the shriek from the funnel of another.

'Let's get out of here before we are deafened,' Nicholas said.

And in the street Meg stood and stared for a minute or two. As Birmingham girls she and Joy were used to traffic, but neither had ever seen so many horse-drawn vehicles before, though there were also a great many petrol-driven cars, lorries and trucks, all jostling for space along the road and avoiding the tram tracks.

'Isn't that rather dangerous for the horses?' Meg asked.

'I suppose,' Nicholas said. 'Probably borne of necessity, though.'

'What d'you mean?'

'Well, petrol is hard to get. They're rationing it now.'

'Rationing petrol already?'

'Yeah,' Nicholas said. 'And there's talk of rationing a few other things too. Remember,' he said, 'until Will came for me, I had nothing to do with myself but read the papers and listen to programmes on my aunt's wireless, so I'm pretty clued up about the war.'

'Good,' Meg said. 'Glad one of us is.'

Joy left them there to get her tram, and Meg and Nicholas began to walk, passing the line of taxis without a glance – taxis were not for the likes of them. They went along Station Street and then Bristol Street. Meg was too tense to talk much as she neared her home, and Nicholas didn't speak either because he could sense the tension running through her. When they reached Bell Barn Road he wanted her to come with him to Rosie's, but she was anxious to see Doris, to see if she had news of the children. He hesitated for a minute, wondering if he should partly prepare her; tell her some of the concerns his aunt had told his mother about.

'What?' Meg said.

No, thought Nicholas, maybe it would be better to say nothing and let her see things as they are, so he said, 'Nothing, what d'you mean?'

'You looked as if you were going to say something.'

'No . . . Aunt Rosie said to come up. She said she'd like to see you.'

'All right,' Meg said.

She gave a wave and walked on. Because their house was on the street, it had another door to it in the entry, and this was the one she opened now as she stepped inside. The first thing she was aware of was the stench,

317

thick and rancid, the sour smell of squalor that hung over everything. She swallowed the nausea and went on, unease growing with every step. She noted a pile of dishes in the sink that looked as if they had been there days; there was thick dust everywhere, a filthy grate with ashes, days old, spilling from it; lino that stuck to her feet and cobwebs festooning the ceiling.

And in the middle of this filth, Doris lounged on the settee.

'I've come to find out about the kids,' Meg said.

'What kids?' Doris snapped. 'They was evacuated.'

'Yes, but they're not there. They weren't on the list. No one knows where they've disappeared to.'

'Ain't nowt to do with me,' Doris said. 'I sent them off to the school like they said and it was their concern then.'

'Aren't you the slightest bit bothered that three young children are missing?' Meg asked angrily.

'Not really. Like I said, I know nowt, so you go and shout at someone else.'

'They took stamped postcards with them,' Meg persisted. 'Did you get a postcard?'

'No I d'ain't get a bleeding postcard,' Doris yelled. 'So you bugger off and leave me alone because I don't want you here.'

With a sigh, knowing there was no point staying, Meg turned to go and had reached the entry door before Doris shrieked, 'And don't you go writing to your dad about this. He has enough to think about without worrying about bloody kids.'

That's one thing Meg had no intention of doing. Fighting men didn't need other things to worry about, especially when they couldn't do anything about them anyway.

'Any luck?' Rosie asked as Meg came in the door.

Meg shook her head. 'Claims she knows nothing.'

'That's what she told Robert when he went down to see her when we got Susan's letter. As far as she was concerned, it was good riddance.'

'And she's not going to lift a hand to help find them. Now why doesn't that surprise me?'

'Maybe we should go to the police.'

'I know, and I shouldn't hesitate,' Meg said. 'Except I worry how it will affect Dad. I don't want him worrying about things here if I can help it.'

Nicholas came in the door then, and Meg asked him to go and tell Terry about the missing children. 'He ought to know and there's a chance he has heard from the kids because they'd hardly write to Doris.'

'No problem,' Nicholas said. 'What are you going to do?'

'Something I don't want to do and that is to go and see Richard Flatterly, if I can.'

'That creep,' Nicholas said. 'Anyway, isn't he living near Penkridge now?'

'Only weekends, I think,' Meg said. 'I know he once used to have offices in Great Colmore Street, so I'll try there first. It's a long shot but he just might know which billeting officer was dealing with the children at Rugeley. Miss Carmichael didn't, but Flatterly is on the council and there is just a chance the billeting officer might have been employed by the council as well. If I draw a blank on this, I really think we will have to go to the police.'

'Yeah, I suppose so,' Nicholas said.

'I should get going if you want to see Richard Flatterly,' Rosie warned Meg. 'Time's getting on and some of those offices shut early.'

When Richard Flatterly saw Meg come in the door he said to the receptionist and his secretary, 'You two do the blackout and then you can go.'

'Yes, Mr Flatterly,' the two girls said, glad to be allowed to leave early.

When they had left, Flatterly led the way to his office and told Meg to have a seat opposite him on the other side of the desk. Immediately she told him why she was there. He seemed to find it immensely amusing that Meg Hallett should seek his help to find her missing siblings.

'But you were involved with the evacuation,' Meg said, puzzled.

Richard looked at her scornfully. 'The administration side of it, that was all. I didn't get involved with the actual children,' he said.

'But you must have known the billeting officer?'

Richard shook his head. 'I never had any need to know, and I never clapped eyes on her that day either. She had long gone, and the children chosen and off to their foster homes. Everything had seemed to run like clockwork.'

'Except for three children gone missing,' Meg said hotly.

'Look, I knew nothing about that until Kate saw your cousin in Rugeley,' Richard said. 'She hadn't told me there was any sort of problem because she didn't think there was then. If she had told me that they weren't in the billeting list earlier, I would have thought, as she

320

did, that they had returned home because they couldn't be housed together. They wouldn't be the only ones. Many of the kids didn't want to be evacuated anyway, and would seize on the first opportunity to go back home. How old were the children, anyway?'

'My sisters are eleven and nine and my brother is six,' Meg said.

'So your eldest sister should have been well able to see to the others, and Kate would have thought she had insisted on them going back home.'

'But nobody checked. That's what I can't get over.'

'Kate wrote to your stepmother.'

'And didn't it bother her that she didn't reply?'

'Apparently you had told her some rather unflattering things about your stepmother, and if she thought of it at all, she probably thought it wasn't in her nature to reply. But she probably didn't have time to think about it anyway, because she was run off her feet trying to meet the needs of the children and the people who took them in, and attempting to educate them at the same time.'

'I know all this,' Meg said impatiently. 'But however it was managed, three children have gone missing and no one seems to know a thing about it, or care either.'

'Well, if you were nicer to me,' Richard said insidiously, sidling round to where Meg was sitting, 'I could maybe see if I can find the name of that billeting officer,' and he slid his arms around her shoulders as he spoke.

'Get off me, you creep!' Meg cried, throwing his arms off as she leaped to her feet.

'The offer is there,' Richard replied tersely. 'I should think about it – if you care for those brats as much as you claim you do.'

He smiled mockingly, but she saw the tic beating in his temple and the flashing fire in his eyes and knew he was very angry. Her fury and frustration matched his, though, and she snapped out, 'I came to appeal to your better nature, but I see I have wasted my time – you obviously haven't got one. I think it's time the police took a hand in this.'

Flatterly definitely didn't want Meg to involve the police. Once they started sniffing around, no end of things could be uncovered and he wouldn't want them to look at him too closely. Suddenly he grabbed Meg's arm in a vice-like grip, so tightly that she yelped in pain as he said threateningly, 'I hardly think we need that sort of unpleasantness.'

'Let go of my arm,' Meg said, struggling to free herself, but it only made Richard hold tighter. 'You're hurting me,' she cried. 'Let me go.'

'Just so we understand each other,' Richard said, releasing her so quickly she staggered.

'Don't you dare lay a finger on me again,' she warned, as she stood rubbing the red weal he'd made on her arm.

'Or you'll do what exactly?' Richard demanded with a sneer. He smirked at her lasciviously as she fell silent. 'They could all be found safe and sound,' he said, eyeing her carefully.

'You don't know where they are,' Meg said. 'You would have said before.'

'And what if I do?' Flatterly asked, a self-satisfied smile on his face. 'What would you give to have them returned to you?'

Meg stared at him and felt revulsion flood through

her body and she said, more bravely than she felt, 'What if I was to tell Kate about this?'

'Go ahead,' Flatterly said. 'She won't believe you. I've already told her about the way you used to come on to me when I was collected the rent, flaunting yourself, offering yourself to get the rent reduced.'

'But . . . but that isn't true, none of it,' Meg said hotly, getting to her feet. 'Kate wouldn't believe that. She knows me.'

'Correction,' Richard said, crossing the room to stand in front of her, 'she *knew* you, and was very surprised you had turned into such a slut.'

Meg felt her heart plummet. She had thought Kate her ally and friend. She had noticed a coolness in her attitude, but put it down to her being busy and, as Joy had mentioned, it being a long time since she'd left school. That was true enough but she had thought there had been some rapport between them and felt saddened that it seemed to have been eroded away.

And now to find Flatterly had been blackening her name to Kate filled her with frustrated rage and while she was still collecting her thoughts he leaned forward so his face was inches away as he hissed threateningly, 'You whisper one word of this to Kate and I will say you came after me, seeking me out when you knew I would be alone and offering your body in exchange for information about those brats you have such feeling for. I would tell her how I had to fight off your advances. Who do you think she will believe?'

Meg felt her heart sinking for she knew who Kate would believe Flatterly over her any time. 'If you want to see those children again,' he went on 'I will do my best to help, but you know what you must do. In fact,' he said, pulling her towards him, 'we could start right now.'

Meg was transfixed with terror for a moment as she felt his whole body pressing into hers. She felt him harden, and when she felt his hand slide between them and start to undo his zip, she found the almost super-human strength to throw him from her and escape to the other side of the desk. She leaned on it, gasping, eyes desperately searching for the exit.

Flatterly was also a bit breathless but he fastened up his trousers and said, 'All right, I will not force you yet, though I could. But the time will come when you will be begging me to take what I want to save those kids. And by then,' he warned her with a smirk, 'the price might be higher. And don't forget,' he added, 'no police. All sorts of nasty things happen to children if police are involved.'

Meg was so frightened for her young sisters and little brother that she was finding it hard to draw breath. Richard saw this and it amused him. 'Think it over, my dear,' he said gloatingly. 'I'm sure you'll come to your senses in the end.'

TWENTY-ONE

Meg went back to her aunt Rosie's house for it had been decided that for her week's stay Rosie's son Dave could stay at Nicholas's house so Meg could have the attic. There was only Dave at home now because his older brother, Stan, had been called up as soon as he turned eighteen and was in the Royal Warwickshire's like her dad and Uncle Alec.

Robert had arrived from work. The meal was ready so Meg waited until they were seated round the table before she told them what had transpired in Flattery's office. She had thought to tell them an edited version, but in the end she decided that she had protected Flatterly long enough and they all sat agog: Rosie, Robert, Nicholas, Dave and even Terry, who'd come in during the telling. Eventually, aghast at Meg's words, Robert cried,

'You mean this man tried to . . . That he nearly—'

'If I hadn't managed to push him off, he would have raped me,' Meg stated simply. 'I knew that I was taking a chance because he showed his true colours that time he was collecting the rents.'

'What do you mean?'

Meg recounted the flirty and suggestive remarks that led to touching and then one day he had nearly got what he desired when he'd pushed his way into the house. 'But,' she said, 'Ruth bit him on the bum and caught him off balance and then he cracked his head on the wall which meant I was able to shove him into the street and close the door.'

'Well, well,' Robert said. 'Why didn't we hear about it? I'm surprised your father—'

'I never told Dad,' Meg said.

'Why not?'

'Think about it, Aunt Rosie. What would Dad have done if I had told him? He'd have decided Richard Flatterly needed teaching a lesson. Then the family would have been thrown out. How could I have had that on my conscience?'

'Dad could just as easily have done nothing at all about it,' Terry put in.

'Oh surely, Terry—'

'I bet Doris wouldn't have believed Meg's account of things.' Terry said 'And she's able to convince Dad that black's white.'

'I know that Doris influences him far too much,' Robert conceded. 'But surely not when it concerns a man's daughter? He knows what kind of girl Meg is.'

'I thought Kate Carmichael knew me,' Meg said bitterly. 'She taught me for years.'

Rosie well remembered the name Miss Carmichael that was seldom off Meg's lips.

'But now,' Meg continued, 'because she has a passion for Richard Flatterly, though she needs her head seeing to, she believes his version of events.'

'Her opinion don't matter,' Terry said, who hadn't a high regard for the teaching profession in general.

'It might not matter to you, Terry Hallett,' Meg said angrily. 'But it matters to me.'

'I can understand that,' Rosie said. 'It's horrible to be thought of so badly when there is no reason and you are unable to correct it.'

'And it reflects on the way I was brought up,' Meg said. 'I was so pleased when I went to Mass that Sunday and saw she was there too and living no distance away. It was like a link with home and I thought we might be able to meet up some time. But all she has eyes for now is Richard Flatterly, who drives up every weekend.'

'Drives?' Robert said. 'He doesn't use the train?'

'No. Why?'

'Just wondering where he gets his petrol from,' Robert mused. 'The ration is only three gallons a week, and even that can't be got at times.'

'Must have his own private tanker then,' Meg said. 'Because he has enough for the bus as well.'

'Bus?'

'Yeah, the Catholic kids are spread about, see, on isolated farms and places like that, so Flatterly and Kate collect them up for Mass on Sunday morning In this small bus she got hold of somewhere. Richard isn't a Catholic so he waits for her outside church.'

'Look,' Rosie said impatiently, 'it wouldn't surprise me at all to find Flatterly was buying black-market petrol. All things being equal, I'm sure by rights he should be in the Forces now. Amazing what money and influence can do. But far more important is what he said to Meg about the missing children. Do you think he knows where they are, Meg?'

'I'm not sure,' Meg admitted. 'At first it was like he really didn't know anything, and then he changed tack and said I had to be "nice" to him before he would tell me more.'

'The dirty swine . . .'

'I agree, Uncle,' Meg said. 'I have no trust in Flatterly, and yet he could have some knowledge or ways of finding out where they are.'

'We should go to the police.'

'I agree, but how can we with the threats against their safety that Flatterly made?'

'He was just bluffing.'

'Uncle Robert, I cannot gamble with the children's lives.'

'Well, Flatterly at least needs a trouncing for what he put you through,' Dave said.

'Yes, he does,' Meg agreed, 'but I don't want anything to happen to him.'

'Why not?' Nicholas said. 'No man should be able to get away with treating you so badly.'

'Maybe he shouldn't, but he's going to,' Meg said determinedly. 'If anything happens to him, it could impact on the children if he has any lead to them at all – never mind the fact that he is your landlord. He would have you out of these houses before you could say "Jack Flash".'

'Hitler might do that anyway if ever these bombs come hurtling from the sky, as people say will happen.'

'No need to pre-empt it, though,' Meg said. 'The streets are not too comfy this time of the year.'

328

No one was happy with that, and the three younger boys looked towards Robert, so they were disappointed when he sighed and said, 'Meg is right. No one is to lay a hand on Richard Flatterly. The risks are too great.'

Later that night, however, as they undressed for bed, Rosie said, 'You've got a very odd smile playing around your mouth. What are you thinking about?'

'I'm thinking,' said Robert, 'that there are more ways of killing a cat than drowning it.'

'What d'you mean?'

'You'll see in time,' said Robert maddeningly, but Rosie, try as she might, could get him to say nothing more.

That evening May called up at Rosie's to see Meg and Meg told her about the missing children and going to see Richard Flatterly to see if he could throw some light on where they could be.

'Is this Richard Flatterly the rent man we are talking about?' May asked.

'The very same.'

'Bet you got a great deal of help from him,' May said sarcastically. 'There's only one person Flatterly cares about, and that's himself. Wouldn't spit on a body afire in the gutter, that one. But God, how worrying to have the kiddies missing like that.'

'It is, May,' Meg said. 'No none seems to know where they are, and Ruth of course is lost to us for good. There is only me and Terry left and I am so bloody miserable.'

'I know, bab, I know,' May said, and put her comforting arms around Meg.

* * *

As her week's leave drew to a close, Rosie thought Meg might stay on in Birmingham and readily offered her a room with them and even offered to try and find her a job in the factory she worked in. Meg was grateful to her aunt for she thought a great deal of her and so she couldn't really admit to her how she longed for the week to speed past so that she could return to her friend Joy and the Heppleswaites who had made her so welcome on the farm, far away from Birmingham and its terrible memories. She wanted to go to bed; tired enough from physical work to sleep deeply without the nightmares that haunted her at night and took way her appetite.

She knew that Rosie and the others were all worried about her, but she couldn't assure them she was fine. She was filled with a sense of failure for her quest to find her missing siblings had come to nothing.

Years later, Meg was to remember that awful train journey back to the farm. Nicholas decided not to come back with the girls, and in a way Meg was glad it was just her, meeting Joy outside New Street Station early Monday morning as arranged. She was also very glad that they had a carriage to themselves. Joy looked at her friend's drawn face, which in the scant week in Birmingham seemed to have lost all its colour; it was as white as lint. Her cheeks were almost gaunt and her eyes looked quite desolate.

Joy touched Meg's arm. 'Tell me,' she said, and Meg told her of Doris's reaction to the missing children and of Richard Flatterly trying to rape her when she went to see him to see if he knew anything at all to help as he was supposed to be in charge of the evacuations from Birmingham.

'He couldn't,' she said. 'Or wouldn't and so I am no further forward in finding the children. And in the end, there is one person really to blame for all this and that is me. I shall feel guilty about letting them down for the rest of my days, because I put my needs before theirs and I shouldn't have done that.'

'You're far too hard on yourself,' Joy said, and Meg suddenly looked so immeasurably sad that the tears trickled from Joy's eyes too and, as the two girls held each other tight, their tears mingled together.

Will was waiting for them at the station with the horse and cart. His weather-beaten face broke into a wide smile as he saw the girls alight from the train. For his sake they attempted a smile back, but Will wasn't fooled; he was also concerned by the lines of strain on Meg's pale face and the forlorn look in her eyes. He said nothing about it, for he left that side of things to Enid, whom he knew had been concerned as to what Meg might find on her first visit home.

He lifted up the girls' cases as if they weighed nothing at all and tossed them into the cart, saying, as he did so, 'By, you two are a sight for sore eyes and no mistake. Place hasn't been the same without you pair to liven it up, but Stephen arrived home a few days ago for a short spot of leave so that bucked Enid up a bit. Like a dog with two tails she was.'

Meg felt her heart quicken 'Is Stephen still here?' she asked.

Will nodded. 'Till the day after tomorrow. He's looking

forward to seeing you again and he was very impressed when he saw that field we reclaimed . . . Anyway, Enid thinks you never get fed properly in them cities so she has made a rich beef casserole and one of her special apple pies to celebrate your coming back.'

Meg hadn't eaten properly for days and even the thought of food made her feel sick. So she truly hoped she could at least make a stab at the food Enid had taken such trouble over.

Joy, watching her face, covered the silence that could have become embarrassing by saying, 'Oh, lovely, Will. And Enid is right in a way, because although there is probably enough food in the city – or at least till rationing comes in – it just doesn't taste the same.'

It was just the right thing to say, and Will had a big grin on his face as he jiggled the reins. 'Come on then, Dobbin.'

'Oh, I don't know why you are bothering, Will,' Joy said. 'Dobbin has two speeds, slow and stop.'

Will gave a wheezy laugh. 'You're right there, lass. When all's said and done, we'll get home eventually and nothing's spoiling, but I know two people who will be impatient to see you both.'

Enid was impatient and excited, but her smile of welcome faded a little when the girls came in the kitchen door and she turned from the range and caught sight of Meg's face. Her heart contracted, and so did Stephen's, for Meg looked so wretched and unhappy. He knew her so much better now, because of the letters they had exchanged in which they had both found that many more things can be committed to paper than can be said face to face. He thought her a wonderful girl with

332

a heart big enough to encompass the whole world. He would have been happy for just a small part of it and, young though she was, he had been determined to speak to her, but seeing her suffering, he wondered if now was the time.

She managed a watery smile for him as he helped her off with her coat and she said, 'In your last letter you never mentioned leave.'

'Because I didn't know,' Stephen said in that lovely musical voice she had loved from when she first met him. He pulled a chair out for her at the table as he went on 'It was a spur-of-the-moment thing, as they so often are. As soon as I was told, because you had told me you were going to be in Birmingham, I sent a letter to the house.'

'I never got any letter,' Meg said. 'I was staying with my aunt.'

'Does she live far away?'

'No, no distance at all. Doris could have come up with it or, failing that, sent word and I would have called in for it.'

'So you had no idea I had written?'

'No,' Meg said. And that doesn't surprise me, but I would have come home sooner if I'd known.'

'That stepmother of yours wants locking up, if you ask me,' Enid said as she put a steaming casserole on the table and Joy followed behind with a bowl of buttered potatoes. 'Your house was the only address I had for you, see. You'd think she'd have said.'

'Yes, wouldn't you?' Meg said. 'Like any normal human being might. But she doesn't operate using ordinary rules.'

'Anyway, you're here now,' Will said. 'And that's all matters. Let's eat while the food is hot. Can't have good food going to waste.'

Stephen noticed straight away that Meg, who had once had quite a voracious appetite, was just pushing the large helping of casserole his mother had served around her plate. She made no attempt to eat it and took no potatoes at all.

Just the sight of the food on the plate made nausea rise in Meg's throat. Joy ate hers with gusto and said it was delicious, but Meg said nothing. Her head was down and her eyes seemed fastened on her plate, and Joy wondered if she was crying. She felt a well of sympathy fill up inside her as Enid said gently, 'Can't you eat a wee bit of it, Meg? You definitely need more meat on your bones.'

Meg lifted her eyes, brimming with tears. She shook her head and her voice was little above a whisper: 'I'm so sorry.'

'Don't be sorry,' Enid said. 'For it's obvious something ails you. Have you been ill?'

'Not ill,' Meg said. 'Just very sad.'

Joy was well aware Meg was near to breaking point. She said, 'Meg, would you like me to tell Will and Enid and Stephen what happened to you in Birmingham?' and she wasn't surprised when Meg nodded. But Meg, unable to bear hearing about it again, left the table and slipped out of the door, glad of the chance to be alone.

It was a while later before Stephen came to find her. He was overwhelmed with sympathy for what she had gone through and that is what he said when he found her in the orchard among the sweet-smelling trees. His words seemed to open the floodgates, and his arms went around her as she cried as if it was the most natural thing in the world.

Meg felt strangely comforted and she cried out against all that had happened to her and, more importantly, to her sisters and little brother. 'I can't help feeling that it's all my fault really,' she said at last, though she felt no desire to move out of Stephen's embrace.

'How could it be?' Stephen asked.

'Well you know Mom put them in my charge.'

'And when you mother did that she had no idea that there was going to be a war,' Stephen said. 'Nor that in the event, parents in industrial cities were advised to send their children to safer locations.'

'No, I suppose not.'

'Well, it was your father who signed for the children to be evacuated,' Stephen said. 'So you couldn't have done anything to stop it. And even if you stayed in Birmingham you wouldn't have known they had disappeared. Joy told me of your old teacher who is here with evacuated children and how she bumped into your cousin, Nicholas, and it wasn't until they talked together that anyone realised there was any sort of problem.'

'There were the postcards,' Meg said. 'I would have known if no postcards had come.'

'Would you?' Stephen said. 'Or would you just assume that your stepmother wouldn't tell you. She didn't let you know I had sent a letter.'

'Nor did she give Dad my address when he was called up,' Meg said. 'He wanted to say goodbye, Nicholas told me, but Doris said he said she didn't know where I was.'

'And she did?'

'Course,' Meg said. 'As soon as it was official that we were staying here I sent her the address to send to the children. So I suppose you're right. If she said she hadn't received the postcards, my immediate thought would be that she was lying and I might think she kept details of where the children were to stop Dad seeing them. I'd think of all that before I'd think of them going missing.'

'So you see,' Stephen said and he squeezed her a little tighter as he went on, 'None of this can be your fault. It is really worrying that you don't know what's happened to your brother and sisters, but you must stop blaming yourself.'

Meg lay back against Stephen. Nothing had altered, Stephen had no magic wand to change anything and yet she felt comforted and felt the guilt that seemed lodged in her heart lessen.

'It seems quite amazing that we can talk together like this when we haven't know each other that long,' she said at last.

'Do you still think that?' Stephen asked. 'I feel I have got to know you so much better through your letters and I love it that you are so open and honest too, so I will be and tell you from the heart that I love everything about you.' Meg struggled from his arms and he held her hands as she stared at him, 'You do?'

'I do,' Stephen said. 'You must know how I feel about you?'

Meg remembered Joy claiming that Stephen was sweet on her. She had refuted it at the time and wasn't absolutely sure that things between them had changed that much. So she said tentatively. 'I think . . . I mean I know you like me.'

'*Like* be damned.' Stephen said. 'I love you.'

Meg gazed at him in stupefaction and Stephen said, 'You have stolen away quite a large chunk of my heart, Meg. There are not many minutes of the day when I don't think of you. You have even got between me and my sleep.' He sighed and went on, 'I wasn't going to speak of this today because you are very young and vulnerable at the moment. But they say this leave is embarkation leave and so I may not get another chance.'

Meg hadn't spoken, As she looked into Stephen's eyes it seemed as if the scales had fallen from her own and she felt her heart swell with love for him. Stephen however thought she was silent because he had spoken words she had never expected to hear. He berated himself inwardly for being a fool. He had frightened the girl – and small wonder – and so he said, 'I'm sorry. Meg, please forgive me and forget anything I said.'

'Why? Didn't you mean it?'

'Oh, I did, every word but . . .'

'I . . . I don't know much about love, love like this between a man and a woman,' Meg said hesitantly. 'I only know that my heart is jumping all over the place and I really think I love you too, Stephen Heppleswaite.'

'Oh, my darling girl,' Stephen cried in delight, 'That will more than do to be going on with.' He caught her up in his arms and kissed her, Meg had never been kissed in that way and she sighed in contentment and Stephen smiled at her as he said 'Shall we go in now before they send out a search party for us?'

'Yes, I think we had better.'

Everyone in the kitchen knew that something special had happened between the two young people who came in hand in hand, but Enid couldn't blame her son for telling Meg how he felt. She knew that a week's leave wasn't given lightly so she was pretty sure it was embarkation leave. However, remembering what Joy had said had happened to Meg in Birmingham, she did say, 'You didn't have to come back, Meg, not if you weren't up to it. You could have stayed on, claimed compassionate leave. We'd have understood that you needed to be with your own folk.'

'I wanted to be back here where I feel I am doing something useful and working really hard so that I can sleep,' Meg replied. 'I've not done much of that lately.'

'Nor eat, neither,' Enid said.

'Sorry,' said Meg.

'Nothing to be sorry for,' Enid said. 'But we have a hefty afternoon of apple picking in front of us and you'll not perform at all well on an empty stomach. Do you think you could have a bit of apple pie and custard?'

Meg nodded. 'Yes, I think I could manage that,' she said determinedly.

'Good,' Enid said. 'I did the plums and damsons while you were away and made a bit of jam, but the apple trees are heavy with fruit just now. And so apple picking is what we will be at next.

TWENTY-TWO

Meg and Joy thoroughly enjoyed apple picking, even the teetering on ladders to reach the upper branches of the fragrant trees. Everyone helped – Will and Stephen too – and they were taking over the milking so the girls didn't have to break off their work in the orchard.

The girls soon found that apple picking wasn't as straightforward as they had imagined. The different kinds of apples were earmarked for certain things, as Enid explained as she led the way to the orchard that afternoon. Will and Stephen carried ladders while she carried numerous hessian sacks, and the girls a selection of wicker baskets. 'There are some cider apples, which we'll pick first,' she told the girls, weaving between the trees, 'as they are grouped together at the back end. There are lots of them,' Enid went on. 'You two love a glass of cider, don't you?' she asked the men.

They nodded enthusiastically. 'Not half,' said Will. 'We make a big batch every autumn.'

'I'm right glad you are here,' Enid told the girls, 'because I think my days of mounting ladders are over – though to be honest I was never one for heights anyway, but the men can't do everything.'

There were dozens of trees in the hollow facing them, some of the branches bowed down with the weight of the fruit, the windfalls liberally littering the ground, mixed in with the fallen leaves.

As the afternoon wore on, Enid fetched Dobbin attached to a small cart, and as each sack was filled, they were loaded onto the cart for Dobbin to pull to the barn where the cider press was kept.

Full darkness had fallen by the time they had stripped all the cider apples from the trees. 'Tomorrow, we shall have the whole day at it,' Enid said with satisfaction as they made their way back to the farmhouse. 'Get a lot done then.'

Later than night, in bed, Will said to Enid, 'Shocking tale young Joy told us about Meg earlier.'

'Dreadful.'

'I knew it was terrible what happened to the young one, and it must be hard for Meg to be parted from her with such finality, but she at least knows she's safe.'

'You thinking of the others?'

'Don't tell me it hasn't crossed your mind?'

''Course it has.'

'Point is, I know the threats that man Flatterly made so that she wouldn't go to the police, but I think he was bluffing.'

'What if he wasn't, though?'

'We can tell the police about his threats,' Will said. 'I talked it over with Stephen earlier. He said that something must be done as well. He thinks it's monstrous that three children have just disappeared and that it's small wonder Meg is in a state. She is troubled; you can see it in her eyes though she is working as well as ever. I think our lad cares a great deal for that young lady.'

'I know he does,' Enid said. 'They are both young, but we are at war and Stephen is in the army so they haven't time to hang about . . .'

'You think there is some understanding between them?'

'I wouldn't be a bit surprised.'

'And how would you feel about that?'

'Couldn't be more pleased.' Enid said. 'I would really get the daughter I've always wanted. But just now I want to help her find her family.'

'And me,' Will said. 'I have been fretting about it all afternoon and evening even before Stephen spoke to me.'

'And he thinks we should go to the police?'

'He thinks it's the only thing to do.' Will said. 'He would go himself but he is off the day after tomorrow. The point is if we do nothing I'll feel we are abandoning these young children, and anyway Stephen said we might be in trouble with the police ourselves if we don't tell them.' Enid looked at Will with fear-filled eyes. She'd never been in the slightest trouble with the police and didn't want to be now. Yet she said, 'Meg has just been coming to terms with this herself. Wait till Stephen has gone back and she has settled back on the farm – where she seems at her happiest anyway – and we will talk to her.'

The next day when Meg woke she told herself that there was to be no sadness that day for it was Stephen's last for some time and she pushed all her concerns to the back of her mind, determined that he should leave with happy memories. They had agreed the night before to milk the cows together to get that job out of the way, so the first time they met was in the cowshed and when Stephen smiled over at Meg she felt her stomach give a lurch. She blushed as he smiled back and had she but known it, that flush to her face made her look prettier than ever,

Will looked from one to the other and then glanced over to Joy with a grin and a slight shrug. Meg was unaware of this for she had eyes only for Stephen until Joy said. 'Come on you two love birds there are cows to milk.'

Seeing how it was between Stephen and Meg and knowing the limited time they would have together, Will directed them both to take the cows back to the field while he and Joy cleaned out the byre. As they walked down the lane hand in hand behind the lumbering cows, Meg said, 'I'd like to stop time. You know, just this one day, because when this day is gone I may not see you for ages.'

'I know,' Stephen said. 'Some of the chaps say it's mad to get involved with girls when there is a war on. That it's best to love them and leave them.'

'Oh, that's a horrid way to think and treat people.'

'Oh, I agree and you need have no worries about me,' Stephen said. 'I am a one-woman-bloke and that woman is you and I think I knew that really the first day I saw you.'

'Is that why you asked me to write to you?'

'Yes,' Stephen admitted. 'I knew you weren't ready to see me as any other than a friend.'

'I'm ready now. Stephen,' Meg said. 'I love you and

in a way wish I didn't because I will worry about you even more.'

They had reached the cow's field and Stephen didn't speak until every cow was in the field and the gate secured, then he said to Meg, 'I'm sorry I know I am laying another burden of worry on your shoulders and I can do nothing to lessen it but I would like to leave you something to remember me by.'

He held out his arms and she went into them willingly and he kissed her again. This time however it was a proper kiss that sent the blood pulsating in Meg's veins and engendered strange sensations to rise in her body and when they eventually broke apart she was breathless and her cheeks were pinker than usual. 'Oh, Stephen.'

'Oh Meg,' Stephen said. 'How I wish I could spirit you off for the day.'

'Me too,' Meg said with a rueful smile. 'But we have the apples to pick.'

'Ah yes. We have the apples to pick,' Stephen repeated and they went back to the farmhouse hand in hand.

They picked apples all day and yet it didn't seem such an onerous task for though the day was cold there was no wind. It did Enid's heart good to see how easy Stephen and Meg were with each other as she saw them laughing together and teasing one another and she sent a silent prayer that they were going to have some sort of future together some day when this dreadful war was at an end.

Stephen was leaving the next day, but the girls were up anyway, helping Will with the cows. Stephen had arranged for an army truck to pick him up at the head of the lane and Meg felt her stomach give a lurch as she heard the rumble of it on the road. Stephen put his arms around Joy and his mother, who was trying not to weep, and his father clapped him on the shoulder, his voice was very gruff as he bid him farewell. Then he hoisted his kitbag on his shoulder and caught up Meg's hand and together they walked up the lane. Before he got into the truck he took Meg in his arms and gently kissed her on the lips. 'Goodbye my dearest Meg'

Meg's stomach felt as if it had a lead weight inside it and tears sprang to her eyes but she wouldn't let them fall as she said, 'Oh please take care, Stephen. Don't try to be a hero. I love you and I want you to come home to me.'

'I love you too,' Stephen said. 'And I promise that I will take no more risks than I have to as a serving soldier. 'Write to me often and let me know that I'm not forgotten.'

'As if,' Meg with a watery smile.

'Are you getting in this truck or not?' the driver called out.

'I'm coming.' Stephen said. 'But you can't expect me to rush when I am leaving someone precious behind.'

And with that he kissed Meg on the cheek and swung himself up in the truck with the other returning soldiers who began ribbing him about keeping them waiting. Meg shed tears as she walked back down the lane, but by the time she reached the farmhouse she had rubbed all signs of tears from her face, though she knew like his parents she would miss and worry about Stephen every minute of the day.

*　　*　　*

It took another full day for the apples all to be collected and the following day they were sorted. Some went to make jam; a lot of cooking apples were to be dried and put into jars in the larder – 'So they are there and handy if I want to make a pie or a crumble,' Enid told the girls.

Other cooking apples were peeled and sliced into rings – the cores as well – because Enid said the apples dried better that way, and then each slice was dipped into a solution of water and coarse salt to stop them going brown before they were threaded through with string and hung from the rafters in the barn.

The girls helped Enid with this and then, as they returned to the kitchen, Joy said, 'There's still a fair few left.'

'They are stored in special dimpled trays,' Enid said, fetching them from a large cupboard in the kitchen. 'Every apple has to be checked – one bad apple will send the whole lot bad in short order – and straw must be laid between each line of apples so no apple will touch another. When we are done they will be stored in the hay loft.'

'It's a different world, isn't it?' Joy said, as she and Meg prepared for bed that night. 'All this work provides cider, jam, the makings of pies and apples to eat, whereas in Birmingham we would just buy things from the shops.'

'I know,' Meg said. 'I think it makes you appreciate the food more, somehow.'

'Oh, definitely,' Joy said.

'Well, that's the apple picking all over for us,' Meg said. 'You heard what Will said at dinner. He wants us in the fields tomorrow, picking the root veg before the frost comes and destroys it all and the ground's too hard to plough.'

'Yes,' Joy said. 'And I'd say we have to go quick because the autumn has come in with a vengeance. There is a definite nip in the air in the morning.'

'And at night,' Meg added. 'Just at the moment I am perishing, so are you going to get into bed or what?'

'What?' said Joy, and lobbed a pillow at Meg and a giggle escaped from her.

Joy caught sight of her face and she said, 'It isn't a crime to laugh, Meg.' Joy said

'How will it help if you are miserable?. Come on, you're right, it's more than just cold. Let's go to bed.'

Meg was glad enough to snuggle down but was almost afraid to go to sleep, and when she eventually did, her sleep was threaded through with nightmares.

While Meg and Joy might think apple picking one of the nicest jobs on the farm, harvesting the autumn root vegetables had to be one of the worst. It was back-breaking work, and cold following behind the reaper pulled by the horse and scrabbling in the dank, moist earth for the beetroot, which had to be lifted first before any frost could get to it.

No one returned to the farmhouse till milking time, but Enid would come out mid-morning with flasks of hot tea and jam spread liberally on slices of her lovely bread. Dinner could be hot baked potatoes, slices of cheese or ham or hard-boiled eggs and some sort of pudding, and before they stopped to get the cows she would come out again with tea. Meg was immensely grateful, as was Joy, for they knew from talking to other Land Army girls that many employers weren't as considerate as theirs.

However, the only time that Meg's hands were warm was when they were clasped around the warm cups. This wasn't a job you could do so well in gloves, and each night when she went into the farmhouse, her hands and stockinged feet would throb as the feeling came back into them.

Day after day it went on, each morning colder than the one that went before, and yet each morning they knew how important the work was, Britain was losing merchant ships on a daily or sometimes twice-daily basis; for each one sunk, as well as the tragedy of sailors losing their lives, there was the loss of vital food stuffs and important materials . . Twelve merchant ships had been lost by the time the HMS *Royal Oak* was torpedoed on 14 October.

They were all upset but it galvanised the girls to work even harder, knowing that with all the stuff not getting through, what they were doing was vital work. They were struggling with the field of sugar beet then carrots, turnips, swede, onions and potatoes to be gathered in. They never complained about their aches and pains to Will as it would have done no good, but they moaned a bit when they were in bed at night.

'I mean, I don't think human beings are meant to bend and straighten as often as we're expected to,' Joy said. 'We're not made that way.'

'I do sometimes feel that I am going to snap in the middle,' Meg confessed.

'I know my back is aching so much that sometimes

I think I won't be able to straighten it at the end of the row,' Joy complained.

'Or if we manage to straighten up, we won't be able to bend again to do the next one,' Meg agreed.

The weather didn't help. The biting wind alone was bad enough, but when that wind drove rain from leaden grey skies to lash into the girls like stair rods and they were forced to hunt in slurried mud for the vegetables, then it was sheer misery. In a way, though, Meg was glad of the gruelling schedule. The days were busy enough to keep the thoughts of the missing children and worries about Stephen at bay and at night she was tired enough to fall into a deep and often dreamless sleep.

Will's respect for the girls strengthened as October came to a close and November began, which was initially even wetter than October. As he said to Enid, 'That relentless rain and cold would sap the heart out of anyone, and yet they toil on regardless.'

'Not for much longer, though, surely?'

'No,' Will said. 'They're on the last furrows. Another couple of days should do it.'

'When Meg's finished the harvest, you must tell her what you did.'

'There's nothing to tell, is there, though?' Will said. 'Don't see the point of upsetting her for nothing.'

Although Will and Enid had had no business with the police, they knew Fred Pearce, the village bobby in Penkridge, very well. He had been at school with Will, and his eldest son, Luke, had been one of the farm hands who had been called up with Stephen. So without a word to Meg, on their weekly trip to Penkridge to charge up the accumulator, the first Saturday after the girls' return home, he'd left them to their own devices and had called in to see Fred unofficially. He told him as much as he thought he needed to know.

'It's the safety of the children I am concerned about, and this man Flatterly.'

As soon as he mentioned the name, he saw Fred stiffen. 'What is it?'

'You mean Richard Flatterly?'

'Yes. Do you know him?'

'I know of him. Some bigwig in the council,' Fred said. 'Be difficult to find anything about him without him knowing, and if he was to make a complaint about me,' Fred drew a finger across his neck, 'I'd be for the high jump all right.'

'Look, Fred, that's all very well,' said Will. 'But no one should be above the law, and these are young children we are talking about.'

'From what you told me, your land girl didn't think he had anything to do with them at first.'

'No,' Will had to admit. 'He arrived after it was all over and all the children ticked off and sent to their foster homes, but then he claimed he would tell her more if she was "nice" to him.'

'She rebuffed him, I presume?'

'Of course she did,' Will snapped. 'I told you: she isn't that kind of girl at all.'

'Well, I would guess he knows nothing and just has a fancy for your girl.'

'According to Meg, it's the schoolteacher he has a fancy for.'

Fred shrugged. 'Some men are like that. As long as

349

he doesn't try and marry the two, I can't arrest him for that.'

'There's still three children missing.'

'Yes, I grant you that is worrying. But these evacuees, you know, a right headache they are giving us, taking off for home at the slightest provocation.'

'Meg is recently back from Birmingham and they're not back there.'

'Fair enough, Will, I will pass the word around, especially to the police in Rugeley, seeing as that is where they went missing from,' Fred promised. 'And to put your mind at rest, I will make discreet enquiries about Flatterly – but they will have to be very discreet – and see if I come up with anything. But don't hold your breath.'

So far Fred had come up with precisely nothing, no sign of the children, and he had found out nothing nefarious about Flatterly either. As one wet day followed another, Will couldn't help feeling that if it was bad for his land girls, it could be far worse for three missing children.

It was hard, too, for the British Expeditionary Force, which set off for France in the biting wind and the icy rain. The Royal Staffordshire Fusiliers and the Royal Warwickshire Fusiliers were part of that force.

TWENTY-THREE

With the harvest safely gathered, and much of the surplus sold off in the markets, along with the excess eggs and butter, the work on the farm got a little easier, though not necessarily so pleasant: one of the first jobs was muck-spreading. That involved transferring manure from the pile behind the farmhouse to the fields via Dobbin and a muck cart, and then after it was laid all along the rows, it had to be dug in through the soil so that it would be ready for planting in the spring. It took some time and it didn't help that the ground was rock solid, for now frost often gilded the hedges and trees, reminding them all that winter was not far away.

There were still the cows to milk twice a day and feed with hay, since the grass was sparse and frost-rimed. Now that the piglets were no longer feeding from the mother, Will moved them to an enclosure at the side of the farmhouse, where the bracken was too dense to plant anything. 'Pigs will love it,' Will assured Meg, and they did seem to; the girls watched the powerful snout of the mother grubbing up the soil.

'What's she doing?'

'Searching for roots and bulbs and insects,' Will said. 'She will feed them to the babies but in a few days they will be digging their own.'

'So don't you have to feed them when they are in there?' Joy asked.

'Oh, yes, they'll still have their pigswill. After all, have you ever seen a thin pig?'

'Honestly, Will,' Joy said, 'till I came here I'd never seen a pig, not close up, like. It isn't something we have a great deal of in the streets of Birmingham.'

Will let out a bellow of laughter. 'I suppose not,' he said. 'Well, this little lady still gets her pigswill.'

So there were still the pigs to feed, and the dogs, and the corn to scatter for the hens and the eggs to collect. And this was the time of year when all the fences had to be inspected and repaired if necessary, and the well had to be cleaned because it usually got partially blocked with leaves in the autumn.

One day Will came in to breakfast, after leaving the churns at the head of the lane, carrying a pile of post. He distributed the post as he said, 'How do you two feel about creosoting the barn and byre today?'

'All right, I suppose,' Joy said. 'If you trust us.'

'You've never let me down yet,' Will said. 'Anyway, it's a case of needs must. The postman was telling me that they are lopping trees in Cannock Chase, so I fancy taking the horse and cart and getting a few logs for the winter. You be all right with that?'

''Course,' Meg and Joy said together.

With a little thrill of excitement, Meg noted one of the letters was from Stephen and she put it with the others and slipped them into her dungarees pocket for reading later.

'One thing about this Land Army,' Joy said, as they started on the fence, 'is that it's harder work than I imagined, though the food is good and gives you energy. But it does mean we've had the chance to do lots of things we've never done before.'

'Yeah,' Meg agreed. 'We would never have had these experiences without the war – and yet it seems to be wrong to feel pleased about something so horrible.'

'I know what you mean,' Joy said. 'And even though some people are calling it "The Bore War", saying nothing's happening, we know about the ships sunk and the sailors losing their lives trying to bring food and other supplies in. Anyway, I suppose we need to get on. I'd like this finished by the time Will gets back.'

'Don't think you need worry too much,' Meg said. 'Enid said that Will might be some time, that it's a fair distance.'

'Well, anywhere's a fair distance, the pace Dobbin goes at,' Joy pointed out, and Meg, laughing, had to agree.

Enid was right. It was afternoon before Dobbin came clopping down the lane, pulling behind him a cart laden down with thick branches The girls unloaded it all before unshackling the cart and dealing with the horse, while Will ate the dinner Enid had kept back for him.

After Will had eaten, they tackled the wood together, Will chopping the branches down with an axe and the girls using a two-handled saw to turn them into manageable logs. The air was icy, with a keen, biting wind, and yet the sweat ran from them and though their hands were blistered, at the end of it, the woodshed was full.

That night Meg was writing letters to go with the Christmas cards she had bought in Penkridge the Saturday before. There were not that many of them to send: one each to her dad and Terry, her aunt Susan and Nicholas, her uncle Robert and Aunt Rosie, one to May, and an especially nice one for Stephen. She hadn't felt right contacting her American relations, because when she wrote to tell them that her father and Doris were getting married, though nothing was said, their responses were stiff with disapproval.

Meg never felt able to write again, and though she was sorry to lose the link with her mother, she was glad in one way, because they would think it odd if she were writing that she didn't mention the children, especially as previously her letters had been full of them and especially the cute things Ruth said and did.

That night, as they undressed Joy said. 'One thing bothers me, if you don't want to tell your dad what's being going on, what the devil do you write to him about?'

'Here,' Meg said. 'The sort of things we do and that.'

'Doesn't he find it odd that you never mention your brothers and sisters?'

'Don't think so. He doesn't say so,' Meg said. 'He asked at first if I'd seen them, but when I said that I hadn't that much time off, he sort of accepted it.'

'And what do you write to lover boy about?' Joy said with a grin.

'If you mean Stephen, I will say that it's none of your business,' Meg grinned back.

354

'He writes reams to you.'

Joy was right, he did. She felt she was really getting to know him well, and she was telling him some of her innermost thoughts too. But she wasn't sharing the details with her friend. There were some things not for sharing.

It was a pleasure to go into kitchen those days in December, the spicy smells rising in the air as Enid prepared for the festive season. The cake had been made weeks before and Enid had said ruefully she couldn't get the fruit she had put in the Christmas cake other years because it just wasn't in the shops, so she had added lots of diced carrot for sweetness. But she had poked lots of holes on it and poured sherry over it at regular intervals. The smell of it was so pungent and alcoholic that Meg reckoned she could eat by the spoonful.

Enid's sister, Lily, was coming for Christmas, as her evacuees had gone home, Enid told the girls as she called them in for a stir of the pudding on Christmas Eve.

Meg wasn't surprised. 'They must be some of the last to leave,' she said. 'Just lately, every Saturday in Penkridge, there seem to be fewer and fewer evacuees running about.'

'Are Lily's coming back after Christmas?' Joy asked.

'Lily thinks not,' Enid said. 'Really she said they all hankered after Liverpool and missed their mother and their friends and their lives really, I suppose. I'm a bit sorry they left because they helped Lily come out of her shell and be a bit more sociable. Anyway I'm glad she is here for Christmas.'

'I'm glad, too,' Joy said. 'I do like her . . . Oh, but the smell of that cake is tantalising me.'

'Well, the top goes on tomorrow,' Enid said. 'If rationing comes in it might be among the last cakes I'll make – certainly one of the last I'll ice. I'll have to be careful with my sugar so had to make mock marzipan from haricot beans and ground rice, so I hope it tastes all right.'

'Haricot beans and ground rice!' both girls chorused, grinning.

'Yes, and a bit of sugar and marg,' Enid said. 'It was a tip on *Kitchen Front* – you know – that comes after the eight o'clock news on the wireless. There was no marzipan to be had, not for love nor money, so it was that or nothing, I hope it doesn't taste too bad.'

'We can take it off if it's awful,' Joy said.

'Doubt we'll notice if it's got icing on top as well,' Meg said.

'Well that's it, you see,' Enid said. 'I haven't got enough sugar for proper royal icing. I'll just put a skimmed layer over.'

'Stop talking about the icing,' Joy said. 'It's the cake that matters.'

Enid laughed. 'Go on,' she said. 'Will is waiting on you and you have the pudding well stirred anyway. Just make sure you have made your wishes.'

Meg made her wish, and both Joy and Enid knew what she would wish for. For all the good it will do, Meg thought to herself as she made her way to the byre. I am no longer a child believing in miracles.

Despite the fact that there would still be cows to milk on Christmas Day, they all elected to go to Midnight

Mass, even Joy. There had been a flurry of snow early on, but it was dry when they climbed into Will's cart, the stars twinkling in the inky black sky, though there was no moon visible. It was incredibly cold, and Meg and Joy were glad of their thick overcoats, which kept the life in them on the short journey to Penkridge.

Meg loved Midnight Mass at Christmas. It always seemed such a marvellous, almost magical time. As they approached the church porch, she heard the organist playing carols softly, the age-old traditional tunes that had been sung for generations. And then she opened the door and stepped into the church. Dark green holly with its bright red berries, interlaced with trailing ivy, festooned the walls. Two large vases filled with white Christmas roses stood either side of the altar, and to one side of them was the crib surrounded by winter primroses; the other side of them stood the large tree with the star on top, bedecked with candles.

Even the priest looked impressive, his white satin vestments decorated with gold embroidery, which sparkled in the light of the flickering candles. He was attended by four small boys dressed in red under sparkling white surplices.

Then the peace that had begun to steal over Meg fled instantly as, just two rows in front of her, she saw Kate Carmichael and Richard Flatterly. Meg turned and would have moved to another pew, but everyone had followed her in and they wouldn't be able to leave without making a commotion, so she knew she had to stay put.

However, instead of attending to the Mass, she again went over every word that Flatterly had said to her in

Birmingham. She knew he had effectively blackened her name with Kate, and she had felt so bitterly ashamed of what she must think of her that she had avoided her every Sunday since. On the rare occasion they had come close to one another, Kate had made it abundantly clear she wanted no friendship with Meg, and if she acknowledged her at all it was with just a slight incline of the head.

This had been incredibly hurtful to Meg at first, and she couldn't understand why Kate could believe such lies from Flatterly so easily. But though he made her skin crawl, she imagined he could be very persuasive if he chose; Kate would also want to believe him because she cared for him – Meg noted that they held hands when they stood up.

She had almost decided not to take communion to avoid passing them when she returned to her seat, but she knew not to take communion on Christmas Day would totally shock Will and Enid and she had no desire to do that. And so she filed out with the others. Though she kept her head lowered as she returned to her seat, she felt Richard's eyes boring into her.

She was glad when the Mass was over and that Will – aware of the little time they'd have in bed – didn't linger. Dobbin clopped his way through the still night at quite a brisk pace for him.

'I think the cold's getting to Dobbin too,' Enid said.

'Yeah,' Will agreed. 'Probably fantasising about a relatively warm stable and a feed of hay.'

'Don't blame him,' Joy laughed. 'But I'll pass on the hay, if you don't mind. I'd rather have some of that delicious-looking broth I saw Enid making today.'

'Me too,' Meg put in.

'Put new heart into you, that will,' Enid said. 'I knew we would all be hungry, not eating before – and you had nothing either, Joy.'

Joy shrugged. 'Seemed mean of me to eat when you couldn't.'

'Well, we'll soon have something inside us,' Enid said. 'It's just to heat up. I usually do something like this if we go to Midnight Mass. A body needs something that sticks to the ribs in this weather, I think.'

Meg was hungry – starving, in fact – and so was Joy, but neither girl was used to late nights any more and Meg felt almost too tired to eat, though even the smell of the broth put in front of her was so flavoursome it made her feel almost light-headed.

'Force yourself,' Will said, seeing Meg's eyes closing in spite of herself. 'You'll not sleep well on an empty stomach and I don't want you passing out on the floor of the byre in the morning.'

Meg knew what Will said made sense and she half roused herself. 'I'll do my best,' she said.

'And so will I,' Joy said. 'Just at the moment, though, I feel I could sleep on a clothes line.'

Even Meg slept too deeply that night to dream, but still the alarm seemed to go off remarkably early and she stumbled around the room getting dressed, disorientated and clumsy. The two weary girls met Will in the byre. He looked as fit as a fiddle and he laughed, but gently, at the girls' tired faces.

'Doesn't it bother you what time you go to bed?' Meg asked him.

'Not once in a while it doesn't,' Will said. 'I have

been doing this for so long now that my body clock wakes me up the same time whatever hour I go to bed. 'Course, wouldn't like to do it for a long time or anything. Best thing is to get these cows sorted and back in the fields and the byre cleaned as quick as we can because breakfast will revive your spirits.'

After breakfast, as Will drove the horse and cart into Penkridge to fetch Lily, the girls released the dogs from the barn and fed them, let out the chickens and scattered corn for them while they collected the eggs, encouraged the sow and piglets into their enclosure and poured swill into the shallow bath. When they eventually returned to the house, Enid had tidied away all the dishes from breakfast and was well on with preparing the Christmas dinner.

She refused all offers of help, saying she thought the girls had done enough, and so they went up to their room to fetch the presents they had bought. As Will was having his after-dinner smoke using a rackety old pipe that was falling to pieces, they'd bought him a new one. And then Enid said how he loved a cigar at Christmas, so they'd bought him a box of those too, and chocolates and a fluffy blue cardigan for Enid. They bought chocolates for Lily, too, not wanting to leave her out, but not knowing her well enough to get her something more personal.

Will, Enid and Lily were all stunned by the girls' generosity, though both Will and Enid said they shouldn't have spent their hard-earned money.

'You let us keep a goodly portion of what you give us in wages,' Meg said. 'More than most land girls are getting – and you treat us like one of the family.'

'Yeah,' Joy said. 'This is just a mark of our appreciation.'

'What considerate girls you are,' Lily said. 'Must say, I didn't know if it was that good an idea when Will said he'd applied for Land Army girls, but I've been proved wrong.'

'Oh, most of the village thought that way at first,' Enid said. 'And maybe some were a bit rough and ready, but from what I hear they are all prepared to work, and that's what it all boils down to in the end – not the way they speak, or their table manners.'

'You're right, of course.' Lily said. 'I mean, look at the children I had, that I had to be nearly shamed into taking in, for all I had the room, and I got real fond of them, even the mischievous boys. I'm sure I would have made some hand of them if I'd had them longer.'

'You think they have gone for good, then?'

Lily nodded. 'Pretty certain they won't be back. It's a bit of a pointless exercise coming to places of safety like Penkridge for a few months when it was as safe in their own home towns. And then the children and the mothers get fed up being separated so the children go back home. But I bet the bombs are going to fall on the cities in the end.'

'Well, the way I see it is, they have to,' Will said. 'We are at war with a barbaric nation. I don't think they've learned anything from the last lot, and we know their capabilities in the air. Don't think we're going to get away scot-free.'

'I don't either,' Joy said. 'But why have they done nothing yet?'

'Oh, don't worry,' said Will. 'I think the bombs will start falling soon enough.'

'But today is Christmas Day,' Enid said. 'So for this one day, no more talk of war.' And then turning to the girls she announced, 'I have got a wee present each for you two as well.'

Neither girls had expected that, and they went bright pink when Enid presented them with sheepskin slippers. 'Noticed you didn't have any,' she said. 'And these stone-flagged floors are too cold just for stockinged feet.'

'Oh, thank you,' Meg said. 'We didn't really go a bundle on slippers at home, except for the younger ones, because there never seemed the money, but my feet have often felt cold here when I have taken my boots off, so I'm very grateful.'

'So am I,' Joy said. 'And they are by far and away the nicest slippers I have ever had.'

'I have something for you too,' Will said gruffly, and he handed each girl an envelope inside which was a five-pound note. He lifted his hand to still their protests. 'Listen,' he said. 'Each week we pay you less than the boys because that was the wage I was told to give you, and also, out of that you have to pay something for your keep, so this money is by way of a little bonus.'

'But it's too much,' Meg protested.

'Not at all,' said Will. 'You said you gave us things as a mark of appreciation; well, this is to show how much you are appreciated.'

'I don't know what to say,' Joy said. 'I mean, thank you, of course, but . . .'

Meg could say nothing, not without crying; Enid saw her eyes glittering with tears and said with mock severity,

'I shall know what to say if you don't take your places at the table this minute. I have a dinner spoiling.'

They sat not far from a range piled high with logs the girls had sawn. The bird Will was carving was one that had been running around the yard the day before; along with it they ate potatoes and the swede and carrots that they had lifted from the ground. Even the flagon of cider that Will brought in from the barn was made from the apples they had picked, and Enid produced what was left in the sherry bottle after dousing the cake, in case they would prefer it. Meg wasn't keen on the sherry, though she drank the small glass Enid poured, feeling it was impolite to refuse, and then refilled her glass with water from the jug at the table – or Adam's ale, as Will called it.

The meal was delicious and they all did justice to it. Afterwards there was the pudding they had stirred, for which Enid had made white sauce.

'Oh, that was just luscious,' Joy said as she finished the pudding, 'and I am ever so full now.'

'And me,' Meg said. 'Point was, I didn't think I wanted any pudding at all, and yet when you brought it out steaming to the table, my mouth started to water.'

'Enid is a very good cook,' Lily said. 'She was always better than me.'

'I wasn't, Lily,' Enid protested. 'I just had more practice, that's all.'

'Well, I suppose that's it really,' Lily said. 'I didn't usually bother much for myself but I had to get a grip on myself when I had youngsters to feed.'

'Will you miss them if they don't come back?'

'D'you know, I think I will,' Lily said. 'But cooking

363

for them made me appreciate good food and that was a truly delicious meal, Enid.'

'It was indeed,' Will said. 'Thank you, Enid. Now if you ladies don't mind, I would like to sit by the range and smoke one of my new cigars.'

No one had any objections, and as Will settled himself, the woman began tidying away. By the time it was all done, washed, dried, put away, and the kitchen to rights again, Will was fast asleep. Meg wasn't surprised and confessed she was fair jiggered herself. 'Midnight Mass is lovely,' she said. 'But when you have to get up early to milk cows or whatever, it makes a body very tired on Christmas Day, especially if you are not used to keeping late hours.'

'Well, I wasn't at Midnight Mass,' Lily said. 'And had a lie-in till I went to Mass at nine, so why don't you three sit and rest yourselves now and I'll make us a cup of tea?'

'Just the job,' said Enid, sitting down at the table with a sigh of relief. 'You may as well cut into the cake when you are at it.'

'Oh, yummy!' cried Joy.

'Goodness me,' Lily said, with a smile at Joy's very good figure, 'where do you put it?'

Joy shrugged. 'My mother always reckoned I had hollow legs,' she said, winking at Enid as she continued. 'But I can eat what I want here as they have it run off me.'

'Anyway,' Enid said, 'we are eating this cake as it may be the last of the proper cakes if rationing comes in.'

'Oh,' said Lily in enquiry, looking at her sister.

'Don't tell her?' pleaded Joy.

'I've no intention of,' Enid said. 'There is something different about the cake this year, and that isn't that it's not iced properly because I ran out of sugar. It's something else.'

Intrigued, Lily tried the cake a little cautiously and declared it first-rate and was very surprised when she was told about the artificial marzipan and the preponderance of carrots. The marzipan did taste strange,' Joy said. 'But it wasn't unpleasant.'

'No, and you couldn't tell about the carrots at all,' Meg said. 'They were all mixed up with the other things'.

She glanced across at their ration books behind the clock on the shelf above the range. 'Rationing is not going to affect you much, is it?' she asked.

'Not yet,' Enid said. 'It's looks as if they're only going to ration bacon, ham, sugar and butter in January. I am due a side of bacon when the pig is killed on the neighbour's farm, we make our own butter, and we can use sugar beet to supplement our sugar ration. But that, I think, will be the tip of the iceberg.'

'Yeah, but even when meat is added, like they say it will be, you can supplement that with rabbits or chicken, can't you?' Joy said.

'Oh, yes,' Enid agreed. 'We are much better off than city folk. As long as I can get feed for the hens, we will always have eggs too, and we can always have as much milk as we want. Oh, the city folk won't starve, and I suppose it's fairer everyone getting the same amount, not like it was in the last war, but it isn't going to be easy when it really starts to bite, especially for those with children to feed.'

'Yeah,' said Meg. 'I bet no one in Birmingham is looking forward to it.'

Meg was wrong, however. Frank Zimmerman was looking forward to rationing coming in because he had a little black-market business going. At the moment all he had was petrol, lots of it in barrels in the spare bedroom. He didn't ask where it had come from and probably wouldn't have been told if he had asked. He knew only that the petrol was the extra given to certain sections of the community like doctors, farmers and government officials, and coloured pink to prevent people stealing it. But if it was filtered through bread from one barrel to another the pink staining was removed and those barrels were delivered to him.

People would come under cover of darkness with cans and if they could pay the inflated price asked they could have as much as they wanted. It was relatively safe, for the darkness in the blackout was really dense. The Government had in the end relented and allowed shielded torches to be used and shielded headlights on cars after so many people had been killed or injured, but nothing much could be seen in the fuzzy pencil of light so anyone who wanted to stay hidden had a good chance of success.

The black market and the drugs were already bringing in a lucrative living. Doris had kicked off at first when she realised Frank was keeping wooden barrels of petrol in the flat, saying it wasn't safe.

''Course it is, you stupid cow,' Frank snapped. 'It's safe as houses until someone sets light to it.'

'Are you sure?'

"Course I am,' Frank said. 'So shut up about it or you'll just make me bloody angry and you'll know what that will mean, don't you?'

And she did, because he controlled her supply of opium that she now couldn't do without, feeding her addiction. It meant she would do whatever he asked her to, like travelling down to China Town to get in the fresh supplies of opium, though he knew she was always nervous going there, and being extra 'nice' to certain people.

TWENTY-FOUR

The New Year celebrations were fairly muted on the farm; everyone believed that 1940 could only be worse than 1939. New Year's Eve was Sunday and so Lily came home with them after Mass and stayed to see in the New Year. Coming up to midnight, they clustered around the wireless, and Will poured everyone a glass of cider, which Meg much preferred to sherry. As they took their glasses, Big Ben began to sound the witching hour.

'I won't wish for a Happy New Year,' Will said, as the booms stopped. 'Let's hope instead that we will survive whatever is thrown at us.'

'Yes, with the Lord's help,' Enid said, raising her glass. 'For surely we are on the side of right?'

'And I'd like you to drink to something else,' Lily said. 'The day before yesterday, I received a letter I'd been more or less expecting. It was from Christine, you know, who I was looking after. She said they have decided to stay in Liverpool. Well, having those children pulled me into the war, which, despite Stephen's call-up, I was trying to pretend had nothing to do with me. I began to realise that war today isn't between two

368

battling armies on a field; it affects each and every one of us, and so I have decided to join the WVS.'

'Oh, Lily, that's wonderful news,' Enid cried.

'And yet much overdue,' Lily said. 'I have licked my wounds for long enough. I am not the only one to taste tragedy, and there will be more of it before this war is won. Everyone can't just go into decline as I did.'

'You were hurting.'

'I was selfish,' Lily corrected. 'I never let go of the memories. I kept revisiting them in my mind's eye. Meg puts me to shame.'

'Why me?'

'Because of your stoicism,' Lily said. 'After losing your mother, you brought up your brothers and sisters, but the war has taken your father and the children from you, and your stepmother no longer wants you.'

'Yes, and I have been making decisions of my own about that,' Meg said firmly. 'Richard Flatterly has been the bane of my life for years and, because of the emotional state I was in, what he told me in Birmingham affected me so much I couldn't think what to do. I should have gone to the police there and then. I reckon he has more to hide than I have.'

'I wouldn't be at all surprised,' Will commented drily.

'Anyway, I am fed up being frightened by him,' Meg said determinedly. 'I am going to see the police and report the disappearance of my brother and sisters as I should have done in the first place.'

Enid looked pointedly at Will, and Meg caught the look. 'What?' she demanded. 'What is it? You know something?'

'No,' Will said. 'Nothing like that. I only wish we did

know, but I did go to see our local beat bobby because I thought all of us might get into trouble if we didn't report the missing children.'

'What did you tell him?'

'That you were upset,' Will said. 'That you had only just found out they were missing and I didn't want to raise your hopes – which was true – and could he make some discreet enquiries? He's a good man. Known him years.'

'And what did he find out?'

'Nothing, I'm afraid,' Will said softly.

'Nothing?

'No,' Will said. 'He contacted the police in Rugeley. One or two evacuees said they had seen your sisters and brother in the hall. One girl said that one minute they were there and the next they were gone.'

'But she didn't see anyone actually take my siblings away?'

'No,' Will said. 'But she said it was hard to see anyone really because there were so many people in the hall.'

Meg's shoulders sagged. 'So you don't think there's any point in pursuing this?'

Will didn't, but that wasn't what Meg wanted to hear, and so he chose his words with care. 'It's always worth having a word with the police and maybe bringing it into their mind again, because three children just going missing like that is worrying and should have high priority. But they seem to have had very little to go on, and Rugeley is a bit like Penkridge: most of the children will have gone back home now anyway.'

'Yes, I've thought that too,' Meg said. 'It's a bit of a dead loss really.'

'We will drink to it anyway,' Will said. 'Toast you and Lily, because we never know what 1940 will bring us.'

Meg drank obediently but she felt very dejected. She knew with each passing day it would be harder and harder to find out what had happened to her three siblings. If she allowed herself to think about them all the time she would be no good to herself or anyone else, so for the moment she resolved to do her best to draw a line under the whole heart-breaking affair.

Meg was finding that a winter in the countryside is very different from winter in a town. Everything took three times as long, for a start. When the snow tumbled from the thick grey clouds, after milking the cows had to be moved into the low lean-to holding shed off the cowshed. They disliked being kept in there, but there was nothing else to do. Each one was then led into a stall and the manger filled with hay; Meg knew that they would need mucking out before the evening milking and if the lane was blocked with snow, that had to be cleared before Dobbin set off with the milk churns, lest he slip.

The yard also had to be kept clear so that the hens could peck amongst the cobbles for their corn, because if they didn't eat enough grit with their food, their shells were too soft. That caused a problem if it iced over in the night, because the cobbles were like a skating rink the next day and had to be liberally sprinkled with rock salt.

The pigs couldn't be moved to their enclosure either, which again necessitated more cleaning out. In fact, the only ones who seemed delighted with the snow were the dogs, who burst from the barn with wag-tailed eagerness for what the day might bring, and then cavorted in the snow-covered fields with such wild enthusiasm they made Meg smile.

Still, most of the dank days were bitingly cold or were battered with wind-driven snow, or icy, sleety rain, and Meg was soon heartily sick of the winter. Easter was early too; 7 February was Ash Wednesday, the start of Lent, when they had all decided to give up taking sugar in their tea, a logical choice because it was now being rationed. Eventually, as one day folded into another, the snow ceased to fall, the ground became less rock solid, the cows were able to return to the fields and the pigs to their enclosure, and life got a little easier. By Mothering Sunday, 3 March, everyone could feel the days loosening their icy grip.

Traditionally, Mothering Sunday – about halfway through Lent – was the day when the girls 'in service' would return home so that they could see their mothers and visit their mother church, and they would usually come with a simnel cake as the restrictions of Lent were relaxed for that day. So, as a surprise, Enid had also made a simnel cake, which she said was made possible by the saving of the sugar ration. After tasting the cake, they all agreed that sacrificing the sugar in their cuppas had been worth it.

'I think even when Lent is over we should take less sugar,' Will said. 'It will do us no harm to be a bit more careful.'

'And it won't just be with sugar,' Enid said. 'Tea is supposed to be being rationed by the summer.'

'Tea?' Will cried in anguish.

'Yes, Will, tea,' Enid repeated. 'Each person will be getting just two ounces – it said on the wireless.'

'Two ounces?' Will said. 'That's beyond the pale, that is.'

'It's another way of saving our ships,' Enid told him. ''Cos the man on the wireless said most of our tea comes from Ceylon. Anyway, if that's the ration then that's the ration, and there's nothing we can do to increase that. We will have to suffer it like everyone else.'

Will was still flabbergasted but said nothing further, though the disgruntled look on his face made the girls smile.

'He's not used to rationing affecting his life in any way,' Joy said as they got ready for bed that night.

'Well, to be fair, none of us is.'

'I know, and I think it will be an eye opener for many of us – and not a pleasant one at that. But the rationing restrictions in January didn't make even a dent in Will and Enid's lives, did it?'

'No,' said Meg smiling. 'But I do see what he means in a way, because there is nothing like a reviving cup of tea when you're tired or cold – or just about any time, really.'

'You'll have to drink milk,' said Joy. 'Enid said that as long as they do their quota, they can have as much of the milk as they want for their own use.'

'It's not quite the same.'

'Better than nothing, though,' Joy said. 'I reckon we'll do a lot of making do in this war before we are finished.'

Just days after this conversation they started the spring planting, and were again out from dawn to dusk.

'What's your cousin at these days?' Will asked, when they had been at it a week. 'We could do with another pair of hands.'

'Oh, I don't think you'll get Nicholas back here, for all he enjoyed himself so much,' Meg said. 'He thinks he's far more use in Birmingham – just for now, anyway.'

'Why? What's he doing?'

'Anything that needs doing, I think,' Meg said. 'Apparently he's with a working party sort of preparing for war. They've dug more trenches and sawed the railings down from everywhere. You were right, Will – everyone seems to want scrap metal.'

'Yes, well, I would say a great deal of metal is used to fight a war.'

'Nicholas says they have taken iron railings from the edges of parks, private houses, and even surrounding ornamental gardens and fountains. He says wrought-iron gates are a thing of the past. At the moment, though, he's busy erecting Anderson shelters for people who can't do it for themselves. A hundred thousand were delivered to houses in Birmingham before Christmas. They're for people who have gardens so it was no good for our lot. But he said you have to dig a pit and then put the erected shelter into it and pack earth and sand-bags all around it and on top, so it's sort of buried, and he said – especially now with the men away – lots of households need help.'

'Oh, I can see that,' Will said. 'That's valuable work all right,'

On the farm, though, little was happening to show there was a war on, Meg thought, and with the long hours spent working at the planting, and with the rest of the farm work to be done too, while she hadn't forgotten about the war it wasn't at the forefront of her mind every day. This changed one Tuesday evening in early April as they returned to the house to find Enid standing stock-still in front of the wireless.

'What is it?' Will asked.

'It's just come through,' Enid said. 'Hitler and his bloody armies have occupied Denmark and now Norway, and seemingly with minimal resistance, for even the commentator said neither country appeared to have put up much of a fight.'

Later, more details emerged. 'The Royal Navy were there ready to go to Norway's aid,' Will said. 'But they never asked for help and didn't even bother to mine the fjords. I mean, how stupid can you get? Might as well have lined up on the shore and shook the invading Germans by the hand.'

Enid nodded in agreement. 'People say he will go for Belgium and Holland next.'

'I think he will, too, but things will not go all his own way there.'

'Why not?' Meg asked.

'Well, Belgium and Holland are protected by the fortress that they say is impregnable and it guards three strategic bridges. If they were to fall into German hands, then those countries would be wide open.'

'But this fortress will stop that happening?'

Will nodded. 'That's what they say.'

'What about France?' Joy asked.

'They have got something called the Maginot Line, which was built to protect France after the Great War.'

'What is it?'

'A line of heavily manned forts that run from the Swiss border to the Ardennes forest,' Will said. 'And they stopped there because they say the forest is impassable.'

'So we're more or less safe then?'

'As safe as anyone can be in a war of this magnitude,' Will said. 'And you are safer here than in Birmingham, so that's one thing you don't have to worry about.'

Although Meg was concerned about her father and now Stephen, and Joy about her brother, they had been somewhat reassured by Will's words. So when Meg turned seventeen just a few days later, they felt justified in having a little party tea for her. She was delighted by the bottle of California Poppy perfume that Joy gave her, and the silk stockings from Enid and Will, and she put both her presents away in the drawer to be used when she went to Mass. She also had cards, not only from those on the farm, but also from her aunts Rosie and Susan and Nicholas, and even Terry. She also got a beautiful one with a red silk heart on the front from Stephen. Enid lined all the cards up on the mantelpiece and the letters Meg put away for reading later.

The days grew warmer as April gave way to May. Meg often thought it was hard to think of fierce battles being enacted not far away and the only real concern for them was the lack of letters. Stephen used to write as regular as clockwork every week, and Meg's father nearly as often but day after day slipped by with no letters. There had been nothing from Joy's brother either, for her mother wrote that she had heard nothing for nearly three weeks and he had never gone so long without writing.

'Maybe it's just that it's difficult for them to send letters where they are,' Meg said.

'Aye, that must be it,' Enid said, but she went on with a sigh, 'and they say no news is good news.'

'Yes,' said Meg. 'So shall we try not to worry until we have something to worry about?'

'We'll do our best, young Meg,' Enid said. 'But worry is the one thing that's very difficult to get rid of.'

'I know,' Meg said. 'I find being busy helps.'

Just a couple of days later, news came through the wireless of an aerial attack on the Dutch airfields. The word *Blitzkrieg* meaning 'Lightning War' entered their vocabulary, and the Blitzkrieg visited on the airfield left the Dutch with only twelve operational planes. There was no defence against another savage Blitzkrieg against Rotterdam a few days later, leaving over 900 people dead. The report said that Allied troops were hampered trying to enter the city to help by the vast numbers of Dutch trying to get out of it. At the same time German paratroopers were dropped on top of the supposedly impregnable fortress. It was in German hands in twenty-four hours and the Low Countries lay open to invasion. The news was as bad as it could get. As Will said, 'Holland and Belgium have surrendered, and really they were left with no option, but we only need France to fall now and our lads will be buggered because the bloody Germans will be able to cut them off.'

No one said anything because no one could think of anything to say, and the only sounds in the room were Will's heavy, agitated breathing, the crackling of the fire in the range and the ticking of the clock on the mantelshelf.

The wireless was never off now, as daily the family waited for more news. Then, on the evening of 14 May, as they were just finishing their dinner, Anthony Eden, who was the Secretary of State for War, broadcast a message from the BBC.

Since the war began, we have received countless enquiries from all over the kingdom from men of all ages who are for one reason or another not at present engaged in military service, and who wish to do something for the defence of their country. Well, now is your opportunity. We want large numbers of such men in Great Britain, who are British subjects between the ages of seventeen and sixty-five, to come forward now and offer their services in order to make assurance doubly sure. The name of the new force which is now to be raised will be the Local Defence Volunteers . . . It must be understood that this is, so to speak, a spare-time job, so there will be no need for any volunteer to abandon his present occupation.

'What's all that about, do you imagine?' Meg asked.
'I think they're worried about invasion,' said Enid.
'Stands to reason,' Will said. 'Look, I'm not trying to frighten you, but it is as well to be prepared. The point is, if France falls – and every other country in Europe has folded so far – then only a small stretch of water separates us.'
Will was so right. Suddenly no letters were arriving.

The waiting was dreadful and every day the news worsened; now the Allies were in retreat. Will brought a map home from Penkridge the following Saturday and, after studying it said, 'The way I see it, there isn't anywhere to retreat to but the beaches.'

'And then what?' Enid asked fearfully.

'What do you bloody think?' Will snapped at Enid in a way he had never done before, because a knot of worry was tearing at his heart. When they heard the request that all owners of boats of all types, shapes and sizes capable of crossing the Channel should contact the navy, they didn't see what use they could be. It was afterwards, when the veil of secrecy was lifted, that they discovered that the job of the smaller boats was ferrying the soldiers from the makeshift pier heads they had set up on the beaches to the naval ships anchored in deeper water. With the ships filled to capacity, the owners of the little boats would load them up with as many men as they could, before heading for home and, once there, go back and start all over again.

The picture in the papers that Will brought from Penkridge showed the boats bobbing about in the choppy waters as if they were at some jolly regatta. The reality was totally different, for these brave men were bombed and strafed with machine-gun fire just like the ones on the beaches and those on the big ships, and many perished, but they carried on regardless.

It was known as Operation Dynamo, and together the small boats and naval ships rescued 192,000 British and 140,000 French soldiers between 27 May and 4 June 1940. It was an amazing feat, despite the fact that many had been left behind on the beaches. Daily they

379

all waited at the farm to see if their loved ones had been among the lucky ones who had arrived home in Blighty.

Just before Operation Dynamo was over, Joy received a telegram from her mother to say her brother was home but injured and in hospital. She sobbed in relief. Enid put her arms around her and wished that she'd had similar news. The Heppleswaites said she must go home for a few days and be a comfort to her mother and see her brother for herself, and that they would manage.

So Meg was on her own that first Saturday in June, for although Will and Enid had offered to take her into Penkridge with them, she had so many more jobs to do with Joy away that she'd decided to stay and make a start on those. She was weeding one of the potato fields when she saw an army truck stop at the head of the lane.

She strained her eyes to see better, but the two dogs who were with her suddenly took off. Though she tried to call them, they didn't take a blind bit of notice of her.

A man got out of the truck, awkwardly because one leg was encased in plaster. 'You're sure you'll be all right?' the driver of the truck asked him, getting out to stand beside him. 'That lane looks a bit dicey.'

As the man opened his mouth to reply, he was very nearly completely overbalanced by two dogs leaping up at him, wild with excitement. The blood seemed to stop in Meg's body, for it was Stephen. Stephen, and he was alive! Oh God, he was alive!

She pelted up the lane towards him as the driver was saying with a laugh, 'There's two glad to see you home, at any rate.'

'They're not the only ones,' Meg said, pushing the dogs out of the way and putting her arms around. Stephen. Her heart was hammering in her chest as she threw her arms around him, nearly overbalancing him again, 'There are no words to tell you how pleased, oh and so relieved to see you,' she cried. 'Welcome home, my darling love.'

'Blimey,' said the driver, and he had a big grin on his face as he eyed Meg up appreciatively as he got back in the cab. 'No wonder you were in a hurry to get home.' And then he turned to Meg and said, 'Good day to you, miss. Look after him well; one of Britain's heroes, he is.'

The driver gave a wave of his hand as he set off, and Meg put her arm through Stephen's and they began their staggering walk down the lane, with the dogs running in front of them.

'I am so glad that you're safe,' she said. 'You have no idea . . . Your parents will be over the moon. Why did you tell no one you were coming?'

'Because I'm not supposed to be here,' Stephen said.

'What d'you mean?' Meg said uncertainly.

'The doctors said I wasn't well enough to travel.'

'Won't they come looking for you?' she asked anxiously.

'I doubt it,' Stephen said. 'It's not like going AWOL from the regiment. I escaped from a military hospital. And it was a nice enough place but I thought I had been there long enough. I wanted to come home and so I sneaked out.'

'But how did you get here?'

'Well, I got a train as far as Wolverhampton and just outside the station got talking to a fellow soldier,' Stephen said. 'He'd been sent to meet the train to get supplies for the camp at Flaxley Green, just outside Rugeley. I couldn't believe my luck, and when I told him where I lived he went out of his way to take me as far as the head of the lane. And by the way,' he added, drawing Meg to her stop and kissing her lips gently, 'it's just so lovely to see you again.'

'And you,' Meg said. 'Oh, Stephen, I'm all of a quiver inside.'

'I'd forgotten just how beautiful you are' Stephen said, 'and just how compelling those dark eyes are.'

'Stephen!' Meg said in embarrassment. 'I bet you say something similar to all the girls.'

'All the girls,' Stephen repeated. 'Are you kidding? There have been no girls in my life but you. Unless,' he added with a grin, 'you count the nurses. Some of them were very cute, but there was this god-awful matron who would bawl you out if you even looked wrong at them, never mind throw in a bit of flirting.'

'Hmm, well, I would say the god-awful matron was needed,' Meg said. 'Especially if the wards were full of young men like you. Now here you are home, can you manage the step?'

''Course I can,' Stephen said. 'Don't start fussing me. I can't stand that.'

'I don't call asking someone a civil question fussing,' Meg said a little testily.

'No,' Stephen said. 'I'm sorry. I'm a bit tired.'

'And sore, I'd warrant,' Meg said, seeing the lines of pain creasing Stephen's face. 'Which is probably why the hospital said you weren't recovered enough to come home. Still, you're here now, so you go and sit down and I'll put the kettle on and make us some tea.'

And when they had the tea before them, Meg told him, 'Your parents don't know whether you're even alive or dead. I wouldn't be surprised if your mother doesn't have a heart attack when she comes in and sees you.'

'I'd hoped they might have heard something.' Stephen said. 'I was out of it when I arrived at the hospital first. I'd been in the water for hours and I was raving with fever, and had lost my dog tag and everything. They didn't think I would survive. One of the doctors told me that my leg was shot to blazes. Under this plaster cast it's one hell of a mess. By the way, where's Joy?'

'Her parents were told that her brother was alive but injured and in hospital, so she's managed to get off to see him.'

'Her parents were lucky,' Stephen agreed. 'And I'm sorry no word has got through to Mum and Dad and you. You must have all been worried sick, but even if I had my dog tag intact, or could tell them who I was, the army are going to find it difficult to locate everyone, because we were coming back in dribs and drabs, on little fishing boats or on those naval ships not bombed out of the water. Then some were severely injured and some weren't going to make it and though they were rescuing men till two days ago, I would hazard a guess there were still plenty left on the beaches; others just disappeared. How do they account for all those men and send the appropriate telegrams? It will take a long time for some to be informed, that's for sure.'

'Of those left,' Meg said, thinking of her own father, 'would they be taken to a POW camp?'

Stephen shrugged. 'They should be,' he said, 'but I don't know. People said they weren't taking prisoners.

But if they were, that would cause a further delay in informing the army and relatives.'

'I can see it must be very difficult to try and account for everybody,' Meg said. 'But it's awful just waiting and waiting and hearing nothing but bad and then worse news on the wireless.'

'I can imagine,' Stephen said. 'That's why I wanted to come home. I wanted to come and see them, show them that I am alive when a good few aren't. The two farm hands, Luke and John . . .' He trailed off.

'Both killed?' Meg touched his hand.

Stephen nodded. 'We were wriggling across the beaches together and when we saw the Stukas diving we tried to burrow into the sand, but there was no time. They strafed us with bullets, killed Luke and John outright and peppered my leg. I would have been one of the ones left behind on the beach if fellow soldiers hadn't risked their lives by carrying and dragging me to one of the pier heads.'

Meg was silent for a time, digesting the full horror of his story. 'Will used to buy the papers and we saw the pictures,' she told him, 'but being there must have been truly terrible,' and she gazed at him and felt a jolt in her heart at realising how close he had come to death. Their eyes locked and Stephen leaned forward. Meg left her chair and kneeled on the floor in front of him and held his hands . . 'Can I kiss you?' Stephen said huskily. 'It's what I've dreamed of and that has kept me alive.'

How could Meg refuse that? 'Oh, Stephen,' she murmured as their lips met and Stephen's arms encircled her. It was only Meg's second proper kiss and she never

384

wanted it to end and she let out a moan of desire that surprised her.

'Meg,' said Stephen but as they eventually drew apart but Meg lifted her head for she had heard the rumble of the cart over the cobbles in the yard and she got to her feet . .

'Here are your parents coming home,' she said, glancing out of the window, 'so I shall go back to hoeing the turnips.'

'There's no need to do that,' Stephen told her.

'Oh, I think there is,' Meg said. 'They will want you to themselves for a while.'

As she walked towards the door, Enid came through it carrying shopping bags in her hands. Stephen had got to his feet and was holding onto the mantelshelf for support. Meg watched the blood drain from Enid's face, the bags fell from her hands as her mouth dropped open, and then she let out a shout of pure joy and ran across the room crying, 'Stephen, my darling, darling boy.' She held him so tightly and with such enthusiasm as tears spurted from her eyes. Her love for her only son and relief that he was alive was almost tangible, and Meg felt a lump form in her throat. She turned and headed quietly out of the door, her emotions churning.

The following day, Stephen received a letter from the military hospital, demanding his return.

'Will you go back?' Meg said, when he read the contents of the letter out at the breakfast table.'

'Not likely.'

'Can you just refuse?' Meg asked. 'Won't you get into some awful trouble?'

'No, I don't think so,' Stephen said. 'Look, there is no point in taking up a hospital bed when I can just as well be treated at Flaxley Green camp, which is no distance at all; they will have medical facilities there.'

'So will you tell them that?'

'Yes,' said Stephen. 'I'll tell them that I will recover much quicker in the bosom of my family. And,' he added with a grin at Meg that caused her heart to give a lurch, 'that I have my favourite girl in all the world to mop my fevered brow.'

'Huh,' Meg said. 'What did your last servant die of?'

'Overwork,' Stephen said sagely and the two fell about laughing. Enid glanced at them and then at Will. She loved to hear Meg laughing. and she was delighted for she already loved Meg like a daughter and there was no one better she could have chosen for her son.

Joy was also aware of the stronger feelings developing between Stephen and Meg as soon as she returned. On her first night home, as they undressed for bed, she said tauntingly, 'Stephen still just a friend then? 'Then added, 'Don't bother answering because you're blushing and that answers the question.'

'It just happened when he came home from Dunkirk,' Meg attempted to explain. 'I thought, what if he had died like his two friends he still misses so much, and that sort of opened my eyes to just what he means to me.'

'You don't have to justify yourself to me,' Joy said gently. 'If I was nasty I could say "I told you so", but I won't because I'm so pleased for the pair of you.'

'Thanks,' Meg said. 'Sometimes it feels wrong to be so happy when the war is going so badly.'

'So will it go better if you go round miserable?'

'No, but—'

'Look, Meg, we're at war,' Joy said, holding on to her friend's hands. 'No one knows what the future holds for any of us so grab happiness where you can. Enjoy your time together and never feel you shouldn't.'

Joy's words did make Meg feel better, but there was no doubt that the war news was more worrying than ever as German bombers pounded the coastal towns. The newspapers were filled with distressing images of dispossessed and traumatised families sitting in the ruins of their homes, and stories of those left dead or badly injured. Everyone knew invasion was a real and very likely possibility as they read of beaches rendered out of action, laid with anti-tank mines. and coils of barbed wire with pillboxes erected behind them. As France fell, the Battle of Britain began in the air and householders were issued with leaflets entitled:

If the invader comes;
what to do – and how to do it

'It isn't much use,' Enid said, casting her eyes over it when it arrived through their door. Meg had to agree. All it did was tell people to stay where they were till they received further instructions.

This was reinforced by posters appearing telling them, 'FREEDOM IS IN PERIL – DEFEND IT WITH ALL YOUR MIGHT', and other useful or not so useful pieces of advice.

People were advised to hide food and maps and

disable bicycles not in use. All cars were supposed to be hidden away and immobilised, and all directional signs were painted over both on the roads and at railway stations, which proved thoroughly confusing to ordinary people trying to go about their daily business. The more nervous citizens began to see paratroopers or German spies behind every tree.

TWENTY-FIVE

In mid-June Aunt Rosie sent a telegram to Meg asking if she could come over and see her on the farm the following Saturday. Meg felt heavy-hearted; she knew that only a matter of great importance would bring her aunt to Penkridge. Enid knew it too, and she sent the boy back with the message that she could come and welcome, and that someone would be there to meet her off the train.

On Saturday morning Meg rattled through her jobs but was totally unable to eat breakfast.

'Just a wee bit,' Enid urged, looking at Meg's white, drawn face.

Meg shook her head. 'I would be sick if I tried,' she said. 'All I want is for the time to speed by until I see my aunt.'

Stephen was quietly watching Meg biting her lip in consternation, and tenderness flowed through him as he saw how she suffered. He wished he had some way of easing things for her.

When the train pulled in and Rosie alighted, Meg gave a sigh and ran towards her. Rosie put her arms around her young niece and Will was glad she looked a kindly sort of person. It eased his mind somewhat. Rosie shook hands with Will as she thanked him for looking after her niece so well. And then she said, 'How far is the farm from here?'

'Three miles or so,' Will told her, wondering why she wanted to know.

'So we could walk?'

'You could, but we have the cart outside.'

'Yes, thank you,' Rose said. 'But it will give me a chance to chat to Meg as we go.'

Will took the travel bag that Rose had been carrying and said briskly, 'Well, I'll relieve you of that anyway, and when you are ready there will be a welcome and a meal at the farmhouse.'

'Thank you,' Rose said, 'you are so very kind.'

As she watched him walk away, she put her arm through Meg's and led her from the station. 'Now, Meg,' she said as they walked slowly together, 'I'm afraid I have bad news about your father.'

'Just tell me, Aunt Rose,' Meg said. 'Dad's dead, isn't he?'

Rose nodded. 'Yes, I'm sorry, my dear, he is.'

Meg turned to her aunt and said matter-of-factly, 'I knew already, really, you know. I faced it when I didn't hear anything.'

'How do you feel, my dear?'

'I feel nothing really,' Meg said, 'and yet I remember the great father he was to me for fourteen years. It was after Mom died that I realised what a weak man he was and it was that weakness and loneliness and need that gave someone like Doris such power over him. But now he's gone anyway.'

'He was left behind at Dunkirk,' Rosie said. '"Missing presumed dead" was what the telegram read.'

'Even if he was left alive, he probably wouldn't have stayed that way for long,' Meg told her aunt. 'Stephen, the son of the house, is home from Dunkirk and he heard that the Germans were taking no prisoners.'

'Yes, and I think if he'd been alive he would have turned up in some POW camp by now. Apparently the telegram came about three weeks ago but Doris didn't tell me immediately.'

'Well, that's not your fault, Aunt Rosie,' Meg assured her aunt.

Rosie was feeling extremely uncomfortable, but knew that Meg deserved to know it all. 'Doris might not have wanted us to know the facts about your father, but she was quick enough to tell others.'

'What others?'

'The orphanage where Ruth is,' Rosie said. 'As soon as she got that letter, she went to there to tell them that Ruth was now technically an orphan because she was no blood relation, but she has grandparents living in Ireland who would probably take her in.'

'But you're a blood relation' Meg cried.

'Course I am,' Rosie said. 'But Doris didn't tell them about me and when I tried and said I was ready and willing to have her, they said the adoption was going through now and Doris had given her permission so it was out of their hands. Tell you, I was blazing mad but there was nothing I could do.'

'Oh they'll be ready and willing all right.' Meg said bitterly. 'It's what they always wanted.'

'You're right,' Rosie said, 'they were only too eager,

and arrangements are being made to transfer the child to Ireland.'

'Oh, dear God!' Meg exclaimed, because this was her worst nightmare. This was the very thing her mother had warned her about. The thought of her little sister in the hands of her maternal grandparents was almost too painful to think about. She couldn't bear it, she really couldn't, and she felt herself falling and the road coming up to meet her.

When Meg's eyes eventually fluttered open she was surprised to see Stephen sitting by her bed. He didn't say he had been sitting there for some time watching her tortured face and remembering all that this young girl had already suffered. For a moment Meg was a little dazed and bewildered, and then everything came flooding back and she gave a groan. 'How did I get here?'

'You fainted on the road, and no wonder you did with all the news your aunt came with,' Stephen said. 'Lucky for you the doctor was passing just minutes later on his way to see a patient and saw you prone on the floor and your distraught aunt trying to rub life into your limbs.' He didn't say that when he saw the doctor carrying Meg's unconscious form from his car that he had pulled up in the yard he thought she had died.

'Oh God, is she . . .?'

'Unconscious, that's all,' the doctor said briskly. 'Had some bad news. Her aunt will explain it to you. Enid, can you show me where to lay her and turn down the bed?'

Enid went off to do as the doctor asked and the

doctor followed and Stephen turned his attention to the woman who had climbed out of the doctor's car and was standing in the farmyard looking a bit lost. She introduced herself as Rose and said she had come to tell Meg of the death of her father.

Now Stephen said to Meg, 'I'd just like to say how sorry I am to hear about your father. We left far too many good men on these beaches.'

'Yes, but it isn't just Dad,' Meg said. 'Dad is just one more thing, if you like. It's the others, everything, and I don't know whether I will be able to live with the guilt, the shame.'

'Guilt and shame of what?' Stephen said. 'From what your aunt was saying downstairs, you were more sinned against than the sinner yourself.'

'Aunt Rose doesn't know the half of it,' Meg cried, distressed, but Stephen knew that Rosie did know more than Meg was aware of and she had tried to explain what she had said to her niece that had caused her to collapse. It was not the death of her father,' she said. 'Telling her who would be adopting Ruth was like the last straw. It all hinged on the promise Meg made to her mother as she lay dying.' Meg had told them all about that and Rosie described Maeve's parents, how unpleasant they were, and the harsh upbringing Maeve had endured at their hands. 'Hard to understand it,' Rosie said. 'For Maeve was lovely, kind and warm-hearted to a fault.'

Rosie looked at the people grouped around the kitchen table listening to her every word and went on, 'Meg would have probably thought that an easy promise to make because all the years of Maeve's marriage her parents had never been over to see her and she certainly never went there. They never even exchanged letters. Maeve told me that herself.'

'So these grandparents don't really know this wee child they want to adopt?' Enid said.

Rosie shook her head. 'They have never even seen her,' she said. 'She was very premature and was in hospital when they came a few days before Maeve's funeral.'

'So what are the Social Service thinking of?' Enid said. 'Even if they were the best grandparents in the world they are strangers to this poor wee mite.'

'Yes, and they are as far from the best grandparents in the world as it is possible to be,' Rosie said grimly. She went on to explain how they had wanted to take Billy and Sally back with them after the funeral and what an idyllic life they told Charlie the children would have in Ireland to tempt him, but that in the end he had refused to be parted from them.

'No one breathed easy till they went home, though,' Rose said. 'And now this.'

That was when Stephen stomped his way painfully upstairs and took up vigil by the bed. Now he picked one of Meg's hands and said, 'Please don't upset yourself. Rosie has told me everything, and none of it is your fault.'

'I have failed my mother, failed them all.' Meg said. Her voice broke and she gave a cry of anguish that tore at Stephen's heart.

The tears came then, not gentle easing tears but great sobs that shook her whole body, There was no way on God's earth that Stephen could have stopped his arms going around her and he shifted to the bed so he could hold her tight, upset himself at witnessing such pain affecting the girl that had a special place in his heart.

The people downstairs heard the howl Meg had made and her sobbing, and Enid crept up the stairs to see if she was all right, pushed the door ajar. What she saw stopped the heart in her throat for she saw her son holding Meg as if his whole life depended on it and from the look on his tear-stained face she knew with certainty that no one else was needed in that room. She turned and went quietly downstairs.

'She is all right,' she said when she reached the kitchen.

'Stephen's still with her?' Rosie asked

'Oh, yes, and suffering alongside her,' Enid said. 'They need no one else just at the moment.'

When Meg's tears were finally spent she felt light-headed and empty, and she still lay against Stephen, glad of his arms around her. She didn't protest when he pushed the hair back from her face so tenderly and gave her a gentle kiss on the lips before saying, 'Believe me my darling girl, none of this is your fault.'

'Even if I were totally blameless it wouldn't change the outcome one bit,' Meg said. 'And I am helpless to do anything about my little sister's adoption.' Then she gave a gigantic sigh and, as if she had mentally straightened her shoulders, said, 'So I must learn to deal with it.'

Stephen had immense respect for Meg's courage. 'Are you able to go down yet?' he asked. 'They will be wondering, but if you are not willing to face it, my mother will, I'm sure, bring you some food up on a tray. I couldn't manage to carry it with my gammy leg.'

'No, I'll get up,' Meg said, but when she got out of bed her legs felt very shaky and Stephen steadied her. 'It's like the blind leading the blind,' he said with a wan smile. 'How I wish I could catch you up in my arms and carry you.'

'No need for that,' Meg said. 'I'm quite all right now. Shall we go down?'

Everyone was very gentle with Meg and even the doctor called in on his way back from tending his patient to see if she was all right. She said she was fine, though she didn't think she would ever be fine again. But she refused the tablets he wanted to give her, saying she had work to do and she'd found working hard was the best medicine.

She was sorry to say goodbye to her aunt, but as the days passed and the battles in the air continued, she thought more about her father. She felt bad that she hadn't mourned him more.

'It's because it hasn't really sunk in yet,' Joy said when she confided in her one night as they undressed for bed. 'It isn't as if you are living at home and he was coming in the door every evening. I mean, the only thing different is that you won't be getting the letters he used to send and I know that you often struggled to find things to say in your replies.'

'Yeah, I did,' Meg admitted. 'But what I will miss most of all will be him just being there. In one way, too though, I'm glad that he never knew of the duplicity of his so-called wife because Aunt Rosie said she was carrying on with others even before Dad was called up. She said she didn't believe it at first, but plenty of people had seen men going up and down to that flat she had used to have on Bristol Street so in the end she followed her and they were right. And Nicholas says she's taking opium.'

'How does he know that?'

'Says that anyone can smell it on her and I smelled it in the house but didn't recognise it. The place stank of dirt and squalor and neglect, but overriding all that was a floral smell, sickly sweet, coming off her. Nicholas says that's opium.'

Joy was quiet for a little moment and then she said quietly. 'I know it's harsh, but your dad might have done Ruth a favour putting her in an orphanage. Better there than living with some drug-crazed nymphomaniac.'

'I can even agree with that,' Meg said. 'But now she is going to my mother's parents, which is the last place on earth that Mom would have wanted her taken. I am certain sure they will abuse her and she is too far away for me to do anything about it, and I find that hard to take.'

Joy put her arms around Meg and hugged her tight.

'Don't be too kind or I'll blub,' Meg warned. 'I've found the solution to heartache is hard work and I am just thankful that there is so much of it here.'

A week later and not a million miles away, as the sky was just beginning to darken, three children were crawling out of a sizeable hole they had made in the very back of the barn where they had slept for the last ten months.

Jenny was excited because she had thought of running away from this place for ages and when she found some rotten boards at the back of the barn it had been easy to work at them until she, Sally and Billy had made a hole large enough for them to wriggle through, but small enough to be hidden with a pile of sacks from the eagle eyes of Lady Hammersmith. But when she had first broached escape to her brother and sister, neither had been keen.

'I'd rather stay here,' Billy said. 'At least Lady Hammersmith doesn't hit us and she's sort of kind.'

'Yes, but we don't get enough to eat,' Jenny said. That was true; they were often hungry. Not that Lady Hammersmith got much more. Jenny and sometimes Sally prepared her meals for her, and she often ate less than a bird and said that people eat less as they get older. That was all very well, Jenny thought, but they weren't older and were sometimes starving. Often they lived on only bread and milk.

'If we got to Meg she would sort it out,' Jenny said confidently. 'We need somewhere where we can be together, have enough to eat and go to school.'

'Oh, I don't mind not going to school,' Billy said.

'Don't be daft,' Jenny said. 'We've all had months off already. Do you want to grow up an ignoramus?'

'Too late,' Sally said. 'He already is one.'

'Shut up, you,' Billy said, who had no idea what an ignoramus was but thought it didn't sound a very nice sort of person to be.

Sally wasn't taking any notice of Billy, though, because something else was bothering her. 'But, Jenny, we don't know where Meg is.'

'Terry will know, though, so we'll make for there.'

'That's miles away,' Sally said. 'How will we know the way?'

'How did we get here?'

'By train.'

'Then we find the railway line and go in the opposite direction.'

'Oh, that's clever,' Sally said.

'Common sense, that's all,' Jenny told her. 'And if it turns out to be a long, long way, then we can try hitching a lift, but not till we're well away from here. Agreed?'

'Agreed,' said Sally and Billy.

Before they set off that night, though, Jenny sneaked into the kitchen and stuffed a large loaf and cheese into a bag.

'Isn't that stealing?' whispered Sally.

'No, it's necessary,' Jenny said shortly. 'Just at the moment our need is greater than Lady Hammersmith's.'

They knew the direction the railway lay in, because they'd heard the trains on a fairly regular basis. It was a fine night and still fairly warm. There was only a half-moon shining through the dusk, but as the darkness deepened, twinkling stars appeared and though they'd set off in fairly high spirits, they found it depressing to trudge mile after mile in the dark next to a railway track. But they kept moving, one foot before the other, desperate to put as much distance as possible between themselves and Lady Hammersmith before their disappearance was discovered. They had been walking at a fairly robust pace for about two and a half hours when Billy keeled over onto the railway, literally fallen asleep on his feet, and Jenny called a halt.

'We can't stay by the railway line – we will soon be spotted,' she said, but fortunately they found undergrowth not far away, which they crawled into, glad of their overcoats Jenny had insisted they bring, which they used as coverings. Billy and Sally were soon asleep but Jenny lay awake feeling the burden of responsibility lying heavily on her.

She heard a train rattle past along the track they had just left, but saw nothing but the fire truck at the front: the rest of the train was blacked out. There were the snuffling and rustling of small nocturnal animals all around her, and she heard the hoot of an owl and the thin howl of a dog fox on the prowl before eventually her eyelids fluttered shut.

They were wakened by the cold in the very early morning. The sun was not up but there was a glow on the horizon, so Jenny knew it was early. She broke the bread in half and did the same to the cheese and then broke that into three pieces. It was a very meagre breakfast, but not even Billy raised a complaint and they were soon on their way again.

After walking for another hour, and when the tip of the sun was just visible, they saw a station in the distance.

'That will be Lichfield,' Jenny told the others.

But as they drew near, there were no signs to say where it was. 'There was signs once, look,' Billy said, pointing to the signal box.

'Someone's painted over it,' Sally said.

'What an odd thing to do,' Jenny commented.

There were no signs anywhere and no map either,

though there was evidence that there had been both. The station at that early hour was quiet, but there was one train waiting at the station and Jenny asked a man boarding it, 'Excuse me, but is this Lichfield Station?'

'Yes,' the man confirmed.

'Why ain't there no names?' Billy burst out.

The man looked at him rather strangely. 'To confuse the enemy,' he said. 'In case they should invade.'

'Goodness,' Jenny said. 'Are they likely to?'

'What planet you been living on?' the man said. 'It's all everyone talks about. The Germans would have been here now if it hadn't been for the RAF who are doing their level best to stop them Names of stations and signposts have been painted over and maps removed, so that if they come they won't find it so easy getting about. You really didn't know all this?'

Jenny shook her head and decided to tell some semblance of the truth. 'We were evacuated to a really remote farmhouse, but now we must get back to Birmingham because our mother is sick.'

'Oh, sorry to hear that,' the man said. 'This is the train you want. Be setting off in a few minutes and takes you right into New Street Station.'

There was nothing to do but get on the train, because she knew the man would think it strange if they didn't, and anyway an idea was forming in Jenny's head. The man made for the front of the train so Jenny, grabbing hold of Sally and Billy, pushed them the other way.

'We have to get off,' Sally said.

'Maybe,' Jenny said. 'Let's go to the back of the train and see if we can get into the guard's van.'

'Why?'

'You'll see.'

It seemed a long way to the end, and any minute they expected the train to move, but they eventually reached the guard's van and Jenny peeped through the window. The guard was in there taking luggage from the platform and packing it in the van, and Jenny chewed on her thumbnail and wondered how to get in without him seeing them.

'What we doing here?' Billy asked.

'Ssh,' Jenny cautioned. 'If we can get into the guard's van we can travel all the way to Birmingham in it.'

'Without paying?'

'Have to be without paying, won't it, Sally?' Jenny said. 'Less you've got some money stashed away somewhere.'

'Hardly.'

'Well, then,' Jenny said. 'There're plenty of crates and sacks we can hide behind.'

As she watched, suddenly the guard was called away. Quick as a flash, she opened the door and, pulling the other two behind her, led them to some crates right at the back of the van.

'How will we know where to get off if all the stations haven't got no names?' Billy whispered . .

'Ssh,' Jenny said, because the guard was back on the train and closing the big sliding doors. There was a piercing whistle and then the train was on its way. It was hard to keep in the one position, Jenny realised, though she was cheered by the miles the train was eating up. She stretched her legs as far as she could without their being seen because she was afraid of cramp.

402

Eventually she felt first Billy and then Sally sag against her as they succumbed to sleep, lulled by the movement of the train. How Jenny wanted to join them. She hadn't had much sleep all told but she knew she couldn't risk that. The train seemed to be stopping at every station and at each one the guard's van was opened to offload some stuff or take more on board. She could see when the doors were open that the stations were small, no bigger than Lichfield, and in some cases much smaller. Jenny was fairly certain that they would know Birmingham by its size, but if she allowed herself to go to sleep they could go sailing past.

When the guard's van doors opened to the one of the bustling platforms of New Street Station Jenny knew straight away. She shook Sally and Billy awake. They were bleary-eyed and stiff but saw as Jenny did that the guard had so many packages to unload they could easily be discovered. Fortunately he was so occupied that it was easy to slip out one by one when his back was turned, and on that teeming platform no one noticed them. They sat on a bench while Jenny shared out the remaining food, and then they set out on the last leg of their journey to Bristol Street and Terry.

At the same moment as the children were walking towards Bristol Street, Dan Wainwright – a grocer in Rugeley – was sitting facing Sergeant George Newbury. 'Might be nothing in it,' Wainwright said. 'But it was with them Germans we found hiding out last week after parachuting out their plane. I got to thinking that if she found one, she'd likely harbour him – and then get

403

killed in her bed, most likely – 'cos she's as nutty as a bleeding fruitcake.'

'Now, now, Dan,' the sergeant chided. 'That is no way to speak about Lady Hammersmith.'

'Oh, come on, Sarge. Everyone knows she's tuppence short of a shilling.'

'All right, so she is a little strange,' conceded the policeman. 'And stranger still since the army commandeered her house and she had to move into the Lodge, but what makes you think she's harbouring anyone?'

'The food she buys,' Dan Wainwright told him. 'She don't understand the rationing and can't get it that she can only have so much stuff and no more. She's always on about it, and then she buys lots of bread 'cos it's not on ration, and my Bessie does the milk round and she says Lady Hammersmith has two large jugs to fill every day and she sometimes has three. So what is she doing with all that food if she isn't feeding someone else as well?'

The sergeant thought for a moment. 'It is strange, I'll give you that. I've had no reports of any planes going down, apart from that one last week, but we'll go up and have a look anyway.'

The policeman was very gentle with Lady Hammersmith, especially when he noted the vacant eyes and manner, and thought it a shame that the family that lived in Rugeley for generations should die out with this vague old lady, because the family's four fine sons had been killed in the Great War. But he explained about the food, and asked her politely why she needed so much, being a lady on her own.

'Not that much food,' Lady Hammersmith said. 'Mr Wainwright won't let me have any more. I see it on the shelf and I have money but he won't let me have it.'

'You buy bread.'

'Oh, yes, he lets me buy lots of bread.'

'But why would you want so much bread?'

Lady Hammersmith gave a toss of her head. 'That's my business.'

'Are you sharing it with someone else?'

'Don't want to tell you,' Lady Hammersmith said childishly. 'You'll take them away.'

Them? The policemen thought, and a memory stirred in his brain of the missing children the copper at Penkridge had told him about. Said they were three young evacuees gone missing from Rugeley and he had never heard that they'd been found. 'Lady Hammersmith,' he said, 'you know it's wrong to lie?'

The lady nodded her head slowly and he said, 'So you must tell me. Have you got children living here?'

He saw the slump of her shoulder and heard the sigh that escaped from her before she said, 'Not here, not in the house.'

'Then where are they?'

'In the barn at the back of the Lodge,' Lady Hammersmith said.

'I must see them,' the policemen said and, with another sigh, Lady Hammersmith led him to the barn, released the padlock and opened the doors. The barn was completely empty.

'They're gone,' she cried.

It was obvious there had been people there: there were beds made up of hay and bedding, and also left behind were three gas masks. Two were children's ones, made to look like Mickey Mouse. Now the policeman was worried.

'Where are the children, Lady Hammersmith?'

'I don't know,' she replied. 'They were here yesterday.'

'You haven't hurt the children in any way, Lady Hammersmith?'

'Of course not.' There was nothing wishy-washy about Lady Hammersmith's denial. 'I wouldn't hurt children,' she went on. 'That would be a dreadful thing to do. But I don't know where they are now.'

Sergeant Newbury couldn't doubt her sincerity, and when he found the hole at the back of the barn, he guessed they had run away. Later, searching in the house, he came upon the stamped postcards they had been given to send home to say they had arrived safely.

But these poor children had not been able to send anything back. No wonder the family had been frantic, but at the time they had had nothing to go on; no lead to finding them at all. He had thought at the time it made no sense, sending unaccompanied children all over the country. Certainly adequate care had not been taken if three young children could be spirited away and disappear for over ten months.

Finding the children was now a priority, but as Sergeant Newbury drove back to the station, he began to wonder if the children might not be hiding away locally somewhere – they would have no money for bus or train fares and no idea where Birmingham was from here.

He called on the doctor as he reached the village, told him what Lady Hammersmith had done and advised him to visit her. 'Maybe her days of living on her own up there are at an end,' he said. 'She needs looking after.'

'It was only ever a matter of time,' the doctor said. 'Leave it to me.'

Sergeant Newbury was only too glad to do that and, once back at the station, he ordered a search of the area, certain the children were not far away.

Back in Birmingham, the children were just opening the door to Drummond's shop. Terry, who was serving behind the counter, looked up as the bell tinkled. His mouth dropped open as he stared at his siblings in absolute amazement. The waiting customers also looked and their chattering stopped; for a couple of seconds there was absolute silence, though not all of them knew who the dirty, bedraggled children were.

Jenny's relief at seeing her brother was immense. She had brought her sister and brother this far, and now she wanted someone else to take charge. 'Terry,' she cried. 'Help us.'

Terry completely ignored the customer he was in the middle of serving and almost vaulted over the counter. Seconds later he was hugging Jenny, Sally and Billy tight, as if he would never let them got again. And though he wept with the children, through his tears he was asking them where they had come from and where they had been all those months, and the children seemed too overwrought to tell him anything as they continued to sob.

Neil was also astounded at the arrival of the children, whom he knew Terry had been worried sick about, and he told his uncle and the waiting shoppers the story as far as he knew it. The customer looked at the little distressed group with sympathy as Billy pulled himself away from Terry's embrace, scrubbed at his eyes with his coat sleeve and said, 'Have you got any food, Terry, 'cos I'm starving? We're all starving.' Terry looked at his two sisters and they nodded their heads enthusiastically.

Mr Drummond laughed. 'First things first,' he said to Terry. 'Feed the troops and ask questions later. Take them up to my wife and I'm sure she'll find something.'

With rationing the way it was, though, Mrs Drummond was a bit stumped. 'Will porridge be all right?' she asked. 'You can have treacle to sweeten it.'

Jenny felt herself relax, for she felt safe now she had arrived. Porridge was at least familiar. She wasn't sure that she could speak without crying and a nod seemed awfully rude. Fortunately, Mrs Drummond seemed to understand how upset they were, and while she made a big pan of porridge, Terry helped them off with their outer clothes and showed them where the bathroom was, knowing Mrs Drummond wouldn't let them eat with such dirty hands. Within a few minutes of their arrival, they were sitting at the table watching Mrs Drummond ladle thick and creamy porridge into three bowls.

They ate ravenously, though Jenny reminded herself that she was twelve now and could not fall upon the food like some wild animal, as Billy was doing, but she wanted to and did not rebuke her young brother. Mrs

Drummond's eyes met Terry's as they both realised how truly hungry the children were. When Billy finished before his sisters and lay back in his chair with a sigh of contentment, Mrs Drummond smiled as she said, 'Could you manage some toast?' and he gave her a big beam as he said with gusto, 'Oh, yes please.'

The girls had some, too, so it was a little while before they were able to satisfy Terry's curiosity.

'Can you tell what happened now?' he said at last. 'No one seemed to know where you were.'

'We didn't know either,' Jenny said.

'Why didn't you send the postcards and tell people?'

'Because Lady Hammersmith took them off us,' Jenny said. 'She'd said she would send them for us, but I never thought she did.'

Terry shook his head. 'No one received any,' he said. 'Who's Lady Hammersmith?'

'The woman who took us off,' Jenny said, and then the story came tumbling out.

'Everyone kept telling us no one would take on three children,' Jenny said. 'So we went right to the back of the room 'cos I didn't want someone to come in and just choose one of us. And then the fire door opened beside us and Lady Hammersmith peered round.'

'Only we didn't know it was Lady Hammersmith then,' Billy said.

'No,' Jenny said. 'But even if we had . . . none of us had ever been evacuated before and they told us people would come and choose the children they wanted to live with them and when this elegant woman beckoned me over to her I went, and so did Sally and Billy because

I was holding their hands. She didn't want either of them, just me, but I said I wouldn't go if she didn't take us all. She didn't argue, she just put us into this old jalopy of a car and drove for miles out into what was like the middle of nowhere.'

'She stopped by this barn,' Sally said. 'Told us we'd be sleeping in there.'

'And you two pulled a face,' Billy said. 'But I never 'cos I thought it were exciting to sleep in a barn and she'd made it real cosy.'

'She had,' Jenny agreed. 'There were plenty of blankets and the hay beds were very comfortable and warm.'

'And she brought us loads of food at first,' Sally said.

'Tons,' Jenny agreed. 'The pantry was stocked.'

'Where was it from?'

'The Big House,' Jenny said. 'She used to live on her own in this huge mansion of a place with an army of servants and then the army commandeered it.'

'You can hardly blame them,' Terry said. 'Why was she on her own?'

'There was no one else,' Jenny said. 'She told us her brothers had been killed in the Great War and her sisters succumbed to Spanish flu and her broken-hearted parents died shortly afterwards. Now there's just her.'

'She's not married herself?'

The children all exchanged glances before Jenny said, 'No . . . she's a little . . . strange.'

'Crazy?'

'No, just strange.'

'But kind,' Billy said. 'She didn't even shout at me when I pulled all the flowers up in the garden thinking they

410

was weeds. I mean, how was I expected to know the flipping difference?'

Billy's indignation made Terry smile and he realised how much he had missed his little brother, missed them all.

'She was kind,' Jenny said. 'And she had no one. All the servants left when she moved to the Lodge. I think she was just looking for a girl to train up because that's what I would do: lay out her clothes and do her hair, help Sally to clean the place and cook her meals. She had never had to look after herself and didn't know how to do it, and Billy would help now and again.'

'You must have known that something was wrong?'

'Yes, of course we did eventually,' Jenny said. 'But what could we do? We were miles away from everywhere and because no one had visited we assumed no one knew we were there. Whenever Lady Hammersmith had to go out we were locked in the barn and she would give us piles of books to read. We talked about escaping a lot but we'd nowhere to run to and were pretty sure that no one in the village would take three children on. And anyway, we all liked Lady Hammersmith and felt sorry for her.'

'So what made you do it in the end?'

'The food,' Jenny said. 'Or should I say lack of it. We'd see what she brought back from the shops and it was just a scrappy piece of cheese and meat and bacon and a tiny amount of marge, butter and sugar. Sometimes there would be a small bowl of eggs left, and that was always a good day, but most times we lived on bread and milk.'

'That will be because of rationing,'

But of course they knew nothing of rationing and, Terry realised with a sinking heart, they didn't know either that their father hadn't returned from Dunkirk, nor about Ruth being sent to Ireland, and he badly needed Meg's wisdom to know how to deal with it all.

TWENTY-SIX

Meg was in the field scything the hay when she saw the telegraph boy turn in the lane. Her heart flew to her mouth, especially when she saw the boy speak to Will, who was scything the area abutting the lane, and he pointed in her direction. Her mouth felt incredibly dry as she took it from the boy, and her hands shook so much she could barely rip it open, but when she did, she crushed the letter to her breast and tears spurted from her eyes. Enid and Joy, fearing bad news, were by Meg's side immediately, their arms around her, and Stephen, sitting on the upturned barrow with his bad leg stretched out in front of him, lumbered to his feet and crossed the uneven hay field with difficulty.

But then they all realised that the tears Meg were shedding were tears of joy and she spluttered, 'They're alive, the children. They're alive.' She passed the telegram to them to read.

CHILDREN RETURNED HOME. SAFE WITH TERRY. PLEASE ADVISE.

'I must go to them,' Meg said, and as she spoke she

looked around the hay field guiltily; she knew if she returned to Birmingham she was leaving Enid and Will in the lurch. But the welfare of the children had to come first.

'Of course,' Enid said.

'Any answer?' the telegraph boy asked, and Meg said there was, but Enid held up her hand.

'Wait,' she said. 'I have an idea. Why don't they come here, all of them, your brother Terry as well? The boys can bunk in the rooms we had made in the barn and we'll get another bed into your room for the girls to share. Give them a wee bit of a holiday in the fresh air and good country food to build them up. You need to be together with all you have gone through.'

'It's a lovely idea,' Meg said. 'I don't know whether Terry would get the time off.'

'And you won't know unless you ask him,' Enid pointed out. 'Look, the boy is here waiting for your answer.'

The children were ecstatic that they were going to see Meg, but Terry didn't think he could ask for time off for himself.

'Why not?' asked Nicholas, who thought – as Enid did – that the family needed to spend time together. 'Someone has got to take the kids, anyway.'

'I know,' Terry said. 'I wouldn't like them to go anywhere unaccompanied again, even though they are resourceful. Fancy sneaking on to the guard's van.'

'Yeah,' Nicholas said, for both of them had been impressed.

414

'But I don't want to put them at that sort of risk again.'

'So what're you going to do? Deliver them to Meg and hightail it back here?'

'Something like that.'

'She'll be up to her eyes haymaking now,' Nicholas said. 'And not able to give that much time to them straight away. I'm sure she expected you to stay a bit.'

'Well I can't.'

'So Meg is going to tell them about the loss of their father and little Ruth being sent to those awful people on her own?'

'It isn't a nice thing to do, you know.'

'Well, I'm glad you recognise that at least,' Nicholas said, and added, 'I really think that you should step up to the mark; be a proper big brother and a support for Meg.'

Terry was furious and glared at Nicholas. 'You have no right to say that.' But even as the words were leaving his mouth, he knew Nicholas was right. 'All right,' he said. 'I'll have to square it with Mr Drummond.'

'I have already spoken to him,' Nicholas said.

'You have? Why?'

'I've offered to take your place if I could persuade you to go with your brother and sisters. He thinks you should, by the way, so he agreed.'

After two days of searching Rugeley, calling on farmers to check their outbuildings and combing fields, Sergeant Newbury put a call through to the police station in Steelhouse Lane and filled the desk sergeant in on the whole story. 'I think they've made for home and are probably there already.'

'I'll get someone check it out now,' the desk sergeant promised.

That same day he was able to report that he had seen and spoken with the children; they were safely back in Birmingham but would shortly be spending the summer on a farm near Penkridge with their sister who worked there as a land girl.

'Oh, that is good news,' Sergeant Newbury said. 'I can rest easy now.'

'They seemed quite concerned about Lady Hammersmith,' the desk sergeant continued. 'They know she did wrong but they don't want her punished for it. They say she never meant to harm them and she was always kind.'

Sergeant Newbury recalled the last time he had seen Lady Hammersmith, her eyes vacant and her mind elsewhere, but what he said was, 'Tell them not to worry. Lady Hammersmith is in a lovely comfortable home where there are people to look after her and care for her.'

'Oh, that is good news, sir,' the desk sergeant said. 'I will make sure that is passed on.'

He made a point of visiting the children again to tell them and, as Jenny said, 'We can really look forward to our holiday now. Lady Hammersmith was on my conscience a bit.'

They weren't the only ones looking forward to the holiday. Meg was ecstatic that the children would be coming to the farm, and Stephen saw her true radiance shining out of her. More than ever he realised the cloud she had been living under. For Meg, though, there was still deep concern about Ruth, but if she allowed herself to think of that small child's future, it hurt her unbearably, so for the sake of her own sanity she had to push it to the back of her mind. She had to put on a happy front for the children, as Aunt Rosie had told her how they had also suffered.

So she was there to meet to meet them at Penkridge Station, and thought her heart would burst with happiness as she hugged them all tight. Back in the farmhouse, Enid exclaimed at their pasty complexions and remarked on how thin they were, and Joy and Meg smiled at one another over the children's heads, knowing Enid would see it as her bounden duty to feed them up.

Meg always believed in meeting trouble head-on, and the same went for unpalatable news, and so straight after a delicious roast chicken dinner followed by apple crumble and custard, Meg took the children up to the room she shared with Joy. Terry, mindful of Nicholas's censure, followed her. Meg sat on the bed, and with Jenny one side and Sally the other, the boys standing in front of her, told them gently of their father's death.

There were tears, but not the outpouring of grief she had half expected, and it saddened her a little that the children had become so distanced from their father.

'It doesn't seem real yet,' Jenny said thoughtfully. ''Cos he's still away and that. Maybe we might feel it more when the war is over and all the other dads come home.'

'I dunno,' Billy said. 'I wish he wasn't dead, but I didn't much like him as a dad when he was with Doris.'

Meg thought about censuring Billy for saying that, but realised that it was so similar to what she had said to her father before his marriage that she hardly had the right, especially with Jenny and Sally nodding vigorously in agreement with their young brother.

'You can hardly blame them feeling that way about Dad, Meg,' Terry said to Meg later as she showed him around the farm. 'He brought it upon himself. And if you want the truth, though I didn't want him to die either, he was so besotted about that Doris that it's maybe better he died with the memory of her intact than to come back to see what she is reduced to. She's moved back into the flat she had in Bristol Street permanently now. And there is a man living with her. Tell you something else as well: Richard Flatterly is a fairly regular visitor.'

'Richard Flatterly? What's he doing there?'

'Well,' said Terry. 'Maybe he is a lover of the white powder himself or perhaps he's a lover of Doris's wares?'

'Ugh,' Meg said. 'Wouldn't surprise me about Flatterly, anyway. He's a horrible slimy toad. I can't understand what Kate Carmichael sees in him but they are definitely in some sort of relationship.'

'Are they? Bet she wouldn't like to hear that he had been visiting our Doris then.'

'Maybe not, but how do you know?'

'Uncle Robert told me.'

'And how does he know?'

'He's keeping tabs on him.'

Meg was surprised by that. 'Why?'

Terry shrugged. 'He won't tell me,' he said. 'All he would say is that he is nearly ready to make his move and I will know all then.'

'I hate people who just tell you half of a thing.'

'Me too'

Meg gave a sigh. 'Come on, we best go in.'

'Are you sure you should tell the others about Ruth as well as Dad today?'

'Well, if they'd have been really upset about Dad I might have waited a bit, but they weren't that bothered, were they?'

'No,' Terry conceded.

'So let's get all the bad news out of the way,' Meg said. 'I'll tell them after tea.'

Jenny was no fool, and when Ruth had been taken to the orphanage, she had known that they probably wouldn't be able to get her out again. So she wasn't as surprised as Billy and Sally when Meg said that someone had offered to adopt Ruth, although she felt a deep sense of loss because she had loved her little sister dearly. But she told herself that if someone wanted to adopt her they would look after her well, and she imagined a young couple unable to have children of their own, perhaps, and visiting the orphanage and falling in love with Ruth's winning smile.

That mental image shattered into a million pieces when Meg told them who the adoptive parents were. Her lips curled back, and Sally and Billy, who had almost been taken to Ireland with Liam and Sarah Mulligan, began to scream and shriek. And when Meg

419

attempted to hold them they lashed out with hands and feet as tears cascaded down their cheeks.

The sounds of their distress brought Will and Enid to see if they could help, but it was some time before the children were in any way calmer. When Enid heard what it was about she asked, 'Is there nothing can be done to stop this adoption?'

Meg shook her head. 'Nothing,' she said.

'This is dreadful, Meg, my dear girl,' Enid said. 'Simply dreadful.'

Meg knew to her cost that there was nothing to be gained by constantly talking about it and keeping it in the forefront of everyone's mind. The children had to learn to cope – as she did – with the loss of their little sister.

They were subdued for a few days and she was very gentle with them, but the rhythm of the farm helped them recover as it had helped Meg. She watched Will teaching them how to build a haystack as he'd taught her and Joy when they had arrived on the farm a year ago. She saw her sisters bringing the solid old horse up the lane to load the trailer, and they would fetch the eggs in the morning. They all had a go at milking, too, Terry and Jenny being not bad at all. Billy and Sally played endlessly with the dogs. They were not at all used to getting such constant attention, and Will said they would have both dogs ruined, but he said it with a twinkle in his eye so they knew he wasn't really cross.

All in all the children fitted into living on the farm as if they'd always lived on one; they seemed to grow taller with sun-kissed cheeks and brown legs and arms, and Meg saw the tension seeping out of them. So Meg should have been happy and content, but she wasn't because she was missing the closeness and time with Stephen. She hadn't been aware there was anything wrong at first because her time had been taken up with her brothers and sisters; then she wondered if that was it – that he was jealous of the time she was spending with them.

But he seemed fine with the children. Terry thought him a fine fellow and Stephen seemed to have endless patience with the younger ones, and when he teased them sometimes it was always gentle teasing. But for her there seemed to be barely a glance any more, and little conversation. He had been to the hospital and had his plaster removed not long after the children arrived. He'd always discussed what the doctor had said in the past but not this time, and when she'd asked him how it had gone his answer had been a shrug and a muttered, 'S'all right.' She was concerned, but with so many in the house, and the farm being so busy, finding any time alone to ask him what was wrong was almost impossible.

As one fine day after another followed the hay was gathered in, and then all the signs were that it would be a bumper harvest that year, the first bombs fell on Birmingham. No one was sure it was Birmingham at first, for the announcer on the wireless just said, 'A Midland town', but as the skirmishes went on, certain areas were mentioned that they all recognised. Then, on Sunday 25 August, a raid of some magnitude was visited on the same 'Midland town', and this time they mentioned the extensive damage to a shopping area known as the Bull Ring and the ancient Market Hall. There was also damage to the High Street, New Street and the surrounding area.

Meg's eyes met those of Terry and Joy, for they knew that the surrounding area could easily be where their houses were, but they didn't want to speak of it in front of the children.

It was Billy who said, 'That ain't a Midland town – it's Birmingham, ain't it?'

There was no point denying it. 'Sounds like it, Billy.'

'And the man said bombs damaged the Market Hall. Hope the flipping animals are all right?'

'Huh, trust you to think of the animals first,' Meg said. 'People are more important, and I hope everyone is safe. All I can say is, thank God it's Sunday and so the Bull Ring would be empty, not like it is weekdays. And Saturday especially.'

In Birmingham there was another raid the following evening, but just before the sirens went, there was a thundering knocking on the door of the flat. Doris knew Frank was expecting Richard Flatterly, so she opened the door with no sense of alarm and then was nearly knocked on her back by the men who burst through it so violently the door juddered on its hinges. The panicky eyes of Frank and plainly terrified ones of Doris were trained on the two beefy men framed in the doorway, both holding baseball bats in their hands as the siren shrilled out.

They just stood and waited till the noise abated slightly, by which time Doris was shaking from head to foot and

Frank wasn't much better, for the men were Big Bert himself and his henchman, known for their brutality.

'Well then, Caudwell,' he said to Doris, 'I think you owe me some money and I'm here to collect it and then give you the biggest hiding of your life for giving me the run around.' He strode across the room and grasped Doris painfully by the chin. 'You will find it isn't a healthy option to run out on me.'

Doris was unaware of the drone of the approaching planes for her whole attention was on the man in front of her as she stammered, 'I have no money, Bert. Honest to God.'

'Think I'll buy that, darling?' Bert said, and slapped Doris on either cheek saying, 'That's a taster for what's to come.'

Clusters of incendiaries rattled around on the roof of the flat. One went down the chimney, fell out in the grate of the spare room still alight, and when it tumbled from the grate, orange and yellow flames began to snake across the floor.

'You have got one minute to give me some wads of cash or I will break your fingers for starters,' Big Bert growled threateningly. 'And then every other bone in your body.'

Frank, hoping to appease them, was on his knees before the cupboard where he kept his cashbox when suddenly an explosion ripped through the flat, then another and another as the barrels of petrol were set alight and turned the flat into a raging inferno.

Richard Flatterly, approaching down the street to do another deal with Frank, was blown across the road in the blast from the first explosion, his clothes ablaze.

Robert, who had been tailing him some distance behind, rushed up and doused the flames with his own overcoat. Then finding him still alive, he alerted a policeman and Flatterly was taken to hospital under police guard.

TWENTY-SEVEN

The holidays were drawing to a close. Enid took the children into Penkridge the first Saturday in September as they were starting at the village school the following Monday and she declared they needed new clothes and footwear. They all ended up going except Stephen and Terry, who decided to stay at the farm as well and keep him company.

On the way there Meg listened to the children chatting and laughing together in the back of the cart, so very different from the nervous bedraggled stick-thin ones that had first arrived at the farm. The changes in them were not just physical either; Meg was delighted to see their old personalities beginning to emerge again and she marvelled at their resilience.

It would soon be all change. Terry would be returning to his job in Birmingham and the children would be moving to Penkridge to live with Lily. The Heppleswaites and Lily had looked into this and found that as Lily had already had evacuees living with her who had returned home, there was no problem in her taking in the Halletts. The children were all looking forward to this. They had met Enid's older sister a few times and liked her a great deal.

In fact, despite the war still raging the Halletts seemed to have survived the turbulent waters that had once threatened to submerge them. Terry thought about this that morning as, with the jobs all done, he and Stephen had made a bite to eat and were sitting over a cup of tea. He acknowledged that the only one who seemed unsettled and unhappy was Meg. No one else might have noticed this but Terry he knew his sister well and had seen her face looking quite bleak at times. He even knew what was making her unhappy and that was the way Stephen was with her. He had known of their budding relationship because she had spoken about Stephen in her letters, and if she hadn't he might have guessed anyway by the amount of times she mentioned him. When they had met he thought him splendid and was pleased and relieved that his sister had found someone special.

However, he soon realised that things were not running smoothly for her and he wondered what had gone wrong between them. He even wondered if he should speak about it to Stephen when they had the place to themselves.

He might well have done just that, but he suddenly heard a car approaching down the lane. This was such an unusual occurrence that he crossed to the window just in time to see a taxi drive into the yard and stop before the farmhouse door. His eyes grew wide with astonishment when a woman got out of the taxi holding a suitcase in one hand and the hand of a little girl in the other.

'What the . . .?' exclaimed Stephen, who had joined

Terry at the window, but Terry was already out of the door and running across the cobbles.

'Teddy,' the little girl cried, not ever able to say his name properly, and Terry scooped her up in his arms, holding her tight while tears fell from his eyes. After a long while he watched the taxi travel back up the lane, then turned to Kate Carmichael and said, 'I don't know what this is all about, but if you have come to upset our Meg, you can just sling your hook and leave our Ruth where she belongs, with her family.'

'Believe me, Terry, I mean Meg no harm,' Kate said. 'In fact, I have come to beg her forgiveness.'

Mollified, Terry introduced Stephen and put Ruth down to explore her surroundings. His mind was teeming with questions, but when he attempted to ask them, Kate said Meg should hear first.

'Meg?' Ruth said.

'She's in town.' Terry said. 'Back soon.'

'Back soon,' Ruth repeated.

'Yes, I wonder what she will make of you.'

All in all they hadn't long to wait – just about an hour – but it seemed the longest hour of Terry's life. In the end he left Stephen and Kate Carmichael talking and took Ruth to show her around the farm. She loved all the animals and didn't even mind the smelly pig, but her favourites were the two boisterous dogs and she clapped her hands with glee when Terry threw balls for them both, and showed Ruth tricks that his sisters had taught them. They were there in the yard, still playing, when the cart rumbled in and the Hallett children saw the sister they thought they would never see again, playing with their big brother. Meg was out of the

427

cart before it stopped, almost staggering towards Ruth, so great was her shock at seeing the child. Then she lifted her into her arms, and Ruth wound her arms around her neck and gave a great sigh of contentment: 'Ah, Meg!'

There were tears in Enid's eyes and Meg was totally unable to say anything at all. It took a little while for her to gain control of her emotions and then she carried her little sister into the farmhouse and set her on the floor, and saw Kate Carmichael for the first time.

'What's all this about?' Meg asked, watching Ruth touching each of her siblings in turn as if she couldn't believe she was back with them. 'What you doing here?'

Kate ignored Meg's angry tone, knowing she had reason to speak to her that way and said, 'I've brought you news of the death of your stepmother.'

The words brought Billy's head up. 'She's dead?' he asked in delight.

'Yes, she is.'

'Well, thank God for that.'

'Billy!'

'What? I'm not going to cry over her.'

'I'm not asking you to.'

'Leave it, Meg,' Terry said, trying valiantly to stop his own face from breaking into a beam of happiness. 'Let's hear the rest. Did she die in a raid?'

'Yes,' Kate said, 'but not in the way you might think. She died on Monday but there was a fire and so there were problems with identification. The fire was because an incendiary fell down the chimney and ignited the illicit petrol stored in wooden barrels in the spare room.'

'She was a black marketeer,' Terry said. 'I knew she was up to summat fishy. Fancy Doris being a black marketeer.'

'Yes, her and a man called Frank Zimmerman,' Kate said.

'Who's he?'

'A friend of her ex-husband, I believe,' Kate said. 'Oh, and that is another thing: looking through her records the police found she was probably never properly married to your father. Her husband went on the run after killing someone and somehow she had a hand in it. Apparently she was in a lot of debt and had to leave the North. Certainly when she met your dad her husband was alive, though he was killed later.'

'Why marry Dad then?'

'I don't really know,' Kate said. 'Because he was available and in full-time work, so there was security for her and she probably thought him easy to manage.'

'Oh, I'll say he was,' Terry said with feeling. 'Putty in her hands, he was.'

'It was a way of changing her name as well in case anyone was looking for her,' Kate said.

'So when did this Frank whathisname turn up?'

'No one is quite sure about that, but when he did she was back with him doing drugs and then, with the war starting and rationing, anything going, I suppose.

'But how come we've got Ruth back?' Meg asked.

'Well, that's down to your father,' Kate said. 'He left a document behind when he went to war, a legal document drawn up by a solicitor and witnessed, stating that if anything happened to him or Doris, you were to be the children's legal guardian till they come of age. The solicitor had charge of it and, hearing about

Doris's death, took it to Rosie and she took that to the children's welfare department. Nicholas came to find me and asked me to stand as character witness for you.'

'Character witness?' Meg cried incredulously. 'But you believed all those lies Flatterly told you about me.'

'I know,' Kate said. 'Please forgive me. I should have known better. I seem to have had blinkers on where that man was concerned.'

'I hope they are well and truly off now,' Stephen said. 'Meg has told us all a little bit about him and he is a nasty piece of work and needs teaching a lesson.'

'Oh don't worry, Stephen, he is being taught a lesson right now,' Kate said. 'He is in hospital and very badly burned. He was caught in the blast and that was because he was going to the flat to get his supply of cocaine. In his car around the corner were three petrol containers. He told me he got extra petrol because he was on the council. He also told me he had a defective heart and so was passed as medically unfit for the services, but that wasn't true either. In fact, he paid another man who did have a defective heart to stand in for him. It was your uncle Robert who found out about this man and went to see him. To save his own skin he spilled the beans about everyone he has helped, and Richard Flatterly was top of the list.'

'What will happen to him?'

'If he survives, and he is so badly burned there is doubt about that, he will probably hang.'

'Shall you be upset?'

'Not in the slightest,' Kate said. 'I have a father who was badly injured in the last war and a brother fighting

430

in this. Richard Flatterly deserves all that he has coming to him.'

'This is unbelievable,' Terry said. 'That was what Uncle Robert hinted at but wouldn't tell anyone about.'

'Can't blame him for not telling you,' Stephen said. 'Couldn't risk it getting out.'

'I understand now,' Terry said. 'He said I'd know soon enough.'

'So was this paper enough with what you said about Meg to get Ruth out of that place?'

'Well, it wasn't just me,' Kate said. 'Nicholas did his work well: he brought the solicitor, the priest and the doctor as well as me. The doctor was marvellous. He said how good you were with all of the children, Meg, and the little mother you have had to be to Ruth – the only mother she has ever known – and he could not recommend that she should go to strange people living in another country when she has a loving family here. Added to that your father hadn't ever signed the forms that allows a child to be adopted. No one had checked that, apparently.'

'I wonder why he did that?' Meg said.

'Well, we'll never know now,' Kate said. 'But you were so fond of the child maybe he thought if you married or something and you had the chance of bringing her out of there sometime it would easier if he hadn't signed the forms.'

'There have been tales of children adopted without any forms, though.'

'Maybe,' Kate said. 'But in Ruth's case they also had the letter, and important people knew those forms weren't signed. The priest is in a position of power in

Catholic orphanages and he was firmly on your side. Anyway, they also brought up the question of your age.'

Meg groaned. 'No getting round that.'

'There is if someone is there to oversee you until you turn eighteen,' Kate said, 'which the doctor pointed out is less than a year away. Rosie offered straight away.'

'Ah, but the children are starting school here now,' Meg said. 'Everything is settled and I don't fancy taking them back to Birmingham if the raids are going to start.'

'We don't want to go anyway, do we?' Billy said, appealing to his sisters, and they shook their heads in agreement. 'No we don't.'

'And it would mean leaving here,' Meg said. As she spoke her eyes, full of meaning, lighted on Stephen. Only Terry noticed him turn away and the hurt flood over Meg's face as she finished, 'and I'd hate that too.'

'So what's wrong with me and Will?' Enid said. 'I know we're not relatives, but—'

'I don't think that matters,' Kate said. 'You will have to have someone to verify that you are respectable upright citizens. You know, a doctor or a priest.'

'Well,' Enid said. 'Either or both would vouch for us. I suppose it could all be done by letter?

'Oh, yes,' Kate said. 'If you let me have their addresses before I leave the authorities will probably contact them direct. They had a meeting and decided that till it's all signed and sealed Ruth stays with you.'

'And quite right too,' Enid said.

Much later, after a lovely meal, during which Kate had been astounded to learn what had happened to Jenny, Sally and Billy, she was preparing to leave when she suddenly said, 'Oh, Meg, I nearly forgot. Your aunt sent you these. She found them when she was clearing out the house.'

'Letters from America,' Meg said, opening the package.

'Yes,' Kate said. 'Rosie said she hoped you didn't mind, but she opened the first one and scanned the first page in case it was upsetting, but told me it was anything but. They are full of concern for you.'

'I have a lot to tell them, and a new address for them to send letters to,' Meg said. 'I'm so glad to get these because they are a link to my mother.'

Jenny and Sally wanted to put Ruth to bed, and now that Meg had learned to manage the horse and cart she offered to take Kate to the station. Stephen asked if he could go with her. She guessed that he wanted the chance to talk, but nothing was said in front of Kate, who apologised again for her bad behaviour towards Meg and promised to make it up to her. Meg assured her she had nothing to make up, but she would value her friendship, and they were both quite emotional as they said goodbye.

They hadn't gone far along the road on the way back home when Stephen asked Meg to stop the cart. He took her hand and said, 'Meg, please listen to me. I have been cool and distant with you and have hurt you and I am very sorry.'

'It was more that you have confused me,' Meg told him, honestly. 'I thought we were friends, at least.'

'Oh, Meg, I wanted to be so much more than a friend,' Stephen said.

'Wanted to be?' Meg repeated. 'Is it over between us, Stephen?' Meg asked.

Dumbly Stephen nodded.

'But why?' Meg cried. 'What have I done?'

'Oh, my darling,' Stephen said. 'You have done nothing. I am doing this for you. I'm releasing you.'

'Releasing me for what?'

'To find someone new. Someone more worthy of you.'

'Stephen, what are you on about?

'You'll thank me in the end,' Stephen said almost as if Meg hadn't spoken.

'I don't want anyone else.'

'Meg, you're only seventeen years old.'

'I have worked that out,' Meg said. 'But that isn't my fault.'

'You have your life I front of you,' Stephen said. 'And you are so beautiful, you could have anyone.'

'Don't be silly,' Meg said. 'I'm not at all, and I don't want just anyone.'

'Meg, I am a cripple,' Stephen said. 'I only have one good leg. The other is baldy pitted and scarred and I have only half a right foot. In fact, I have scars all over my body and I am not at all the man I was when I walked off to war. As for my foot, they say that though they will be able to build my shoe up, I will always have a pronounced limp and the leg itself will never be anywhere near as strong as the left. I've spoken to the doctor and that's what he said. I don't even know if I will be able to farm and it's all I can do. How can I marry you like this if I'm not able to provide for you properly?'

'What are you on about?'

'What d'you mean?'

'I asked you why you felt the need to release me.'

'And I told you.'

'No, you didn't, you told me some rubbish about your foot.'

'Doesn't it matter to you?'

'Not in the way you mean,' Meg said. 'It matters to me only if it gives you discomfort.'

'No, it doesn't hurt now, but it looks awful, grotesque'

'Who cares, because I don't,' Meg said.

'You can't mean that?

'Yes I can,' Meg said. 'I bloody well can. Don't you tell me I don't mean what I say.'

'What if I can't farm?'

'I'd say you are looking on the black side of this totally, Stephen.' Meg said. 'Maybe there will be things you can't do and ways of doing things you may have to adapt to make life easier, but are you intending to sit in the armchair all the days of your life because of a limp?' And before he could answer she went on, 'In Birmingham we had a rent man with a really pronounced limp and it didn't stop him doing anything because he didn't let it.'

Meg saw the doubt still on Stephen's face and she realised his confidence had taken a severe knock. At that moment, seeing his vulnerability, she loved him more than ever. She took his hand and said gently, 'Stephen, your body is no longer perfect, it's battle scarred, but I fell in love with the person not the body. Think of your good friends Luke and John? Wouldn't they love to be standing here beside you now, and looking forward to living their lives, limp or no limp?'

Stephen nodded. 'They would,' he said. 'I suppose you think me rather shallow?'

'Will you stop trying to guess what I am thinking?' Meg said. 'You're wrong, anyway, because what's in my head at the moment is that I think I love you and your gammy leg and your bloody foot.'

'Only think?' Stephen said with a tentative smile that caused Meg's heart to flip over. 'Well, if you would only shut up for five minutes and give me a kiss,' Meg told him, 'I might be able to give you a more definite answer. But only do that if you have given up all thoughts of releasing me. I am where I want to be.'

'Are you sure?' Stephen said. 'You are so very young.'

'I can't help being young,' Meg said. 'And being young doesn't stop me knowing who is in my heart and that is you Stephen Heppleswaite and only you.'

'Oh, my darling girl,' Stephen cried. 'I love you so much. I never dreamed you could still want me.'

'Hush,' Meg said, 'Of course I still want you and I will love you till the breath leaves my body. And,' she added with a coy smile. 'I am still waiting for that kiss,'

Stephen's lips descended on Meg's. She felt a shaft of desire shoot through her. After all that had happened to her in her life she knew that that wonderful kiss sealed a love that was strong and true and would stand firm against all that life might throw at them, and Meg felt that at last she had come home where she belonged.